ALPHA WOLF
DARKMORE PENITENTIARY
Book 2
Caroline Peckham & Susanne Valenti

*This book is dedicated to all the readers who think
it's okay to find psychos attractive.*

*It is NOT okay for you to fanatasise about hot,
sweaty men choking someone out.
It is definitely, definitely NOT okay to bite your lip while
reading about a shirtless, crazy guy with abs cut from
stone getting stabby. Being stabby is NEVER okay.
It's also NOT okay to rationalise the minds of the guys in this
book because they have dark and twisted pasts, even when their
little sad backstory brings a tear to your eye – especially then!*

Here is your map of Darkmore Penitentiary.
Your rights have been revoked, your punishment has been decided, your sentence is about to begin. Fight for your place like Fae, or die and be forgotten. This is your one chance for redemption. May the stars be with you.

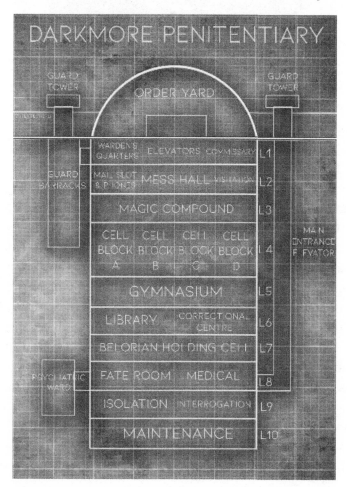

I was locked in my cell with my chest heaving and my ears ringing. I'd felt Rosalie's pain, captured by the agony of losing her, the possibility that she was going to die. If the Belorian had gotten to her, it was my fault. I'd sent it that way. But then as quickly as it had begun, the pain had subsided and I'd felt the connection to her still thrumming keenly through my veins. Wherever she was, she was alive. And I had to thank the stars for that small mercy tonight.

I hung a sheet over the bars and paced my cell. No one could see me. Which meant no one could see the cuff key in my hand either. I'd pulled it from the pocket of one of the most notorious thieves in Solaria while he'd been manhandled up the stairs beside me. I'd almost succumbed to the temptation to use it, tear my way out of this cell block and hunt down my mate. But I'd managed to maintain an inch of sanity. The guards were crawling the walls tonight. My block alone was teaming with them. Magic or not, I wouldn't have gotten two paces beyond my cell before they'd have disarmed me.

Fuck. So what now? How did I deal with this raging hurricane inside me? I needed an outlet. I needed to fight someone or something. No...

I stopped pacing, a thought latching in my mind. I needed to see Rosalie. I had to hold her in my arms and kiss her until she couldn't breathe. Not being able to see that she was okay with my own two eyes was driving me to insanity. And with the chaos going on out in the halls, no one would be checking my cell anytime soon. At least, I had to hope not.

Screw it.

I hurried to the back wall, unlocking my magic and casting a silencing bubble before creating tools out of ice to carve the bricks free. One by one, they came loose and I piled them up carefully, my heart hammering out of tune. I knew I wasn't doing the best job of this, but my mind was hooked on her. My girl. My enemy. My mate. It didn't matter about all the hate that lived between our people, nothing in this world could stop me from being with her tonight.

When I finally had a large enough hole to fit through, I carefully cast an illusion spell in place behind me, making the wall appear intact and creating a body-shaped lump in my bed that would fool a guard at a glance. But anyone looking closer would see through it pretty quick.

There was so much chaos in Darkmore right now though, I was just going to have to pray to the stars that I had a window of opportunity here.

I moved through the space behind the cells, counting the blocks as I moved closer to the girl I ached for. I'd had eyes on her for a long ass time and knew exactly which cell she resided in. I could just picture her there, laying on her bunk, the way she'd probably scowl at me for coming uninvited, but then she'd give in as she realised I wasn't on the offensive tonight. I just needed to hold her in my arms and feel her heart beat against mine. *By the sun, what is happening to me?*

I'd try and fight this feeling normally, but the mate bond wouldn't rest right now, like the moon itself was encouraging my actions. I needed to feel the weight of her in my arms, her soft lips against mine, her throbbing pussy around my – *alright fuckwit, let's not get carried away.*

I finally made it to her cell and pressed my ear to the wall. There were shouts sounding out from her cell block, but I couldn't tell if it was the guards or the cellmates so I cast an amplifying spell to hear better. Then I shut my eyes as I focused and recognised Plunger singing the colours of the rainbow like that wasn't creepy as shit. Apart from that, I couldn't hear any guards calling orders close by. And that was going to have to be good enough.

I pictured her in there, just aching for a strong Wolf to come and kiss her lonely lips.

Shadowbrook to the rescue.

I cast a sharp ice pick in my hand and worked on easing one of the bricks out of the wall until I could see into her cell. My heart crushed in my chest as I found the space bare and all oxygen stopped flowing into my lungs.

"Rosalie?" I hissed just in case she was in one of my blind spots by the wall. But no response came. "*Love?*" I growled, fear starting to slice at my chest.

"Shadowbrook?" Roary's voice carried from the vent to my right, anger lacing his tone. "You piece of shit. I'll break your legs for stealing that key."

"Where's Rosalie?" I snarled, ignoring his threat. If Roary wanted to fight me Fae on Fae then I'd be more than happy to rise to the challenge, but right now all I cared about was finding my mate.

There was a tense pause then Roary finally answered. "I heard she's in the hole," he muttered. "A couple of guards were just discussing it in our block."

"Fuck," I hissed. "For how long?"

"I don't know," he said sourly. "You'll return that key to me, Shadowbrook. She left it in my care. She *trusts* me."

I ignored the sting in my chest at the implication she *didn't* trust me. It was hardly surprising; I didn't trust her either. But the fact that she was my mate meant I still expected things of her that I was never gonna get. It might have been unreasonable, but I was going to blame the moon for it and just focus on my girl for now. If I started questioning my sanity over this then it would be one hell of a long night because as much as I wanted to deny it, Rosalie Oscura had wound her way under my skin and I was fairly certain there was no cutting her back out again now.

"I'll safeguard it for her myself," I growled. "And I'm sure she'll suck my dick in thanks." Might as well rub it in, seeing as Roary Night was always sniffing around my girl. He knew she was my mate now so he could back the fuck off if he knew what was good for him.

"Final warning," Roary snarled, a low Lion's growl sounding from his cell. My spine prickled and I bared my teeth at the challenge.

"Get. Fucked," I said calmly then shoved the brick back into place, sealing it with ice before turning back in the direction of my cell.

My heart hammered out a furious tune as I made it back there, slipping into the safety of my own personal cage and fixing the wall by making a paste from the crumbled mortar and sealing it all back up. When I was done, I got up and took the key from my pocket, turning to face the bars just as the sheet was suddenly pulled off of them. I had the key poised to lock my cuffs when my gaze slammed into Officer Rind's, his beady eyes narrowing on me like I was waving a red rag at a bull – or Minotaur as the case may have been. My gut clenched and my heart catapulted into my throat just before he shouted out in alarm and dove into action.

"Back-up needed! Code fifty-two!" He shot vines at me through the bars that snatched my wrists just as I raised my hands in surrender.

There were already four guards racing up behind him, magic swirling in their palms and fear made my heart lurch. If I gave them even a flicker of an excuse to kill me, they'd do it. So I let the key fall from my hand, the little metal triangle tinkling across the floor as I dropped to my knees and let Rind bind me with more vines. My world shattered into a million pieces as the cell door was opened and I was hauled out of there, forced face first onto the ground as an officer knelt on my back and made sure my cuffs were switched on once more, locking my magic away. As the feeling of my power faded from my grasp, I'd never felt so helpless. Rosalie needed me wherever she was, I could feel it in my heart and soul. And instead of going to her and being the Wolf she needed, I was back at the mercy of our captors, I'd lost the key and the stars only knew what punishments I'd have to endure now.

My Wolves were howling, but I couldn't muster a howl in return as shock took hold of me. I'd been caught in possession of a cuff key. They'd slap a minimum of ten years on my sentence when I'd been just about to get out. I'd only had a few weeks left in this hell, the taste of freedom had been coating my tongue and breathing my name on the wind. And now it had been ripped away from me.

All because I couldn't fight the urge to stay away from my fucking mate.

Fuck.

Fuck.

FUCK!

"Get him down to interrogation," Officer Nixon's raspy voice reached me and my blood chilled. "We need to find out every spell he's cast. Any traces he could have left around the prison. And for the love of fuck, toss his cell." Footsteps marched into my cell as I was dragged away. The paste I'd used to fix the walls wouldn't leave a magical signature, only the tools I'd created would. But they were long gone, so there was nothing to find in there. And I sure as shit wouldn't be squealing my secrets to Mr Quentin. But that didn't mean it wasn't going to hurt like a bitch.

***

I was with the creepy ass psycho, Quentin, for three full days before the interrogation was over. I didn't breathe a word of the truth, nothing about Rosalie or Roary, or whatever plans they were hiding with that key. I bit my tongue, doing what any self-respecting Fae would do and refused to snitch a word of the truth while I was cut open and subjected to all manner of poisons before being healed from the brink of death. It wasn't pretty. And it sure as hell was going to leave an imprint on me, but I'd faced interrogation with Quentin before. His gifts were strong, but not that strong. And I knew how to hide information when I had time to prepare. It was all about covering memories with new ones, thinking through each one I wanted to conceal and rebuilding them to cover the secrets they held. So long as I was ready to face him, nothing he did would ever break me. He'd tried to use physical torture to weaken me first, but I'd been trained by the biggest, baddest Lunar I'd ever known on how to handle pain. So there was no chance of that working on me. The real wound that would never heal was the sentence handed to me the day I was returned to gen pop.

Officer Nixon strode beside me with a smug sort of smirk on his thin lips; he was a tall asshole with a bald, shiny head and bushy black brows. "So I hear you're gonna be here for another fifteen years. Ten for stealing a cuff key and five more for the intent to use your magic for devious purposes. You might get another five if they can prove you released the Belorian." He glanced at me as if looking for signs of guilt in my features. "And *my* how the rumours spread fast in this place. Half the inmates already think you're guilty. And a lot of them are real pissed since their little friends got eaten by the monster you let loose."

"I didn't let it loose," I growled, an edge of warning in my tone, though what I could actually do to this fucker was pretty limited. And would probably serve me with another few years in this place. *Shit, how am I gonna explain this to my sisters?*

Guilt mixed with dread inside me. I'd been so close to release. So. Fucking. Close. I'd been counting the weeks, the days. There'd been times I could almost taste the fresh air waiting for me up there above the ground.

I swallowed a whine, keeping my expression hard and impenetrable as Nixon's arm brushed mine.

"Of course, I can always look out for you in here, One," he murmured. "You scratch my balls and I'll scratch yours, eh?" He gave me a suggestive look, his tongue wetting his lips in a slow and creepy as fuck motion and my upper lip curled back.

"You put your balls anywhere near me and I'll rip them off and stuff them down your throat," I snarled and his hand moved to rest on his shock baton.

"Say that again. I dare you," he hissed as we made it to level two and approached the Mess Hall.

I didn't want to be sent to the hole - or back to fucking Quentin for that matter - so I swallowed my tongue and Nixon lifted his chin like he'd won a point. In the real world, I would have ripped his intestines from his stomach and choked him with them by now. But hey ho, life in Darkmore was a piece of shit. *And now I have fifteen more years to look forward to.*

Eyes fell on me and chatter broke out as Nixon left me to join the inmates in the Mess Hall and my Wolves howled excitedly, rising from their seats.

I tried not to panic or fall into a hopeless shell of a person, but it wasn't easy. I'd had plans. A life to return to. A gang to lead. But now...I had nothing. Nothing but more time to waste, more of my life to pour down the drain.

An Experian Deer Shifter was walking my way with his tray in hand and I had the urge to slam it up into his face as fury took hold of me and my muscles shook with adrenaline. I clenched my fists and contained the urge as he scurried past me, averting his gaze. *No point in earning myself more punishments right now.*

Harper made it to me first and I wrapped her in my arms, nuzzling into my Beta as more of my pack surrounded me, running their hands over any part of me they could reach as they tried to comfort me.

"I'm so sorry, Alpha," Harper said, the words choked and I brushed my fingers over her dreadlocks.

"It's not your fault," I said in a dark tone.

"How long did they give you?" she asked, leaning back to search my expression.

"Fifteen years," I said a little hoarsely and her eyes widened in horror before she wrapped herself around me again with a mournful howl.

My gaze locked on Roary Night across the room where he sat alone, but there were plenty of his Shades lurking close by. He surveyed me coolly and I scowled back at him. He was going to fight me over stealing that key then losing it. I knew it. I just didn't know when.

I turned away from him, instinctively hunting the room for Rosalie. It was too much to hope that she'd be out of the hole already, but my gut still sank in disappointment. I was just lucky I hadn't ended up down there myself. But as I'd just been told that my youth was going to be well and truly stolen from me in this place, I wasn't going to be too grateful about it.

"Any word on the Oscura leader returning?" I muttered to Harper, a knife's edge to my voice keeping my concern over Rosalie concealed.

"I heard Cain gave her a month in the hole," Harper said excitedly, glancing up at me with joy in her gaze and I hitched on a smile to match hers.

"Perfect." *Fuck. My. Life.*

I was a ball of testosterone, ready to be unleashed. The Order Suppressant may have kept my Wolf buried in me, but it couldn't keep my instincts at bay. And the mate bond was a power of its own, driving me to be with her, find her, free her. I didn't know where it ended and I began. But I was a slave to it. A slave to *her*. A month in this place without her sounded almost as bad as the extra years on my sentence right now.

My eyes wheeled onto Cain across the room, his muscular arms locked across his chest as he glared at everyone like he'd happily douse us in Faesine and set us all alight. It was a miracle they didn't do that sometimes. But official executions in this place weren't as common as they used to be. Not since new laws had been brought in to protect the scum of the earth. All because of some fancy ass inmate who someone with power had wanted to protect – but I wasn't going to sneer at that blatant use of influence if it helped me out. Not so long ago I could have earned myself a death sentence for stealing that key.

It was all such a fucking joke. I was innocent to the core –

of my convicted crime at least. And I'd tried to keep my hands clean to ensure I lived out my sentence and not a day more. My pack were hand chosen by me, most of them in here for gang related crimes against the Oscuras. You didn't get away with that shit in Alestria these days. But some of them were bad people plain and simple. There was no avoiding that in a place like this.

I swept a hand over my hair, pulling away from my pack and moving to sit at a bench while my Wolves brought me offerings of the best breakfast foods available today. I tucked into a bowl of oatmeal with honey and fruit, sullen as I thought of my girl trapped in the hole again. She was probably losing her mind missing me, touching herself ten times a day as she dreamed of my cock.

Now that my sentence is longer, we have all the time in the world to be together.

I jerked at the thought, rejecting it with all my being. I might have been a positive kind of guy, but I wasn't going to find reasons to be happy about staying here for another fifteen fucking years. *Ergh.* As I processed it, the reality sank in a little deeper and I dropped my spoon into my bowl, my jaw clenching as I tried to think of a way out of this. I needed to appeal. Which meant I needed lawyers. But I was all but broke on the outside world since I'd spent every penny I had on lawyers for the first appeal I'd lost. The rest of it was keeping my family with a roof over their heads and I sure as shit wasn't going to strip that away from them.

Harper started massaging my shoulders and my skin prickled at the touch. It would have felt natural once, her touching me like that. But since I'd been mated, I rejected all other Wolves. All other women for that matter. It was a cruel kind of fate. I'd been banking on getting out of here and putting as much distance between me and Rosalie as possible. Now I was stuck in Darkmore, still pining for her, still turning away my own pack.

"*Enough,*" I growled sharp enough to make Harper spring

away.

She whimpered and I looked to her with an apologetic frown. "Sorry, love, I..." I didn't have an end to that sentence, so I just sighed and looked away. I'd lost everything. And all I'd had to hold onto in here was that my time would soon be over in this place. I'd been so close to freedom. How could I have fucked it up over an Oscura girl? It was shameful. And the worst thing of all, was that a small part of me was happy. Because now I didn't have to leave her. Now I could stay and see her and hold her and devour her. I'd have to endure this hell for far longer than planned, but so long as that meant I could have her, I wasn't as upset as I should have been about the idea. And I had to think the stars were having a huge laugh at my expense.

***

It had been almost three months since Rosalie was put in the hole and I was in a state. I didn't sleep, I didn't eat. My pack thought I was losing my mind. Sometimes I thought I was too. I set Veiled Wall jobs every day to find out as much information as I could about what was going on with her. But no one had the answer as to when she was being released. No one but Cain. The asshole who'd put her there and who held her fate in his hands.

I was done pretending she meant nothing to me. I had to risk it. I couldn't do this alone anymore. This secret was feasting on my insides. And it was going to kill me if I didn't let it out soon enough. So I came up with a plan that would kill two birds with one stone and summoned Harper to my cell.

"Hey Alpha," she said with that worried look they'd all been giving me for weeks. Months really. Ever since Rosalie had arrived and fucked up everything. Made me obnoxiously happy and unbearably *un*happy simultaneously.

I was in my jumpsuit with the arms tied around my waist, my chest bare. Harper cocked her head at me as I moved past her and tugged down the sheet over the bars to give us privacy.

"I need to tell you something that you can't tell anyone else. And I need you do something for me that is a big ask...but I have no one else to turn to and I trust you Harper."

Her brows pulled together. "Anything."

I sighed, taking her hand and pulling her away from the door, lowering my voice to nothing but a murmur. Man, I missed silencing bubbles. This place had ears even without the gifts of people's Orders.

"I have a terrible secret," I said, swallowing thickly. "Something that could shatter the foundations of our pack, that could make all of them lose faith in me. Could make *you* lose faith in me." I knew what I was risking here, but this couldn't go on any longer. And maybe, just maybe Harper would pull through for me. She'd been a loyal Beta, but this would push the boundaries of that loyalty to their limits. Possibly snapping them for good.

"What is it, Alpha?" she asked a little fearfully.

"Will you swear not to tell the others?" I asked, making a mental note to perform a star deal with her the next time we were in the Magic Compound.

She nodded firmly, no question about it in her eyes. "I promise."

"I...fuck, how do I say this?" I laughed, sounding slightly deranged and her frown deepened. "I've been...mated to an Oscura. The moon chose us. I didn't want it, I fought it. I'm still fighting it, but it was out of my hands-"

"Who?" she gasped, looking horrified as she shook her head in denial.

"Rosalie Oscura," I croaked and she winced, her face twisting in revulsion, refusal. A possessive energy filled me that made me want to snap at her for looking like that, beat her down for daring to suggest Rosalie was anything but perfect. But that was wrong. All so fucking wrong. "It's been months now. I hid the mark." I turned, pointing to where I'd placed the new tattoo of thorny roses around it – practically the same

14

fucking tattoo as she had winding up her body which I'd realised after getting the damn thing done. Why did everything I do these days revolve around her, intentionally or otherwise?

"Oh my stars," she gasped, her fingers grazing the silvery crescent moon mark as she found it amongst the tattoo. "Alpha this is...this is terrible!"

"Shh," I hushed, her, spinning around and shoving her against the wall as I cupped a hand to her mouth. "You will tell no one," I demanded and she nodded beneath my hand. The threat was clear. If she broke this promise, I would kill her. As simple as that. I lowered my hand, letting her speak as my next request burned my throat, my tongue. "It's why I can't bear to sleep with you all anymore, why I can't fuck a single one of you. I'm hers whether I want it or not. I'm *hers*, Harper. Body and fucking soul."

Her eyes practically bugged out of her head as she nodded again, continuing to nod as she tried to process that.

"So I need...someone to cover for me," I said slowly. "So that the pack understand why I'm avoiding them. And I know it's a lot to ask of you, Harper, but I need you to be that someone. To pretend to be my mate."

Her jaw dropped as she gaped at me. "But Alpha-"

"I know what I'm asking you to sacrifice. But your sentence is up in six months. Then you'll be free to go and be with as many Wolves as you want. It's not so-"

"Ethan," she growled, using my full name for once and I growled in response, sensing the challenge in her words. "I can't be without the contact of the pack. I can't – I'll go mad."

I nodded as I accepted that, drawing in a deep breath. She was right. It was too much. I couldn't make her go against her own instincts for that amount of time, it would be insufferable. As I was well fucking aware. "Well...maybe I can arrange ways for you to be with another Wolf or two under my watch. Some mates enjoy that. It's not unheard of."

She nodded, seeming to respond better to that idea. "And you'll be there too?" she asked hopefully. I'd admittedly been with Harper in the past, but I was used to the Wolves vying for my attention. I'd laid with plenty of my pack and others besides. But being an Alpha meant I didn't ache for them like they did for me. Most of them wanted to please me, it satisfied them to do so. And she was missing that just like the others were.

"Yeah, I'll be there," I said firmly and a small smile tugged at her lips.

"I'll keep your secret."

"You'll need a mark." I raised a hand to trace the place behind her ear where Rosalie had hers. My gut twisted sharply at the thought of anyone else standing in her place, even if it was just a farce. But this way I could have a solid explanation for my pack as to why I didn't want their attention. I didn't have to let them know the truth which would lead to my downfall as the Alpha of the Lunar Brotherhood in Darkmore. Because how could anyone follow me after that?

"Will you do it?" she asked.

"No, I've offered protection to Alvin Zion to keep this secret. He did this." I pointed to the tattoo covering my mark and she nodded, looking slightly hurt that I'd told someone before her.

"I was afraid of what would happen if I told you, love," I said gently and she nodded with a sigh.

"I understand…but how are you going to deal with this?" she asked. "Ryder Drac-"

"I don't want to discuss the fate of my old leader," I warned. "It won't be like that."

"Promise me," she pleaded.

"I swear," I said firmly. "I'll find a way to fix this."

"I've never heard of a mate bond being broken before but… I'll look into it for you," she said, hugging me tight. "I'm so sorry this happened."

I wanted to say 'me too' but that would have been a lie. I wanted to be sorry, I wanted to *want* to take it back. But now I was mated with Rosalie, all I really wanted was to keep her as mine. Forever. It was conflicting as shit.

"Thank you, Harper." I hugged her tight for a moment, some

of the weight on my shoulders easing.

I wasn't used to living the hard life. I ruled from the top. No one had ever affected my status quo until Rosalie had come along and fucked shit up. But by the stars I was going crazy without her. I needed to figure out a way to get her out of the hole. And I knew that wasn't for purely selfish reasons either. Three months in that place alone was enough to crack the toughest of nuts. And as strong as my mate may have been, no one was immune to that shit. Especially when I could feel the pain of being in that place eating at her like it was eating at me. I swear Sin Wilder was as sane as a sober nun when he went in there. Alright, maybe as sane as a drunk nun who'd had a stint in Starfall Asylum. But still. He was definitely fifty percent crazier these days than he used to be.

"We can announce it when the tattoo is done," I said and she nodded, beaming at me, happy that she was helping me in this. But she couldn't hide the darkness in her eyes over the reason for that help.

The bell rang to announce it was time to head to the Magic Compound and a breath of relief left me at the thought. I needed to set more jobs on the Veiled Wall to see if there was any more information on Rosalie's release. Whoever was gathering info on the matter for me probably thought the Fae setting the jobs was entering stalker territory when it came to Rosalie. But thanks to the wall being anonymous, I didn't give two shits.

I headed out of my cell with Harper and my Wolves howled as I approached them, running my hands over their heads before leading the way out of the cell block. I crossed the bridge and we were led to the Magic Compound. Our block was the first to arrive, but I frowned at the added security by the gateway that led inside. Fourteen fucking guards stood sentinel around it and Officer Cain was right there to usher me forward.

"In," he commanded, opening the door and I smirked threateningly in his face as I passed by, stepping through the door which shut sharply behind me.

Officer Lyle looked sweaty and more pale than usual behind the barrier of glass that parted us as he ran a hand through his red locks.

"Hey gorgeous, you look a little flushed today," I switched on the charm, but he didn't seem to be in the mood to bite.

"Hands," he instructed.

I put them through the holes with a frown and he placed a cuff key into the lock. Instead of turning it halfway to release my magic, he twisted it fully around and the cuffs fell from my wrists with a clatter.

"What the-" I started, but before I could finish that sentence, he'd snapped two shiny new silver rings onto my wrists in their place and gestured for me to go into the compound. "What's with the new cuffs?"

"Security upgrade," he said simply, giving me a slight smile as he softened for a moment. "Now go."

The door into the compound was open but I lingered a moment longer, looking back at the guards who were all staring in at me, their shoulders rigid. I guessed they wanted this changeover to go smoothly, and the looks on some of their faces said they were out for blood today, so good luck to anyone who tried to cause trouble.

I stepped into the compound and headed over towards our usual benches, sitting down front and centre before resting my elbows on my knees and flexing my fingers. I created a chalice of ice and filled it with the purest water before taking a sip while I watched the rest of the inmates slowly be re-cuffed and let into the compound. I examined the new bands on my wrists, the metal shimmering a little as it caught the light. I couldn't see a keyhole on either of them and I wondered how the fuck they came off.

I finished my drink, melting the ice and pushing my finger under one of the cuffs, tugging to assess its strength.

"They're as strong as a milkman's asshole."

I looked up at the deep voice, finding Sin Wilder grinning at me like a deranged motherfucker – and I guessed that was what he was, so it fit the bill. His bulky muscles were filling out his jumpsuit and his sleeves were rolled up to reveal endless ink on his dark arms.

"How'd you get in here before my pack?" I growled. "And what makes you think a milkman has a strong asshole?" Not sure why I wanted to know the answer to that second question, but call me Curious Clive.

"I don't queue unless the notion takes me. And it didn't take me today," he commented with a shrug, playing with flames between his fingers. I shifted upright, lifting my chin in case the psycho fancied taking a shot at me. There never seemed to be any particular reason he flipped on people, so it was always worth being prepared. "And to answer your second question, I'd have to kill you if I told you, so are you sure you wanna know?"

"Pass," I drawled, shrugging, but now I was seriously fucking Curious Clive about it.

Sin picked up the wall ball and tossed it against the wall and I turned my attention to the gate as Roary fucking Night stepped through next before my pack. Were all the assholes in Darkmore playing top dog today? Because I was the only number One around here. Though since Sin had seen me and Rosalie together, he was still messing with my damn head by pretending he owned me. Of course, I had to play along with that shit until I could get some leverage on him in return. Which I was working on daily.

"Someone's mighty keen to find out when little Rosalie Oscura is getting out of the hole," Sin said thoughtfully as he bounced the ball against the wall again and he glanced down at his hand where magical writing would be revealing itself to him about the open jobs. "You wouldn't happen to know anything about that would you, kitten?"

"Fuck off," I growled and Roary glanced our way as he wandered towards the wall.

"First thing you've ever said that I agree with," he snarled venomously, glaring at Sin and that got my interest real piqued. He'd tried to beat my head in over the key not that long ago, but he'd never looked at me with as much hate as *that*.

Roary had caught me in a sour as shit mood the day after my return from Quentin and had gotten in a few good punches when he'd sprung me in the library. For some reason, he'd decided not to challenge me with magic or tear into me in his Order form in the yard. No, Roary Night had wanted to spill my blood with his bare hands, and he'd gotten his wish. But I'd left plenty of dents on him too. Roary had broken my nose before the guards had intervened. And maybe I'd relished some of that pain in penance for being fucking stupid enough to lose that key. Looked like they'd been planning to change the cuffs though, so we would have lost access to our magic anyway.

As my pack spilled into the compound, I got to my feet to seize the opportunity before they arrived, striding toward Sin and Roary, flicking my fingers as I cast a silencing bubble. "Oh yeah? And why's that, asshole?"

Roary looked to me like he was assessing whether he could be bothered to tell me. But with another glance at Sin – who had a deadly ass glint in his eyes – he did. "Sin set the Belorian loose. Rosa could have died. We all fucking could have."

"That true?" I rounded on Sin with acid in my veins. My intel from the wall jobs suggested Rosalie had been captured because she'd been cornered by the Belorian on level eight. Cain had found her before it had killed her then locked her up for attacking him. But why she would have done that, I couldn't figure out.

Sin shrugged. "She asked me to."

"She explicitly told you *not* to actually," Roary hissed, taking a step toward him and squaring his huge shoulders.

"Why would she ask you to?" I questioned Sin.

"That's not your concern," Roary snarled and I narrowed my gaze at him.

Sin frowned like he was trying to comprehend something as he looked at Roary. "So, you're saying...I'm responsible?"

"Yes fucktart, that's obviously what he's saying," I snapped.

"But why would you even have discussed something like that?" There was definitely something I was missing here.

Sin threw his head back, laughing manically and flames danced around him in a breeze created by his air Element. Crazy asshole.

"Well that's some news," Sin said, abruptly stopping laughing and baring his teeth at Roary instead. "So how do I get her out?"

"I dunno, ask Cain nicely, he's the one who put her in there," Roary said sarcastically then strode away beyond the wall without a backwards glance.

Sin turned his gaze to the outer fence where Cain was still guarding the entranceway, a thoughtful yet deadly expression slipping over his features.

"Why did you release it, Sin?" I demanded, but he just ignored me, walking away like I wasn't there and my spine prickled with irritation.

I dropped the silencing bubble and strode back to my bench, a growl in my throat. As much as I wanted to carve Sin's face off and serve it up in a pie, I still had mine and Rosalie's secret to protect. So when it came to him, I was currently collared and fucking leashed. But I had a bunch of my pack members and anonymous Veiled Wallers running circles around him, digging into his shit to find anything I could use against him. And sooner or later, something would surface and I'd put him back in his damn place.

I met with my pack and plucked Harper up from her seat, taking her hand and drawing her away from the others. I cast a silencing bubble around us and an illusion that blurred the movements of my mouth just to be safe before having her strike a star promise with me not to tell my secret. When it was done and the magic bound us to seven years of bad luck if we broke it, I sought out the guy I needed for the next stage of my plan.

I spotted the little dude, Alvin, just as he yelped and was knocked on his ass a hundred yards away. A Pegasus built like a brick shithouse was responsible, leering over him with his huge muscles on display in his white tank, the arms of his jumpsuit tied around his waist. His biceps were painted with colourful ink just like most of him and his gang were. The leader stood a step behind him, her hair cropped short and painted like a rainbow complete with glitter. She was nicknamed Sparkle and the huge guy to her right was Glitterpuff, I shit you not.

Sparkle had had it in for me ever since word had circled that I'd been found with the cuff key. One of her herd had been killed by the Belorian and I was apparently being held responsible. But if a bunch of ponies thought they could challenge the strongest Wolf pack in Darkmore, they were going to be laughed right back to their little green pastures.

I strode over and Harper kept at my heels as I leaned down, hoisting Alvin up by the scruff of his neck. He was so light, his feet left the ground for a moment before I placed him back on them and he nodded to me in thanks before slyly shifting behind me and my Beta.

"Hands off, Sparkle. The rat's mine." It wasn't an insult; Alvin was a Tiberian Rat shifter. From what he'd told me, the reason he was in here was because he'd been caught snooping on some very powerful people and had been leaking stories about them to the press for months. Though I got the feeling that wasn't the full story. You didn't end up in Darkmore for shit like that. But everyone in here had their secrets and his story was his to keep. It was one of the few things we had control over in here.

"Then why was he wandering over here into *our* territory?" Sparkle growled and the rest of her herd came up behind her, whinnying their approval.

I took in the range of colourful tattoos on their arms and necks and the symbol they all sported which represented their gang. The Twisted Horns. The colourful Pegasus branded on them appeared to be leaping toward me through a cloud. Its coat was white and its wings spread wide, but instead of a horn it had a shining silver knife coated in blood. Arching over it was a shimmery rainbow with the name of their gang running through it. Among the other tattoos were more rainbows, clouds, wings and horns, some surrounded by words like *this is your one and only horning, you have been horned, glitter is fitter, talk to the wing (or I'll stab you up)*. Across Sparkle's collar bone were the words *rainbow is the new black*.

It would have been hilarious if I hadn't seen first hand how ruthless this gang could be to anyone weaker than them. They really would stab you through the chest with their horns out in the Order Yard and I'd seen more than one of the small Orders be trampled to death by them out there.

"This whole side of the wall is Lunar territory," I snarled. "You can go and try your luck carving out your own territory with the Oscuras if you want, Sparkle. But everywhere here is *my* domain. So challenge me for it or get out of my face."

She bristled and a few of her herd stamped their feet in rage. "Why's the rat so special to you, Shadowbrook?" She narrowed her light blue eyes at me.

"That's none of your business, love," I growled, my hackles rising.

"Humour me," she insisted, an edge to her tone like she really was considering challenging me today. And with the mood I was in, I would have relished the fight.

"He's a decent tattoo artist. There's not many of those about judging by the art on your herd," I snickered and Glitterpuff snorted aggressively beside me. As if I was gonna be intimidated by an overgrown My Little Pony though. "Now take your tiny glitter gang and fuck off."

"My gang is growing every day," Sparkle snarled, a warning in her tone. "Remember that, Shadowbrook."

"Noted." I flipped her the bird and turned away, clapping a hand to Alvin's shoulder and nearly knocking him onto his ass again from the force I used. "Stay out of trouble."

"I will," he said quickly, bowing his head to me, about to scurry away when I tugged him closer.

"I need another favour," I murmured to him and I cast a silencing bubble around us before explaining about the mark I needed him to tattoo onto Harper. When he agreed to do it tonight, I made him swear to keep his silence then let him go and sent Harper back to our pack.

I hunted down Cain beyond the fence and strode over to him at a casual pace, though my heart was beating a mile a minute as I closed in, anger racing through me. I swallowed down the words I really wanted to say to him – *let my mate go you blood-sucking piece of shit* – and slapped on a winning Shadowbrook smile.

"Officer," I said politely. "I suppose I ought to thank you for locking up my arch nemesis."

Cain's stormy grey eyes scraped down me, his mouth set in a flat line and I wondered if I'd ever seen the bastard smile. It was like he'd had it permanently removed at birth.

He said nothing, so I went on.

"It's been a while though now, should I be preparing myself for her strutting back in here sometime soon like the queen bitch she thinks she is?"

Cain ran his tongue across his teeth and my gaze shifted to a shiny new device hanging around his neck. What the fuck was that?

"She'll be rotting in there for a while longer," he said in a hollow tone.

A snarl caught in my throat and I tried my best to school my expression as rage clawed up my spine. "Don't tell anyone, but I'm kinda missing the challenge of beating her down. Do a guy a favour and send me back a worthy opponent. I promise you can enjoy watching me spill her blood. I've seen the way she pisses you off." I dangled the juicy carrot in front of him but didn't get the reaction I expected. He took his lightning taser from his hip and pointed it at me, his fangs lengthening as he glared. "Get out of my sight, One."

"Oh, come on," I pleaded, but it came out as a snarl, my anger overflowing.

"Last warning," he hissed and I clenched my jaw, backing up, my muscles tight.

I spent the rest of my time in the compound pacing and furious, giving up on posting jobs to the wall about my mate. I had my answer. Cain was going to keep her locked up as long as he damn well fancied. And it sounded like that was a long fucking time.

When our time was up in the Magic Compound, I was ready to draw blood and go to war to get Rosalie back in my arms. But I had to bury those feelings down and let them rot in my stomach while the pain of the mate bond called me to her so fiercely that it made my bones ache.

Before anyone left the compound, Cain lifted the strange new remote around his neck and pressed something on it. The cuffs on my wrists blocked my magic off and I gasped at the suddenness of losing it as everyone around me did the same. A soft blue glow emitted from the cuffs and the metal shimmered like stardust.

With a sinking feeling in my gut, I realised I wouldn't be getting out of these ever again unless a guard allowed it. And I had another fifteen years to pine over my freedom without even the perks of a stolen cuff key to make my life a little more bearable. But there was one thing I longed for more than the sweet bliss of magic rushing through my veins at all times. Rosalie Oscura. And I was starting to think I'd pay any price to get her back.

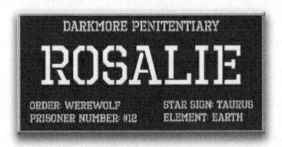

DARKMORE PENITENTIARY

ROSALIE

ORDER: WEREWOLF   STAR SIGN: TAURUS
PRISONER NUMBER: #12   ELEMENT: EARTH

I kept my eyes closed in some foolish, pathetic attempt to convince myself that none of it was real. That my world hadn't been condensed into this tiny rectangle. That I couldn't walk more than six steps before meeting a wall. That it wasn't true that I hadn't breathed fresh air or seen the moon in so long that I'd lost count of the days.

If my eyes were closed, I could almost convince myself that I could feel the gentle caress of moonlight on my skin. That my flesh was shivering with the desire to shift instead of the bone numbing cold which had just taken root in me so deeply that I didn't know how not to shiver anymore.

I could try to force myself to believe that the scent of mould and mildew came from the moss in the forest surrounding me or from a brook like the one at the base of my Aunt Bianca's vineyards.

I could almost believe I was standing there, in that peaceful valley which belonged to my family, with my pack running to meet me through the trees. I could imagine my aunt yelling at us for being late to dinner and if I tried really, really, hard I swear I could nearly smell the bliss of her cooking on the wind, tempting us home.

Fuck. *Home.* I missed that place like nothing I'd ever known. My heart ached for the feeling of the wind in my hair, the taste of the family wine on my tongue, the sound of laughter and bickering and howling on the air from a hundred Oscuras and more.

And when I went deep inside of myself like this it didn't

seem so far away anymore. Like maybe this tiny cell was just a nightmare. My brain twisting the memories of the things my papa had put me through into this fresh hell. Maybe I could believe I was sleeping and I was about to wake up safe and warm in my bed-

Or at least I could until the guy in the cell across from me started screaming again.

I flinched minutely as I was dragged forcefully from the vision I'd been working so hard to create. The perfect forest I'd been fighting to make myself believe in faded to nothing more than four walls with dirty, red/brown bricks and scratches gouged into the mortar from the various Fae who had existed down here over the years. I called it existing because I knew for a fact that it wasn't living.

Bile rose in my throat as I cracked my eyes open and faced my own reality. I should have expected this to happen really. Fate always had liked to kiss me on one cheek while slapping me on the other. I'd managed to survive the Belorian, find out some seriously fucked up shit about the things that went on down in Psych and now I was paying for that good fortune by living my nightmare.

All thanks to one man who had chosen to take control of my life and toss me away like the trash he clearly thought I was. Mi vendicherei. *I'd get my revenge.* Mason Cain was going to learn what happened when you spat in the face of an Oscura Clan Alpha soon enough. Not that I'd seen him since the day he'd thrown me in here. Codardo. *Coward.* He'd have to face me sooner or later though and things were going to change when he did.

Of course, my schemes of vengeance and retribution had taken a back seat for the last few months in favour of the hell I was currently living in. Cain had sworn to leave me down here for a month. The last time I'd seen Hastings, I'd asked him how long it had been, praying that my time was almost up and this endless eternity would finally relinquish me from its grasp, because I was sure that I had served my time already. And I had.

I'd been down here almost three months now and there was no sign of me being let back out. No sign of Cain. No sign of hope.

Had I been a total fool for believing that I could pull this off? I'd come here thinking I could break myself out and bring Sin and Roary with me, but here I was, sitting in a tiny box of darkness, all alone and forgotten by the world.

What would Dante be thinking? My cousin hadn't wanted me to take on the insanity of this task, but he had understood why I felt I had to. But now it had been months without a word from me and I knew he and the rest of my family would be going out of their minds with worry. They should have been informed that I was in the isolation unit, but I couldn't be certain of that.

The only thing I could be certain of these days was the fact that I was trapped here. With nothing but the memories of my papa's voice to keep me company.

"Your momma was a whore, only good for one thing and I'm starting to believe that you're no better. Perhaps I should stop trying to make you into something you clearly aren't capable of becoming and let the members of my pack put you to work the only way you're good for?"

"I'll do better, papa," I begged, the pain of my broken fingers excruciating and making it almost impossible to focus enough to speak.

Felix stared down at me as I fought not to tremble beneath him and I looked back. A small, foolish part of me ached to meet his gaze full on and hold it, stare him down and challenge him, lunge for his throat with teeth and claws. But I didn't. Perhaps that was how all of this was going to end. With the taste of his blood on my tongue. But I didn't think so somehow. More likely I'd be the one bleeding out on the carpet if that were to happen.

His lip curled back in that sneer he saved especially for me and he lurched forward suddenly, catching my wrist and making me scream as my broken fingers were jolted.

"Let's see then shall we, runt?" he asked, dragging me through the house and out onto the porch.

I almost fell as he hauled me down the front steps before dragging me across the yard, heading for the bonfire that always seemed to be burning and the three men who sat around it drinking beer.

Papa's pack always lingered close by. There wasn't a time that I could think of when there hadn't been at least five of them in or around the yard. In fact, this group of three was the smallest I'd ever found here.

"My darling daughter isn't making good progress with her pain control lessons," Papa announced as the three huge Wolf shifters turned their attention on me. They weren't even blood related Oscuras. None of Felix's pack were aside from his other children and with the way he always talked about the strength of his family, I had always wondered why, but I never dared question it.

"You need some help with her again?" Bert asked, eyeing me like a tasty rabbit who'd just crossed his path.

A few months ago, Papa had made me run into the woods and warned me not to let any of his pack catch me for a full day or he'd punish me worse than ever before. These three had been amongst the Fae to chase me out into the dark beneath the trees.

But I was fast. My Wolf form big and swift and built for speed in a way none of the other Wolves I'd ever met seemed to be.

I'd run into the forest with the mountains set firmly in my sights and managed to evade every damn one of them. I'd wanted to keep running, never look back and never feel the solid weight of my papa's fists striking my flesh again. But fate had turned on me then, too. A blizzard had picked up and snow had fallen thick and fast. Even in my Wolf form, I hadn't been able to pick out the scent of anything to eat and the path across the mountains had become more than treacherous. I'd near died from the cold despite my thick coat and eventually, I'd been forced to turn back. I'd been gone a week and had feared my return more than anything, certain that I'd be punished for disappearing for so long.

Instead, upon my return, Papa had praised me for remaining undetected for a full week and had swept me into his arms, placing kisses on my cheeks. For a full burning evening, I'd believed that everything was going to change. He'd made sure I was well fed, given me a new blanket for my room, praised me and called me his *figlia* - daughter - *in front of his whole pack.*

But of course, the next day he just made it clear that he expected more from me now than ever. He'd pushed and pushed as he subjected me to what he liked to call pain control training which meant he would injure me and then expect me to perform tasks for him while making myself ignore the pain.

"Perhaps," Papa said in answer to Bert's question. "I'm just trying to decide if she's even worth the effort I'm putting in to training her. It occurred to me that she might be more useful as a pack whore instead."

Ralph chuckled, his muddy brown gaze trailing over my thin body and I stiffened at the look he was giving me. I might have only been eleven, but I knew well enough what sex was. Papa's pack took part in orgies regularly and publicly. I'd seen all three of these men fucking various Wolves out on this lawn, but up until this moment, there had never been any suggestion of me participating in that.

"She hasn't even got any tits yet," Ralph joked.

"Take your clothes off, runt, and show them what you've got to offer," Papa said casually and for the first time in my life, the idea of getting naked in front of other people disturbed me. I'd been shifting since I was three years old so stripping down or even just bursting out of my clothes was a pretty standard practice for me. More people had seen me naked than I could count, but this was different and I knew it.

"I guess it doesn't matter about her tits if you just go at it doggy style," Curt put in and the three of them laughed, though I was almost certain that none of them were actually interested in doing the things they were saying. I'd seen the way they looked at other Fae when they wanted them for sex and there didn't seem to be any of that predatory darkness in their gazes as they looked at me.

"Strip off, Rosalie," Papa suggested. "Let them see what their new pack whore is working with."

"No," I growled, jerking away from him and cradling my injured hand to my chest. "I'm not a pack whore."

I knew what he meant by that term. There were enough of them hanging around here in the evenings and on the weekends. They were low ranking Fae, Wolves with little strength magically or physically who bought their way into the edges of the pack by offering themselves up as servants to the main pack. They ran around after them like little bitches and had sex with them whenever the mood struck, but that wasn't me. I wasn't born to serve. It was the one thing I was certain of about myself and I wasn't going to ever pretend otherwise.

"Well," Felix said. "I think you'd better prove it then."

He glared down at me with a dark and hungry look in his eyes which promised I would pay dearly if I didn't manage to do what he was demanding of me, but I knew him well enough to understand that this was no empty threat. He would force me to my knees for these men or others in his pack if I couldn't be what he wanted me to be. And even if they didn't want me for that now, I knew it wasn't long until they would. Another few years and I'd be a woman instead of a girl and they'd take whatever they wanted from me then unless I managed to show them exactly what I was made of so that they didn't dare try.

A soft whimper caught in my throat as I glanced down at the three broken fingers on my right hand, but I fought it off before anyone could hear it.

I took a deep breath, focusing on everything aside from the pain until I could almost block it out entirely and then I shifted.

The change ripping through my broken bones was agony unlike anything I'd ever known, and I couldn't help but hold my front paw off of the ground as I settled into my Wolf form between all of them.

"Fuck, she's big," Curt murmured as my Wolf form put me on eye level with my papa for once. I was already bigger than a fair few of the adult Wolf Shifters in the pack and it was becoming clear to me and everyone else that I was going to become one of the biggest, most powerful Wolves among us in time. I just wasn't sure how Papa felt about that.

"Good," Papa purred, his eyes lighting with the knowledge of *how much that must have hurt me. Every other time I'd tried to shift since he'd taken a hammer to my hand this morning, the pain had forced me back into my Fae form. "Now run a circuit of the property. If you can make it back to me within five minutes, I'll heal your hand and we won't have to call off our training. If not, you can sleep in the barn with your broken fingers to remind you of your own failures."*

I turned and ran without trying to make any protests. I knew they would fall on deaf ears anyway. But it took me almost five minutes to circle the property when I was fully fit, doing it with my paw screaming in agony seemed impossible. But I refused to back down. I wanted him to heal me. So I was going to run like the damn wind and make it back there in five minutes even if it killed me.

I flexed the fingers of my right hand as I fought against those memories, trying to centre myself in the present and cursing myself for falling asleep. Felix always haunted me in my dreams. But down here in the dark, it was harder than ever to stop him from doing so during the day too. Not that I knew it was daytime. For all I knew, the sky could be dark way, way, up above me. Sometimes I felt the faintest prickle against my skin which made me almost certain that the moon was shining somewhere up there, calling my name and missing me like I was missing it.

I would give everything I had just to run beneath the moon one more time. Not that I had anything now. Down here I was nothing and no-one. I was forgotten and alone. I was all the things my papa had threatened that I would become.

I tugged my arms inside the sleeves of the black sweater which made up part of my Isolation unit uniform until I was hugging my chest within the confines of the baggy, rough material. My fingers traced the curves of my tattoo there, following the lines of the scars I'd hidden within it. A man who was supposed to be my enemy had given me that tattoo. He'd shown me that I could take the pain of my past and turn it into something beautiful, powerful, unstoppable. My tattoo symbolised my family, my Element, my undeniable strength and perseverance. But it also hid my weaknesses too. I disguised my scars because I couldn't bear the pain of the memories that went with them. I might have been able to use that pain to my advantage, but that didn't take the sting out of them. Sometimes I just felt like that little girl who had been beaten and broken and forced to bend to my papa's will. Even after I'd thought I'd escaped him and gone to live with my Aunt Bianca, he'd managed to come for me again, one final time. And it was hard to ever believe that I was totally safe from him even now I knew he would never be able to come for me again. Especially as he still haunted me in my dreams.

For the briefest moment, as my fingertip slid over a scar along my ribs, it was like I could feel the white hot, blinding pain of that blade carving into my flesh. Sun steel. The most deadly weapon known to Fae. The damage it caused impossible to ever fully heal. I could almost feel the vines that bound me to that cold, metal table, almost smell the tang of old alcohol on my papa's breath. Almost hear my screams.

I lurched off of my uncomfortable cot in the corner of the room and threw myself over the toilet as I began to heave, shoving my arms back through the sleeves of my sweater. But there was nothing in my empty stomach to come up. I just heaved until I fell back on my ass panting, and the terror and pain of those memories finally faded enough for me to breathe again.

I almost felt like that once more, this tiny cage bringing back all the memories I held inside me of all the times I'd been pinned at that man's mercy. Locked in the dark and left to suffer for him. And now I suffered at the leisure of another.

Cain might have hated me for what I'd done, or what he believed I'd done, and though at first, the idea of that cut me up inside, I'd come to realise that it didn't matter. I might have done some things with no motive beyond my desire for him, but I had used him too. I still would, given half the chance. He'd shown me who he really was, and I wasn't fool enough to ever doubt that again.

So in place of any misguided feelings I might have started to believe I had felt for him, I'd placed two solid facts which I could state with truth and venom.

I saved his life.

He left me to rot.

And if I ever got out of this stinking hell and there was even the slightest part of me left able to fight then I would direct all of my hatred his way for what he'd done to me.

Mason Cain was a dead man walking.

He just didn't know it yet.

ARIES. VAMPIRE. FIRE.

COMMANDING OFFICER

CAIN

DARKMORE
PENITENTIARY

Twelve was supposed to be out of sight, out of mind. So why was she out of sight, but so deeply in my fucking mind that I couldn't think of anything else? It was like I'd chained her up inside my own fucking head and she was scratching at the walls, tearing out chunks of my damn brain. *Bitch.*

I hated her. I fucking *loathed* her. But I was obsessed with her too. No, I was possessed *by* her. That girl had some sort of magic about her that could bypass the cuffs and worm its way under my flesh. She'd used me. Manipulated me. Made me think that I – she – we –

"Fuck," I gritted out.

I was in the guards' gym, working my body to its limits as veins bulged in my arms and sweat poured over my naked chest. No matter how hard I pushed myself, nothing worked to force her out. Even after all this time.

I'd considered leaving this forsaken fucking place, but then I'd be facing the pathetic truth that I tried to ignore as much as Faely possible. I had nowhere to go. Outside of these walls, I had nothing and no one. In here, I had one thing that kept me sane. A purpose. To keep the monsters of the world contained while ensuring I didn't end up joining them myself. Because if I left here seeking another life, I knew how it would go. The bloodthirsty creature in me wouldn't rest. I'd find ways to feed it. I'd go too far. And one way or another, I'd be hauled back here in cuffs. I knew that on some base level.

I already pushed the boundaries of legality on too many

occasions. Attending underground hunts was the least of it. And now Twelve had shown up with her pussy hypnosis and innocent eyes. She'd had me by the balls. Had me risking the one thing that I'd claimed as my own. A job I'd worked tirelessly to secure. Which I'd given everything to because the alternative was becoming what had always been expected of me. And I'd thought for half a fucking millisecond that what we'd had was real. That I'd found a girl who not only sought out that monster in me, but coaxed it from the dark and accepted it as a part of me. But what she'd really been doing was making an idiot out of me. Of course she hadn't *liked* me. I was the most unlikeable fucker in Solaria. I had nothing to offer a girl, nothing but perks in a hellhole like Darkmore. And it was blindingly obvious now that that was what she'd wanted from me. *So why hadn't she let me die?*

I threw the fifty pound dumbbell in my grip across the room with a roar of rage, panting heavily as heat coursed under my skin. It was Saturday. The staff who weren't working were home with their families, seeing their friends. This place was a ghost town. And that was the way I liked it. But why did my life feel just that much more hollow since Twelve was no longer a constant in my day? And that was saying something considering the size of the void that lived in me.

Why did I go over and over in my mind the moment she'd saved me from the Belorian's poison? Picking through my reaction, the relief I'd felt waking to her, the heat of her mouth against mine, then the icy prickle of betrayal as I realised how long she'd been using me. She'd been up to something. She was *always* up to something. And though I'd known that all along, I'd still let her use me, let her manipulate me with my lust for the hunt. I'd handed the girl my balls and locking her up had felt like my only option.

The first few days, I waited for her to talk. For the Warden to call me to her office and not only strip my position from me, but hand me to the FIB for abusing inmates. I'd hunted the pretty little Wolf. She could have easily put on her big eyes and spilled a few tears while she told them how I'd abused her. But she never talked. And I didn't know why.

I swallowed the throbbing lump rising in my throat, ignoring the twist in my gut that always came whenever I thought of her. Alone in the hole. Pawing at the walls. And I was *constantly* thinking of her.

I didn't go down there, didn't go near the place. I was working double shifts again, content to spend long hours overseeing the inmates rather than spend any time alone with my thoughts for too long. Not that it helped a whole lot. But it was better than being here, like this, with the quiet pulsing loudly in my ears and my thoughts running wild. But Warden Pike had insisted I take time off this weekend, so now I was trapped with myself and a thousand thoughts of her.

I strode from the gym, heading down the grey corridor and into my quarters. I moved through the bare room with its single bed and blank walls, marching into the en-suite and kicking out of my shoes, dropping my pants and stepping into the shower. I turned the water on so hot that it burned and shut my eyes to try and focus on the heat, letting it sear my flesh and draw all of my attention. Except that it didn't. Because when I closed my eyes, *she* was there staring back at me, those big hazel irises glinting, drawing me in, promising things I had accepted would never be mine a long time ago. Her magic was so strong that maybe she could Bedazzle Fae even with those cuffs in place. She was a temptress like none I'd ever known. I found myself obsessing over everything from the taste of her blood to the secrets in her eyes. I wanted it all. I wanted to cross every boundary and barrier that kept me from her and seize her as *mine*. It was more than a need, it was a base instinct. One I grappled with every day because that was exactly what she could never be.

My cock hardened as she took up residence in my head and I growled my fury at that reaction to her. My body was a fucking traitor. I knew the truth now. I knew what she'd wanted from me all along. Her magic had been free; that bitch had gotten hold of a fucking cuff key and somehow Shadowbrook had ended up with it. Had he been working with her? It didn't make sense. And then he'd come asking me about when she was getting out of the hole, and if that wasn't shifty as shit then I didn't know what was.

I growled. Whatever it was, she was up to no good. And she'd been playing me like a fucking fiddle.

And yet as angry as I felt, as much as I wanted to crush her for manipulating me, I hadn't breathed a word about the cuff key to Warden Pike. Call me a fool, a fucking half-brained moron, but I had, for reasons beyond my comprehension, kept her dark little secret. Maybe it was because she'd kept my secret, or maybe I'd never intended on telling the warden at all.

I'd ensured the situation was neutralised anyway by encouraging Pike to upgrade all of the cuffs in the prison, so it wasn't like the key would do her any good now even if she had still had it stashed away somewhere. But that didn't explain why I hadn't exposed her. She would have had ten years slapped onto her sentence for it. And I kept telling myself that was another reason why I'd held my tongue. I didn't want her around any longer than I was already going to have to put up with her. *Sure, asshole, that's why you did it.*

I wrapped my hand around my cock then bared my teeth as rage built inside me like the fires of the sun lived in my flesh. I jerked off over her almost as often as I bled inside over her. I despised myself for it. But I despised her more.

I let go of my hard on and threw my fist into the white tiles instead, again and again, until they cracked and shattered beneath my blows. With my Vampire strength, I soon had a sizeable hole pounded into the wall, the remnants of the tiles coated in blood from my split knuckles. I let the pain of crushed bones in that hand steal me away as I clenched my teeth through the agony. But nothing would steal *her* away from my mind. No matter what I did, or what I endured to rid her from my fucking soul, nothing worked.

I finally had to accept that Rosalie Oscura was here to stay.

And I might just go mad and end up in Psych over her one day soon. Then maybe the drugs pumped into my veins to silence me would be some kind of mercy.

***

I sat in the warden's office as Pike placed a white binder on the desk between us.

"The new cuffs have been quite the success, don't you agree?" she asked, straightening a pen beside the binder so it lined up exactly.

"Yes, ma'am." I touched the remote around my neck. I could key in a specific inmate's cuffs at any time and check the status of their magic, switching them on or off at a press of a button. I could also shut off the entire prison's magic or switch it on. But there was a code and a magical signature scanner for that so even if some shady asshole got hold of it, they wouldn't be able to use it.

"I have a few more upgrades in the works, but most importantly, this one." She opened the binder, pushing it toward me and I took in the blueprint of the prison and the newly highlighted magical barrier that ran deep into the earth, circling the entire underground complex.

"What is that?" I asked curiously.

"The biotech company who created the Belorian have been working on it for a while now. It's going to cover a few blind spots I've been concerned about for some time." She tapped on the blueprint, pointing out the gaps between the detectors in the earth surrounding Darkmore.

"The chances of someone tunnelling out there are slim to zero," I pointed out. "And the detectors are placed randomly. It would take a miracle to get through them."

"Yes, but I must account for miracles," she said slyly. "The new barrier will ensure that absolutely no miracles can happen in Darkmore Penitentiary."

I nodded, satisfied by that response. Any layers of protection that kept the psychos where they belonged was good enough for me. "When will it be put in place?"

"Six weeks," she announced, beaming with pride. "It's going through the final trials then the lab guys said they can have it up and running within a week once they come to install it. Will you let the other guards know?"

"Of course," I agreed.

"Good." She leaned back in her chair. "The Belorian is well healed since its escape, but I've asked the lab to have a few more in the pipeline in case anything happens to it. We can't afford to have gaps in our system. We have a reputation to uphold, but better than that, we will improve upon it."

"Good to hear, ma'am," I said.

"How's your report coming along on inmate Twelve? She should have started correctional classes by now, is her time in isolation drawing to an end?" She arched an eyebrow and I fought the urge to shift in my chair. I hadn't started the damn report I was supposed to hand in about her. I needed to suggest classes based on her behaviour. But every time I went to do it, I ended up worked into a rage again.

"It's...coming along. But I'm eager to ensure she learns her lesson since her attack on me before she's released." I'd had to come up with some reason to cover why I'd locked her in there. And that was the simplest one which justified the length of time she'd been isolated. My throat tightened at the thought of her in there alone for all this time, but I pushed away any uncomfortable feelings on the matter and lifted my chin. "Another few weeks at least. New inmates need to have the message driven home."

"Well you're the best at what you do so I'm sure you know what you're doing."

"I do," I agreed. But I didn't. I was keeping her in there for selfish reasons as much as anything else at this point. Because I knew that the second she was let out, I had to be ready to regain control over her, resist her manipulation, figure out what the fuck it was she wanted from me and ensure I never crossed the line with her again. Even as I thought of my past mishaps, playing cat and mouse with her down on the maintenance level, my mouth watered over her blood and my cock twitched with the memory of her body pressed to mine.

Fuck. I've got to get a grip.

"Alright, make sure that report is sent to me before she's released though. I want her behaviour being corrected as soon as she's back in gen pop."

"Yes, ma'am," I agreed, rising from my chair as I sensed this conversation was over.

"Oh, and Officer Cain..." Pike steepled her fingers together, eyeing me with a stern expression. "I am aware you have been neglecting to visit Twelve. But she is still under your supervision. Don't forget your duties."

I paused a moment, hoping I wasn't detecting any suspicion in her tone, but I concluded that she was just towing the line with me when she didn't elaborate. "Yes, ma'am."

I walked for the door, my legs like lead as I turned the handle and stepped outside. The air was too thick as I dragged it into my lungs.

My fate was written for me. I'd run out of time to try and get these rampant feelings under control over the Wolf girl. I had to face her. And I hoped to fuck I was strong enough not to fall prey to her again.

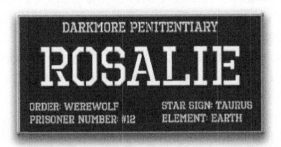

I never should have let my tears fall. That was the real lesson I was learning here. It wasn't about me having a total lack of emotion. I didn't think I'd ever be able to stop myself from feeling anger or longing or fear. No more than I could stop myself from feeling the pain of the injuries he gave me and forced me to battle through. It wasn't about becoming some emotionless monster who felt no pain. It was about making the world believe that it was so.

My tears gave me away just like a whimper of pain would. What I was really being taught in my papa's home was how to construct a mask for myself and how to never take it off. At least not where anyone else could see.

I should have known better than to cry. I'd been here long enough to know it only made him angry, and he always loved a reason to punish me. I didn't know if I feared the beatings more or the lingering torture of this kind of punishment. Locked in the dark.

I wondered if he'd had this place carved out just for me. It was little more than a crawl space beneath the front steps of the house. The dirt was dry and cold beneath me. So dry that it made me cough if I breathed in too deeply.

There were thin cracks between the wooden planks that made up the stairs so during the day I had a little light, but that was when it was most likely that Papa would come too.

He sat on those steps and used his water magic to form little drips which splashed down onto my skin and made my heart leap and pound with fear. Sometimes they were ice cold, sometimes scalding hot so they burned me where they landed. I couldn't even move to avoid them. The space down here was only just big enough for me to lay down flat in. I couldn't sit up, let alone stand and I could hardly even roll over. He made me crawl inside when he wanted to punish me this way and if I didn't do it, he gave me injuries to nurse during my incarceration too.

Every time a set of heavy footsteps would pass overhead, I'd flinch and cower like a little pup, whimpers of fear and panic rising up in my throat like bile which I was forced to chomp down on. Because if he heard me, it would only get worse. Sometimes the footsteps passing overhead weren't him. Just another pack member coming and going. And I didn't even know if that was worse because the fear of his arrival was even more paralysing than the tiny space I was crammed into. I was desperate for him not to come while knowing with all certainty that he would.

But this time, while I lay in the dark and waited for his arrival, I refused to let my fear rule me. I kept my breathing calm and my eyes shut as I let myself daydream about the kids I used to see playing out in the park by my mamma's old apartment before Felix Oscura had found me and taken me away. I used to watch them laughing and playing and imagine myself amongst them. I'd seen enough of life outside of my own to understand that I was missing something vital. And if there was a single thing in this world which I was determined to claim for myself then it was that. Normal. Freedom. Happiness. So if I had to learn to play this role for my papa to earn it then so be it.

Heavy footsteps sounded overhead and I expelled a slow breath as they paused. Little tendrils of dust were knocked loose from the steps above me and fell over my face, but I didn't flinch. I just waited.

When the silence dragged and my heart was racing so fast that I could hardly draw breath, my lips parted and words spilled from my tongue without me ever giving them permission to do so.

"Can we get this over with? I was hoping to do something better with my day than just sit down here like a stronzo."

The pause that followed my outburst had fear coursing through my veins for several achingly long seconds before Papa's rough laughter rang out. His boots thumped back down the steps and the little door he'd installed on the side of them to lock me in here swung open as he unbolted it.

His hand latched around my ankle and I stifled a scream as he dragged me out from beneath the steps until I was laying on my back beneath him in the faint moonlight which shone through the clouds.

"What do you suggest we do tonight then, runt?" Papa asked, his eyes flashing with warning but there was something else there too. Like a hunger, a need. There was something he wanted from me and even though my heart was racing and I had to fight not to let my hands shake with fear, I raised my chin and forced myself to speak again.

"I want to sleep in my own bed tonight," I said firmly. "So tell me what I need to do to make that happen."

A slow and deadly smile spread over my papa's face which really should have filled me with fear, but I was beyond that. I didn't care what he did to me or what he demanded of me. I just wanted to take some small measure of control back over my own destiny. So I'd do whatever it took to get what I wanted.

"It looks like someone has finally realised how to stand up for herself. Maybe you're not a runt after all. Come on, there's something I want to show you. If you can watch without giving away a sniff of those delicate little emotions of yours then I'll give you your bed and I'll throw in some dinner too. So what do you say, Rosalie? Do you think you can handle that?"

"Yes," I growled because I didn't care what it took. No one else in this filthy, stinking place was going to swoop in and start taking care of me, so that meant I was going to have to do it for myself. I'd paint on the mask he wanted me to wear so perfectly that no one would ever be able to tell what I was really feeling again. If my papa wanted to make me into a monster in his image then that was what he was going to get. I just hoped I wouldn't forget the girl I buried beneath the mask, because I got the feeling she wouldn't get much time to see the light again any time soon.

Papa strode away from me across the yard and I followed, stripping my dirty clothes off as he did and shifting into my silver Werewolf form. I inhaled deeply, trying to ignore the stink of my papa and his pack that filled the air around here and focus on the fresh breeze that blew in from the mountains with a sweeter scent. There was a promise of freedom on that wind. Something I yearned for in the depths of my soul.

Papa gathered his clothes between his teeth so I copied and when he took off across the yard, I made sure to keep up.

He ran flat out and I raced to match his pace, shivering in pleasure when the moonlight breached the clouds for a moment and trailed along my spine. I wished I could howl a greeting to it, but the clothes in my mouth made that impossible, so instead I just silently thanked it for its company.

The moon was the only true friend I'd ever known. And as sad as that was, at least I knew it was reliable. Come rain or shine, night after night it would be up there in the clouds, waiting for me.

Felix raced well beyond his yard and through the fields which surrounded his property. He owned everything out here for miles and the darkness of the night seemed to hold all kinds of his secrets in its shadows.

As we ran towards a huge warehouse on the edge of the trees, the cloying scent of blood hit the back of my throat and I had to fight not to slow as I realised where he was taking me. I'd never been inside that building before, but this stench of blood and death always lingered around it, so it was easy enough to guess what happened here.

Felix ran straight towards the doors and one of his pack mates pulled them open to admit us.

When we arrived inside the barren space, Papa dropped his clothes and shifted back into his Fae form. He quickly pulled his clothes back on and I hurried to follow suit.

"Come, Rosalie," he growled. "You can watch and learn. Assuming you can control those emotions of yours, you'll have a full belly before resting your head on soft pillows tonight."

My stomach rumbled hopefully at the prospect of that and I hurried along at his heels as he led me through the warehouse to the *very centre of it.*

My gaze had been stoically fixed on Papa's back, so when he stopped, I came up short. He stepped aside, his gaze fixing on my face as I was given a view of the woman he had strapped to the metal table in the centre of the cold warehouse.

Her face was bruised and swollen, her nose looked broken and blood stained her chin.

"Help me, child," she begged as her brown eyed gaze fell on me. "Get me out of here, he's going to kill me. I have a family. I-"

Felix punched her hard enough to knock a tooth skittering away across the concrete floor and I fought with all of my strength not to flinch as she wailed.

"Get comfortable, runt," Papa said as he picked up a roll of leather from a small shelf at the foot of the table and slowly unravelled it. "I like to take my time ridding the world of Lunar scum."

The woman began sobbing as papa pulled a stunning golden blade from within the folds of leather and held it up for me to see. Even in the flickering light from the old bulbs glowing overhead, the blade somehow managed to catch the light.

My breath caught in my lungs as I stared at it, wondering how someone even began to create something of such power and beauty.

"This is a sun steel blade," Papa explained as he saw where my attention had settled. "The only material known to the stars which will scar a Fae beyond the power of healing magic. It burns like the light of the sun itself lives within the metal when it cuts too. You have no idea what art I can create with this beauty, pup, but you'd do well to pay close attention and learn. Because this spot right here is where all scum and traitors end up. So if you've got any grand ideas of turning that hatred you feel for me into anything violent then just know that I won't hesitate to lay you out here and carve you up too. Blood of mine or not, once you're a part of my pack, the only way out is death."

I shuddered as the memories pushed in close, relief spilling through me as the guy in the cell across from mine started screaming again and yanked me out of them, forcing me to wake up before the worst part. Fuck, I hated that man. Even now, after all these years, I still hated him with the fury of all I was. Sometimes I wished I could force him to face me as I was now, with the full extent of my powers Awakened and my Wolf grown to full size. That bastardo would have quaked in his fucking boots if that day had ever come.

The screamer began slamming his fists against his door, crying out for a guard to come and let him out. He tried that shit at least six times a day, crying and begging and fucking screaming until my damn ears felt like bleeding. It never did him any damn good either. The guards were probably getting off on his pain.

My chest ached with a heavy sort of ache as I looked around my dark cell and shifted off of my uncomfortable bunk. There was no chance of me sleeping again with that nightmare lingering and his screams echoing throughout the entire isolation unit. Some of the other inmates would start yelling at him to shut the fuck up soon, but I didn't know why they bothered. It never made a lick of difference. And sometimes I welcomed his noise just to break up the fucking silence. Because sometimes the silence was too damn loud down here.

The only time he ever stopped was if the Vampire in the cell at the far end of the block yelled out for him to stop, though it didn't happen often. Every fucker in here fell silent if he commanded it. At first, I hadn't understood why, but I'd managed to get Hastings to tell me a little about him when he took me for my shower one day. Apparently he was a big stronzo, more powerful than any other Fae in Darkmore and one day a few years ago, he'd flipped out and killed over twenty Fae in the Magic Compound before the guards could disable him after losing an appeal to get out of here. The way Hastings had told it, the poor bastardo had been locked down in the hole ever since. He was just too strong for them to risk setting him loose in gen pop again.

I dropped into a set of push ups and tried to clear my mind of the memories of that woman's screams and the way my papa had smiled while he carved her apart with a deadly precision that ensured it took hours for her to die. I hadn't moved an inch throughout it. Hadn't looked away. Hadn't even blinked as far as I could remember. And now every single moment of that horror and all of the others that had taken place in that cursed warehouse lived on forever in my memories.

I tried my hardest not to think about my own scars and what it had taken to cause them. I pushed myself into the workout, making my body burn and ache in the only way I'd found to block out those memories down here.

My stomach growled in protest as I finished my set and started sprinting back and forth from one wall to the other. Six steps either way with a sharp turn as I slapped my hand against the back wall and then the door. It was all I had to keep me sane down here and the only way I could think of to pass the time aside from counting sheep and drowning in the darkness of my childhood.

One day I might have a whole Wolf pack's worth of my own pups and I could shower them with love and kisses to make up for all the shit I'd been denied. But it was hard to picture that while I was stuck in here. It was hard to picture anything beyond these four walls if I was totally being honest with myself. Though there was one thing which came to mind more often than I would have anticipated. Or rather one Fae. Although thinking about him invariably led me down a road of thinking about the other alphas who had caught my eye in this hell hole and I didn't know whether to just put it down to the fact that I hadn't gotten any in a really long time or if it was the fucking mate bond.

But that was just me bullshitting myself really. Because I knew it was the mate bond. I wasn't such an insatiable sex addict that I really believed I would have been fantasising about him this much aside from that. *Fucking Shadowbrook.*

I swatted at the crescent moon shaped mark behind my ear in frustration as it tingled and I was filled with the urge to run with him beneath the full moon. I wanted him to take me in his arms, hold me close and kiss me until I couldn't see straight. I wanted him to make all of this pain and worry in me fade away and just lock me in his arms and never let go.

I finished my sprints and turned my head up to the ceiling and howled, cupping my hands around my mouth to make the sound travel as far as possible, though I knew it wouldn't reach the man the moon had chosen for my mate. But maybe, in the deep recesses of his heart, he might feel me calling out to him the way I sometimes imagined I could feel him too. Not that I should really care whether he was pining for me or not. He'd gone to the effort to hide our bond with ink just to try and escape the shame of being bonded to someone like me. He hated me that deeply, based on nothing but the blood which ran in my veins and the family that had birthed me. It was pathetic. And I hated him for it. Even if I did miss him like crazy too.

Fuck my life.

I tugged the fugly black sweater off of me so that I was left in my tank as I dropped into an ab workout.

I was finally beginning to warm up and exercise was about the only thing that allowed that down here. The thin, scratchy blanket they provided me with certainly didn't do much to warm me. On the odd occasion that the nightmares from my past didn't wake me up, the shivering always would.

When I finished up with that, the itch in my mate mark was beginning to feel more like a burn and I fell back to lay on the cold concrete floor, cupping my hands around my mouth and howling again.

A beat later, I could have sworn I heard an answering howl. No, that wasn't right, I hadn't heard it. I'd *felt* it.

I sucked in a breath as a wave of pain and longing swept through me and I cupped my hands around my mouth as I howled again, long and low, the sound echoing in the small space that had been my prison for so long.

As that tug in my chest came again, I gasped, certain that somehow, somewhere, Ethan was answering me. The thought of that filled me with so many emotions that I didn't know what to do with them. Anger, frustration, hurt, envy, and so much fucking longing. I ached for the feeling of his hands on my body, his lips against mine, his soul close and heart pounding for me.

A sob escaped me as a tear slipped down my cheek, rolling down over my ear and sinking into my hair. I tried to choke it back, but I hadn't cried since that first night in here, at least not while I was awake. I'd fought against this hopeless, painful feeling with everything I had and now the dams were breaking and I knew I was helpless to stop it.

I rolled onto my side and curled in on myself as my mind stayed fixed on Ethan for a long moment before moving to Roary. I'd promised to get him out of here and all I'd managed to do so far was screw everything up and get myself locked away in a box in the pits of hell. I was so fucking useless. It was no wonder he didn't want me. Maybe I really was the same stupid pup he thought I was. Bigger tits and a cockier attitude didn't make me anything special. Maybe I was just full of shit and so desperate to fulfil the promise I'd made to rescue him from this hell ten years ago that I'd even managed to bullshit myself into believing I could.

Fuck, I missed him. I'd been missing him for so fucking long that it shouldn't have even been possible to ache for him more than I had been before I came here, but I was. Everything was different here. Before he'd been this unreachable fantasy and now he was more like the keeper of my tortured heart. It might have been bloody and ruined but it still beat for him. I was pretty sure it had since the very first time I'd laid eyes on him when he didn't even know I existed. Shit, sometimes it still felt like he didn't know I existed. I was just the dumb pup who'd come here spouting promises I was unlikely to ever keep now. Cain had forgotten me down here. He'd wanted to prove to me how little I meant to him and the world and he'd done a fucking good job of that.

That tug in my chest resounded through me again and I was sure that somewhere Ethan was in just as much pain as I was. And even the thought of that just cut me deeper, knowing my pain was hurting him and that I couldn't go to him.

I buried my face in my palms and sobbed as the utter hopelessness of my situation suffocated me and I was forced to consider the fact that I might just die down here. All alone and forgotten in the dark. As useless and pathetic as my papa had always claimed I was.

"Shit."

I almost didn't register the soft curse that came from behind me, but the rush of warm air from the corridor beyond my cell washed over my skin and forced me to accept that it was real.

A hand brushed against my shoulder half a second before I was rolling over and scrambling backwards until I hit the wall at the rear of my cell where I could glare at the guard who had found me in my weakest moment with as much venom as I could muster.

And of course it wasn't just any guard. Mason Cain stood in the doorway, highlighted by the fluorescent lights out in the corridor as he just fucking stared at me like I was supposed to be the one to break this silence between us.

"Twelve," he began hesitantly.

"Vaffanculo," I spat venomously, meaning it more than I think I'd ever meant that phrase in my entire life. *Fuck you.*

He took a step towards me and I stood as fast as I could manage, refusing to cower at his fucking feet even after he'd found me like this. I almost blacked out as I stood so damn fast thanks to the fact that I hadn't eaten for...well, I had no fucking idea because I had no fucking clock to go by, but I'd worked out that the food only came twice a day and tasted like utter shit. Perks of being in the hole and all.

Cain shot forward and caught my arm to steady me and I shoved him off with a deep snarl, baring my teeth at him, all fucking Wolf, reminding him that he was cornering a wild predator right now even if he had found me sobbing.

Cain released me and took a step back like he realised I was about three seconds away from ripping his throat out with my damn teeth even if my canines weren't as sharp as I would have preferred for the job.

I sucked in a breath as I shoved my tangled, knotted black hair out of my face and raised my chin, refusing to wipe away my tears. I wasn't going to be ashamed of them.

"I..."

"Is it time for my weekly shower?" I sneered. "Have you come to watch me freeze my tits off when they switch on the cold water so that you have something fresh to jerk off over later? Because I'm sorry to inform you, stronzo, that they aren't as big as they used to be. Two small meals a day plus a shit ton of exercise has made me lose weight during my time in here."

"I'm still your CO, Twelve, you can't speak to me like that and expect to get away with it," Cain growled.

"And what the fuck are you going to do about it, bastardo?" I taunted. "Extend my time from one month to three - oh wait, you did that already, didn't you? Or is it six now? Maybe a full year? Maybe you're just waiting for me to lose the plot entirely so that you can ship me off to Psych for one of your little experiments?"

"What do you mean by that?" he demanded, looking like he might try and grab me again and I snarled even louder than the first time.

"Lay a fucking finger on me and I swear to the stars that I'll rip your fucking cock off with my bare hand and flush it down the toilet before you even stop screaming."

"Watch your mouth," he warned, the angry asshole in him rising to the surface fast enough.

"What are you gonna do to me then, boss man?" I snarled, taunting him even though I knew I might live to regret it. But he'd already seen me broken, already knew exactly what being locked down here was doing to me, so it wasn't like there was any point in me trying to hide it.

Cain's gaze narrowed before he shot at me in a blur of motion. I was flipped up and over his shoulder before I'd really had a chance to even brace for it and the world blurred around me as he carried me out of my cell at full speed.

When we stopped, I found myself in the single shower unit that had been my only reprieve from my cell for the past weeks.

"Strip," Cain commanded, taking a step back.

I spat at his feet and cursed him. "Make me, stronzo."

His eyes darkened at the disrespect in my tone but I just sneered at him. He'd made an enemy of me and I wasn't ever going to forget it.

With a cluck of his tongue he shot at me again, pushing me back against the beige wall tiles before hooking his fingers into my sweatpants and shoving them down.

My tank went next, ripped off of my body with such savagery that the material tore in two instead of making it over my head.

"Is this what you want?" Cain growled at me as I stood beneath him in my horrible, shapeless prison underwear. "You want me to keep going?"

"I don't want anything from you, figlio di puttana." *Son of a bitch.* I shoved my panties down and tugged my bra off while he just stood there glaring at me like he had some fucking right to be angry with me.

When he didn't move out of my personal space, I stepped forward, knocking into him as hard as I could so that I could force his shoulder aside and stalk into the single shower unit.

I kept my back to him as I waited for the water to pour from the showerhead above me and tried not to gasp too loud as the stone cold water crashed down over me.

I remained as still as I could while the water soaked me, washing the worst of the sweat and grime from my body as I began to shiver. I hadn't been lying to Cain when I told him I'd lost weight and the tight muscles across my body had stolen a lot of the feminine curves from my flesh which also didn't help when it came to keeping warm. I'd probably be shivering for the rest of my day back in my cell. I wouldn't have the energy for another workout until the food arrived and I had no idea when that would be.

I reached for the scratchy bar of soap, which I was sure they bought with the intention of making us as uncomfortable as possible, and began scraping at my skin.

The longer I stood there, the harder the shivers wracked my body, but I refused to get out until I was fully clean. Leaving us filthy half the time was just another form of torture they offered the residents of the hole and I refused to make it any easier on them. I'd survived far worse than a cold shower in my lifetime.

"Why the roses?" Cain asked from behind me and I gritted my teeth as I moved on to scrubbing the soap into my hair. My beautiful, waist length black hair which was now so full of knots and tangles that I feared it would all have to be cut off if I ever did make it back to gen pop. They didn't even let me brush it, let alone have shampoo and conditioner and I'd never realised before now how important such small luxuries had been to me.

I chose to ignore the stronzo watching me shower and kept scrubbing my hair, but of course he wouldn't just leave it alone, pushing the issue of my tattoos as if he actually cared.

"Are they just because your name is Rosalie and you thought it would be a cute thing to get inked on your body?" he taunted.

I looked over my shoulder at him, knowing he was looking at the vines which curled over my ass and back from the tattoo which ran up the entire left side of my body.

"Every bloom on the vine represents someone I would gladly die for," I growled. "A morte e ritorno." My family's motto rolled off my tongue like an old friend. *To death and back.*

"So it's just gang bullshit then?" he asked and I tsked as the shivers in my body made it hard for me to even form a coherent response.

"When I was fourteen, something happened to me that left me scarred in every way a Fae can be, inside and out. I didn't want to spend the rest of my life looking at the evidence of what had happened to me and re-living it over and over again. So a man who had lived through just as much agony as I had taught me how to take my pain and turn it into strength."

I never spoke about that. Ever. But something about this smug stronzo just made me want to prove him wrong in all things. And as much as I shouldn't have given a shit what he thought of me, I wasn't going to let him make light of my darkness. Fuck him. Besides, this wasn't some deep and meaningful chat, just me informing the bastardo that I was never going to be afraid of him because I'd known true fear in my life and nothing he did to me could ever come close to that. "So I don't care if some prissy little stronzo like you wants to sneer down his nose at me and pass off everything about me like you know me. Because you have no fucking idea what it is to live my life or walk in my shoes. Becoming one of the Oscura Clan Alphas took more sacrifices and pain than you could ever comprehend with your idiota brain. So why don't you go back to lording it over me and enjoying the way this perceived power of yours gets you all kinds of hard, because I have nothing to say to you."

I began washing the soap from my ruined hair as best I could considering the tangles and I jolted as the water crashing over me warmed suddenly.

The suds spilled down my body and for one, long glorious moment, I bathed in the utterly amazing sensation of warm water caressing my skin. It was a damn shame that I couldn't enjoy it.

I blew out a breath of frustration and whirled around to face Cain, stalking out of the shower towards him and baring my teeth.

"I don't want your pity, stronzo. I don't want a single fucking thing from you," I snarled, grabbing the scratchy towel from the hook on the wall and scrubbing at my now pink skin.

"It's my responsibility to make sure you don't get sick and die on us, Twelve," Cain replied in a dark tone. "That wasn't pity, it was me making sure you don't get hypothermia and make me drag your peachy ass off to medical."

"Fuck you."

"And just for the record, I didn't grow up in some suburban daydream like you seem to believe. You're not the only person in the world who's had it shit."

I lifted my gaze to his and for a moment, I could have sworn that what I found there wasn't hatred at all. But I didn't care. He'd long since lost any chance of me feeling anything other than that for him.

My skin was tingling with my anger and for a moment I didn't even realise that it was more than that. I wasn't just angry, I was buzzing with a raw and potent energy and a faint, pale glow was beginning to form along my skin.

Cain's brows rose as he noticed it too and a dark smile curled my lips up as I glared at him.

"I curse you, Mason Cain," I hissed, every bit of venom I held in my soul for him rising up to the surface of my skin. "In the name of the moon that rules me, I curse you and wish you nothing but pain and misery." The glow on my skin grew brighter until I could feel my entire body buzzing with the power of my moon magic. I had no fucking idea how it worked but whenever I'd used it before, it had come just as easily as breathing to me and that was exactly how I felt now.

"How are you doing that?" Cain demanded, his gaze flicking to the illuminated cuffs on my wrists which were blocking me from using my magic. But this wasn't Elemental magic. This was something intrinsic to who I was, something soul deep and linked to my Order and my Wolf and even with the Order Suppressant locking that part of me away, I could still access this well of power that ran deep within my veins like moonlight when I needed it most.

"Ti maledico," I repeated in my family tongue. *I curse you.*

Cain shot forward and shoved me back against the wall, his hand clamping tight around my throat as he used his bulk to crush me. "Stop what you're doing," he demanded in that alpha asshole voice of his and I just smiled like a fucking psychopath as the contact between us made the silver glow spread out to encompass him too.

I gripped his wrist as my smile widened, whispering the words that the magic asked of me. "La luna maledetto." *Moon cursed.*

The moment the words left my lips, it was like all of that unearthly power shifted through my body, warming my skin and rushing to the point of contact where I held his wrist in my grasp before flooding into him.

He swore as he released me and the silvery glow left the room as I panted from the exertion of using my Order gifts even if I wasn't entirely sure what I'd done with them.

Cain ripped the button securing the cuff of his black shirt open and rolled the sleeve back as he looked down at the spot where I'd been holding him. A silvery mark adorned his skin on the inside of his wrist in the shape of a single rose on a thin vine.

"What the fuck is that?" he demanded, holding it out for me to see and I just looked back impassively.

"That's what the moon thinks you deserve, stronzo. It's no good asking me. I'm just a vessel for her will."

"Bullshit. You knew what you were doing when you cast that spell," he snarled, rubbing at his wrist like he thought the mark might come off. *No such luck there, sunshine.*

"Prove it," I taunted and it wasn't even total bullshit, because I didn't fully understand what had just happened, but to me the use of the word curse had been prevalent enough to clue me in.

Cain growled angrily, shooting forward and ripping me off of my feet before tearing back out of the room and through the long hall of the isolation unit until he reached my cell. We sped inside and he dropped me down, snatching the scratchy towel I'd been wrapped in from my body before thrusting a pile of fresh clothes into my arms.

"We have unfinished business, you and me," he warned as he backed up and I just smiled my cherry pie smile as I saw him rattled.

"No. We don't," I replied. "I have nothing to say to you. You're less than nothing to me. Just an asshole with a superiority complex and a vendetta. I hope you sleep well at night knowing how big and tough you are, pushing girls around and locking them in cages when you have their magic and Orders locked away and they can't fight back. You'd just better hope you never meet me outside of this place, *Mason,* because I would take great pleasure in ripping your head from your body with my teeth and using my earth magic to bury you deep beneath the ground where not even the worms would find you."

The door slammed in my face and I was plunged into darkness again, left to dress myself using only the light cast by the glow of my cuffs. I sank down onto my cot, feeling insanely worn out by the use of my gifts, but just before I could lay my head back against the hard bed, my fingers found a wad of material on the cot and a smile bit into my cheeks. Officer asshole had forgotten to grab my old sweater when he ran off. I might actually be able to sleep tonight without shivering.

Thank the stars for small miracles.

But as I tugged it on and lay back once more, I released a long sigh and the smile slid from my face. I may have won a few small battles today, but I was still losing the war. And as the four walls surrounding me seemed to close in once more, I knew the nightmares were coming for me the moment I closed my eyes.

Blue balls was my name. And raging hard ons was the game.

By the sun and that dipshit of a moon, why did I decide on waiting to fuck someone special after my time in isolation? Why couldn't I shove it in the nearest eager hole and be done with this agony? Old me would have. Old me was loose and had no standards. But dammit, I'd promised myself Rosalie Oscura and now she'd been shoved in a hole not even Plunger wanted to dick. I had to suck up this pain. But I was done waiting for my wild girl to be set free. Especially because I missed looking at her. And when she said stuff. And did that fluttery thing with her eyelashes.

I was attached to my little wild girl and I was tired of Roary glaring at me like I'd ridden all of his moms and slapped his dad while I did it. Was it *so* wrong that I'd let the Belorian out? Was anyone really *that* upset about it? Anyone who'd died was dead, and anyone who hadn't wasn't dead. So why were people still angry? And why did I feel...uncomfortable about it? There was a knotty, twisty lump in my stomach and an even sharper one in my throat whenever I thought of Rosalie. And I always thought of Rosalie. Not just her perky tits either, which was saying something. *Those tits are extra perky though...*

I ate my dinner on my own table with two helpings of gravy on my meal and four pudding pots piled up beside me. Roary Night was glaring at me again and I let my jaw fall slack to show him my mouthful of half chewed food, making him grimace and turn away. Ignoring social customs was one of the biggest weapons against society I'd ever learned to wield. If people thought you were deranged, they stayed the fuck away. Being unpredictable made me terrifying, even to guys who were bigger and stronger than me. Not that there were many of those around. But there was something about disrupting the norm that outright unsettled people. What they didn't realise was that I wasn't crazy. I was as free as a fucking bird. A caged bird, but still. These fuckers didn't even have the potential to spread their wings. Whereas the second I broke out of this place, I'd be back to my lawless life and no one would ever catch me again. Happy, wild and scaring people shitless.

Rec time was my favourite part of the day and I scoffed down my food and four puddings, not even slowing to savour their creamy middles as I devoured them before abandoning my tray on the table and heading out of the room. I glanced back to see the big Bear Shifter, Pudding, gathering the pots. He always did weird shit like that. I guessed one Fae's trash was another Fae's treasure. But it beat me what he wanted them for. If I had to guess, I would have said he was building a carefully constructed pudding pot outfit. It's what I would have done with hundreds of pudding pots.

I headed downstairs past glaring guards posted around the place. I marched into the gym and the icy cool air conditioning rushed over me, making my senses sharpen. The taste of chocolate pudding still sat on my tongue and it reminded me of Rosalie again. Of when she'd brought me a pot down in isolation. A growl caught in my throat as I thought of her down there where I'd been. It made me angry. Kept me up at night. Made me beat in heads daily just to get some relief from the furious emotions racking my body. She was my own special brand of pudding made of my darkest fantasies and my cock's personal temptation. She tasted like rainbows and the best fuck I was yet to have. She was sweet and pure and dark and wild. And I would make her sin for me so good that she'd never be able to forget me. Even when I was just some Incubus she'd screwed, I was still gonna be the best Incubus she ever screwed. Just as soon as I'd gotten a read on her desires.

I headed past another guard into the locker room, grabbing a pair of shorts in my size from the dispenser on the wall before stripping off and tossing my uniform into a locker. It didn't actually lock, so it kind of defeated the purpose of its name. Which was the opposite of me and my name. Guess they couldn't have inmates stashing shit up in here though. But there were far less conspicuous places for that in Darkmore anyway. If the guards thought they had us under control, they were living in a pretty illusion. And I was fine with that so long as I could continue quietly defying them, and loudly defying them too when the occasion called for it. With the burning heat of rage pounding through my limbs right now, I was starting to think it was time to send out invites to my up and coming defiance.

I pulled on the black gym shorts and pushed my feet back into my sneakers before heading out into the gym. My shoulder thumped against someone walking in and Roary Night growled at me as he waited for me to get out of his way.

"Move, Wilder," he demanded.

"Or what, pussy cat?" I shoved past him and Officer Hastings glanced between us uncertainly, his hand going to his baton.

I painted on a wide smile for the kid and strode over to the boxing ring which was standing empty. I gloved up and climbed inside, hungry for a fight today to release the beast which was constantly roaring inside me since my wild girl had been taken away. I usually challenged people in the Magic Compound, but I fancied feeling flesh on flesh today. Real Fae contact. Because the last time I'd gotten any of that was too many months ago for my brain to comprehend.

Incubuses needed the touch of other Fae, especially sexual touches. I had to stand in bushes like a creeper out in the Order Yard and feed on the sexual energy of anyone getting down and dirty. The Wolf packs were good feeding grounds for that with their orgies. The Oscura Clan had been having one every time they went to the yard as they consoled themselves over the loss of their Alpha. And I swear I'd cry wanked along with

61

them too a couple of times. But I'd made a vow to myself which I was keeping. Plenty of Fae had propositioned me since I'd returned to gen pop, but there was only one person I wanted to bury myself in. The pretty little Wolf who'd brought me pudding.

"Hey," I called out to a guy working on his bicep curls. He looked over his shoulder with a frown, his eyes widening when he realised who'd spoken to him. "Come here and fight me."

He parted his lips, then he shook his head, tossing his weight down and heading away at a purposeful pace. *Chicken shit.*

I propositioned a few more inmates and somehow managed to clear this whole section of the gym. I growled in annoyance and ached with frustration. *Why does no one want to play with me?*

Roary was the only one left down this end of the gym, deadlifting two hundred pounds. As he finished a set and mopped at his brow with a towel, I took in the rippling muscle on his torso and the sweat soaking his golden skin with a smirk.

"Hey, Night!" I called and he looked to me with a dark scowl. I wanted to feel the wrath of that anger full force. I was ready for it. "Come fight me."

"No one wants to fight you, asshole," he deadpanned.

"But why?" I demanded, hanging my arms over the edge of the ring as I frowned, curious and confused.

"You don't play by the rules, for one. You're a crazy motherfucker, for two." He shrugged, striding over to a water fountain and taking a few gulps.

"Real fights are unpredictable," I reasoned. "If I bite off an ear or two it's only because I'm fighting like I would in the real world." I had *maybe* done that the last time I'd fought in the ring, but boohoo. It was just an ear. And three fingers. "Come on, Night, you're always glaring at me. You want this fight. I know you do."

Roary turned to me, wiping his mouth with the back of his hand. His hair was pulled into a top-knot and a thick layer of stubble on his chin told me this Lion was getting lazy with his grooming routine. His upper lip peeled back and his eyes turned venomous. "Yeah I wanna fight you, Wilder. But you know why I won't? Because you want me to. And I'm not giving anything to the guy who got Rosa sent to the hole. You hurt her, so I'll hurt you. Not the way you expect it though. But the way you deserve it," he snarled and my throat thickened and my chest did that knotty thing again.

I paced in the ring, tearing off my gloves and tossing them to the ground. "Fight me!" I demanded, pounding my chest.

He turned his back on me, the biggest fucking insult a Fae could offer another Fae and something snapped inside me. There wasn't much left in my head to snap, but something sure as fuck did. And it had everything to do with Rosalie Oscura.

"I didn't want this!" I bellowed, gaining the attention of everyone in the gym.

Officer Cain pushed through the door at that moment and I saw red, violet, fucking magenta as that asshole moved further into the room. Sucked air out of this space, dared to fucking breathe this close to me when I felt like *this*. Like I was a monster pure and simple, and I needed death to survive.

It wasn't my fault Rosalie was in the hole, it was *his*. *He* was the one who'd caught her. *He* was the one who held the power in this place. *He* was the one who'd kept her locked up for month upon month in the dark.

I released a roar of rage and dove out of the ring, my feet hitting the floor as I swiped up two dumbbells and launched one across the room in the direction of Cain. It smacked into the back of a guy doing squats and he cried out as he fell down under the weight of the bar on his back. I kept throwing dumbbell after dumbbell and people screamed and started running.

Officer Hastings was closest to me as the guards shouted orders I couldn't hear and he started tearing toward me with his baton raised.

Roary Night stared at me with wide eyes as I shoved past him, leaping over a bench with the heavy weight of a dumbbell in my grip as I kept my eyes focused on Cain. I'd either kill him or get myself sent to the hole to see my girl. Either way, this would be worth it.

"Die devil teeth!" I shrieked, jumping onto a bench and springing off of it again as I raised the dumbbell above my head, soaring towards him like the wings of death.

His eyes were wide as he stared up at me and I swiped the dumbbell at his skull, but instead of the satisfying crack of crunching bone, my hand sailed through his fucking face and I stumbled as I landed. An illusion. *Shit a brick.*

A hand latched around my neck from behind and I was thrown with incredible strength onto the floor and the weight of a furious rhino landed on my ass. I finally got the contact I'd been craving for months and despite my bloodthirst, I still arched up into my enemy as he wrestled to pin my hands behind my back. I laughed manically as he muttered about me being a raving lunatic and *fuck* his hands were rough against my skin.

"Did you touch her like this?" I panted, getting off on the idea. "Did you pin the Wolf girl down like this, Officer?"

"Shut the fuck up!" He cracked my head against the floor, but my laughter only heightened.

He totally had.

My rage was twisting up into lust until I was lost to the cravings of my Order and the ache to see my girl. My emotions collided and set off fireworks in my head. Maybe I was mad after all, but it was all for her right now and I didn't care what the consequences were. People died for all kinds of reasons in this place, but for me it was going to be my balls combusting and my dick falling off from lack of use. It would have been funny if it wasn't so damn sad. And all because of one girl.

Cain yanked me to my feet, my cuffs now locked together behind my back as he marched me forward through a sea of furious looking guards. Two of them were helping out the guy who'd been crushed under his barbell, healing him as best they could, but that injury was gonna need a medic going by the angle of his neck adjacent to his spine. *Nasty shit that. Real unfortunate.*

"Clean this place up!" Cain ordered. "I'm taking Eighty-Eight to the hole."

I tried not to smile – alright, I didn't try that hard. I beamed like the Cheshire Cat and when I was marched past Shadowbrook's pack, I tossed that pretty boy Wolf a wink. Because I was going to see our girl. And he wasn't. *Sucks to be you, kitten.*

DARKMORE PENITENTIARY

ROSALIE

ORDER: WEREWOLF   STAR SIGN: TAURUS
PRISONER NUMBER: #12   ELEMENT: EARTH

"Oh I do like to be beside the seaside!"

The sound of singing jolted me out of my latest stint of self pity and horror filled memories and I pushed myself to sit up-right as it slowly drew nearer.

"Do you ever shut up?" Officer Lyle's exasperated voice sounded over the singing and my heart lightened at the throaty laugh which followed his words.

"Never. Not ever. I'll sing until my cock is blue and I'm humping the floor for some relief," Sin chuckled. "Oh I do like to be beside the blah, blah, blah, diddly dee da, da, da."

I pressed my ear to the door as he was led closer and couldn't help but smile at the sound of the cell door beside mine opening to admit him. I really hoped he wasn't back down here for murdering someone again, but I had to admit that I was more than okay with the idea of having him for a neighbour. My last one had done nothing but sob on and off for their entire sentence and had never once spoken to me.

"You know the drill, Eighty-Eight," Lyle said. "Strip off and change into the isolation uniform. Then we can leave you to enjoy some alone time."

"You're not fooling me, kitten," Sin purred throatily. "You just want a long, hard look at my Incubus cock. If you really want something to write home about, you could slip me some of that Order Suppressant and I could show you a real good time."

"Perhaps we'll just stick to you getting changed for now," Lyle suggested dryly and I waited as Sin did as he was asked and the heavy door finally closed again.

Sin instantly started up his song once more and a real smile pulled at my lips at his unbreakable spirit. When the heavy door which secured the isolation unit closed in the distance, I scrambled over to the small vent at the base of the wall connecting my cell to his and banged my shiny new cuff against it to get his attention.

"Who's that trying to ram down my back door?" Sin asked curiously and some movement through the metal grille caught my eye as he came to lay down and look through too. It was so dark down here that there was no way I could see him by the light of our cuffs alone, but somehow just knowing he was so close made the ache in my chest unfurl a little.

"Hey," I breathed, reaching out to brush my fingers across the grate dividing us as if I could imagine it was really him I was touching.

"Sex pot? Is that really you, honey bee? Oh, kitten, I've been missing you something chronic. When I swore not to fuck anyone until I'd had you, I didn't expect you to up and vanish on me for three months. I've been jerking off more than I was when I was locked down here for months by myself and that's saying a damn lot. In fact, I wish they'd put me back in my old cell because there was a crevice in that wall which felt like a rough, grainy pussy if I rubbed my dick against it just right and I'm gonna miss that bitch more than you can imagine this week."

Laughter tumbled from my lips, surprising him into silence but that was nothing to how shocked I felt. I hadn't felt anywhere near close to laughter in all the time I'd been trapped down here and yet within a few minutes, Sin had me grinning like an idiot.

"Holy shit, sweet thing, make that noise again. You have such a dirty laugh I just came a bit, give me a second to get my cock in hand and we might really have a party ready to get started."

"By the stars, Sin, don't you ever think about anything other than sex?" I teased, though I couldn't deny that deep, gravelly voice of his calling out to me in the dark was awakening more than a little desire in my body. He had a way of talking that just bypassed the crazy of his actual words and dripped sex all over me in deep and sensual tones which really made me curious about those Incubus skills of his.

"When I'm this close to your sweet ass? Unlikely," he purred and there was a definite sound of shifting material that followed his words.

"What are you doing?" I asked, a frown tugging at my brow.

"I assumed we were doing this thing," he said, a slight hesitance to his tone.

"What thing?"

"The whole phone sex thing sans phone. I swear, baby girl, I do dirty talk like no one you've ever met, you'll be coming even if you don't wet your fingers in that sweet, tight pussy of yours."

I laughed again and if I was being honest, that time I did catch the hint of sexy to the noise. But it was definitely unintentional. Probably.

"I don't think we've made it to that point in our relationship yet," I teased, though I had to admit that I was seriously tempted to take him up on his offer. My body was wound so tight that I was just bursting for some kind of release and I was certain that Sin would be a man of his word when it came to dirty talk.

"Right," he sighed. "Because you're mad at me for releasing the Belorian...unless you're not? Because Roary seemed to think that you were, but I told him that you were the one who told me to do it and then he said that you didn't but I was pretty sure we were talking in code when you said that, so help a guy out and cut me the truth, apple pie, because if you need to hate fuck this anger out of the air between us, I'm down for a bit of choking and heavy spanking, I just wanna get your safe word locked in first..."

"Wait," I spluttered, trying to fish the parts of that out that mattered. "You seriously believe I *wanted* you to release that fucking thing? You know it nearly ate me, right?"

"Nearly being the operative word, sugar tits. I bet it got your adrenaline pumping real good, huh? You wanna know what else can pump real good?" Sin asked and I had to fight away the urge to blush because goddamn that man was frustrating as fuck, but I was seriously lacking in recent orgasms and he was distracting as hell. At least I couldn't see him because if I was looking at that gorgeous face of his I was pretty sure that my resistance would be cracking even faster than it currently was.

"Sin," I growled and dammit, that growl was kinda sexual, but I was going to ignore that. "I've been locked down here for three months because of that thing."

"How so?" he asked curiously.

"Because it cornered me down by Psych and I had to let Cain see me using magic."

"Had to? Was it life or death?" he asked curiously.

"Yes," I growled. "And then the damn thing stabbed him with one of those poisonous spines on the end of its tail and he almost died."

"Almost? Damn. You shoulda finished him off, hot cakes, and you coulda saved yourself all of this time down here," Sin suggested like that was the most obvious thing in the world and sure, *now* it seemed that way. But at the time I'd been caught up in the ridiculous idea that Cain's death was intolerable to me, that he meant something to me, that we had something worth risking everything for. *More fool me.*

"I realise that now," I huffed. "But at the time I was obviously deluded as fuck because I opted to heal him instead."

"Oh fuck, you just killed my boner. Why the hell would you save that motherfucker's life?" Sin cursed. "I was pretty close to coming, too."

"What?" I demanded. "You're not seriously jerking off in there are you?"

"No. Not now, obviously," he replied pissily. "All that talk of saving assholes turned me right off."

"What the fuck, Sin? I thought we were having a serious discussion," I snapped. *Gah, he was so damn frustrating at times.*

"Well, I just thought you were really fucking bad at dirty talk and I was trying to spare your feelings," he grunted. "But now I know you're a guard lover, I don't know what to do with my cock."

"Maybe just put it back away?" I growled.

"Put what away?"

"Your cock, stronzo," I snapped.

"And we have lift off! Tell me how much you hate me for letting the Belorian out then, baby doll, and let's see how fast I can finish," he purred and the distinctive sound of his hand slicking up and down his cock made me blush, and bite my lip and consider things I didn't want to be considering right now because I was meant to be mad as all hell with him. But I'd also been so damn lonely down here for so damn long that it was hard not to just enjoy his company despite all my reasons to be mad.

"No," I hissed before buttoning my lip. He wasn't going to get away with this shit that easily and I certainly wasn't going to let him hate jerk off over me. Was that even a thing? Damn stronzo seemed to want to make it a thing. So I was going to give him the one thing that he couldn't use for any kind of sexual gratification - silence.

"Please, carina, I'm so hard and I've been aching for you for so long," he groaned and okay, I was maybe a bit flattered by the idea of this sexy as fuck Incubus saving himself for me, but I'd never admit it and I sure as shit wasn't replying. Plus, had he just called me carina? As in Faetalian for cutie? Because I knew for a fact he wasn't Faetalian. I'd read his file front to back and it was as short as it was sweet. Sin Wilder - or Whitney Northfield as he'd been christened - was a street kid from outer Iperia and he shared zero heritage with me. So maybe he'd made the effort to learn that for my benefit which I irritatingly couldn't hate on either because that was sweet as fuck. Even if it was just meant for dirty talk purposes.

"There's got to be something I can do to make you forgive me. Something you need..." he pressed and to be fair, I did still need the ingredients to neutralise the Order Suppressant.

"I could maybe forgive you, if you got me a Sunstone Crystal and a Nevercot Plum," I said slowly, wondering if he could pull it off.

"Maybe? Come on, bella, stop teasing me. I'll get you that Sunstone Crystal you need for your hocus pocus with the escape plan. And the Nevercot Plum too. I'll get 'em for you so good, you'll want to reward me for it with a night between those bronze thighs of yours. Hell, I can just bury my face down there and see how many ways I can use my tongue to make you come. Ball park figure I'll be going for is sixteen - did I ever tell you that I once met a guy whose ultimate fantasy was a Basilisk Shifter who had only shifted his tongue into snake form? I can shift it and make you feel things you've never even imagined, kitten."

"Are you ever just serious?" I asked him, raising an eyebrow even though he couldn't see me.

Sin groaned and huffed out a frustrated breath. "Fine. I'll put my dick away if you really want serious," he said. "But you'd be the first woman who ever wanted that from me in my adult life."

"Really?" I asked.

"Yeah," he said and there was a bitterness to his tone that made my gut twist. "When people figure out my Order they tend to be after one thing. In fact, I've never had anyone make me work for it like you do. Never had anyone make me work for it at all."

"Sin," I said softly, wishing I could reach out and touch him. "That sucks."

"Yeah well, what do I care? I can be every fucker's dirtiest fantasy and know for a fact that I'll be the best lay they ever have. What more do I need?" he said dismissively but there was a hint of anger to that statement too.

A long beat of silence passed between us and I sighed. "Tell me something about you," I said. "Something real. Not sexual. Something you care about."

He tutted like he didn't believe I really gave a shit about that, but I just waited for him to go on.

"I like fixing up old cars," he said eventually. "Like really fixing them up, the full works. Complete engine re-build, interior overhaul, paintwork, the lot. I had this fucking stunning old Minostang which I painted cherry red. It was like the ultimate sex on wheels car...err, I mean, forget the sex part of that, but you get the drift."

I smirked up at the ceiling as I imagined Sin camped out beneath the hood of an old engine, grease smeared up his arms and making those tattoos all dirty. It definitely wasn't a bad visual.

"My nonno used to have this old Faevette, bought it from new back in the sixties and it was a fucking beaut," I said.

"I bet," Sin purred. "Maybe if you really break my ass out of here, I can take you for a drive down the coast some time? The Cerulean Sea gets to just the right temperature for skinny dipping by midsummer and the Ammabond beach stretches on for miles and miles with nothing but pure, white sand. I was gonna buy myself a house right on the seafront there one day."

"Oh yeah?" I asked, closing my eyes as I pictured that slice of paradise. "I've barely ever left Alestria. My family is there, my gang, my whole world really. But I think I'd like to see that."

"You wanna date me, kitten? I promise I'll make you purr if you do."

I laughed and he groaned again.

"I thought you said no sex," he accused. "You can't offer up that dirty laugh and expect me not to get hard for you, sugar plum."

"I can't control how much you like my laugh," I protested and it didn't escape my notice that I'd laughed more in the last hour of his company than I had in the entire three months I'd been stuck down here. I mean I'd only have to have laughed once for that to be true, but still, I actually didn't feel like utter shit right now and that had to mean something.

"And I can't control how much I like making you laugh, beautiful girl," he said seductively and a shiver raced down my spine at his words. Fuck, a night with Sin Wilder was definitely going to be something to remember. Maybe I should have been considering his offer more seriously. Dating him would be one hell of a ride.

"How long were you down here before I got you out?" I asked him softly and he blew out a breath.

"Too long, kitten," he sighed. "Too fucking long."

A loud bang from the corridor outside made me flinch and the sound of several guards' footsteps pounding along the walkway drew my attention to the door.

A moment later my door swung open and the bright light from beyond it illuminated Hastings standing in the doorway with Officers Rind and Nichols behind him like two big, cumbersome statues that had been oddly placed. I swear those guys never even blinked. I didn't really know many Minotaurs so maybe they were all like that…or maybe these two were just all brawn and no brain.

"Good news, Twelve," Hastings said, offering up a bright smile as he looked down at me where I lay on the floor. "Your time in the hole is officially up. You are about to re-join gen pop."

My heart lurched as I looked to Sin, whose face I could just see illuminated through the grate now that the light from the corridor was spilling in.

"They only gave me a week this time, poppet. But if you wanna help me pass the time better, you could always flash me the goods." He winked like a cocky bastardo and I snorted a laugh as I rolled over to get up.

"Come find me in a week and we'll see," I said, winking right back and he groaned.

"That's a promise, sex pot."

Hastings moved to take my arm as I got to my feet and he offered me a small smile as he led me towards the door.

Rind and Nichols fell in behind us as we walked down the corridor to the exit and I waited patiently as Hastings flashed his security badge at the scanner before pressing his palm to the device so that it could confirm his magical signature.

I resisted the urge to moan in pleasure as we stepped out of the isolation unit and Hastings led me straight to the elevator.

"Oh shit, it's embarrassing how much I've missed my old cell in D block," I cooed as he hit a button and we began to ascend.

He was still holding my arm and I looked up at him with a flutter of my lashes despite the fact that I knew I looked like shit right about now. By the stars, my hair alone was enough to turn anyone off, but I was flirtatious by nature and I'd rather cover up my utter relief at escaping that hell and my desire to sob over it with an attempt at acting naturally than embarrass myself with the truth.

"Even better than that," Hastings said, grinning at me in that cute choir boy way that made the good girls swoon as he leaned closer like we were sharing a secret. "We just dropped the masses off at the Order Yard. I assumed you'd wanna free your inner Wolf after all this time."

I blinked stupidly, then threw my arms around him with an excited squeal. "Thank you, ragazzo del coro," I gushed, squeezing him even though I knew this wasn't exactly his doing and more a matter of perfect fucking timing, but I didn't give a shit. I hadn't had a hug in a damn long time and I was so excited I could burst. Wolves needed hugs dammit and okay, he wasn't returning my embrace or anything, but this was more than I'd had in months so maybe I was going a little bit limpet on his ass.

"Step back, inmate," Hastings warned, pushing me back gently but firmly and I released him with an apology, biting my lip like I was embarrassed as I batted my eyelashes again. Thank the stars that they were so long naturally because I definitely didn't have the luxury of mascara in here.

The elevator came to a stop on the first floor and Hastings guided me out of it and along the corridor to the elevators which led up to the Order Yard while I tried not to bounce with excitement and failed miserably.

Hastings pushed the call button and then I pushed it again. And again, jamming my fingers down on it over and over as I tried to force it to hurry the fuck up and Hastings tried to hide a smirk as he watched me.

When the doors finally opened, I hurried inside, grinning widely as Hastings caught my eye in the mirror and couldn't help but smile back. I nuzzled against him before I could stop myself. But he was like a cute little Wolf pup with those big eyes on and I guess being a Cerberus at least meant we had the canine thing in common, so I was pretty sure he got my need for the contact after so long alone.

Rind and Nichols were glaring at me and I dutifully put some space between me and my little choir boy as the elevator began to ascend and the sweet, sweet scent of the antidote washed over me, releasing my inner Wolf from the prison inside me.

We finally reached the top floor and the doors slid open, offering me a view of the lockers in the room which opened out onto the yard where I could be freer than I'd been in fucking months.

"Be careful out there. We'll leave your jumpsuit and standard uniform waiting here for when you return," Hastings called, but I was already gone, running and stripping out of the ugly ass isolation unit uniform and tossing stuff everywhere without a care for if I ever saw it again.

I sprinted out into the trees and cupped my hands around my mouth as I spotted the moon lighting up the dark sky above me like it had been waiting here for me this entire time. I howled, long and low in greeting, sure that my bare ass was as pale as the moon itself after all those hours in the dark. The next time I was out here in the sun I was gonna need to spend some time tanning up butt ass naked. Maybe I could join Roary on his favourite rock – though he'd probably go all Lion over it and wouldn't let me.

In the distance I caught the sound of my pack howling in reply and a ferocious joy spread through my chest at the thought of re-joining them. But before I could even shift, another howl pierced the night sky from the opposite direction and my heart skipped a damn beat.

I turned towards the sound of it with my pulse thundering and my breath catching. He was here. Waiting for me. And I needed to see him more than anything in the entire world right now.

"Ethan," I breathed, leaping forward and shifting in the blink of an eye, four huge, silver paws hitting the dirt and my claws gouging deep into it.

I howled again, the sound so much better in my Wolf form as I let every beast running in the dome tonight know that Rosalie Oscura was back.

I took off instantly, diving into the trees and racing towards him. I didn't even have to think about where he was, I just knew. I could scent him on the air, taste him on the breeze and every inch of my flesh was aching with the desire to reunite with him as the mate bond drove me his way with an insatiable desire.

I thundered through the pine forest then emerged in a sandy desert before racing on to a snowy tundra. Up ahead, I spotted a river crashing down a long slope and as my feet splashed into it, a solid black Wolf just as big as me emerged from the jungle which began on the other bank.

My nose was full of the pure, masculine scent of him and my heart raced with joy as I spotted this beast of mine, my equal, my *mate*. This want in me was a feral, desperate thing and it was as undeniable as it was irresistible. He was mine and I was his and there was absolutely no denying it in that moment.

We leapt at each other, colliding and rolling through the shallow water of the river in a tangle of limbs as we yipped and barked like a pair of excitable pups, nuzzling each other and planting wet licks on each other's snouts.

Ethan rolled on top of me and tried to pin me down and I

barked a laugh as I fought my way out from beneath him before taking off down the river.

He barked at me as he took chase and I howled at the moon again as I raced on, loving the feeling of my magic replenishing as the wind whipped through my fur and the river water splashed over my legs.

We ran on past rocky hills and a deep, dark lake before rounding the water's edge and racing towards a tall waterfall that stood there.

I dove through the cascading water, skidding into the cave beneath it on wet paws a moment before Ethan leapt in behind me. He growled playfully and the two of us fell into a tussle once more.

I managed to pin him beneath me and he shifted back into his Fae form suddenly, laughter tumbling from his lips as he smiled widely and his muscular body glistened with moisture from the waterfall. I shifted too, falling over him as a girl once more, my flesh instantly heating with need and desire everywhere as it met his.

"I missed you so fucking much," Ethan murmured and there was something pure and potent in those words which had me admitting my own true feelings too.

"I missed you too, Ethan," I breathed and as he leaned up to capture my lips with his, I gave in instantly.

There was no denying this bond between us, this need. It was urgent and hungry and irresistible.

He kissed me slowly, his mouth teasing mine and the taste of something so much purer than any words we'd ever exchanged on his lips. That kiss lit me up from the inside out, made me feel worshipped, adored, wanted, desired. Like I really was his true mate, his one and only, the beginning and end of all he needed and would ever need.

"I couldn't fucking bear knowing you were hurting so much down there," he growled. "I wanted to tear this entire prison apart to get you out. It hurt my fucking soul to know that you were locked up in the dark."

"I'm out now," I said, kissing him again and tasting his tongue, not wanting to think about that place. I just needed to enjoy this freedom. Enjoy him. "Now make me forget I was ever there."

Ethan growled hungrily, the beast in him showing as he tugged my bottom lip between his teeth and I moaned with longing.

His hand slid between us and he growled deeply as he slicked his fingers straight up the centre of me and I gasped. Fuck, I needed this. I needed it more than I'd even realised. My whole body was a ball of tension that desperately needed releasing. And who better than my very own Alpha Wolf to set me free of it?

"Fuck, you're so wet," he gasped as he slid two fingers straight inside me, making me moan his name needily.

His thumb found my clit and I swear I was already a goner. I arched my back and moaned for him and he was either casting magic between my thighs or I was just so fucking turned on right now that I was already a forgone conclusion.

I found the solid length of his cock and wrapped my fingers around it, moaning at the silky smooth feeling of it in my hand, the bead of moisture crowning the tip just for me which I rubbed down his length as I began to stroke him.

I didn't know if I'd ever been this turned on before. I fucking needed this. My body was aching for it and I was already panting and moaning on the edge of oblivion.

He sucked my nipple into his mouth and pumped his fingers a few times, driving his thumb down over my clit in the perfect way to have my pussy clamping tight and a moan of pure fucking ecstasy tearing from my throat.

"That's my girl," Ethan purred like a satisfied tomcat as he watched me come for him with his eyes alight with need. "Are you going to let me live out my fantasies now?"

"What fantasies?" I asked breathily as he continued to pump his fingers in and out, milking me for every bit of pleasure he could get.

"I've been dreaming about bending you to my will for a long fucking time, love," he growled, his free hand gripping my ass tightly as he pumped his fingers in again. "I promise I'll make it worth your while if you submit to me for a little bit."

He kissed me again, his tongue invading my mouth and halting my protests as he lifted me up, withdrawing his fingers from my aching core and leaving me panting with need. I wasn't nearly done with him yet and he knew it.

Ethan moved me until I was kneeling over him then shifted out from beneath me, making me growl as he got to his feet and walked behind me.

I stood too, turning to face him and refusing to let him do what he clearly was hoping for.

"I'm not your pack whore, Ethan," I snarled.

"I know that, love," he replied, smirking at me in a way that had me aching even more as my gaze strayed to his hard cock which was just begging for more of my attention. "But you look like you need a good, hard fuck and I'm willing to bet you've never let any asshole bend you over before. You don't even know what you're missing out on."

I growled, but I had to admit that I had thought about it once or twice, but I'd never really expected to allow anyone to do it. I was an Alpha, I didn't bow to anyone, but I was feeling pretty weak right now and I needed to feel him inside me sooner rather than later. Maybe it wouldn't be the worst thing in the world to try it out…

Ethan didn't give me any longer to consider it, lunging at me and wrapping his strong arms around me as he tugged me close and kissed me like he was aching for it. His hand fisted in my hair and I moaned as he tugged until I tipped my head back and he could drop his mouth to my nipple, biting down hard enough to make me gasp.

The moment I closed my eyes, he clapped a hand down on my ass and spun me around.

"*Ethan*," I snarled in protest, but he used his grip on my hair to keep my back to him before forcing me to bend.

My hands hit the rocky wall of the cave we were hidden in a second before he drove his dick into me hard enough to make me scream.

I wanted to turn around and rip his damn throat out for that move, but as he began to thrust his hips hard and fast, I was left unable to do anything but moan in pleasure and fight against the urge to beg for more because fuck him but oh, *fuck him.*

His hand clapped down against my ass and I moaned again, loving the way his balls struck my clit every time he slammed into me, the head of his cock driving into this fucking perfect spot so deep inside me that I wasn't even sure I'd ever felt it like that before.

Ethan's fingers dug into my hip, gripping me around the bone as I fought to meet him for every single thrust, holding myself up using the wall as every slam of his body into mine almost had me seeing stars.

Fuck his cock was so big and so perfect and I was never ever going to let him know how fucking amazing this felt, but I was definitely going to let him believe he'd overpowered me again in the near future.

He was groaning and murmuring my name like a prayer as he pounded into me with the bestial savagery of our kind, showing me that he was every inch the Alpha. Every. Fucking. Inch. And as much as I wanted to hate that, I fucking loved it.

I was panting and moaning and begging and it wasn't long before an orgasm tore through me unlike anything I'd ever felt before. My pussy clamped tight around his thick shaft and he growled as he fought against the urge to follow me into oblivion, instead pausing while his grip in my hair turned painful.

The second the biggest wave of ecstasy had passed me, he was moving again, somehow faster, deeper, this fervent kind of energy to his movements which demanded more and more of me. And I was more than willing to give it, my hips slamming back to meet his until he was coming with a deep, animal growl that almost had me coming again too.

Ethan pulled back and thrust into me once more, spanking

my ass hard and forcing me to come whether I liked it or not. And fucking hell, I liked it. Being dominated by him was going in my hall of fucking fame to be played on repeat in my fantasies every time I was left alone in my cell and needing some help getting myself off.

He took his sweet time before pulling out of me and as I straightened, he relaxed his grip in my knotted hair before turning me around and kissing me again.

"Fuck, you're just so..." he trailed off as he worshipped my mouth, his touches soft and gentle now that he'd had his fill of me, like he was trying to caress the aches back out of my skin and I was sure that if he could, he'd be healing me right about now. But I was kind of glad he couldn't. That tender ache between my thighs was like the shadow of where he'd been buried within me and I couldn't say I hated it. He was mine and it was just another thing to prove it to me.

"You missed me then?" I teased, pushing my hands into his silky blonde hair and loving the way his tongue slid over mine before he gave me an answer.

"You have no idea, love. My pack thought I was losing the plot. You're an impossible secret to keep."

"Why keep it then?" I murmured because right now, I didn't want to have to go back to pretending with him. I wanted to be able to touch and hold him whenever I felt the urge to and I didn't see why some old gang war that had lingered on inside this prison had to dictate what we did or didn't do. "We're both Alphas. We could merge our packs and be the strongest gang leaders in here."

Ethan laughed without humour, but he clearly didn't think I was being serious.

"You're crazy, love. And maybe I like that a little too much."

"Come on, Ethan, how are you going to keep hiding this? If you've been pining for me the way I was for you, then-"

"It's fine. I came up with the perfect cover. My pack thinks Harper is my mate. She got a fake mark and everything-"

"What?" I jerked back like he'd struck me and he frowned as I glared at him with unconcealed outrage on my face. "So you're just pretending that some other, lesser bitch is your mate? How the fuck did you convince them that she's your equal? *Harper?* Are you fucking kidding me?"

"She's my Beta anyway. It's not that hard to believe," he snapped and I snarled at him.

"She's fucking *nothing,* and you know it. She can't come close to what you feel between us and I don't believe for one fucking second that you can fake it like she does."

"You don't know shit about my pack. They believe what I tell them to because I'm their damn Alpha. If that's not how your pack see you then maybe you should consider whether or not you just let me dominate you for sex. Maybe you submitted because you know your place is beneath me anyway, love."

I punched him so hard that he staggered back a step and his perfect nose most definitely broke, but I forced myself not to advance on him even though my body ached with the desire to rip him apart for what he'd just said.

"Fuck you, Ethan Shadowbrook. If you seriously believe that you can disrespect me like that and get away with it then you've got another thing coming. I am not and never will be inferior to you in any way. I'm a fucking Alpha unlike anyone you've ever known. And you'll live to regret crossing me like this."

I shifted before he could reply and leapt back out from beneath the waterfall, howling to the moon and seeking out my pack. My mate could go take a running jump off the nearest cliff for all I cared. He was an itch the bond between us had forced me to scratch but that was all he'd ever be. And one day he was going to live to regret the fact that he'd made that choice.

I'd be long gone, living my best life outside of this hell while he pined away in here and I forgot he even existed.

I howled long and low, seeking out my pack and leaving that motherfucker behind as I tried to forget about him, but the burning rage inside of me felt like magma ripping through my veins. It needed an outlet. It needed something to satisfy it.

I snarled as I raced along the riverbank and dove into the trees of a pine forest, listening to the howls of my pack as I charged towards them, aching for the feeling of them all around me.

I was so angry that I didn't even realise that I wasn't hearing the entire pack until I burst out into a clearing and was greeted by ten Wolves instead of a hundred.

Sonny barked with excitement and leapt at me, his russet brown Wolf form the biggest of the bunch. The others all rushed me too, nuzzling and licking, wagging their tails so hard that I caught one to the eye and winced a little.

I shifted back into Fae form and laughed as they surged closer, licking me and getting slobber all over me until I batted them off and they shifted back into their Fae forms.

"Shit, we missed you, Alpha," Sonny gasped as he wrapped me in his arms and hugged me tight, his dick slapping against my thigh as we just ignored the whole no clothes issue.

"I've cried myself to sleep every night since you left," Esme sobbed as she joined our hug from behind and her huge tits pressed to my back.

"I missed you guys too," I laughed. "But let's put some space between us while we're nude, yeah?"

They reluctantly backed up and I found myself looking around at ten sets of puppy dog eyes on the faces of a bunch of full grown hardened criminals with their junk out. It felt just like home.

"Anyone wanna tell me where everyone else is?" I asked, looking around at the trees as they all started whimpering.

Esme shot a worried look at Sonny then dropped down to her knees in a submissive position.

"You tell her while I go down on her to take the sting out of it, Beta," she breathed, moving forward and kissing my inner thigh before starting to work her way north, but the idea of some submissive cunnilingus was really not doing it for me so I caught a handful of her curls and turned her head away from me with a growl to tell her to back off.

That move put her face to crotch with Banjo which she seemed to think was intentional as she began sucking him off instead. Honestly. Wolves were so ridiculous sometimes and that was coming from me.

"Speak," I commanded, getting tired of the nervous look Sonny was giving me and he nodded, ducking his head in deference.

"About a week after you were sent to the hole, Amira took the pack back by force. I fought hard, Alpha, but..." He hung his head and whimpered and a low growl escaped me. "She claimed I had no right to run the pack in your absence because I wasn't the strongest. Then she..."

"She cast us out," Brett supplied with a whine, taking Sonny's hand. "The ten of us were the ones denying her most vocally, so she cut us from the pack and threatened the rest into running with her. None of them wanted to, but they were afraid."

A deep growl escaped my lips and I bared my teeth as I heard a howl on the wind which I knew was coming from my stolen pack.

"She can't cast you out," I said in a deadly tone, the anger Ethan had left me with rising up in me tenfold now that I had someone to aim it at. "Only the Alpha can do that. So let's go remind that bitch who runs the Oscura pack."

I shifted as they all howled and whooped in excitement and I turned, racing away from them into the dark between the trees. I put my nose to the ground and turned my attention to the hunt.

I hurried on and my ten loyal packmates were soon left desperately trying to catch up to me as I pushed myself to my full speed, the moonlight making my silver coat flash in the dark every time it touched it.

I howled, long and low and full of rage a moment before I burst out of the trees onto a wide open plain of long grass and found my pack there, one scared looking bitch trying to stand tall in the centre of them.

I didn't waste a single second as I leapt at Amira with a ferocious snarl and the Wolves closest to her all scattered with whimpers of fear.

I slammed into her hard, knocking her down into the grass beneath me and sinking my fangs into her throat before she even got a chance to defend herself.

My jaw locked tight and Amira screamed in agony as I shook her almost hard enough to break her scrawny, traitorous neck. I flung her to the ground as the taste of her blood flooded my mouth and pinned her beneath me, snarling with blood and drool dripping from my fangs and a promise of her death in my eyes unless she submitted at that very second.

The bitch clearly had some sense because she shifted fast, baring her throat to me in surrender and whimpering like a little pup as she cowered beneath me.

I lingered there long enough for her to see that I held her life in my hands before shifting back and standing over her.

"Shift!" I commanded in my Alpha tone and all around me, every single Wolf shifted back into Fae form, closing in around us in a tight ring. "This bitch just proved how unworthy she is of the Oscura name!" I cried, placing my bare foot on Amira's neck as I drove her down into the dirt beneath me. "We are a family, not just a gang, not just a pack. *Family.* A morte e ritorno."

"A morte e ritorno!" every single Wolf surrounding us cried, their loyal gazes locked on me.

"Will anyone here speak up for this un-Fae, conniving bitch?" I asked and I let several long seconds pass so that Amira could see how not one of them spoke for her. Not one of them cared.

"Please," she breathed. "I didn't know how long you'd be gone. I was just-"

I kicked her to shut her up and stepped back, allowing her to scramble onto her knees. I'd been waiting for the perfect moment to strike at this bitch since I'd realised she'd sold me out to Gustard. She'd been on borrowed time for far too long and the clock just ran out.

"You are nothing and no one. You are not an Oscura and you are not a member of our pack or any other," I said in my Alpha tone which no Wolf could deny or argue against. "I cast you out. I strip you of your place. And I name you Lone Wolf."

Amira gasped in shock, shaking her head in denial as tears streamed down her face.

"You can't," she begged but I just growled at her.

"I already have." I spat on the floor before her and one by one every single Wolf in the pack turned their backs on her in the highest insult you could offer another Fae before shifting back into their Wolf forms and racing away into the trees until it was only me and her left.

"Run back to Gustard and beg him to take you in and protect you." I sneered, though I was certain he wouldn't. What use was she to him now? Her days of spying and skulking in the shadows were over. She was done. No one in this prison would want to be associated with her now and there was nothing more dangerous in Darkmore than being on your own.

"Alpha, please," she sobbed but I ignored her, turning my back and striding away into the trees.

There was only one Oscura Alpha in this place. And no one would ever forget it again.

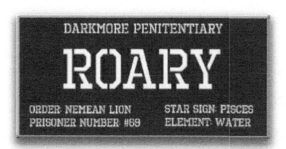

I was back in my cell block waiting for Rosa, having spent the whole time in the Order Yard looking for her. My lead Shade, Claud, had let me know the second she was sighted, but fuck. Why hadn't she come to me? Was she angry with me? Did she blame me for her getting caught? I'd been trying to get down to her that night, but I'd gone and fucked that up by getting injured and – *shit, I have to fix this.*

"She's coming!" Claud appeared at the top of the stairs, rushing toward me and clapping me on the arm.

He scratched the Lion tattoo on his neck, smiling up at me, seeming as anxious as I was for me and Rosa to be reunited. He was the only man in this prison I trusted, even the rest of my Shades would never earn themselves the respect I held for him. He'd told me once that he'd been forced to take the fall for a murder committed by another Lion outside of Darkmore, used as nothing more than a slave by the asshole. I hated Lions who abused their status like that. Who used their Charisma to belittle those who served them. It was the mark of a true Lion to wield their power responsibly, only influencing those who wished to serve, or deserved to. I always followed my father's teachings in that and was proud to say I'd never faltered from it.

Claud was smiling like a damn teenage girl and I jammed an elbow in his ribs to stop him, but he didn't. For all my efforts not to get too attached to anyone in this place, I had failed in that when it came to Claud. He was a good man, a constant in my life and one of the few people I could actually stand in this place.

"Where is she?" I gritted out, shifting from one foot to the other.

"Be patient, Roary," he mocked. "Did you get her a rose like I suggested?"

I balled my hands into fists and shook my head. "She's just a friend."

He laughed loudly and I shot him a look that made him swallow the sound and splutter into a fake cough instead. No one could know the secret feelings I harboured for Rosa. She was family. And she was going to stay that way no matter what my dick thought about the matter.

"Alright, I just don't know why you give her the moon eyes all the time if you're just *friends*," he murmured and I clenched my jaw.

"I do not give her the-" the words fell dead in my throat as she appeared at the top of the stairs.

I carved my fingers through my hair, unsure what to do with my hands. My stomach tightened and I felt sick. Sick to my fucking core at the clear weight she'd lost, the dark circles under her eyes, the hollowness to her cheeks. Her hair was matted too which was a travesty of its own to my kind.

"*Rosa*," I said hoarsely, taking a step toward her before thinking better of it.

She was still moving towards me and I wasn't going to babble some bullshit excuse at her for why I hadn't made it in time to save her from this fate. If she was angry at me, then I would accept her wrath like a true Fae.

She kept moving toward me and my fingers flexed with the desperate need to drag her into my arms. But still, I didn't move. I let her come, waiting for her to strike me, but instead she wrapped her arms around my waist and nuzzled into my chest. A huge breath of relief left me as I crushed her into my body, squeezing her tight.

"I'm so sorry," I growled.

"You have nothing to be sorry for," she said firmly and a knot unravelled in my chest.

"I fought for your cell every day," I murmured. "No way would I have let anyone take it."

"He sure did," Claud chipped in. "He kicked the ass of a very surly Griffin, Miss Rosa."

She smiled widely. "Thank you, Roar," she sighed, sounding tired.

"Do you wanna rest?" I asked.

"Not alone." She clutched onto me and I growled furiously at seeing her like this. I wouldn't stand for it. I'd make this better. Do anything I could to take some of the darkness from my little pup's features.

I glanced over at Claud who mouthed *moon eyes* then winked and ran away before I could berate him. But I just wanted to be alone with Rosa anyway, so I wasn't going to go chasing after his ass.

I led her into my cell, placing her down on my bed before hanging a sheet to give us some privacy. She lay down on my mattress and sighed, letting her eyes flutter closed and the sight made the anger in me ease a bit. She was here now, I just had to do whatever I could to make her feel better.

I strode to the wall opposite and knelt down, pulling the loose brick free at the bottom to reveal my stash of chocolate bars and hair products that my brother helped me sneak into the prison.

I gathered it all up and placed it down on the foot of the bed in an offering.

"Let me take care of you," I commanded. I wasn't going to let her refuse this, I couldn't. My Lion nature was begging me to look after her and I didn't dare let my thoughts latch on to what that meant. I just had to do this. I could no easier stop the sun from rising than stop myself from helping her.

She opened her eyes, propping herself up on her elbows as she took in the pile by her feet. Her lips parted. "Is that a Faero?" she gasped and I snatched it out of the pile, immediately handing it to her, knowing it was her favourite. "You've been holding out on me, Roar."

She smirked a little before tearing the wrapper open and sinking her teeth into it. The moan that left her was almost sexual and my cock jerked to attention at the noise. I tried to ignore it, but she kept up those sounds as she devoured the chocolate bar and I turned to fetch my hairbrush while subtly rearranging my junk. *Rosa's back and I guess my fucking hunger for her is too.*

I approached the bed, standing over it with the brush in my grip. "Move forward," I instructed, picking up the little bottles of hair product from the pile of contraband.

She raised her eyebrows but didn't argue as she shifted down the bed and I slid in to sit behind her, placing down the products between my legs. I gripped her hips and tugged her back a few inches, growling again at the feel of her bones sticking out more prominently through her skin than they should have.

"Cain will pay for this," I said in a deadly tone.

"He already is," she said darkly.

"What do you mean?" I asked.

"Well the moon made me all glowy and shit and marked him with a curse. I dunno what it'll do to him, but I sure as hell hope it hurts." She grinned darkly and a sweet satisfaction filled me.

"You're amazing, Rosa," I said, a purr rattling through my chest.

I was fascinated by her powers and it brought a smile to my lips knowing the moon herself had punished Cain for what he'd done to her. I had to agree with Rosa too, I hoped that curse hurt like a bitch.

I sprayed her hair with tangle teaser and started gently brushing it. She whimpered a little as I worked out the bigger knots, but she never pulled away or asked me to stop. Doing this soothed the deep ache in my chest over seeing her this way. But it wasn't enough. I had to do more. Everything I possibly could to make sure she was okay.

When she finished her first chocolate bar, I pointed to the

pile again. "Eat," I growled and she seemed happy to obey, grabbing up a Fairy Milk bar this time and tucking into it.

"Don't you want some?" she asked.

"No. It's all yours. *All* of it. And I'll get more the next time I see Leon."

"He gets this stuff into the prison?" she asked in surprise. "How?"

"In the pockets of the guards," I lowered my tone just in case anyone was listening beyond the sheet. "Then I steal it back off of them once he gives me my mark. I can't get anything magical in unfortunately or it'd set off the sensors. But I can always get candy and hair products." I smirked.

"Trust the best thieves in Solaria to come up with that," she said with pride in her tone, but those words only cut into my chest.

"I'm not one of them anymore," I murmured.

"Roary..."

"I don't want to talk about me," I said firmly, drawing another section of hair back over her shoulder and starting to work on that. "I want to talk about you. Are you okay? Did they punish you? Keep food from you?" I croaked, running my finger down her spine through her jumpsuit.

"No. But we only got two small meals a day and I worked out a lot as there wasn't much else to do." She unbuttoned the top half of her jumpsuit and suddenly shrugged out of it so her white tank was revealed. "Touch me," she asked and it hurt me. Wolves needed contact with other Fae, it was fundamental. And she'd been deprived of it so long I could only guess at the pain she was in over it, even after running with her pack up in the yard.

I took an elastic from my wrist and gently tied her hair up on her head. My breath caught as I spotted the mate mark behind her ear, the silver crescent moon lightly glistening against her skin. I trailed my finger over it and she stiffened.

"Oh shit-" she started, but I cut over her.

"Ethan told me," I gritted out, my chest tight. "I guess I didn't want to believe it until I saw the mark on you too…"

She glanced over her shoulder at me and I took in a welt on her lip which looked like she'd bitten into it a hundred times. I grazed my thumb over it and she didn't even wince at the contact. My heart was thumping uncontrollably as I drowned in her chestnut eyes. Her strength defied every force on earth, but I still wanted to protect her like she was nothing more than the little pup I'd known ten years ago. Even then she'd had more fire in her soul than nearly every Fae I knew. I dropped my hand from her mouth and my fingertips tingled from the contact with those full lips.

"When did he tell you?" she asked, her voice a husky purr that set my blood alight.

"He found me after the Belorian attacked me," I said and her eyes widened.

"What?" she gasped and I explained how one of its spines had poisoned me and if it hadn't been for Cain finding us, I would have been fucked. "Ethan was going to go after you, and when I said I didn't trust him, he showed me his mate mark."

She swallowed, her throat bobbing as she gazed at me unblinkingly while jealousy clawed at my insides.

"So you two are…" I didn't want to complete that sentence, but I knew I needed to hear it from her lips. That she and Ethan, a fucking Lunar no less, were moon mated.

"Mated, but not together," she said firmly. "I don't know how to explain it better than that."

"So you don't want him?" I growled. "Or he doesn't want you?" Depending on her answer I either wanted to kiss her or tear Shadowbrook's head off for daring to refuse this girl who was moonlight itself. *Think clearly, asshole. I have no right to do either.*

"It's complicated," she sighed, turning away and envy clawed its way up my flesh and screamed bloody murder in my ear.

"Right," I said stiffly.

"What do you care anyway?" she asked lightly.

"I don't," I bit out harsher than I intended. "I mean, I do. Obviously. But only because Shadowbrook's bad news."

She tsked. "Everyone in here's bad news. And he's better news than most."

I fought the urge to grumble like a little bitch and picked up a bottle of argan oil, pouring some into my palms. I gently pushed her tank straps aside and goosebumps rushed across her neck just before I lay my palms on her shoulders and started massaging the oil into her soft skin. She hung her head forward as I worked the tension out of her muscles with firm circles and strokes.

I wet my lips as I worked along her shoulders and fought the urge to lean in and chase my touches with kisses. I put it down to my instinctual need to care for her, but who was I really bullshitting? I wanted her like I'd never wanted any girl. Being apart from her for this long had only confirmed that. I'd pined for her every night and day. I was beyond denying it to myself, but that still didn't mean I'd cross that line. Especially as she was apparently someone else's fucking mate.

I just had to protect her. And that would have to be enough to sate this primal need in me.

"I missed you, Roar," she said with a sigh and my throat thickened.

"I missed you too, Rosa," I said gruffly, not calling her little pup for once, because right now she seemed anything but a pup. She was a beautiful woman who'd been hurt and damaged in this cruel place. And I'd sworn to protect her. I'd let her down so fiercely that it killed me.

When she was half melting under my touch, I released her hair from its tie and continued working through the knots.

"I'm never going to let them take you away again," I promised her, teasing my fingers through a matted section of hair, using the argan oil to loosen it.

"You can't promise that," she said. "Besides, I knew the risks."

"You didn't know Sin would free the fucking Belorian," I

snarled and her shoulders tensed up, probably twisting up some of those muscles I'd just relaxed. I tutted, figuring I'd work on them again as soon as I had her hair done.

"I think he was trying to help," she said. "Though he sure as shit will listen to me next time. And I guess I did get into Psych..."

"What did you find?" I asked immediately. I'd forgotten to care about fucking Psych after losing Rosa and nearly dying because of that monster in the halls. But she'd gone there to find Sook Min. And our plan had hinged on that Polethius Mole Shifter.

"Roary, it was awful," she breathed, her tone setting my pulse pounding.

"Did you find Sook?" I asked in concern.

"Yeah she...fuck, I dunno what they're doing down there, but it's not good. I saw them take something from her."

"What do you mean?" I asked anxiously.

"She was in this operating theatre and they did something that took this...light from her."

"Light?" I frowned.

"I don't know what it was, but they put it in a jar. And then Sook started convulsing and – and...she didn't make it."

I rested a hand on her back, swallowing against the lump in my throat.

"It was horrible down there, Roary. They're doing something terrible, I could feel it. I saw other Fae and there was something missing from them too. That light...it's like it was their soul or-"

"Oooh getting oily in here. You're basting her up real nice there, Lion man. Wanna put those big, strong hands to good use on my tight little hiney when you're done?"

I twisted around at the sound of Plunger's voice and found him tugging the sheet aside on my cell. I bared my teeth at him, snarling viciously as his eyes ran over Rosa in front of me. He was in nothing but his tight white underpants and some sort of red sauce was seeping through the material.

"Oh don't mind my leakage, boy," he said, rocking his hips from side to side so a wet sloshing sounded within the material. "Tomato sauce is great for smoothing out my johnson. Gets it all *kinds* of soft."

"Get the fuck away from my cell or I'll rip your fucking *johnson* off," I snapped as Rosa growled her own warning.

"Suit yourself," Plunger chuckled. "But your hand would slip right off my shiny smooth shaft so you'd have to keep on trying to tug and tug my devilsome dick in that big fist of yours."

"Get the fuck out!" I bellowed, about to get up to force him away when he dropped the sheet and chuckled as he left.

I shuddered as I turned back to Rosa, realising I'd wrapped my arm around her and had dragged her against my chest on top of the products between my legs. The scent of the argan oil on her skin and the tempting, sinful scent that was entirely her beneath it made me want to lean in and rake my tongue along her throat. She was the only thing in the world which could force that image of Plunger out of my head so fast.

She turned her head back to look at me and my dick swelled against her ass as I released ragged breaths.

I cleared my throat, remembering myself as I pushed her off of me before I got rock hard.

"So, Sook Min is dead," I prompted, knowing my tone was cold, but I needed to get her mind straight off the matter of my throbbing dick and back onto the real issue here.

She turned away again and I started back on the last section of her hair, gently running my brush through it. "Yeah," she said sadly. "And may she rest with the stars, but now we have no Polethius Mole Shifter for my plan and...fuck, we really need one. They're the only Order capable of sensing the detectors buried in the ground surrounding the prison and we can't risk digging any tunnels unless we can be sure we won't hit one of them. If we do, we'll be blown to pieces before we even realise what happened."

I gritted my jaw, trying to bite back my next words, but we really had no choice. "Plunger's our only option."

"Fuck no," she snarled wolfishly.

"There's no one else," I sighed. "And trust me, if there was, I'd say so. I mean, we can always wait to see if a newbie shows up, but those Shifters are rare as it is. We could be here for years before another one arrives."

"Why Plunger?" she groaned. "I swear the stars don't want me to get out of here."

"They do," I grunted. "And even if they give up on you, I won't. I'll get you out if I have to tear down the whole prison, Rosa. You will not stay here."

"Aren't I the one who's supposed to be rescuing *you*?" she teased but whimpered as I tugged through the last big knot in her hair.

"Sorry," I murmured. "And yeah, you are. I'm just making sure you keep your word."

She laughed softly and the sound made me even harder. My cock was seriously not getting the off limits message and the lack of blood in my head was making me consider its case.

"So what are we gonna do about these?" She reached back to catch my hand, running her thumb over the new magic blocking cuff on it. Her touch made my skin warm and I remembered power sharing with her right here. It had felt so good being connected to her like that and I ached to do it again someday.

"How hard do you think it would be to get one of those remotes when it's time to break out?" she asked and I shook my head.

"I've been paying close attention and those things have magical signature detectors on them. Unless we could get a brand new one and register it to one of us, I don't see any way to get these cuffs off. Not without getting a guard to do it for us," I laughed, but she didn't, like she was considering everything I'd said.

"I'll work it out," she replied eventually just as I combed out the last of her hair and sat back to admire its shiny gleam. She groaned in appreciation as I ran my fingers through it.

"I know you will," I said, having total faith in her, though things weren't looking too good.

"We're going to need a new place to tunnel out too," she said. "Now we can't get into the walls, we're gonna have to find somewhere we can dig. Somewhere we won't be found."

"Are you really expecting Plunger to dig us out of here?" I didn't scoff, though maybe I should have. The amount of obstacles I could see with that one idea alone were endless. He didn't have access to his Order for one. And you couldn't dig out of the Order Yard, the magical dome went just as deep underground as it did above, containing us in an unbreakable bubble.

"Yeah," she said. "That's exactly what I'm expecting."

She looked tense again, so I started massaging her shoulders once more and she tossed me a mischievous look over her shoulder.

"Any chance you wanna do my whole back?" Her eyes glimmered hopefully and I was already nodding like an eager Lion cub when she hooked her tank top up and whipped it off.

She turned around, kneeling before me and gesturing for me to get up, but I just stared at her with my heart thumping and my jaw slightly slack. She was more than beautiful, she was stunning. Like she actually froze my limbs in place as good as a shock baton could.

"Move, Roar." She jabbed me playfully and I got up, picking up the hair products and heading across the room to place them back in their hiding place. When I turned to face her again, Rosa had taken her bra off and was lying face down on my bed looking like the embodiment of temptation. *Oh fuck.*

I rearranged my dick again for all the good it would do, trying my best to ignore the way it twitched demandingly at the sight of her like that.

I moved to kneel over her legs and squeezed more of the oil into my palms before laying them on her back. My hands were so big they encompassed most of the skin there and she groaned as I massaged her in firm strokes, trying to focus on all the reasons I had to not try anything with her.

I'm ten years her senior.

I'm a screw up.

I'm her cousin's friend.

She's family.

I'm supposed to protect her.

She's been through a lot, I would be an asshole to take advantage of her right now. And I wouldn't anyway because I don't feel that way about her.

I squeezed my eyes shut for a moment to centre myself as she groaned again and I concentrated all of my energy on her. It became easier then as I worked over every inch of her bare flesh, wanting to wipe away some of the torment of the isolation unit from her body and replace it with something achingly good instead. I was going to get her back to perfect health in no time and watch as Cain suffered under her curse. And if I didn't deem that punishment good enough, I was going to find a way to spill his blood and watch him beg for mercy at my feet. I wasn't a natural born killer, but for her, I would commit any sin. *You will pay Officer Cain, I swear it on the stars.*

As I continued to work the kinks out of her muscles, my dick starting to make its own solid case for why I should lean down and brush my lips over her shoulder.

She's all grown up now.

She needs to be held, it's in both of your Orders' instincts to comfort each other with sex.

She's been into you for a long time, why keep denying her what she wants?

You haven't fucked anyone since she got to prison and you're risking dick rot.

Dick rot is a genuine thing, you don't need to look it up.

She's sooo fucking pretty.

No one will know anyway, it's just between the two of you. Is it really so wrong?

Remember when you kissed her before and you had to jerk off quietly in your cell over it the next day, and the next, and the next? And when you came, you had to pretend you'd fallen out of your bed when she heard you groaning and you even bashed your knee into the wall before she saw you in the morning so you had a bruise to prove it. You don't wanna be that guy again, right?

Rosa moaned as I massaged her shoulder blades and I swallowed a curse, hating my dick, especially because it had some valid points.

I found myself leaning down, following this desperate, instinctual urge in me to kiss her and I gently grazed my lips over her shoulder. She sucked in a breath, going still beneath me and I realised in this position, my cock was now rubbing right against her ass and she felt everything. Eve-ry-thing.

"Don't stop," she breathed heavily and I didn't.

I kissed along her shoulders, pushing her hair aside so I could kiss her neck then worked my way up to her ear, nibbling as I brushed my fingers down the side of her body. She shivered beneath me, pushing her ass back into my hard on and I growled deeply, biting her throat and tasting the sweet oil on her flesh.

"Roary," she begged and I lifted my hips, rolling her beneath me, realising a second too late that her breasts were bare. My gaze dipped to them before I could stop myself and a lump thickened in my throat at the sight of her hardened nipples. She gripped a fistful of my hair, yanking to make me look her in the eye and smirking at me. But I didn't smile back. I was on the edge of pulling away again, my conscience reawakening, but as she tilted her head up towards me, I threw caution to the wind and dipped down to meet her mouth with mine. She came alive beneath me, wrapping her legs around my waist and I rolled my hips involuntarily, the Lion in me taking over as I dragged my tongue across hers, kissing her slow and torturously.

Her lips were as soft as velvet, fitting perfectly against mine. I groaned, deepening our kiss, never wanting to come up for air, because I was sure the second I did, I'd see sense. And I

99

didn't want to see sense ever again. Why couldn't I be reckless and carefree about this? Why couldn't we have each other like this if that was what our bodies wanted?

Because you can't offer her anything. Because you threw away your life and everyone outside of this place knows you as the Night who brought shame on his family. Because you're just some washed up, could-have-been-somebody who is now nobody. And this girl deserves a guy who still has his dignity and his pride intact.

I broke the kiss and I hated myself for it almost as much as she would hate me in a second. I drew away from her, sitting on the end of the bed and dropping my face into my hands.

"Put your clothes back on," I demanded and silence came in answer to that.

I heard her shifting off of the bed and suddenly her hand was in my hair again, pulling hard to make me look up at her. She was in her tank but she'd left her bra off so her nipples showed through it and I nearly swallowed my tongue as she stood over me like that, a flare of a true Alpha in her eyes.

"You either want me or you don't. I'm not your toy. I'm no one's fucking toy," she hissed.

"I know," I said quickly, feeling like such a fucking douchebag.

She shook her head at me. "Claim me right here, right now, Roary. Or I'm shutting the door on that possibility forever. No more bullshit. We're friends or we're more than that. Which is it?"

So many words got stuck in my throat and I had to fight down the Alpha Lion in me who was roaring in my head, begging me to seize this opportunity and claim her once and for all. But that Lion didn't rule the world anymore. Once we got out of here, I had the sum total of fuck all to offer her. And I wasn't going to be the reason she ended up living with some loser who'd she'd eventually realise was the worst mistake of her life.

I bowed my head, a knife driving into my heart as I gave her the answer I didn't want to give. Knowing what I was sacrificing for her. But I'd give anything to make sure she got the life she deserved one day. "We're friends."

She released a low whine of pain in her throat then turned and walked out of my cell without another word.

I couldn't breathe with her gone. I knew giving her up was also me giving up my one shot at happiness in this life. I'd never find a girl who made me feel like she did. But I'd also never forgive myself if I selfishly stole her for myself.

Rosalie Oscura wasn't for me. And it was time I started making my peace with that.

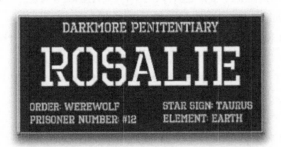

DARKMORE PENITENTIARY

ROSALIE

ORDER: WEREWOLF
PRISONER NUMBER: #12

STAR SIGN: TAURUS
ELEMENT: EARTH

I lay in my bunk after the first semi-decent sleep I'd had in months, finally not dreaming of Papa and the fucked up things he used to do while feeling a different kind of pain instead.

I hadn't really allowed myself to dwell on it too much while I was in the hole because there were more pressing issues on my mind, but I was literally having a personal crisis over it now. Since I'd gotten to this stars forsaken place, four alpha male assholes had caught my eye and silly old me had thought I'd be able to run rings around them just like I had with every other guy I'd ever met. But it wasn't like that with them at all.

Hell, Cain had thrown me in a cell and locked me away for months without a second thought. I'd stupidly convinced myself that he cared about me for something more than the taste of my blood, but aside from the fact that he was half tempted to fuck me, it had become painfully clear that he was never going to see me as anything other than a delinquent scumbag just like everyone else in here. I just hoped my moon curse was causing him problems because as it stood, that was the only weapon I could wield against him and even if I didn't fully understand it, I was certain the moon had my back. That bitch was my people and I knew she had a plan.

Although...I really should have been mad at her too, because I had her to thank for the fact that I was now mated to a man who hated me, despised my family because of some pathetic old fight which should have been forgotten years ago and would rather parade a fake mate around the place and tattoo over his mate mark than ever let anyone find out about us.

Aside from fucking me, he didn't seem to have any real interest in me and that was absolutely not how I was going to be treated. I needed a plan for Ethan Shadowbrook, something to put him in his box and keep him there. I didn't want a mate who treated me the way he did, so I'd take advantage of the fact that he couldn't hurt me while this bond connected us and then I'd leave his ass here when I escaped and make a deal with the moon to sever it. I was a Moon Wolf, I had to believe that gave me perks when it came to things like this.

I mean sure, everyone knew the story of what had happened to the last person to try and force the stars to change their mind on fate and I did *not* want to take the Darius Acrux route. I shuddered at the mere thought of what had happened to him and I wondered if he was up there somewhere thinking the sacrifice he'd made had been worth it. Either way, fuck no. Ethan Shadowbrook was *not* worth it. He was a piece of shit who was so ashamed of me that he was literally pretending to be mated to a *Beta* rather than own his bond with his true match. So fuck him.

Anyway, I was looking to make a bargain to *break* a bond so maybe my situation was completely different to what Darius Acrux had been attempting. I certainly wasn't going to die to get it done though. Me and the moon just needed to have a little chat and I was sure she'd see sense. Weren't mates supposed to be your equal anyway? Ethan may have been as strong as me physically, but he wasn't my equal in the kind of strength that counted. Ever since I'd escaped my papa's clutches, I'd made sure that every single decision I made in my life benefitted my own goals. I certainly wouldn't let shame or fear force me into hiding something so monumental. A true Alpha didn't fear their pack. So what if they were pissed about it when he told them? All he had to do was force them back into line and tell them he didn't give a shit. Alphas set the status quo, they didn't fucking follow it. *Pfft, pezzo di merda.*

I scratched at the stupid mate mark and let my mind move on to Sin. He was actually the one and only guy I was interested in who was more than willing to accept me as I was and would love nothing more than to shout from the rooftops about the two of us being together if he got the chance. Of course, knowing him, he would literally be swinging from the light fittings while doing it and I did still have that niggling feeling that once he got what he wanted from me then he'd move on. But maybe that was just my own prejudice talking. It was clear that he hadn't found many people in this life who had seen him as more than just an object for sexual gratification and seeing as his Order form let him slip into the skin of people's wildest fantasies, I could totally see why he believed that was all anyone would ever want from him.

The assholes who wanted him to shift so they could fuck him didn't want *him*, they wanted the object of their desire, so they wouldn't want to get to know anything about who he truly was. But I was coming to realise that I did. I loved his brand of insane - aside from when it led to psychotic monsters being set loose - but there was a real freedom to him and the fact that he was totally uninhibited that made me want to dive off of the next cliff with him and find out where we landed. Of course, he'd be stuck in the hole all week so there wouldn't be much chance of that, but maybe I'd give it some more consideration for when he was released, assuming none of the asshole guards decided to add to his time like they had mine.

And Roary...ergh it hurt to think about Roary. Shit, it had always kinda hurt to think about Roary, but now he was close and kept reeling me in despite the fact that he swore he didn't want me. So maybe I was just a nice little reminder of home for him. An escape plan, an easy ticket out of here and nothing more. But fuck, when I thought about the way he'd kissed me before he'd pulled away, I lit up like a goddamn Christmas tree from the inside out. My lips still tingled at the mere memory of that kiss and my heart pounded the way it had when I was a teenager and he used to come hang out at my aunt's vineyard. Shit, wanting him hurt so fucking bad sometimes that I was tempted to swear off men for life. Or maybe I should just go take part in a pack orgy and let them work to satisfy me. Surely if they all were putting in enough effort, it would be good... Aside from the fact that the idea of all of those lower ranking Wolves pawing at me and panting over me left me as dry as the Ilorian Desert. *Great. Alpha assholes for life then.*

A low buzz finally sounded downstairs as the guards arrived and I groaned in appreciation as I sat up in my cot.

"Open on three, cell twelve," Cain's voice suddenly came from beyond the sheet I had hanging over the bars at the front of my cell and I cursed his speedy Vampire ways a moment before he tugged it down and my cell door rattled open.

"Morning, Twelve," he said crisply, looking at me like he didn't know me from Adam, before giving his attention to an Atlas in his hand. "We need to have a meeting this morning about the correctional programs you are going to be assigned to and as you have visitation following breakfast, I think now is the best time to have it."

"Sure," I said, smiling sweetly as I hopped out of my bunk and moved to grab a clean jumpsuit from my shelf. "It's not like I need to eat or anything. I've been enjoying playing count the ribs since you left me to starve in the hole."

Cain frowned but didn't say anything as I tugged my jumpsuit on and then added socks and boots to my outfit. Man, I missed dressing the way I liked. I hadn't given much thought to the uniform when coming in here and I'd never been a girly girl parading around in sweet dresses, but I missed the feeling of jeans cupping my ass and shirts that weren't fucking orange. I seriously needed to go shopping once I escaped this pit. Hell, at this point I'd gladly take one of Aunt Bianca's hideous floral dresses over this stars damned uniform.

When I was ready, Cain beckoned me like a dog and turned to stalk off down the walkway. I followed along obediently, glancing at Roary as I passed his cell where he'd moved to stand with his arms trailing out through the bars. He reached for me as I passed but I dodged his hand, not even caring when a frown pinched his brow. He'd made it clear he didn't want the stupid little pup so I was done mooning over him. If he didn't want to touch me in all the right ways then he didn't need to touch me at all.

"Rosa," he called out as I moved beyond him and despite my best intentions, I paused and looked back at him to hear what he had to say to me. "Are we...good?"

"We're perfect, Roar," I assured him with a cherry pie smile that I usually reserved for people I hated but worked just as well to sell bullshit too. "I heard you loud and clear last night. No need for you to worry about the little pup. I'm good taking care of myself."

"Rosa, I-"

"This is not the moment for love's young dream to have a deep and meaningful conversation," Cain barked loudly, smacking his baton against the metal railing at the top of the stairs so that a dull noise rang out around the cell block.

"Oh please." I sneered, flicking a dismissive look Roary's way which actually fucking hurt me deep in my soul, but I had to do it. I had to be done with this because needing him and aching for him and pining for him was too fucking painful. He'd made himself clear and it had to stop. I wouldn't keep embarrassing myself. "He's so old his balls probably knock against his knees when he walks."

"You're getting my balls and my dick mixed up, pup," Roary joked and I rolled my eyes.

"Well it's not like I'd know," I replied before stalking away after Cain.

He stayed silent as he led me down through the cell block, past all the other guards who were currently taking the count.

"I need to count you, Twelve," an officer working by the coop called out as I moved to follow Cain out through the doors, and I paused as he approached with the scanner.

He was tall and bald, the name Nixon printed on his shirt and as his gaze slipped over me, he wet his finger and thumb and slicked his bushy black brows down. *Welcome to ew city.*

I'd seen him around a bit and I knew from my research that

he was dirty, but I'd decided against using him in my plans. Nixon accepted bribes in the form of sexual favours and I had zero desire to get on my knees for a slimy bastardo like him.

"Look deep into the scanner," he said, licking his lips in a way that grossed me out, but maybe that was just because I knew he was a perv.

I turned my gaze to the scanner and waited until a shiny number twelve flashed up to confirm I'd been counted then slipped away from him and hurried out after Cain.

He led me along and I said nothing. We got into the elevator and I said nothing. We arrived up on level one where the guard barracks were and still not a single peep. I had nothing to say to him. So unless I absolutely had to respond to something, my lips were good and zipped.

Cain caught hold of my elbow and I fought the desire to fight him off and let him tug me along the corridor without so much as a growl.

"No smartass questions today, Twelve?" he asked when the silence got so deafening you could have heard a pin drop.

I didn't reply and he tsked angrily. He led me past an open dining area where a few off duty guards sat eating their breakfast and I fought the urge to moan at the scent of cinnamon buns and fresh, properly brewed coffee. Fuck him. He'd probably brought me up here purely to torture me with that smell.

Cain led me to a small office with a table in the centre of it and two comfortable looking office chairs sat on either side of it. He pointed me towards one and I flopped into it with all the attitude of a surly teenager, rolling the chair back and spreading my legs wide like those dudes who acted like their balls were too damn big for their bodies.

Instead of moving to take the other chair, Cain headed back out of the room and I was left wondering how long this was going to go on for. At least I had visitation to look forward to and I needed to see someone from home more than anything in the world today. I bet my Aunt Bianca had been having kittens while I was locked up and my cousin Dante would be cursing the fact that he'd agreed to this crazy scheme of mine.

When Cain returned, he was carrying a tray with two plates of cinnamon buns and two mugs of coffee which he set down on the table between us before taking his seat opposite me.

"So," he began, looking at his Atlas like it held all the answers to every question he'd ever thought to ask of me. "It's beyond time that we get you settled into some of your correctional classes and I've had time to prepare a program for you to follow."

He glanced at my plate of untouched cinnamon buns and I was half tempted to spit on it and throw it in his lap. That did kinda seem like cutting off my own nose to spite my face though, so instead, I reached out and picked it up, pushing it between my lips and moaning loudly as I bit into it. And despite the fact that I was putting on a show solely designed to piss him off, I couldn't deny that the damn thing tasted amazing. We really didn't get much with sugar in it in the Mess Hall and never in the hole. So this baby was going to die a sweet old death in my belly.

Cain gritted his teeth as I worked through the two cinnamon buns with as much overt sexuality as I could manage before finishing by licking the sugar from my lips nice and slow.

"Are you quite done now?" he growled and I smirked at him.

"That depends on what you're referring to, boss man," I said sweetly, but there was nothing sweet about the way I was looking at him.

"Well at least now you have no reason to complain about me starving you," he replied curtly.

"Oh yeah," I agreed. "Two cinnamon buns and I've forgotten all about the three months in the dark with my stomach constantly rumbling. So did you want me to suck your cock now or were you wanting to chase me around a bit and bite me first?"

Cain snarled, shooting out of his seat and tossing the door closed before locking it and throwing a silencing bubble up around us. He grabbed hold of the back of my chair and tipped it back onto two wheels as he snarled down at me and I fought not to react in the slightest to his show of dominance.

"What now?" I murmured and his chest rose and fell rapidly with anger. "Are you going to lie and tell everyone I attacked you again? Throw me back into the hole? Show me what a big bad guard you really are?"

"Why did you save my life?" he hissed, moving so close that our breaths were mixing between us, but I refused to balk.

"Believe me, I've been asking myself that same question a lot recently. Safe to say, it's not a mistake I'd repeat a second time." My heart beat harder at those words, but I refused to take them back. He'd shown me just how little I meant to him and I wasn't ever going to forget what he'd done to me.

"I want the truth," he insisted.

"Yeah well, I want a lot of things I don't get to have, stronzo."

He glared down at me for a long moment, his eyes roaming over my features and the hatred he could no doubt see there plain as day before dropping down over my body.

"If you seriously think I'd willingly fuck you now, bastardo, you're even dumber than you look," I hissed as his gaze fixed on my tits which were somewhat on show seeing as my jumpsuit was half unfastened and I wasn't wearing a bra beneath my white tank, but I hadn't wanted to give him a view of my body when he'd come to get me out of my cell so I'd just thrown the jumpsuit on over what I'd slept in.

He slammed my chair back down onto all four wheels again with an angry growl and moved to stand behind me where I couldn't see him. I resisted the urge to look around at him though, refusing to bow to his intimidation tactics and grabbing my coffee instead.

I moaned again as I drank it, knowing that he hated me playing on his lust like that and playing up to it as much as I could. If the worst I could give him right now was a serious case of blue balls then I'd take it. Let him ache for the girl he couldn't have. I hoped it burned him up with want and need and tortured him as often as possible.

"You aren't leaving here until I get some answers," he said in a low, dark voice which had the hairs along the back of my neck standing to attention, but I still refused to turn. It wasn't like being able to face him made any real difference to my chances against him if he attacked me anyway. I didn't have access to my magic or Order form, so I was already a dead girl walking if that was what he wanted.

"Cry me a river, stronzo. I don't owe you shit," I said, inspecting my nails which were actually chewed to crap after my time in the hole and just pissed me off so I dropped them into my lap again fairly sharpish.

Cain snarled in warning which seemed like the perfect moment for me to reach across the table and snag one of his cinnamon buns. The second I bit down on it, he was back around the table, striking the wood with his baton in some attempt to frighten me, but I just arched an eyebrow at him as I continued to eat...and moan...and suck sugar from fingers suggestively.

"Problem?" I asked sweetly.

"I'm going to give you a choice of which subject you want to tackle first and then I'm going to be getting some answers, Twelve," Cain said, choosing to ignore the food theft and I had to wonder why. He'd never let me get away with shit like this before. Hell, he'd never given me anything like this before. Was the scary Vampire feeling like an asshole? Or maybe it was all just a ploy to get me to open up. A little bribe to get me feeling generous. *Good luck with that, stronzo.*

"Tit for tat, boss man," I purred. "If you expect something from me then I'm going to be wanting something in return."

Cain dropped down into his chair again, scowling at me so hard I was surprised he could even see me. I batted my eyelashes and took a long sip of coffee in response. He really could have done with a few lessons from my papa about how to keep your emotions hidden - not that I'd recommend those to anyone, but if there was one asshole in this world who I might be persuaded to send for them, it would be him.

"I want to know what you were doing down by Psych when the Belorian got free," he began and I couldn't help the twinge of curiosity in me at that question because instead of sounding like he was worried I'd discovered some secret he was a part of covering up, it sounded a hell of a lot like he had no idea about what happened down in that hell. "I want to know what the fuck this curse that you put on me does and how the hell I'm supposed to get rid of it. I want to know why you were down on the maintenance level that day I caught you in there. And why you're wasting your time fraternising with Sin Wilder."

"So, just to be clear, you don't wish to discuss the subject of you grinding your dick into me at every given opportunity or the way the mere thought of biting me gets you hard?" I asked innocently and his upper lip curled back to reveal his lengthening fangs.

"I won't let you sit here and disrespect me like that, Twelve, if I have to warn you again, you'll regret it."

"So what you're saying is that if I were to slip out of this jumpsuit and bend over the table for you, that would go against your wishes?" I fingered one of the buttons on my orange jumpsuit as if I might actually do it and he swallowed thickly.

"Stop trying to distract me. I'm not some doe eyed moron ready for you to Bedazzle with your pouty lips and perky tits," he growled but the roughness to his voice was enough to let me know he'd rather enjoyed that little visual. The cold, hard, carnivorous look in his eyes coupled with that tone had my nipples hardening too, but I'd never admit that to him. Besides I hated him too much to even consider hate fucking him so my tits could forget about that idea. "Let's start with an easy one. Why are you cosying up to Eighty-Eight?"

"You're seriously asking me why I'm eager to spend time with the big, sinful as fuck Incubus?" I mocked. "You may be as straight as an arrow, boss man, but you can't have missed how freaking hot he is. And his dick is *huge*, not to mention he knows exactly how to use it." A vein had begun to pulse at Cain's temple and it was only getting more violent the longer I spoke. "And he *seriously* knows how to use that tongue of his too. I mean, shit, it gets me wet just thinking about him and how hard his cock can-"

"Enough," Cain snapped, the vein at his temple pulsing with barely contained rage. "Tell me about *this* then." He unbuttoned his cuff to show me the curse mark on his inner wrist. The vines seemed longer now, curving away from the rose up his forearm with a second small bud alongside the first flower.

"Maledizione della luna," I purred, my lips hooking up into a delicious smile. "You're moon cursed, boss man. Take it up with her."

His lips parted on what I was sure was going to be a really firm telling off, but his radio blared to life, saving me from the lecture.

"Cain?" Warden Pike's voice came over it. "I need a quick word in my office."

Cain gritted his teeth and I smirked at him. "Run along, boss man...although, if you have a boss then I guess that means you're not a boss man, right? So what does that make you?"

"I won't be long," Cain muttered, leaning over the table and casting a magical chain to connect my left manacle to the table, making sure I couldn't leave. "Try not to get up to anything while I'm gone."

"Aye Aye, Captain Stronzo," I agreed, saluting him with my right hand and he narrowed his eyes at me before shooting out of the room. "And in answer to my question, I think that makes you the little bitch man," I added, knowing he'd be able to hear me with his bat ears and chuckling to myself. It seemed like I'd found a new favourite hobby. Asshole baiting.

I was about to start cursing him for leaving me chained to a table like a dick, when I spotted his last cinnamon bun and his mug of coffee.

Waste not, want not, stronzo. At least this torture had some perks.

ARIES. VAMPIRE. FIRE.
COMMANDING OFFICER
CAIN
DARKMORE
PENITENTIARY

I headed down the corridor as the cursed mark on my wrist began to throb and pain slithered out into my veins, making my fingers curl into a fist as I tried to fight it. The pain was rising though and this had happened before. So I ducked into the men's restroom, pressing my back to the door just before the all-engulfing, blinding rush of agony seized me.

I clutched my arm to my chest, stifling a cry as the pain raced deeper into my body.

I was half aware that I'd fallen to my knees when the visions found me, scraped out from the darkest crevices of my mind. Where I tried to keep them away. But this curse made sure I stared my past in the face and watched myself become a monster over and over again.

I suddenly stood looking down at the boy I'd once sworn to protect, his eyes wide and hopeful, full of all the trust I'd betrayed.

"*No*," I ground out, trying to force the image away, but the damned curse had other ideas as it drew me back to the place where I'd spent most of my youth. The rafters in the old theatre were filled with young boys and girls and a shadow lurked in the corner where *he* slept. That shadow seemed to grow and fear gripped me as I realised what night this was. The moonlight seemed to slip away through the window as he picked out his victims for tonight's games. And I was one of them.

The curse loosened its hold on me before I had to relive that night again and I found myself panting on the restroom floor, feeling the fear I'd felt back then as sharply as if it was happening now.

I pushed myself upright, blinking hard to clear my head then ripping back my sleeve to check the mark. The silver rose had grown again, the thorny vines curling around its base now and reaching a little further up my arm.

What has she done to me?

I moved to the sink, splashing my face with cold water and stuffing away those old memories, forcing them into the back of my head and wishing I could force them all the way out. This curse punished me with the worst memories of my life. I'd already had nightmares before Twelve had marked me, but now they were as clear as if I was really that kid again, living those horrors once more.

I had the feeling my anger with Twelve had brought this episode on and I swore at myself for letting myself be baited by her. Who cared if she was fucking Sin Wilder?

My fangs lengthened and fury built in my gut like acid. *I* cared. Clearly. But I needed to find a way to stop her from riling me or I was never going to keep my head around her.

I scraped a hand over my short hair and sighed, looking at myself in the mirror. I didn't do that often. I didn't like the man looking back. All I could see in his eyes was bloodlust and chaos and darkness. The darkness was what I had to work to conceal at all times. I could never give in to it. My base instincts couldn't be trusted. I had to fight to appear respectable, trustworthy. To Warden Pike, I was the best officer she had on duty. Little did she know, I had broken far too many of her rules. And mostly, I had broken them for Twelve.

I pushed through the bathroom door and lifted my chin high as I prayed to the stars the curse wouldn't overwhelm me in front of Pike. That mark on my arm was like a key to all my secrets. It linked me to Twelve. If she was questioned, forced to go under Cyclops interrogation, they'd find out I'd been hunting her, wanting her. At best, I'd lose my job. At worst, I'd end up with some prison time of my own.

I strode down the hall, knocking on the warden's office door as I drew in a long breath to calm the fuck down.

"Enter," Pike called and I stepped into the room.

She nodded curtly to me from behind her desk. "Good morning, Officer, how are you getting along with Twelve?"

"I'm just about to assign her to her correctional program." My nerves frayed as she gazed at me and I started to fear she knew something, that she was about to expose me. But I must have been fucking paranoid. I'd covered my tracks. It had been months since my last discretion with Twelve.

"Good. Sorry to summon you out of your meeting, but I've just had a call with the Tucana FIB Captain and it looks like we have a livewire being transferred here this afternoon." She gestured for me to sit and I did so before she handed me a casefile.

"Laura Metz has been reprimanded in the past for various misconducts regarding a particularly famous Werewolf."

"Who?" I frowned.

"I'm not at liberty to say, the information has been redacted from her file. She has been arrested for stalking multiple times, but on this occasion, it was with intent to kidnap. Charges have been pressed and the judge deemed a stint in Darkmore necessary to drive the message home."

"That seems extreme considering she didn't actually pull off the kidnap," I pointed out. Darkmore was for monsters, not Fae with half-cocked plans to kidnap celebrities.

"Yes, well the judge took into account the fact that the FIB agent who brought her in lost an arm while subduing her."

"Holy shit," I cursed.

"My feelings exactly," she said, her nose wrinkling. "The arm was utterly obliterated so there was no chance of reattachment."

My throat tightened. Losing a hand was the worst kind of fate for a Fae. Nothing was worse than that apart from losing *both* fucking hands. We couldn't wield our magic without them and those Fae who'd been known to lose both either lost their minds or got so sick, they fucking died.

"She claims it was an accident, but of course, that made no difference in the end even if it is the truth. The damage was done," Pike said with a sigh. "Anyway, I wanted to make sure you would be around to process her at four pm. I want my best officer in attendance."

She always gave me the crazies and the savages. Maybe I wouldn't have formed my obsession with Twelve so quickly if I hadn't had to process her naked ass. I could have ignored her if it weren't for that interaction where my dick had gotten so stiff, I swear I'd had to jerk off three times to fix my hard on later that day.

"I'll be there," I agreed.

"Good. I'll sign up Officer Lucius as her CO. She has experience with wildcards and I know you have your hands full with Twelve currently." She straightened out her already flat shirt and smiled at me. "I won't keep you from her any longer. I want a two week report on her progress once she starts classes."

"Yes, ma'am." I got to my feet and strode to the door, heading out into the corridor and walking back in the direction of the office I'd left Twelve in.

My chest tightened the closer I got to her and the mark on my inner arm prickled uncomfortably, like it was warning me to fucking behave. I growled irritably then unlocked the door and pushed into the room.

She was still in place on her chair, but I glanced around the room for evidence that she'd moved even though she was chained to the damn table.

"You look suspicious, Officer. What in the world could I have gotten up to in here?" She batted her lashes innocently and I pushed the door shut, locking it tight as I tried to contain my temper. She'd had my coffee and cinnamon bun for one. Not that I was complaining. There was a reason I'd gotten four of them when I didn't even like cinnamon. Not a reason I was going to admit to however.

"Knock it off with the innocent act," I said, deadly calm. At least, that was how it sounded and I had to give myself mental kudos for keeping my cool with her externally for once.

"It's not an act though. I *am* innocent," she said, looking offended and I pinned her with a glare, striding forward and splaying my palms flat on the table as I towered over her.

"This bullshit doesn't fly with me, Twelve. I know you."

"Oh you *know* me, do you?" she said tauntingly, leaning back in her chair. "Or is it that you *want* to know me? That you just can't stand how I get under your skin, how you yearn for my blood, my body, my puss-"

"*Enough*," I hissed, leaning forward to unlock her cuff from the table and buy myself a moment to think. "I know you were up to something down in Psych, I know you were using me to get down onto the maintenance level, so what is it you're after?"

She just shrugged and I bared my fangs. "I have no idea what you're talking about, sir. You should really take a few days off, I think you're getting burned out. That pretty face of yours won't stay pretty for long if you don't get your beauty sleep. My aunt Bianca always said-"

"Stop wasting my time," I snapped.

"Beauty routines aren't a waste of time. Look at how I turned out when I was stripped of mine?" She poked at her ribs, pointing out her thinness since her time in isolation and guilt ripped up the middle of me.

I fought to keep my expression neutral, snatching up the course binder from the edge of the table and slamming it down in front of her, needing to change the subject. I was losing the grip on my cool head already and it was infuriating as hell. Why did she affect me so deeply? How did she manage to drive her way under my flesh like a sharp nail intent on piercing its way through my black heart? "I have hand-picked your courses to correct your behaviour."

"Have I been a bad girl, boss man?" She twirled a lock of hair around her finger, fluttering her lashes and I was sure she was piling on the falseness just to enrage me.

I ignored her, flipping the book open to the first course she'd be attending. "Group therapy," I announced with the hint of a smirk as I pointed at the picture of a circle of serene-looking inmates holding hands. "You will be encouraged to talk about your dark and dirty secrets in front of your peers. And keep in mind I will be conducting reports on your progress, speaking with your counsellor to ensure you're making an effort. And if you're not, I'll write you up to the warden."

"Figlio di puttana," she cursed me and my smirk grew.

I flipped a few pages and pointed to her next course. "Guided by the Stars," I read the program title. "You'll learn how to identify the tug of the stars and how to surrender to their will and make better choices."

"What if the stars want me to shank your ass, stronzo?" she goaded, but I didn't bite. I always had thought this course was bullshit.

"The warden believes the stars only pull us toward doing good," I said and she scoffed almost as hard as I had when I'd read through this new program designed by Pike. "Seems to me like telling a bunch of criminals to follow their inner instincts is asking for a fucking riot, but I'm just the muscle around here I guess."

Her eyes fell to take in said muscle for a moment and I cleared my throat as she casually slid her eyes back up to mine. Her cheeks didn't flush, but I could hear her heart pounding harder and for a crazy moment I let myself wonder if she still wanted me on some level.

Focus, asshole.

I turned the pages, hunting for her next course.

"Why did you sign me up to a course which encourages me to follow my instincts, Mason?" she asked in a seductive purr that was designed to taunt me and my cock which was still clearly at her beck and call. *Treacherous bastard.*

"Because the course material is soul destroying," I tossed back in answer. Which was the complete truth. I knew these courses weren't going to correct the behaviour of someone like her. They were designed for delinquents and psychopaths and she was neither of those things. Which was another reason why I was suspicious of her. What kind of Oscura gets themselves banged up in Darkmore for theft? The gang were notoriously wealthy. What the fuck could she have wanted the money for?

"Are you sure you're not just hoping I'll follow my instincts and be bad with you again? Because I assure you my instincts are running in the opposite direction. How long has it been since you hunted someone, by the way? You look *thirsty*." She was trying to get me angry again and the mark on my wrist was starting to burn as I fell into her trap. I wanted to drag her out of that chair and bite her, force her into submission. My hands were starting to shake with the need for her blood, but I would *not* be tempted.

"I don't know what you mean," I dismissed her and she laughed at me. Fucking mocking me.

I flipped the pages until I found the final course she'd be attending. The one I wished she didn't have to attend. Because as her CO, I was required to have one to one sessions with her on a subject of my choosing. A behaviour I deemed important to correct. And the one I'd picked out was fitting for more than just her.

"Impulse control," I announced. "With me. Twice a week. You will learn to-"

"Wait – what? I have to have lessons with *you*?" she blurted, looking horrified and I hated that that hurt. It cut into some fleshy part of my chest and made me want to upend this whole table, hurl it against the wall and watch the blood drain from her face.

The thought of doing that set off the pain in my arm, the curse winding its way into my bones and I hissed through my teeth as I battled to make it stop. But it didn't, the pain kept coming until it rushed into my head and I was vaguely aware of leaning on the table for support as an explosion of agony burst through my skull like a firework going off in my brain. I groaned, my strength nearly giving out as it took hold of me, attacking me from the very depths of my being.

"Mason?" her concerned voice cut through the searing agony of my mind and I cracked my eyes open as it finally started to ease.

"You did this to me," I gritted out. "Fucking cursed me. How do I break it?" There was a hint of desperation to my voice and I despised that.

I found her standing from her chair across from me, watching as my knees half buckled and I clutched onto the table for support.

She reached forward, carefully tugging up my sleeve and turning my wrist over to look at the mark. She traced her fingers over it and the pain eased, warmth spreading where her skin connected with mine and it felt so fucking good, like she was bathing it in pure moonlight.

"I don't know," she breathed. "I've never done this before. I don't know what I did."

I wanted to bite at her, demand she give me a better answer than that, but I could see the truth in her eyes.

"I just follow the magic of the moon, it's never steered me wrong before," she said, a crease forming between her eyes as she stared at the mark she'd placed on me.

I pushed myself up, staggering away from her and clutching my arm as my breaths came in heavy pants.

"You need to go back to your cell block," I rasped.

I rested my back to the door as I made it across the room, trying to swallow down my discomfort at her seeing me like this. "Let's go," I snapped, trying to move on from what she'd witnessed, but the look in her eyes said she wasn't letting it go.

She strode forward, reaching for my arm and for some reason I let her as she pulled up my sleeve again and continued to examine the silvery mark on my flesh. Her touch was warm and tugged on some innate part of me, begging me to draw her closer. The rose had grown once more, the little vines coiling along my skin towards the crook of my elbow.

I tugged my hand free and yanked my sleeve down, my jaw

ticking as I gazed at her. When she was this close, it was hard to remember why I so desperately needed to stay away from her. But the hate in her eyes was a reminder in itself. She didn't want me. She never had.

"I hope you're suffering like I suffered," she breathed and my heart clenched.

I growled low in my throat, grabbing her wrist and turning to yank the door open. I escorted her back to the elevator and released her as we stepped inside together.

My pulse thumped heavily at the base of my skull and I held my breath as we descended. In a space this small, it was all too tempting to think of the blood pounding through her body. The memories of me drinking from her were far too clear and I swear the curse latched onto my thoughts and urged more of those memories into my mind. Of my fangs in her neck, of her urgent moans, of my mouth finding hers in the dark and our bodies becoming a tangled mess of limbs as we clung to each other like two Fae possessed. I blinked hard to try and force them back and was glad when the doors opened.

I pushed her along ahead of me and she seemed happy to remain silent as I walked her back to her block.

"You'll be given a timetable for your classes," I muttered and she nodded stiffly as we reached Cell Block D.

I lowered the bridge for her and she turned to me instead of immediately walking across it.

"Have a shitty day, Officer." She mocked me with a curtsy and headed across the bridge while I seethed at her words.

I locked up the cell block once more and strode back to the elevator. I had a few hours off now and I knew exactly how I'd be spending them. I'd been researching moon curses online ever since she'd put the damn thing on me and had come across a book which seemed promising. It had arrived in the mail this morning and I was anxious to start studying it.

I headed into the guards' quarters, but before I made it to my room, Jack Hastings stepped into the corridor dressed in his uniform, looking ready to start his shift.

"Oh hey, Mason," he said brightly and I gave him a withering look.

"Hello," I said, moving to walk past him, but he sprang into my way.

"This was in the rec room for you. I was about to come find you." He waved a slim package in his grip and my heart jolted at the sight of the Midnight Hospital's emblem on it.

I was about to snatch it from him when I figured he had been about to bring it to me, so I muttered a thanks and held out my hand instead.

He placed the envelope into it with another smile. "Everything okay? Haven't seen you outside of shifts for a while. I could use some help finishing off a box of beers my grandma sent me this evening." He looked hopeful and for once I was almost tempted to agree. With the curse making me relive my past every time I was alone and Pike not letting me take on endless shifts to occupy myself, I was starting to dread the hours of solitude in my room with nothing but the curse's torture to keep me company.

"Yeah. Okay, yes," I said, sounding as surprised as Jack looked over my response.

"Oh shit, really?" he asked.

I shrugged and he beamed, starting to move from foot to foot like a damn excited Labrador.

"That's great. See you at seven?" he confirmed and I nodded stiffly.

He swept past me and I glanced back at him with a frown as he bounded off to his shift like he was having the best fucking day of his life. I didn't know why the kid gave a shit about spending time with me. He'd made plenty of friends with the other guards by now. It wasn't like I was good company. I didn't even like hanging out with myself, so why would someone else?

I shook my head, walking on and heading into my room. I kicked the door shut behind me, dropping down at the desk at the foot of my bed and placing down the package from the hospital. I'd sent the enquiry over to them more than a month ago and part of me had figured they weren't going to respond. But now they had, I was kind of unnerved about unveiling the secrets that lay within that package.

I pushed it aside and picked up the book I'd received this morning, taking in the hardback cover with the picture of the moon etched into the silver surface. I turned over the first page and started reading. It was all about the moon and its powers so I was going to have to wade through it all to find the part on curses.

It was over an hour before I found some useful information and my heart lurched as I discovered a picture of a similar marking to mine drawn on the inside of someone's arm. Though this one was of a lily.

A moon curse can only be given by a Fae who is intrinsically linked to the moon. All Orders of the night have rare breeds that hold deeper ties to this celestial body. But their powers vary greatly between them.

Moon curses have been documented for hundreds of years, despite their rarity. They hold some common attributes. The bearer of the curse will be marked by a flower – the symbolism of which is most likely pertaining to the crime of the bearer* - and they will suffer through nightmares and visions of their darkest memories. With these visions comes intense pain, described as a sharp and agonising burn which travels through the veins and can cause loss of vision and strength. It is unknown exactly what makes the flower grow, but in all recorded cases of the mark covering the entirety of the curse bearer's body, an excruciating death occurs where they bleed from every orifice in their body. A bleeding which no healer can stem.

*See page 156 for flower interpretations.

I will not die bleeding out of my star-damned eyes and asshole thank you very much.

I started rifling through the pages, hunting for any reference to a cure, a way to stop this fucking shit before it was too late. How long did I have? There was no timescale given that I could find. *Fuck. Fuck it. Fucking fuck.*

I made it to the page marking out each flower and my gaze fell on the one for the rose.

The lovers mark.

A lump grew in my throat as I read the words beneath the image of the rose that was so similar to the one on my arm, it couldn't be mistaken.

A moon-gifted Fae may curse their lover for their wrong-doings and have them face the wrath of the moon in penance for their crimes against them. There are only a few recorded cases of the lovers mark and all resulted in death. It is unknown what breaks this curse, but two opposing theories have risen between scientists. The first, that the curse could be broken by righting the wrongs of the lovers' relationship, similar to the familial moon curse, while others maintain that matters of the heart are so fierce, that a lovers mark will always result in death no matter what the curse bearer does to counteract their crimes.

My breathing grew heavy and I slammed the book shut, pressing my fingers into my eyes as the mark started to ache once more.

No. this can't be happening. This can't be fucking happening.

Why did I have to mix it with that girl? Why couldn't I resist her? Why did I have to be such a slave to her?

I was weak, pathetic. A fucking useless piece of shit who couldn't even keep away from a girl he was paid to keep in check.

I shoved the book away and grabbed the package from Midnight Hospital, tearing into it and pulling out the files from within. The ache in my arm fell still as I found myself staring at a picture of a young Rosalie Oscura who must have been fourteen or fifteen years old. She was standing in her underwear with her arms wide, her eyes hard and empty as she stared into the camera. Her left side was covered in silvery scars, the exact place where she had her rose vine tattoo now.

I felt sick looking at that, furious to my fucking core too. My hands shook with the heated rage coursing through my limbs as I read the file that accompanied the photograph. It detailed how she'd been admitted to the hospital after she'd been tortured with a sun steel blade. She'd made several visits, seen the best specialists in Solaria to try and heal away the scars and rehabilitate the nerve damage done to the tissue. There'd been some improvement, but the scars had remained.

I nearly crushed the file in my hand as I stared at what her father had done to her. And I couldn't contain my fury over it.

I needed an outlet. I had to know where her father was now and if he was still drawing breath somewhere in this world, I would find him, *destroy* him. I shouldn't have cared, but I did. I cared so much it possessed me like a demon.

The mark on my arm pulsed with a thrumming kind of warmth different to the pain I'd endured from it before. But I couldn't pay attention to it for long as my rage took over and fire burst from my hands as I paced and paced.

When I could think slightly clearer, I extinguished the fire, shoving out the door and heading to the training room.

Whoever was there was going to get the beating of their life. And I was glad when I walked in and found Officer Nixon practising air magic in one of the magic proof glass units. I'd never liked the guy ever since he'd flashed around some seedy porn in the rec room. He was a depraved motherfucker and I was more than happy to teach him what happened to his little breeze when it met the ferocity of hellfire. Especially when that fire burned in me for Rosalie Oscura.

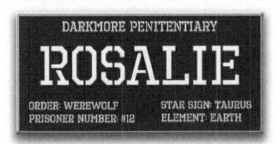

By the time I got to the queue for visitation, the other inmates were already lined up and waiting and I was stuck at the back. Not that that meant anything to me as I just sauntered straight past the line which had formed and offered up taunting smirks to anyone who didn't like it.

Unsurprisingly, at the front of the queue, Roary, Ethan and Gustard were standing in a vague line across the hallway rather than engaging in some kind of effort to force dominance. The guards allowed it because they knew it wasn't worth the backlash if they gave out any kind of preference to any one of the gang leaders.

Just before I could step forward to claim my place between the three of them, a broad woman stepped out of the queue and moved to bar my path, planting her hands on her hips and sneering at me. She had vibrantly coloured tattoos all over the exposed flesh I could see where her jumpsuit was tied around her waist and a mean look in her eye said she intended to follow through on this little show of power.

"If you want to be at the front of the line then you should have turned up on time," she said, stomping her foot in a way that was way too horsey to be a coincidence.

I raised a single eyebrow at her as the other gang leaders and the guards all looked my way. This was a test which I couldn't fail in front of them or they'd claim I was weak, but if I flipped on this bitch in front of all the guards I could end up back in the fucking hole. At the very least I was bound to miss out on my visit and there was no way that I was going to miss seeing my cousin after all this time.

"Get in line at the back where you belong, or we're going to have a problem, mutt," the girl snarled and several of the inmates who had been in line with her snorted and whinnied their approval.

"Tell her, Sparkle!" one of the guys cried enthusiastically and the name was like three percent familiar to me. My Wolves had mentioned something about some jumped up Pegasus bitch trying to make a play for a spot as one of the rival gang leaders in this place while I'd been in the hole. I guessed she'd managed to convince herself she was close to taking my place. But that was a fucking joke.

I clucked my tongue like she was some insolent child and then kept walking. Not around her, but right at her. She had the choice to move the fuck aside or let me crash into her. I wasn't even going to step around her. She was nothing to me and ants scurried aside when Wolves walked towards them or they found themselves crushed underfoot.

Sparkle's nostrils flared in a way that looked kinda cute on a horse face but just gave way too much view up her nose in Fae form.

Her hands curled into fists at her sides and I saw the strike coming at least five seconds before she threw the punch. I didn't even need my Moon Wolf senses to anticipate the moves of this dumb herbivore.

I twisted at the last moment, refusing to allow her to strike my face, but the punch glanced off of my shoulder and that was all I needed. Now, anything I did was just in self defence. And to be fair to the girl, she had power behind that punch. I guessed as a Pegasus she'd pack a pretty harsh kick, but I wasn't too worried about that – I just needed to go for the jugular and this would all be over in the blink of an eye.

My fist slammed into the side of her head, knocking her towards her little herd of followers and I snatched a fistful of her short, rainbow coloured hair with my other hand before she could right herself.

I used the propulsion of her already off balance body to swing her face first into the wall and there was a loud crack as her nose met with rough bricks.

My Wolves started howling excitedly, screaming my name and calling out insults like *hoof whore* and *saddle sore bitch* and *glitter vag* at the prick who had dared to try and stand against me.

Sparkle fell to the floor and I kicked her in the gut as hard as I could before slamming my boot down on her ass.

Sparkle screamed in agony and her herd closed in around us, but I didn't bother going any further. The guards were shouting out for us to stop and even though they couldn't see what was going on now that the other inmates had formed a wall of flesh blocking their view, I had no intention of wasting any more time on this sorry excuse for a Fae.

I stalked away from her and the other Pegasuses parted to let me through as the guards rushed in.

With a sharp whistle, I commanded my Wolves to back off before they got themselves in trouble and by the time the guards had finished shouting and striking at the herd with their batons to return the corridor to order, I was standing in my rightful place at the front of the queue.

Officer Rind grabbed Sparkle and hauled her away while she yelled protests through the blood streaming down her face from where her nose had hit the wall.

Hastings hurried over to me before I could give the other gang leaders any of my attention and I bit my bottom lip as I widened my eyes at him innocently.

"What was that about Rosa-Twelve?" he demanded, his cheeks pinking adorably as he realised his mistake in almost addressing me by my name in front of the other inmates.

"I honestly have no idea, ragazzo del coro," I said, batting my lashes.

He glanced over my shoulder where the sound of Sparkle cursing me colourfully was accompanied by the guards telling her to shut the fuck up as they hauled her ass away.

"Just...stay out of trouble, Twelve," Hastings said eventually, offering me a tight smile. "You don't want to end up back down in the hole."

"No, sir," I agreed, my voice just a touch breathy as I continued to give him my come to bed eyes.

It was a shame the dude didn't have the backbone to be a true Alpha because he really was pretty and his body was stacked, but as I let my gaze trail down him I felt all the stirrings of a wet fish left to dry out on the shore. Niente, nada, nothing. He could spend an hour working magic between my thighs and I was pretty sure all I'd feel was a mixture of mild irritation and boredom. It was a crying shame that my alpha obsession had come to this but even the feeling of Ethan's eyes on me right now was making my skin tingle with want. And he was a total asshole who I hated. Poor Hastings. Why couldn't I just make the easy choice and follow through on what I was making him believe I wanted? Ah well, he seemed happy enough in the dark, so I wasn't going to enlighten him.

"Alright then...I spoke to Officer Cain about your correctional class assignments," he added. "I'll come and find you when it's time for group therapy. As I'm assisting as your CO, he thought it would be good for me to take on some more of those responsibilities."

"Perfect," I agreed with a flirtatious smile. I took a step forwards and lowered my voice just for him, though no doubt the fuckwits surrounding me could still hear. "I like you much better than him anyway, he's such a grouchy bastardo and you're so..." My gaze trailed over him suggestively before I met his eyes again. "Nice."

Hastings cleared his throat, making some effort to smother a smirk and I stepped back.

"I'm just going to see how we're getting on with the visitation rooms," he said, clearing his throat a second time and carefully avoiding the subject of my preference in guards before turning and striding away.

"What the fuck was that about?" Ethan demanded as Roary

snorted a laugh and I rolled my eyes without looking his way.

"Why do you care?" I asked him in the most disinterested tone I could muster.

"I'm just wondering whether or not you're spreading your thighs for a guard," Ethan said scathingly and as I tossed a look his way, the smirk on his face said he thought there was zero chance of that.

"What if I am?" I asked, tilting my head at him curiously. "The last guy I fucked left me seriously unsatisfied so it makes sense for me to try out someone better. And who doesn't like a man in a position of power?"

Ethan snarled like that really pissed him off and I smiled wider as I taunted him.

"And just who was this unsatisfying lover?" Gustard purred, stroking a finger along the beetle tattoo on his cheek as he watched us with his eyes alight like Christmas had just come early.

"Just some Beta asshole trying to play at being the big man," I replied dismissively. "I thought he was an Alpha, but when we got down to it, it became seriously clear that he lacked in the necessary...*power* to get the job done."

Roary snorted a laugh, smirking at Ethan like he knew exactly who I was referring to and Ethan snarled at him too.

"Well, well, I do hope you aren't this careless with all of your secrets," Gustard said mockingly. "Because if I hear you making insinuations about your other one then I may have some concerns."

"What the fuck are you talking about?" I demanded even as a shadow of warning raced down my spine. I still wasn't sure what information he'd stolen from my mind when he'd managed to snare me in his Cyclops powers that time in the Order Yard and this felt seriously like a warning. Fuck, why had I let myself believe that he would have been satisfied by finding out about me and Ethan? Knowing this conniving bastardo, he would have rooted around in my brain for every single secret I owned.

"I think we all know the answer to that," Gustard murmured, looking from me to Roary and finally to Ethan who looked confused as fuck. Shit, he really needed to work harder on his poker face if that was the best he could manage. *Idiota.* "Or maybe not all of us. You really are a cutthroat little bitch aren't you, leaving your own mate in the dark."

"What the fuck did you just call me?" Ethan snarled, puffing his chest up and striding forward like he intended to lay Gustard out here and now, but this seriously wasn't the time.

I moved between them and placed a hand on Ethan's chest. "He's baiting you, asshole. Do you wanna get sent to the hole?"

Ethan growled, but let me stop him as Gustard smirked.

"I know your secret, pup," he whispered. "And I'm looking forward to the whole thing playing out."

"Four-oh-six, go to room nine," Officer Nixon called out and Gustard sauntered away, grinning like he'd just won the fucking lottery.

"What was that about?" Ethan demanded, taking hold of my arm as I bared my teeth at Gustard's back and forcing me to turn and face him.

"None of your business, stronzo," I snarled, turning my anger on him happily enough. "Now get your fucking hand off of me before I break it."

"I want to know what he was just threatening you over," Ethan insisted, his grip tightening.

"She told you to release her," Roary said in a low growl which said he was looking to step in and defend me. But fuck that, I wasn't some poor victim needing a knight in shining armour.

"Why don't you tell the whole prison about us being mated? Then I'll tell you all of my deep, dark secrets," I offered, shifting closer to Ethan so that we were almost close enough to kiss, but despite the heat building between us from our proximity, I had no intention of doing that.

"You know I can't do that," he growled back.

"Can't or won't?" I asked. "Anyone would think you'd been castrated because you sure are acting like a scared little bitch."

Ethan bared his teeth and I gave him my cherry pie smile.

Roary shoved him off of me and I smiled even wider as Ethan whirled on him. "Don't tell me she's got you Bedazzled too? It seems like half the men in this place are sniffing around her like a pack of desperate vultures."

"What's the matter, Shadowbrook?" Roary asked, moving so that his chest was pressed to Ethan's. "Is there some reason why you don't like the idea of me and Rosa sharing a bunk at night?"

Ethan's gaze shot to mine and the look of betrayal on his face made me bark a laugh.

"What's the problem, stronzo?" I asked. "Is there some reason why you don't want me warming another Fae's bed?"

"You can't possibly expect me to believe you actually want this asshole?" he demanded, pointing an accusing finger at Roary. "You shouldn't be able to think about anyone apart from-"

"Apart from who?" I asked, smirking widely as he bunched his fists up with anger, because even now he looked fit to snap. "Is there some reason why I shouldn't be sharing my body with every hot Alpha I can get my hands on?"

Ethan just growled as he shot a look at the rest of the Fae lining the corridor but most of the Wolves and Pegasus herd were still bickering and close to breaking out into another fight so none of them were paying us too much attention.

"You can't," Ethan commanded, that Alpha tone to his voice which forced everyone beneath him to fall in and obey his commands. I felt the power of it crash against me like a storm, but my will was unmoveable and there was no fucking chance of me bowing my head to any command of his.

"Watch me," I purred, tossing him a wink and turning to walk away from him.

"Rosalie!" he barked but Officer Nixon was beckoning me over to room three and I had zero interest in any of my so-called mate's bullshit right now.

I raised a hand over my shoulder and flipped him the finger

as I put more sway into my hips than usual and let him watch my ass walk away. That was a sight he seriously needed to get used to anyway.

Roary's laughter followed me down the hall and I smirked before remembering that he was rejecting me too. What was with all the stronzos in this place? I was going to get a fucking complex soon if I wasn't careful.

"Did you get a good frisk already, Twelve?" Officer Nixon asked me in a low voice as I approached the door. "Because I don't mind giving you a good going over if you haven't? Then maybe you'll find your commissary a little higher this week for good behaviour."

"What the fuck did you just say to me?" I demanded, turning to glare up at him and he just smiled blandly.

"If you want a really big boost, we could go the whole hog and do a cavity search," he said, leaning closer to me.

I was about to punch him in his smarmy face when he swung the door open for me and I spotted Dante sitting inside the room waiting for me.

All thoughts of pervert guards and asshole Lions and unwanted mates abandoned me as a shriek of excitement escaped my lips and I raced into the room at full speed.

I leapt over the table and landed in his lap, hard enough to knock his chair flying and send the two of us crashing to the ground as I locked my arms around him.

"Gah! Calm down, crazy lupa or I'll have to tell Mamma that you lost your damn mind in here," Dante joked as he managed to get to his feet and hauled me up with him, wrapping his arms around me properly as I snuggled against his chest and felt the familiar touch of static electricity on his skin from his Storm Dragon gifts.

"Try not to get too frisky, you two," Nixon said from the doorway, winking suggestively and I sneered in disgust. What the fuck was with him and why the fuck would he think I might be open to his brand of revolting perversions? I was going to have to do something about him if he didn't realise that he needed to back the fuck off of me sharpish.

"He's my cousin, stronzo," I spat.

"Ooo, even naughtier," he said, waggling his eyebrows as he closed the door between us.

"What the fuck?" Dante asked but I just rolled my eyes.

"Never mind the creepy bastardo," I said. "I need to know how everyone is at home and then I want you to tell me all about your birthday plans. I know you wanted to have them early this year, but please tell me I didn't miss out on all the excitement while I was stuck in the hole?"

Dante smirked at me as we moved to take our chairs again. His birthday plans were really just a code for the date I picked for the escape and obviously after missing out on three months of my life while officer dickweed left me to rot in the hole had set me back a bit, but that was okay. Because I was back now and I was ready to get the fuck out of here.

"Did you get all of my letters before they sent you to isolation?" he asked me, clearly needing to know if I'd gotten all of the information I needed on the ipump 500.

"Yeah," I said with a grin. "They were great, thank you. Just what I needed to take my mind off of my problems."

Dante chuckled and cast a glance around the room at the cameras and I was sure they'd be listening into our conversations too so we had to be careful.

"Good. And did your friend ever make it back out of Psych?" he asked casually.

"No," I admitted, releasing a breath and letting him see that there was much more to that story by the look in my eyes, but there was no way I could explain everything that had happened with Sook Min to him here. "And apparently no one ever does, so…"

"I guess you'll have to make some other friends then?" he asked, his brow pinching with concern and I was willing to bet he didn't like how much of my plans had already gone wrong but I wasn't exactly thrilled about it either.

"Yeah." I didn't think that Dante would like the sound of

Plunger all that much, so I just turned the conversation back to our family, his wife, the kids, I wanted to hear about everything and just pretend I hadn't missed it all for a little while.

The time ran away way too fast and before I knew it, Officer Nixon was opening up the door again and telling me to say my goodbyes.

"I actually ran into an old friend the other day," Dante said as my heart sank at the idea of him leaving so soon and I could tell by the way his mouth twitched in amusement that this was about something important which we needed to slip past the guards' comprehension.

"Oh yeah? Who was that?" I asked, ignoring the feeling of Nixon's gaze on me.

"You remember that old Bear Shifter who lived next door to us?" Dante asked and I frowned in confusion because the only people who lived anywhere around the Oscura family home were other Oscuras, but he went on without letting me question him.

"Well he was telling me about this project he'd been working on with his brother which was pretty cool and he set me up with everything I need to take part in it too." Dante arched an eyebrow at me like I was being slow or something and my lips popped open as my brain suddenly clicked onto what he was talking about.

Pudding had said his brother could make a receiver to give Dante so that I could contact him with the transmitters he made out of the chips in the old pudding pots.

"Really?" I asked, my eyes shining with hope and Dante grinned at me as he nodded.

I had to fight not to start squealing with excitement and jumping up and down because that meant I'd be able to call him and speak to him plainly about my plans whenever I needed to from now on which would make everything a hundred times easier.

"Come on, Twelve. I can't give you preferential treatment unless you wanna earn it," Nixon drawled behind me with the barest suggestion to his tone.

It was there though and Dante shoved to his feet so fast that the chair he'd been sitting on crashed to the floor behind him.

"And how exactly do you intend for her to *earn it,* stronzo?" he demanded, rising up to his full height and looking every inch the Storm Dragon he was as electricity crackled through the air.

"I don't know what you're suggesting, son, but if you expect to be allowed to attend visitation again, you'll treat me with the respect I'm owed," Nixon replied, wetting his lips with his tongue and looking way too like the Heptian Toad Shifter he was.

"Forget it Dante," I growled as I placed a hand on his chest, wondering what the fuck had possessed Nixon to try and talk down to the King of the Oscura Clan. "You know you don't need to worry about me. This motherfucker isn't even a blip on my radar."

Dante gave Nixon a death glare over my head and then pulled me into his arms, crushing me close.

"Sei la Fae più forte che conosca, Rosalie. Ci vediamo presto," he growled in my ear. *You're the strongest Fae I know, Rosalie. I'll see you soon.*

"Ti amo, Dante." I squeezed him tight, wishing I didn't have to let go, but all too soon he was releasing me and walking away while I was left to return to my cell once more. But I went with a spring in my step because now, everything seemed to be coming together again.

DARKMORE PENITENTIARY

ETHAN

ORDER· WEREWOLF   STAR SIGN· CANCER
PRISONER NUMBER· #1   ELEMENT· WATER

I'd lost my fucking work assignment since I'd been found with the cuff key. All privileges stripped, so now I couldn't even earn tokens for the commissary. My Wolves brought me whatever I wanted, but that wasn't the point. Warden Pike had my balls in a vice and she was giving them a good fucking squeeze to drive the message home. But I was done being beat down like a naughty pup. I wanted my kitchen job back dammit.

As everyone filed out of the Mess Hall after breakfast and the guards split them up to be sent to their jobs or back to their cell blocks, I lingered in the doorway with my gaze locked on my target. I swept a hand through my blonde hair and hitched on a sideways grin that served me plenty of attention as the inmates walked past me. Girls were biting their lips and giggling, reduced to pools of melted butter at my feet. I could have had any of them. I *used* to have any of them. But then fate had decided to fuck me in the ass and mate me to a girl I could never really have.

Sometimes I wondered what I'd done to piss off the stars. Being a Lunar meant I'd done plenty of bad shit in my time, but nothing unjustified. And being brought up in a gang-run city, what was I supposed to do? Spread my legs like a whore and get fucked? It wasn't in my nature. I'd been seeking glory my whole life. I was born to lead, born to fucking rule. But apparently the stars didn't agree, because they just kept throwing me curveballs that knocked the wind out of me.

Officer Lyle approached and I gave him a smoulder that could have turned the straightest of men gay. And Lyle was definitely not the straightest of men.

"Officer," I purred. "A word."

A faint blush lined his freckled cheeks as he moved to my side and let me walk with him out into the corridor.

"You've done something with your hair," I commented, leaning back to assess his red locks.

He waved a hand dismissively. "No I haven't."

"You have. It's more...fluffy or something." I knocked my shoulder against his and he chuckled.

"It's not fluffy." He patted it down, but a smile was playing around his lips that he was trying real hard to fight off.

"Well either way, I like it," I said, leaning close to him again and he looked up at me with a flustered expression. "Keep doing whatever you're doing to it, Officer."

"You'd better get along now, Ethan," he encouraged.

I sighed dramatically. "Can I re-join my pack in kitchen clean-up this morning?" I asked, cocking my head to one side in that cute as shit way chicks couldn't resist. I was adorable. Fact.

"Oh..." He glanced over in the direction of Officer Cain who was rounding up the crew heading to work on the Cell Block E renovation. Rosalie didn't have a job either anymore since she'd been in the hole. Not that I paid attention to what she was or wasn't doing. "Sorry Ethan, I think your work privileges are still revoked."

"But it's been a few weeks now. Forget the kitchen, I'll take something more menial. You must have something I can do, Officer?" I gave him an imploring look, flexing my muscles as I did so and his gaze dropped down to the ink peeking out from beneath my jumpsuit. "I'll do anything," I said seriously. I was so done wasting hour after hour in my cell losing my mind over Rosalie. And frankly, my dick was gonna fall off if I kept jerking it ten times a day over her too. "Put me on construction. I'm good at lifting heavy things." I quirked an eyebrow and he cleared his throat, shaking his head.

"Construction is a level three job. Besides, the taskforce is full already." Lyle continued shaking his head, glancing over at Cain again like he was going to call him over here any second. And if that peacocking bastard of a Vampire heard what I was asking for, I could say goodbye to my job rights for several more fucking weeks.

"Come on, there must be something I can do. If I'm left to lie in my cell all day, who knows what naughty ideas I might come up with? I'm a bad boy, Officer, I need stability to keep me on the straight and narrow."

Lyle sighed frustratedly, carving a hand through his hair. "Alright…there's one job. But it's not looking for applicants until next week and-"

"I'll take it," I said immediately. "What will I be doing? Working in the commissary? Restocking shelves? Or are you gonna have me washing down the showers in my tightie whities?"

"No," he spluttered. "The library is being revamped. We've got a stockpile of new books being brought in next week to update the catalogue and the warden's decided to have the whole place redecorated and reorganised too. There's damage to one of the back walls where a fire was started and the carpet is so worn that you can practically see the floorboards underneath it. It's going to be several weeks of work and instead of a magical taskforce, Warden Pike figured it would make a good character building job for the inmates."

"Perfect." I flashed my pearly white smile at him, happy as a fly on shit. "Thank you, Officer. I owe you one." I winked at him, leaving him blushing as I headed away into the flow of bodies being corralled back to the cell blocks.

My gaze snagged on Rosalie up ahead and my throat tightened sharply. Since we'd fucked, she'd barely spoken to me. I couldn't believe she was taking the stance that I was an asshole for coming up with a genius plan to cover up our mate issue. She could brand a mate mark on her Beta if she wanted to and I wouldn't't-

I snarled ferociously with jealousy over that thought and several Fae darted out of my way. One even dove straight into the wall to my left, nearly knocking themselves out.

Rosalie glanced back over her shoulder at the noise, her eyes locking with mine. Fuck, the envy I'd felt over the mere idea of that was on another level. *Dammit all to hell.*

I pushed through the crowd until I was walking directly behind her, my breath making her hair flutter.

"Go fuck yourself, Shadowbrook," she said calmly, but there was an electric undercurrent to those words that made the hairs on my body rise.

"There's not much else to do in here, love," I mused. "It's either myself or someone else, so what would you prefer?"

She was slowing her pace and I was too, allowing the crowd to sweep past us, even though most of them were giving us a wide berth anyway. We were suddenly walking at the back of the line alone, and I moved to walk half a step behind her to her right, stealing a glance at the side of her pretty face. Although the word pretty when directed at Rosalie Oscura was an insult. She was the epitome of beautiful. The stars couldn't have moulded a more perfect girl for me. She was my type right down to her bra size.

She didn't answer my question, instead acting like I wasn't there, but that shit wasn't going to fly with me.

"I know why you're angry," I murmured.

"Wow, Ethan. Do you want a congratulations for understanding me telling you why I was angry in plain and simple terms? And it only took you, what, a week?" She fucking slow clapped me and I growled, glaring at her. Alright, so she had told me that she was pissed about Harper. But maybe I hadn't understood it on this base level until now. Her mocking tone meant I was suddenly incapable of giving a mature answer though, my pride too wounded for that. So fuck her.

I could feel her pain as sharply as if it was my own over this situation, but I was happy to hurt us both in retaliation. Because that was just the kind of petty asshole I was. "Well I was gonna try and resolve this, but now I think I'll just go back to my cell and wait for my mate to return. Harper really keeps the bed warm at night. It's nice to wake up with my dick pressed to a round ass again. And she appreciates my spooning, unlike some." I started walking away from her and felt her heart twist like it pounded within my own chest.

"Enjoy the second rate company," she called. "Though I guess me and her have something in common now as we both wake up with our asses pressed against an Alpha's cock."

I stilled and she almost walked into me, instead shoving past me so I was once again glaring at the back of her head.

"Are you really fucking him?" I snapped, hounding her, hating how quickly I'd lost the upper hand. I didn't even need to ask. There was only one Alpha shitbag sniffing around her regularly enough who shared her cellblock. "The long-haired asshole of a *Lion*?"

She tossed her hair and flipped me her middle finger, suddenly pushing through the crowd and disappearing within them.

Roary Night was one dead motherfucker. I was going to rip his spinal cord out and throttle him with it if she really was screwing him. The mate bond meant I didn't want anyone else but her. So why was she different? She couldn't be. But what if she was? *Fuck. Fuck!*

***

My anger didn't cool as the day ground on and by the time I returned to my cell again after lunch, I was seething. Rosalie had been all over Roary in the Mess Hall, laughing and joking with him, the two of them acting like the best fucking friends who also liked to dick each other. I'd noticed it before, but now that she kept suggesting they were sharing a bed, my brain was fit to fucking implode. All I could think about was his hands on her body. A body that belonged to me. *Mine.*

I wanted a fight with him, but I wasn't going to do it somewhere the guards could see, somewhere they could slap more time on my sentence if I went too far. No, I was going to wait until the next time we were in the Order Yard together and I caught him unawares. Then I'd sink my teeth into his throat and drain the blood of my enemy before snapping his fucking neck.

"Are you okay, Alpha?" Harper asked as she followed me into my cell and I kicked my bed so hard that I put a dent in the framework.

"No," I snarled, pacing back and forth in front of her.

She glanced out to where my pack were gathered, looking in at us in concern and I strode forward, yanking the sheet down to block their view. Then I pushed Harper up against the wall, flattening my body to hers and dipping my head toward her mouth. If Rosalie was fucking the Lion, then why shouldn't I fuck Harper?

She tilted her chin up, her lips wet and hungry for mine. I could totally do it. I could just kiss her and fuck her and she'd thank me for it too because I was one hell of a damn lay. I definitely wasn't just butt hurt and trying to prove a point.

I got within an inch of her panting mouth before I yanked my head back so hard I almost gave myself whiplash.

I smacked my hand against the wall above Harper's head and hissed, "Pretend I'm fucking you."

She started moaning, her body grinding against mine in hopes of me giving into her and I moved away as she slammed herself against the wall, committing hard as she moaned and slapped the bricks again and again. I sighed. She was a damn good Beta, bless her heart. But my dick was so soft right now I could have used it as a blanket.

I dropped onto my bed, hooking a newspaper off my nightstand as Harper continued to scream and make sound effects that were so damn realistic, it was like she'd practised them a thousand times. *Kudos girl.*

I flipped through the articles in the Daily Solaria, ignoring the boring politics shit. I'd only ever taken a real interest in it a few years back when the Vega princesses had been vying to take the throne from the Celestial Heirs. Total fucking shit show, but the press had lapped it up and the stories that had come out had been more riveting than prime time television. No one could have predicted the way that would turn out. Glad I was in here when everyone started dying. I swear Darkmore had been a safe haven for a while compared to the war beyond these walls. It would be a whole new world out there when I finally got free. Which wouldn't be for fifteen more fucking years. There could be more wars, more upheavals, more political deaths by the time I was free. Who knew who'd be sitting on the throne by then?

The bell rang to announce the guards arriving and I frowned a second before I realised why they were here. I dove off of my bed and snapped my fingers at Harper to stop the sex noises coming from her mouth before shoving the sheet aside and striding outside.

"Number Three-Oh-Seven," Officer Nixon called out. "Ninety-Four, Two-Fifty-Two, Three-Eighty-Nine, One, Two-Thirty-Eight," he continued reading off the inmates' numbers as I grinned hungrily. Fuck. Yes. Maybe fate wasn't against me after all. Maybe the world was just a dick and those pretty little stars up there really were rooting for me, sighing my name and fingering themselves over their favourite Alpha Wolf.

I ran down the stairs, taking them two at a time as my pack howled excitedly for me and I returned the sound as I went.

There were more guards grouping behind Nixon, a few of them exchanging glances over me winning a spot in the Fate Room lottery. *That's right fucktarts, I'm going to get a glimpse into the future and use it to my damn advantage. And there's nothing your shiny little badges can do about it.*

The guards led all ten of us across the bridge and I bounded along at their heels, anxious to get into the Fate Room and read my Horoscope, roll the dice, read the cards, get some fucking good news for once.

I growled as we arrived outside the huge metallic doors of the Fate Room, the rest of the cell block groups already there waiting to go in. I started pushing through the crowd just as Officer Cain opened the doors up ahead and I was dragged along with the tidal wave heading inside. I snarled and snapped at any fucker who got in my way and by the time I swept into the dark space, I was almost at the front.

I made it to the silver stairs that wound up to the huge Horometer slowly circling on the ceiling, the planets rotating around the large orb representing the sun at the heart of it. I shoved my way past everyone and no one challenged me until I made it to the very last person at the front of the line. Sin fucking Wilder.

"You got out of the hole then," I said irritably.

"Yup. Just now in fact. You been missing me, sugar tits?" he purred, smirking and I didn't bother to answer.

He stepped up to the panel to read his Horoscope and I folded my arms, glaring at him impatiently. He was one of the few assholes who could pose a real challenge to me in Darkmore, so it wasn't worth the aggro of fighting him, especially when he still had a hold of me. I could wait a couple of minutes I supposed. Though he was taking his sweet damn time, humming a song under his breath which I swear was the Jurassic Park theme tune.

"Take your time," I said overly sarcastically, and he glanced my way, his dark eyes narrowing but there was a crazy smile on his lips too.

"Oh I will, kitten." He cocked his head to one side as he read the words on the screen and I ground my jaw as he rubbed his chin in thought, putting on a show just to piss me off.

"We're in a hole underground, deep, deep, deep in the depths of the ground," a girl sang somewhere behind me and I threw a look down the line, spotting Bullseye with her pink hair and petite features. She rocked her head from side to side, continuing her made up song and a frown pulled at my brow. "They put us in the earth like we're dead, dead, dead. Bang, poof, whop, chop!" She giggled, leaning in to lick the back of a girl's neck who moved up a step to put some distance between them.

"Hey," I called to Bullseye. I hadn't had many jobs to offer her lately, but she was still loyal to me. I didn't like the feeling in my stomach over seeing her like this. She wasn't acting right.

"Oh wow it's the Wolf lord, the big Lunar cheese. Awoooo!" She cupped her hands around her mouth, tipping her head back. "How does the moon hear you all the way down here? She must have big flappy ears that are listening all the time to all the little Werewolves scurrying across the earth." She stepped out of the line, running off down into the Fate Room and crawling under a Tarot card table out of sight.

I cursed under my breath, running my fingers through my hair. That was not good. Bullseye was a damn good ally, but if she'd caught the crazy in here, she was no good to me. I wanted to do something about it, but there was nothing I could do to help her. It was just a sad fact in Darkmore. Once someone lost their mind, it was only a matter of time before they were dragged off to Psych.

I turned my gaze back onto one crazy asshole who somehow walked the line of just sane enough to remain in the main prison. Made no sense to me. If anyone needed crazy pills it was this guy.

Sin looked to me, gesturing for me to step up to the screen without moving an inch. "Go ahead, I'm done."

I moved forward, but he didn't step back and I growled in warning. "This is private, get out of here."

Everyone else on the stairs was keeping well away, but Sin was leaning in closer and he suddenly slid his arm around my shoulders, squeezing firmly like he was reminding me he owned me.

"Nah, I'm gonna stay right here, kitten. We're on the same team today, so I need to make sure the stars aren't going to fuck us."

"What are you talking about? I'm not on your team." I shoved him off but he just got closer, nudging me toward the screen and smiling like we were best friends playing around. But that was not what we were one fucking bit.

"You are today," he said. "I'm the captain and you're my little bitch. Say 'aye aye, captain'." He grabbed my cheeks, squeezing to make my mouth move in time with those words and I snarled, shoving my palms into his chest as my hackles rose.

"Touch me again and I'll rip your throat out," I warned.

"You're a very angry little Werewolf," he taunted, still fucking smiling. "And you know what I'll do if you don't play along." He cocked a brow and my jaw locked tight. I'd put so much effort into keeping mine and Rosalie's secret still a damn secret, and this motherfucker was testing the limits of my sanity while he dangled it over my head.

Sin tipped his head back, cupping his hands around his mouth. "Attention inmates of Darkmore Penitentiary-"

I elbowed him in the gut so hard that he coughed out a breath.

"*Fine*," I snapped at him, furious as I moved in front of the screen and placed my palm on it. Sin rested his chin on my shoulder as he gazed down at it to read my private fucking information.

Prisoner Number: #1
Name: Ethan Shadowbrook
Crime: Kidnapping
Order: Werewolf
Star Sign: Cancer
Element: Water
Sentence Remaining: Fourteen years,
eleven months and ten days.

I would have been out of here by now and the reminder of that made my gut sink like a stone.

"Kidnapping, hmmm?" Sin murmured in my ear. "You dirty dog."

I jerked my shoulder up to try and dislodge his head, but he pressed his chin down harder to stay there. I didn't tell people the reason I was in here, it was my fucking business and I despised Sin peeking into my life. My baby sister had tried to solve our money issues on her own, and that had been one helluva mistake which had landed my ass in here. I'd been furious until the moment she'd told me she was pregnant and then what was a guy to do?

"I kidnapped a hobo once," he mused. "Terrible idea. No one realised he was missing. Eventually, I gave him a pair of my shoes and put him back where I found him."

"By the stars," I muttered. "Why the fuck would you do that?"

"He didn't have any shoes."

"I mean why would you kidnap him in the first place?" I growled, shaking my head at him and he paused.

"I was a dumb kid and only had three auras to last me a week for food," he said thoughtfully.

"And you thought kidnapping a hobo for ransom was the answer?" I said irritably.

"Not my finest moment. We still talk sometimes though. Alf runs a shoe shop now out in Iperia, real nice guy, bit ironic that he started up the shoe shop after-"

"You gave him some shoes, I get it. But I don't give a shit about Alf and his shoe shop."

"You should, I get a fifty percent discount there and he casts spells on the soles that make them the comfiest damn feet keepers I've ever worn."

Feet keepers??

My horoscope was on the screen and I refused to go down this rabbit hole of a conversation so I read it before it disappeared.

Hello Cancer inmate.
The stars have spoken about your fortune.
You're feeling unbalanced of late, as though the scales of fate are tipping against you. And with a Sagittarius stepping on your toes, you may feel suffocated. However, you could find that following this uncomfortable path leads you right to where

you want to be. As Mars moves into your chart, you might find it harder to quell your anger in the face of your struggles, but take heart, the road of resistance can sometimes end at an oasis.

"I'm a Sagittarius," Sin spoke in my ear again, his breath hot on my skin. "It's definitely talking about me. My Horoscope mentioned you too, kitten." He grabbed my hand and I yanked it free as he tried to guide me away.

"What the hell are you doing?" I hissed, glancing at the queue of people waiting to come up who were now muttering among one another.

"Just play along, sugar," he encouraged. "We have another little task to do for our favourite she-Wolf."

My eyes widened and I growled. "No," I refused, remembering the Nepula Weed I'd had to sneak out of the Order Yard up my fucking ass. "If she needs something done, she can do it her damn self."

I headed off down the stairs and heard Sin's heavy footfalls following close behind me. I managed to evade him for a while, doing a couple of readings on the Tarot cards and getting the same sort of message as my Horoscope. It looked like I was going to be walking down a rocky road for a while. But there had to be a way to change that.

I headed over to the dice to get some more specific guidance, but before I made it there, Sin appeared again, wrapping his arm around my shoulders and directing me toward the crystal section at the back of the room.

"Pull away and I'll shout your secret at the top of my lungs," he whispered to me and I stiffened in fury but didn't fight him. I just couldn't fucking risk it.

The crystals were kept in giant form here, embedded along the back wall to keep them from being stolen, each of them the height of a man.

Sin guided me into a darker corner that was lit only by the low yellow glow of the Sunstone Crystal in the wall.

"Rosa needs some of this," Sin breathed, glancing over at the camera pointed our way up on the wall. There was no sound on the feed, but stealing from this place was all but fucking impossible with the ever watching eyes of the guards anyway. So whatever plan he might have come up with wasn't gonna work.

I scoffed. "Good luck with that. I'm not going to the hole for trying to get something out of here. They pat down everyone the second they leave."

"Yup," Sin agreed. "They sure do." He reached out, brushing his hands over the crystal on the wall. He suddenly slammed me against it and his mouth landed on mine as he crushed me in place. I was so in shocked that it took me a couple of seconds to react before I shoved him back and threw a punch into his gut.

"What the fuck?!" I snarled as he smirked and my gaze was drawn to the piece of crystal he'd broken off in his hand, twirling it between his fingers beside his leg out of sight of the camera.

"Great," I said hollowly. "Enjoy getting that out of here."

"You need to put it up your butt," he said in a low and serious tone.

"*No*," I balked, but he just nodded firmly.

"They'll strip search me, they always do. It has to be you, kitten," he said simply.

"I'm not doing it," I snarled.

"Rosalie needs our help, don't you wanna help your *mate*?" he whispered and I glanced around, though luckily no one else was in this section of the Fate Room. But that didn't mean he could risk saying that shit out loud.

"Shut up," I growled.

"She needs us, baby cakes," he said. "I'll help you do it, I'll be *real* gentle. I've got a lot of experience with matters of the ass."

"No," I snapped. "Apart from anything else, there's a camera pointed right at us."

"I'm aware." Sin smiled broadly, flashing me teeth and I

scowled. "You're really not gonna help her?"

I clenched my jaw, hating myself for the temptation I felt to bring a smile to Rosalie's lips. It would sure as shit help cut the tension between us too. Maybe she'd even forgive me for Harper...

I was still mad over her comments about sleeping with the Lion, but I could straighten that shit out. Besides, my mate bond didn't let me fuck anyone else, she sure as hell wasn't fucking Roary Night even if she *was* sharing a bed with him. Logic told me that and maybe it was time I started believing it.

Balls, I'm really gonna do this, aren't I?

"Fine, give it here." I moved closer to try and subtly take it from him, but he shook his head.

"There's only one way this is going to go unnoticed." He reached up to trail his fingers along my jaw and I frowned at him before he snatched a fistful of my hair and drove his mouth against mine again. I punched him, trying to fight him off, but he managed to turn me around and push me up against the wall, grabbing hold of my jumpsuit which was tied around my waist.

"Motherfucker!" I growled.

"Just count to ten and fantasise about your mate, it'll be over in no time," Sin laughed and I swung around, fighting him back with furious punches which he took, only laughing harder even when his lip started bleeding.

He started wrestling me and I growled as he knocked my legs out from under me and dropped over me on the floor, his mouth landing on my throat.

"Say my name, baby," he taunted as I thrashed on my back, but he weighed a fucking ton. He lifted his hips and I threw another heavy punch at his kidney, making him grunt in pain as I twisted over onto my hands and knees to scramble out. *Bad move. Shoulda known it.*

He shoved his weight down on me again so my stomach hit the floor and then he did the unthinkable. He started fucking *tickling* me. And I was one ticklish bastard. I laughed, unable to help it as he tickled me until my sides hurt.

"Stop – mother -fucker," I hissed, kicking back at him then realising he was trying to make this look like some fun little hook-up for the cameras. *Asshole.* "You are *not* sticking that up my ass!"

"You always say that until I'm inside you," he said loudly, putting on a show for whoever might care to listen. *Gah!*

He tore my jumpsuit down and his hand went between my ass cheeks, making me clench up like a fist.

"Not like this," I snarled and he leaned over me, his breath on my ear.

"It's the only way, Shadowbrook. Just relax. Lie back and think of the moon," he encouraged and I knew, I just fucking *knew* he was right. If I wanted to do this for Rosalie, this was the only way I was getting that crystal out of here. Especially if they really would strip search Sin when we left. The breath fell from my lungs as I gave in and Sin slapped my ass, making me growl angrily.

"Come on sexy, show me how much you love your big boy," he encouraged.

I'm going to kill him.

I gave in and let him roll me over, feigning a groan while fighting my scowl and Sin released a filthy laugh.

"As if anyone would believe I'd let you top me," I muttered before Sin pressed his lips to mine. He didn't fucking hold back either, sinking his tongue between my lips while I tried my best not to bite it off. It wasn't like I hadn't kissed guys before, but these circumstances were fucking unacceptable.

Sin brought his fingers to our mouths, pushing the crystal between our lips to wet it while keeping it hidden with the angle of his head. Then he lowered his hand, pushing it down into my jumpsuit and I lifted my hips as he shoved his hand into my boxers, biting his lip angrily as his fingers parted my cheeks. I braced myself, growling as he slipped the crystal in, then he removed his hand just as quick.

"Why are you hard?" I hissed as his cock ground into my leg.

151

"I'm an Incubus with blue balls and you're hot, give me a break sweetums," he laughed again.

"Oh yeah, that's the business." My head lurched up at Plunger's voice, my eyes flying open and I found myself staring at him with his jumpsuit hanging open and his hands down his pants as he watched us.

"Mmmm, room for a little more salami in that mandwich?" he purred.

"Fuck off," I barked as Sin got off me, tugging my pants up before yanking me to my feet.

I rearranged my jumpsuit, flinching at the discomfort of the crystal lodged up my ass. *By the sun, the stars really do hate me.*

"Shadowbrook's ass is *mine*," Sin snarled. "Go find your own bottom."

Plunger strode away in frustration and I glared at Sin. "I'm not a fucking bottom. Ever."

"Well, according to every guard in this place you are, those rumours will be spiralling already." Sin grinned and I punched his arm hard enough to bruise. The guy didn't even flinch, he just continued to smile at me like we were friends. "Thanks for the good time, sweet cheeks." He winked and walked away and I was left scowling at his back. I was even more furious when our time in this place ran out a few seconds later and I hadn't even gotten to roll the dice.

I fumed as I strode toward the exit with everyone else, but my anger turned to worry as I made it to the door. The guards were patting everyone down and as I stepped up to Officer Nixon and he started running his hands all over me, I thought two things. The first, that I should have picked another guard because Nixon was a pervert and I'd been molested enough for one day. The second, that I'd just risked more years on my prison sentence for Rosalie Oscura. *I'll risk my reputation, my freedom and a put crystal up my ass for you, love. If that's not worthy of make-up sex, then I don't know what is.*

Nixon finished his far-too-thorough pat down then gestured for me to leave and a breath of relief escaped me. I glanced over at Sin as Cain patted him down then let him go and I glowered at him.

I thought they always strip searched you, asshole.

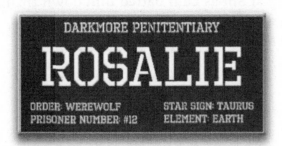

I sat in the rear corner of the Magic Compound with my cuffs turned off and power thrumming through my veins. Now that the cuffs had been changed, I had no need to save up any of my power to dig tunnels or do anything actually helpful for my escape plans, so I was indulging my creative side.

All around me, I'd grown a thick layer of moss and grass filled with all kinds of colourful wildflowers. Surrounding my little oasis of calm, I'd grown a layer of trees and shrubs so thick that aside from the thin patch of ceiling which I could see poking through between the leaves at the very top of my woodland escape, I could actually believe that I was outside. All I needed was the sound of a bubbling brook and I would be in heaven, transported to the tiny coppice just outside of my aunt Bianca's vineyards where I'd made myself a little sanctuary to escape to when I needed to be alone for a little while.

I lay on my back and breathed in the earthy scent of my surroundings as I allowed my eyes to fall closed and just bathed in the moment as I tried to escape reality.

Of course, I couldn't really relax, seeing as I was currently stuck in a massive room filled with cutthroat criminals and assholes who would have liked to see me dead, but the illusion of it was nice enough.

I sighed as I tried to puzzle out many of the new obstacles in the way of our escape and cursed Cain for the thousandth time for throwing me in the hole for so long. If I'd been in the main prison during that time, our plan could have progressed, we could have used the key and maybe we would already be enjoying the sweet taste of real fresh air right now instead of being stuck here.

Whatever the case may have been, there was little point in me wasting time on lamenting it. Cain was currently enjoying the wrath of the moon and I was seriously grateful to that bitch for having my back and cursing him. While he scratched his head over my little curse, he seemed to be actively avoiding me too which was all in my favour because seeing his face made me feel stabby. And if I got stabby with him then I'd be shipped right back off to the hole, so that wasn't ideal.

No. I couldn't waste time worrying about stabbing guards or mentally bitching about the ways my plan had gone wrong. I needed to focus. Onwards and upwards. Literally. Because I really needed to get us all the way up and out of this underground dumping ground for the world's most criminally damaged stronzos.

With my fingers tangled in the moss either side of me and my magic connected to the earth at my fingertips, I felt it the moment someone stepped into my little sanctuary. I curled my fingers into the soil even tighter, inhaling deeply as I readied myself for an attack and slowly began to trail the intruder with vines which snaked along the ground in their wake and swung down from the treetops subtly until my uninvited guest was being stalked through the trees without even knowing it.

The moment my intruder stepped through into my clearing and the silencing bubble I'd put up, I flicked my fingers and they were wrenched off of their feet and yanked skyward as a net of vines closed around them.

"Fuck," Roary cursed and a bark of laughter tore from my lips as I looked up at him dangling above me, but I should have known better than waste time laughing.

Roary whipped his arm towards me and a fat snowball crashed into my face a second later, a shriek escaping my lips as I failed to avoid it.

I used my control on the vines to hang him by his ankles so he was fully upside down and then managed to hook one around the hem of his shirt and yank it down to cover his face so he couldn't see me.

I was gifted a view of his golden abs flexing as he fought to break free, but as I was distracted by my desire to drool over him, he flung a hand out and a damn tidal wave of water exploded from his palm and came crashing towards me.

I managed to throw a wall of dirt up between us before it could hit me, crouching down behind it as the water crashed over the top and droplets peppered my skin.

By the time the water had rushed away and I dispersed the wall of dirt, Roary was no longer hanging from the treetops.

I craned my neck to look for him and a prickle of warning raced along my spine a second before he leapt from the trees at my back. My instincts gave me the time to whirl around to face him, but as his arms locked around me, I was taken down to the ground beneath him.

We hit the ground hard but the moss cushioned our fall as we tumbled across it.

I snarled at him as he caught my wrists and pinned me beneath him, his weight settling between my thighs in a way that felt too damn right to be wrong.

He'd torn his shirt off, presumably when escaping my vines and his bare chest was slick with water as his dark hair dripped down onto my cheeks.

"Yield, little pup?" he questioned, his voice rough and his golden eyes alight with our game.

"Is that really what you think of me, Roary?" I purred, wriggling beneath him in a vague attempt to get free without putting any actual effort into it. "That you can just get me wet with a flick of your fingers and then pin me beneath you and I'll yield like a good, submissive little pup?"

He swallowed thickly at my words, his gaze shifting to my mouth for the briefest moment as the weight of him between my thighs really made me want to moan for him. But I kept my desire locked down tight. I wasn't going to be a slave to that shit anymore and Roary had had far too many opportunities to

156

throw my feelings for him back in my face. It hurt. And I was done hurting for him. At least in any way that he could see.

He'd said it plain and clear. He wanted to remain 'friends'. Nothing more. And I'd swallowed that rejection down as best I could and closed the door on me and him once and for all. At least, that was what I kept telling myself. But whenever we got this close and his eyes burned with something that was far more than friendship, I sometimes felt the door cracking open again and had to slam it shut tight. I wished there was a key to that motherfucker so I could throw it away for good. But maybe a part of me would always be in love with Roary Night. Maybe the door would always be ajar.

He shifted an inch closer to me, his dick seeming much keener on me than he would ever admit out loud and the moment his grip on my wrists loosened a fraction, I bucked my hips beneath him and snatched my right hand free.

I threw a punch into his side and while he wasted time cursing me, I willed thick vines into existence which wound their way around his hands, cutting off his access to his magic. I threw my weight forward, rolling us over and the moment I was on top of him, I wrapped a hand around his throat and smiled widely.

My vines tightened around his hands, rooting them to the soft moss either side of us and I laughed as Roary swore at me.

"What's the matter piccolo Leone?" I purred. "Did you really think you could beat me?"

"I think we both know I'm no little Lion, Rosa," Roary growled, rolling his hips beneath me like he was proving a point and I raised an eyebrow at him as I fought not to show him how much I liked the feeling of his hard cock rutting between my thighs like that. For a guy who was supposed be just my friend, his dick certainly had a lot to say to the contrary.

"Non ne so niente," I breathed. *I don't know anything about that.* "And I don't want to, either."

His brows pinched before he could hide it and I mentally high fived myself for putting his smug ass in his place. Did I love the feeling of his dick rubbing up against me? Hell yeah I did. Did I wish he'd just give in to this heat between us and fuck me until I couldn't think straight? Erm, yeah, duh. But was I going to keep letting him wield his cock power over me? Hell no. I was done with him dick blinding me and making me look like a piccola cagna. Rosalie Oscura was no one's little bitch.

"Looks like we both agree on that then," Roary grunted and I squeezed his throat just a little tighter, enjoying the view from up here, dominating the king of beasts.

"Well, two out of the three of us do anyway," I agreed sweetly, sitting back so my weight shifted to his thighs instead of his crotch and dropping my gaze to his rock hard dick which was straining through the material of his jumpsuit.

"Don't read too much into that, little pup. I just haven't gotten laid in a really long time. My dick got hard over a bar of soap the other day," he said dismissively.

"Well maybe you should go and find yourself a nice Lioness to fuck then?" I suggested as I released my grip on his throat and moved off of him. I refused to acknowledge the sting of pain that suggestion sent spiking through my heart because I wasn't some lovesick little pup with a crush on a guy who was never going to really see me for me. *Fuck my life.*

"You mean like the way you found yourself a Wolf?" Roary asked bitterly as I released my hold on the magic securing the vines around his hands, letting them fall away and he sat up beside me. "How is being bonded to a guy who would love nothing more than the annihilation of your entire family working out by the way?"

I pursed my lips in irritation but I just shrugged. "Ethan can fuck well enough that I can almost forgive the rest of his personality failings," I said casually. "I mean seriously, he can make me come like no one I've ever-"

"Just a shame he'd rather pretend his Beta was his mate than let anyone find out about the two of you then, isn't it?" Roary interrupted waspishly.

I didn't want it to, but that hurt like a punch directly to my heart and I looked away from him as I tried and failed to shove it off.

"I have plenty of practice at being unwanted," I muttered, looking at a patch of wildflowers as I tucked my hair behind my ear, my fingertips tracing over the ridge of the moon mark I'd been given when I was mated to Ethan.

Even now, when I was raging with anger and hurt over him, a part of me still ached for him, urging me to tip my head back to the sky and howl for him to come to me. Stupid mate bond. I refused to listen to it though. I'd survived much worse torture than just pining over an asshole who was ashamed of me.

"He's a fucking idiot," Roary said thickly, grasping my chin and forcing me to look back at him. I tried to pull away, but he held firm, locking me in his golden gaze and making sure I listened to what he had to say. "Any man lucky enough to be blessed by the stars to have you as their mate should be praising their fortune and holding onto you as tightly as they can. You're one in a million, Rosa, you shine brighter than any star and you burn with more heat too. If I was blessed with a mate even half as beautiful and fierce and strong as you then I would wrap my arms around her and never let go. I'd give anything to have a girl like you, little pup."

I let him pull me against his chest and wrap his arms around me, but his words hurt almost as much as Ethan's behaviour did. He wanted a girl *just like me*. He just didn't want *me*. Because I was just the broken little pup who had ruined his life and gotten him locked away down here. I was scarred and flawed and endlessly aching for him and I was clearly never going to be who he wanted.

I sucked in a deep breath, laced with the rich, spicy scent of his bare flesh and then locked all of my unwanted and unrequited feelings away and pushed myself back out of his arms.

"Thanks, Roar, I'll bear that in mind," I muttered, doing a pretty spectacular job of sounding like a wounded little bitch, but there it was.

He frowned at me like he didn't understand why I was upset

and I expelled a hard breath before raising my chin and locking my emotions up tight. If there was one thing my papa had taught me, it was how to present a mask of indifference to the world. If I could hold a resting bitch face through walking on a fractured ankle during his so-called training, I could face down my broken heart just as easily. Surely it should hurt less than that. So why did it feel like it hurt more?

"We need to up our plans again," I said, changing the subject and closing the door again on that bullshit. "I know everything I need to about the ipump 500 to neutralise the Order Suppressant when we're ready to and Sin has promised to get me the ingredients I need."

"And you seriously trust him?" Roary asked sceptically.

"Sin may be batshit crazy, but he isn't a liar," I said a little firmly. "He's open and honest about what he wants and what he is willing to do to get it, and I have to say that I much prefer that to Fae who speak in riddles and bullshit. He told me he already has a plan to get the Sunstone Crystal, then I'm just waiting on him getting the Nevercot Plum and I'm all set. And, I managed to retrieve the Nepula Weed I hid in the wall in my cell because that stronzo Ethan left a brick loose when he came looking for me after he stole the key. Anyway, our most pressing issue is figuring out where we're going to dig from and how we're going to get Plunger onboard without alerting anyone to the fact that we're up to something. If we just start hanging around with that fucking creep, people are going to notice. No one is his friend by choice."

"I actually came here to talk to you about that," Roary said and when I glanced at him I found him smirking like a smug bastardo. "Because I think I've found the perfect place for us to dig our tunnel."

"Oh yeah?" I asked eagerly, shifting so that I was facing him and crossing my legs beneath me.

"Yeah. So, it turns out that the library needs a re-stock-"

"That's not surprising, the books in there are older than my Aunt Lasita," I muttered.

"Yeah, well they want all of the books gone through and a lot of the old shit will need to be removed to make way for some glossy new books all dedicated to helping us improve as Fae."

"You're losing me, Roar, what does this have to do with-"

"It's a work detail. One that will require the convicts on it to spend hours and hours alone in the library stacking dusty shelves. And as we know, there are a lot of CCTV blind spots in the library and I'm sure there's a shelf we could move aside to hide the fact that we're digging a hole..."

My lips parted as I realised he was right. This was exactly what we needed, I just had to figure out how I was going to get some antidote to the Order Suppressant so that Plunger could use his Order gifts to dig the damn tunnel. Then it was just a matter of making sure that everyone on that work detail knew how to keep their fucking mouths shut.

"How many people do they want on the job?" I asked.

"Nine. And Officer Lyle is sweet on me, so he already said I can have a spot if I want it. He's Sin's CO too so with a bit of luck it won't take too much convincing to get him assigned the job as well. He hasn't had any work since coming out of the hole and he's been on somewhat good behaviour - or at least hasn't been caught out doing too many things he shouldn't. So I'm sure we can convince Lyle to give him a spot."

"Okay. So, with Plunger that'll be four. We can't risk the other spots going to unknowns so is there anyone in this dump who you'd like to bring when we run? Because I think to make this work we're going to have to open up the guest list, otherwise they'll have no reason to be loyal and help us cover what we're doing. And the risk of them figuring it out and then blabbing is too high if we try to hide it so we need them in from the get go."

"My second, Claud, has been here a hell of a long time for a crime he didn't commit and still has a hell of a long stretch to go. He's missing out on seeing his kids grow up and he's been a rock for me throughout my stint," Roary said as he considered it. "We can trust him."

"Okay," I agreed. "He's in. I'll bring Sonny too and make up the rest of the count from my pack. I just need a few days to decide on who would bring the most skills to the job."

"What about Ethan?" Roary asked and I sneered in disgust.

"What about him?" I snapped before I could help myself. It was so natural to let my guard down around Roary that I didn't really hold any hope of keeping my feelings from him about much anyway. Besides, if I didn't have at least one person who I could open up to while I was stuck down here then I'd probably go insane.

"He might be an asshole and totally deserve to rot down here, but..."

"Just spit it out, Roar," I growled. "I haven't got all day."

"Fine. He's your mate," he said, matter of fact like that was that and I had no say in the situation. "The moon bound you and despite the fact that you're pissed at him, I'm guessing you feel a pull to him? I know that if Leon is away from his-"

"Your brother's situation is nothing like mine," I interrupted, refusing to let him compare the shit storm of me and Ethan to that. "I'm a Moon Wolf. The moon is on *my* side and once she sees that I have zero interest in remaining bonded to that piece of shit, I'm sure she will do me the courtesy of unbinding us. Capisce?"

"Rosa, I really doubt it's that simple to just-"

"Forget Ethan Shadowbrook," I snapped. "I'm not taking him with me. If he wanted me then he wouldn't be parading around the prison with that Beta trash hanging off his arm as if she's got what it takes to match him. Fuck him. And fuck you if you really think I'd take him with us after he disrespected me like that."

"Alright, alright," Roary gave in. "Just...think about it, okay? I might hate the idea of that dirty mutt having a claim on you, but I hate the idea of you pining for him and unable to ever see him again more. I don't want you to end up regretting the choice."

"Psh." I waved him off. "Don't worry about it. I'm never going

162

to want to spend time with an asshole who isn't man enough to own his feelings for me anyway. I'm no one's dirty little secret."

Roary's eyes met mine and I pursed my lips as I realised that statement practically could have applied to him too. Not that there was anything dirty going on between us because of course he had to be a gentleman about the way he ground his dick against me and then told me to fuck off. *Gah.*

"Well, well, well, isn't this cosy?"

My head snapped around and I leapt to my feet at the sound of the voice approaching and my upper lip curled back in a snarl as Gustard pushed through the bushes to our right and stepped straight into my silencing bubble as if he'd been invited.

"What the fuck do *you* want?" I snarled.

"That's not a very nice way to speak to your newest accomplice," Gustard purred, stroking his fingers along the beetle tattoo on his cheek like he thought it might come to life and creep away across his skin.

"Get to the point before I drown your smarmy ass," Roary growled, water twisting between his fingers as he glared at the man who had had me beaten up twice. Or had gotten his entire crew to do it in his place anyway.

"Before I do," Gustard said, stepping a little closer in his crisply pressed jumpsuit like it was designer chic instead of prison standard issue. "I want you to know that I had a meeting with my lawyer in visitation the other day. He was very helpful. Do you know that I am allowed to make a will via Memoriae crystal and fill it with memories which I would like to have viewed in the event of my death."

"You mean white jasper?" I asked. "Who would give a shit about the creepy thoughts in your head once you're dead and gone?"

Gustard smiled a devil's smile at me and he raised his eyebrows like he knew something so freaking juicy it was making him salivate.

My heart was pounding and my palms were slick because I knew, I already *knew* what he was going to say. But I had to front it out. I couldn't show any of my cards until I was certain beyond any doubt.

"Well, there are some memories in particular which I actually plucked from your young, supple mind when we had that little rendezvous in the Order Yard a few months back. Memoriae crystals are rather hard to come by and as I wanted two for my purposes, it took a little while to acquire them. But I feel certain that the effort will pay off once I'm breathing fresh air once more." Gustard looked like the cat who'd gotten the cream, the gourmet pouches of crazy overpriced food, and an obsessed little old lady to boot.

Roary took a step forward with a growl but I reached out and caught his arm, halting his progress as I glared at Gustard.

"Spit it out you mind raping bastardo. If you have something to say to me, then just fucking say it."

Gustard's predatory smile widened and he lifted his chin like he thought he'd won something. And he had. It was as clear to me as a dick slapping me in the face. No missing it. He had us right where he wanted us.

"I know that the two of you are planning to escape this cesspit with Sin Wilder in tow," he purred, lapping up the way both Roary and I threw hate filled looks his way like it was making his fucking day. "I know you need a Polethius Mole Shifter and that there's only one left in the entire prison. I know what you plan to do to the Order Suppressant pump down on the maintenance level and how you plan to circumvent all of the security measures put in place to stop you. And I believe that it will work. So, here's my offer. Take me with you and I won't say a word to anyone." Silence rang out following his words, but he just waited for us to agree and it fucking killed me to admit to myself that we were probably going to have to.

Why stars? Why him? Of all the fucked up, twisted motherfuckers in here why did it have to be this particular brand of ass eating dickweed??

"And if we refuse?" Roary growled. "Or just kill you here and now and leave your broken body for the guards to find?"

"Well, then in that case, the crystal with my memories containing every dirty little inch of your plans will be handed over to the authorities," Gustard said with a shrug like either option was equally acceptable to him.

"Bullshit," Roary hissed. "I don't believe you got hold of one of those stones, let alone two. They're rare as fuck. Even my family find it hard to come by them and we know every backwater dealer and notable thief in the kingdom."

"It was difficult," Gustard agreed. "But worth it for the cost of my freedom. And the reason I had two created was because I was certain you wouldn't believe me. So sweet Rosalie's cousin Dante will have received one of the pair in the mail this morning. All it will take is a single phone call to him to confirm it and we will all find ourselves on the same team."

Roary looked at me like he was asking permission to tear this asshole's throat out anyway and I gritted my teeth in rage as I was forced to shake my head.

"If you're lying to me, Gustard, then I'll rip your balls off and choke you with them before you die," I spat.

"You'll do well not to speak to me that way again, pup," he hissed. "But for now, I'll give you a pass while you come to terms with your new reality." He smirked at us before tipping an imaginary hat to me and stalking away into the trees again.

"Fuck!" I cursed as soon as he was out of the silencing bubble and the stench of his black soul had left my nostrils. "I'm not bringing that psychopath with us when we leave - do you know what he did to earn his place in here?"

"I heard he killed a bunch of women," Roary muttered, swiping a hand down his face like he was trying to think of some way out of this.

"Killed is putting it lightly. And they weren't women. They were girls who hadn't been Awakened yet. He kept them alive for days while he tortured them to death. He used his Cyclops gifts to find their greatest fears and then brought them to life and tortured them with them. I looked into all the gang leaders before I came here and the things in his file would have given my papa a run for his money."

"Then what the hell are we going to do? We clearly can't let him go free," Roary insisted.

"Well we can't kill him either. At least not yet. I'll have to confirm his story with Dante but it must be the truth or he wouldn't bother with the lie. By the stars, I think we're stuck with him."

"Rosa, we can't-"

"Just for now," I insisted. "We include him in the plans, keep him close, get him on the library team and make sure he knows to keep his fucking mouth shut. Then when it comes to the actual escape, we either incapacitate him or kill him. Either way, we leave him behind when it counts."

Roary growled low in the back of his throat, all Lion as his temper boiled over. It was pretty damn hard to get a Nemean Lion to lose their shit but when they did, it was explosive. And we couldn't afford that right now.

"Roar," I said, trying to catch his attention as he paced back and forth, his muscles flexing as his jaw ticked.

"I'm going to rip him apart," he swore. "No one threatens you and gets away with it, little pup. No one."

I stepped into his path and caught his hand, taking his cheek in my other palm when he tried to look away from me and forcing him to meet my gaze.

"We've got this, Roar," I promised him. "Everything is coming together. Gustard won't derail it. I swore I'd get you out of here and I will."

"It's not me I'm worried about," he said roughly, taking my hand from his cheek and laying it on his chest above his racing heart. "I can't watch you waste your life in here, Rosa. You came here out of some false sense of owing me something and if you get stuck here then that's on me too. Ten years in this hell was almost enough to break me. Watching Darkmore steal your life really would see me destroyed."

166

"We're getting out of here," I snarled. "You and me. We're going to go and find some island in the Cerulean Sea where the sun shines all day long and you can lie in it until you're so bursting with power that you don't know what to do with it. You'll be so freaking tanned that just looking at your stacked abs will blind me. And we'll stuff ourselves with fresh fruit and get drunk and party every night for the rest of forever beneath the moon. I swear it."

Roary stared at me for so long that it felt like he was just drinking me in, and I was caught in the heat of his golden eyes so that I couldn't move a damn inch even if I'd wanted to. And I didn't want to. Because despite what promises I made myself and how much I kept trying to convince myself that I was done with him, I was coming to realise I'd never be done with Roary Night. His name had been tattooed onto my heart the night I'd lost him all those years ago and even if he never loved me the way I did him, I would never be able to erase the mark he'd placed on my soul. And in moments like this, I didn't even want to. I could take a thousand heart-breaking rejections in payment for him spending five minutes looking at me the way he was now. Like I was everything he'd ever hungered for in this world and he'd rip a star from the sky for me if I asked for it.

"You're something special, Rosa," he murmured, the rage in him calming as he ran his fingers down the side of my cheek and my heart leapt out of rhythm. "I've never met a single soul with even half as much fire in their heart as burns in yours. You're wild and captivating and freer than anyone in this place has any right to be. And I promise to get you out of here too. Whatever it takes."

"Whatever it takes," I agreed and I flinched as the point where our hands still met flashed with magic as we unintentionally struck a magical deal to that promise.

Roary barked a laugh and forcibly stepped away from me as he released my hand and shook his out. My fingers were still tingling from the power too, but I just curled my hand into a fist, savouring the touch of his magic for a moment.

"Well, now we *have* to get out of here," Roary teased. "Or the stars will curse us with seven years of bad luck. And in this hell, that would probably be fatal."

I forced a laugh too, biting into my bottom lip as I turned my eyes away from the bronzed perfection of his chest and thought about what we needed to do to make that happen.

"I'm going to need a guard in my pocket," I said slowly as the rest of the plan came to me. "We need Plunger to have access to his Order gifts to be able to tunnel. That means I've gotta get hold of some of the shots the guards give themselves before their shifts start. Each one grants twenty-four hours of immunity so we can probably get away with grabbing three or four of them and then splitting the doses down to give an hour at a time. That way we can still control Plunger and make sure he's doing as we say. I'll just have to get up to the antidote dispenser in the guards' quarters..."

"Maybe I should be the one to carry out any thefts that need to take place," Roary suggested with a smirk and I shrugged.

"Maybe. But either way we need that guard on side, which means I'm going to have to up my efforts. I have Hastings half way Bedazzled anyway so he's the obvious choice. Plus with Cain avoiding me, he's practically my CO so I should be able to convince him to agree to getting me assigned to the library job too."

"Are you sure?" Roary asked. "You're a beautiful girl, Rosa, and I can't deny that you draw people to you like moths to a flame, but Bedazzling a guard into helping you out that much seems pretty extreme..."

"Oh please," I said, rolling my eyes at him like I was offended. "I could Bedazzle *you* if the notion took me. My little choir boy is easy prey."

"Come on, Rosa, I think we both know that you can't rival my Charisma with your fluttering eyelashes and cherry pie smiles."

"Poor, sad, Roary, Bedazzling is so much better than Charisma for a job like this. If you unleashed that shit on him, he'd be off telling everyone and anyone how great you are and how much he wants to suck your dick just to make you smile. Bedazzling doesn't work like that. It's a subtle kind of manipulation that takes a lot of time and effort."

"Sounds a lot like Charisma to me," he muttered.

"Okay, well think of it like Charisma offers out insta-love to anyone who gets a taste of it. The moment they get pulled into your web, they'll be yours to toy with. But whenever you release them from it, they will pretty much go back to how they were without you. Bedazzlement is more like a love story playing out slowly. It feels natural and there's no exchanges or any expectations involved. The mark genuinely likes me which I could obviously encourage with a magical exchange if I was doing it properly, but as that isn't an option in here I'm just getting him to like me the good old fashioned way. It's not forced, just a slow and steady build into them doing things to please me because they actually want to because my happiness makes them happy too. I don't have to give them anything or do anything to maintain it other than be my natural, charming, sweet self."

"So you just flash your tits until he's panting for you so much that he'll do anything to get a shot at some time between your thighs? Besides, I'm pretty sure you're not actually Bedazzling him if you aren't using magic so all you're actually doing is flirting with him," Roary baited.

I rolled my eyes. "Whatever. Doing it without magic just means I'm even better at it. You don't get it because you're as subtle as a pig in a tutu. Point is, Hastings is already falling for my charms which means I'll be assigned to the library before you even wake up from your afternoon nap."

"Good luck with that, pup," he teased just as the bell sounding the end of our session in the Magic Compound rang out to let us know we needed to get our asses out of here.

"I don't need luck. I'm Rosalie Oscura," I taunted before turning away from him and strolling out of the trees.

I stopped at the edge of my tiny woodland and pouted as I looked up at the perfectly sculpted magical haven I'd built. I swear making us destroy everything we created at the end of every session was a torture of its own design. I hated that I had to pull apart the magic I'd spent the last hour and a half crafting for no other reason than some asinine rule. *Assholes.*

"Alpha! Have you got a minute?" Sonny called and I turned to him with a smile as he strode over with a new girl walking at his side.

My chin lifted with interest as I recognised another of my kind instantly and the way she held herself with a confident swagger told me she was strong. Supposedly me and Ethan should have been competing to get the strongest Wolves who turned up at Darkmore to join our packs, but with all of my attention focused on the escape, I'd palmed that work off onto Sonny. He would then introduce me to anyone worth the effort.

"Hey," I said, my gaze skimming over the newbie as she met my eye and held it.

The Wolf in me perked up at the challenge and my lip almost peeled back with a warning snarl before she dropped her gaze in deference and I smiled. Girl had balls but had sense too.

"This is Laura," Sonny said. "She's looking for a pack and obviously ours is the only one worth bothering with in here, so she came to the right place."

"Supposedly the Oscuras are the best, so that seemed like the right fit for me," Laura said confidently. "Assuming you're not all full of shit of course."

I snorted a laugh and arched an eyebrow. "Damn right we're the best. Which means the bar is high for initiation. You think you can keep up if you run with us?"

"Please. Whenever I go to my baby's house I have to run like the damn wind to escape the FIB. I've never met a Wolf as fast as me," Laura said with a cocky smirk.

"Why do you have to escape the FIB when you go to his house?" I asked curiously.

"Well...technically he's married so our love has to remain a secret. We had a wild, steamy affair one weekend when my Academy met his for a Numerology tournament years ago which would have totally ended in a mate bond if the moon had been full and we were outside. But we had to hide what we had because he had *obligations* due to his identity," she dropped her voice and glanced around like someone might be listening to us. "He's kinda famous you see."

"Oh yeah?" I asked curiously but she mimed zipping her lips.

"I'll never tell. I'll protect him with all I have because our love is pure and unbreakable. That's why I have to stay hidden. Our love is constantly being thwarted by that bitch he married calling the cops and telling lies about me, but we're destined. Elysian Mates. These are just the tests the stars have put in place for us, but soon he will come for me and get me out of here and then we will have our divine moment and if that nasty, possessive, ass-eating, manipulative, pussy-blocking twat he married wont step aside, then I'm fully ready to cut a motherfucker-"

"She really is fast," Sonny cut in as Laura seemed about ready to lose her shit and start stabbing someone. I sure as fuck wouldn't want to be the one standing in between her and her 'baby', but I was also getting the feeling that the guy in question might not actually be aware that he was in a relationship with her. Though as I already had murderers and arsonists in my prison pack, I could hardly get picky about a stalker joining up and she looked pretty fucking tough.

"Well, while you wait for your love to come for you, it can't hurt to try out for the best pack in this dump," I said, making sure I didn't let any of my doubts over the reality of her relationship with her 'baby' show.

"Try out?" Laura asked like she'd expected to get in without all the bother of that and with that level of confidence, I was willing to bet she'd be initiated just as soon as we got a chance to run together in the Order Yard, though if she thought she could beat me then she was in for one hell of a race.

I felt Ethan's gaze on me like a physical touch and looked up to find him scowling in my direction so I shot him a taunting smirk.

"Yeah. I can't risk any basic bitches like the Wolves Shadowbrook surrounds himself with getting in to my pack so we gotta make sure you can keep up. But don't worry – I get the feeling that a girl used to running rings around the FIB has got what it takes to become an Oscura," I told her.

Laura grinned like she knew she had it in the bag too and Sonny wrapped an arm around her as he drew her away.

Ethan whistled to get Laura's attention as they passed him by, but she turned away from him like he was irrelevant to her and my grin widened. Girl knew the value of loyalty and wasn't afraid of the big bad Lunar. I got the feeling she'd fit right in with us.

I turned my gaze back to my magical woodland with a sigh and prepared to pull apart the magic I'd used to create it. It was so frustrating. Like nothing I did here was allowed to have any purpose or longevity. How could I take pride in my magic when I knew it would have to be destroyed within hours of making it all the damn time?

"Why so glum, wild girl?" Sin's deep voice drew my attention from the view of my little woodland sanctuary, and I turned to look at him over my shoulder just as he moved up behind me and wrapped his arms around my waist.

"What are you doing?" I growled, batting his hands off of me, but he just tightened his grip, his thick, muscular arms locking me against that broad chest of his as he chuckled.

"Don't make me beg, kitten, I've just spent a week in the hole with nothing but a cold, hard wall to cuddle up to and you know how my kind need physical contact. We can make a trade if it'll suit your Alpha personality more, but just let me spoon you a bit first."

"Your dick is grinding into my ass," I pointed out as I gave in. There were seriously worse places in the world a girl could find herself than in Sin Wilder's arms anyway.

"Yeah. But you like it, so it's all good," he purred, rolling his hips in a way that couldn't be natural for a guy his size and making me gasp as his hard cock pressed right between my ass cheeks.

Roary chose that moment to step out of the trees and he raised an eyebrow at me in Sin's arms before moving closer and extending a silencing bubble over us.

"You know, if you're looking to make Ethan jealous, you don't have to be so obvious about it," he bit out, looking kinda pissed himself, but I wasn't playing into his bullshit. If he didn't want me then he wasn't going to have any kind of say in who else I might pick instead of him.

"Ethan?" I asked in confusion.

"He's right behind us, baby cakes, and if rage and jealousy could feed my monster, I'd be good and stocked up already," Sin joked before whirling me around to look over at Ethan where he stood amongst his pack glaring at us. I'd assumed he'd fucked off after Laura dismissed his ass, but apparently he was still watching me and I didn't know how I felt about that.

Sin dropped his mouth to my neck, kissing me and making a shiver shoot down my spine as I arched my back against him.

"Stop," I protested, but the way I was gripping his arms tight around my waist said something more along the lines of don't stop. *Oh well.*

For a moment, Ethan looked about ready to flip out, go full Wolf and come drag me out of Sin's arms. But then that troll, Harper, sauntered over, took his hand and tiptoed up to place a kiss on his lips. He turned his cheek at the last second so she missed his mouth, but the fury that small act lit in me was instant and filled me with murderous intentions.

I lurched forward with a possessive growl tearing from my throat and Sin's grip locked tighter around me as I tried to leap right out of his arms. He swung me back around like I weighed nothing at all and promptly hid me from view of the conniving little skank and my traitorous unwanted mate.

"Fuck him," I spat before descending into Faetalian as I lost my shit and Roary raised his eyebrows in surprise like he hadn't known I could curse that colourfully.

"Calm down, wild girl," Sin commanded as he fought to keep hold of me and I seriously considered using my magic to escape his clutches so that I could go beat a bitch's face in. "Believe me, your boy doesn't feel an ounce of lust towards that girl. I can feel it. He wants her near his cock about as much as he wants a hoard of angry hornets near it. But if you want to make him feel as bad as you're feeling right now, then I suggest you get back to dry humping me. Or we could ditch the clothes and I could make you scream my name so loud that you forget his? I dunno how you feel about exhibitionism?"

"For the love of the moon," Roary muttered. "Just get your fucking hands off of her so that we can head back inside before the guards punish us for wasting time." He held his hand out for me like he expected me to just leap away from Sin and go running because he'd beckoned.

"You go, Roar," I said, my anger at my situation with him lending a layer of fuck you to my tone. "I'm good here, thanks."

Roary's gaze narrowed on Sin as he casually unbuttoned a few of my jumpsuit buttons while nuzzling against my neck so that his stubble made the most delicious scattering of goosebumps rush across my skin. I stopped his progress on the buttons, but the neck thing felt all kinds of good and it was so nice to be held by someone who wanted me and wasn't afraid to say it, so I made no move to stop that.

"Seriously?" Roary asked, giving me a scathing look that said I was pissing him off, but what did he want from me?

"Why do you care?" I asked him and Sin chuckled like he knew the answer to that.

"I don't," Roary replied. "But I seriously doubt your cousin would want me leaving you here with *him*."

"As if Dante has a leg to stand on when it comes to hanging around with questionable characters," I joked. "Besides, I just need to deconstruct my magic. What do you think we're going to do with two minutes to spare that's so worrying?"

"Is that a challenge, kitten?" Sin asked in a tone that had my toes curling. "Because I promise you, I can make it the best two minutes of your life."

Roary muttered something I didn't hear and stalked away towards the crowd of inmates heading back into the prison and Sin spun me in his arms so I was looking up at him.

"Do you want some help destroying your pretty little woodland, wild girl?" he asked, that same glint in his eye as he'd had when he suggested setting the Belorian free. It should have terrified me, but there was something kinda exciting about it too.

"Why do I feel like I should say no to that?" I asked as he grinned mischievously.

"Because society has spent years trying to make you conform to the rules of social propriety that make for a boring as fuck life. But you don't want to say no because deep down you're just as wild as me and you wanna watch the world burn at my side."

"I feel like I'm going to regret this," I said but I was smiling too as his mood begged for company.

"Not a chance, wild girl, I got you." Sin turned his back and patted on his shoulder for me to hop up and I did so with a laugh, looping my arms around his neck and winding my legs around his waist. "Don't let go," he warned before striding back into the trees.

The moment we reached the little hollow at the centre of them, Sin raised his arms and flames ignited in his fingers. With a flick of his wrists, they shot away from him, catching onto the closest trees to us which instantly ignited.

The flames spread quickly, leaping from branch to branch until we were completely surrounded and I sucked in a breath of exhilaration as he built the blaze into an inferno, directing his air magic around us to fan the flames and cocoon the two of us at the heart of the raging fire.

The flames burned white hot, the colour dancing between orange, red and even blue under his command as it ate through everything around us and destroyed it in a show of magic so powerful it made my heart race.

Sin started laughing as the flames moved closer and closer to us and I knew that I really should have been afraid, but somehow I was so caught up in the beauty and raw power of his magic that the adrenaline pumping through my veins just lit me up as brightly as the flames themselves.

The sound of the roaring fire was deafening and I bit my lip as I looked all around at the destruction Sin wreaked so easily. This was more than just a fire Elemental flexing his magical muscles, these flames were an embodiment of the wild and temperamental creature beneath me. They could be just as deadly as they were alluring.

When the fire finally burned out, there was nothing at all left of the little woodland I'd grown with my power, the last ashes swept away on a breeze of his design. I dropped down from his back and caught his hand in mine.

Sin turned to look at me with a dark and dangerous glint in his eyes that made my smile widen.

"Twelve! Eighty-Eight!" Cain barked from beyond the fence that surrounded the Magic Compound. "Get your asses back to your cell blocks or I'll be placing you both back in the hole."

Fucking ass badger.

"Sure thing, captain," Sin called, grabbing me and tossing me over his shoulder before I could do anything to stop him.

I laughed as he jogged back to the exit where the last of the inmates were heading through the doors and Officer Lucius used her remote to re-activate our cuffs, locking our magic away before we made it to the doors.

Sin carried me right past Cain who barked an order at him to put me down and I wriggled in his grip to make him comply. I wouldn't put it past Cain to throw us in the hole again if he could come up with a good enough excuse and I didn't intend to give him one.

"You wanna come back to my cell and let me peel that polyester off of you, wild girl?" Sin asked in a low tone which really wasn't all that low and earned us a glare from Officer Dickwad.

"That is seriously tempting," I agreed even though we both knew I wasn't allowed in his cell block. "But I think I want a date first. And unfortunately, I don't have time for one with you right now."

Sin frowned at me like I'd just spoken a foreign language. "A date?" he asked.

"Yeah, you know, two people, hanging out and seeing if they actually like each other before they fuck. I've heard it can even be fun sometimes," I teased.

"You...want to date me?" Sin's frown deepened and I rolled my eyes at him.

"Why not?"

"Alright, next time we're in the Order Yard, I'll use my gifts to become your perfect-"

"No," I interrupted him because I was starting to get really damn curious about who the real Sin Wilder was and it was all too easy for him to don a mask when he had access to his gifts. "Not in the Order Yard. Let's just see if we can make some fun for ourselves without our Orders taking over. Okay?"

"I'm not sure where to begin dating someone, kitten," he teased, but there was a look in his eyes that I almost wanted to call vulnerability if that hadn't been utterly insane.

"Well, let's start with a dinner date and take it from there."

Sin opened his mouth to reply, but suddenly Cain was shoving his way between us. "I'm not here to supervise the two of you making plans for romantic liaisons," he growled. "Come on Eighty-Eight, I'll make sure you get back to your cell quickly." He shoved Sin towards the stairwell so hard that the Incubus almost fell down the steps.

"Jealous, Officer?" he taunted as he turned and ran from Cain's angry face. The Vampire shot after him with a growl of rage and I smirked to myself as Sin's howls of laughter carried back to me as he kept running.

"Keep moving, Twelve," Hastings said as he came up beside me and I turned to him with a wide smile as I fell into step at his side.

177

"Have you come to take me back to my bed, Officer?" I asked in a teasing tone and the corner of his lips twitched with amusement before he schooled his expression.

He was bringing up the rear of the group though and there were no other officers close by, so I knew I'd be able to get him to crack with the right leverage.

"You've got work assignments next," he reminded me.

"Not me," I disagreed with a small sigh. "I haven't been given anything to do since I got out of the hole."

"Hasn't Cain reassigned you some work?" he asked curiously.

"No," I replied with a shrug, shifting a little closer to him so that my arm brushed against his. "I think he's been under a lot of pressure from Warden Pike recently, so I didn't like to make a fuss. And I wasn't sure who else to talk to about it."

I slowed my pace so that the other inmates drew ahead of us and within a few flights of stairs, we were practically alone.

"Well...if Officer Cain hasn't had the time to assign you a work detail, I could figure it out for you. I'm your supporting CO after all and I don't mind taking on a few tasks to lighten his load," Hastings suggested, and I sang a song of victory solely inside my own head.

"Would you really, ragazzo del coro?" I asked, placing my hand on his arm and batting my eyelashes at him for a moment. "I'm up for anything."

"Erm..." Hastings cleared his throat and I withdrew my hand as I continued down the stairs, treading the line of flirtatious without coming across like I was propositioning him. "Is there anything you're particularly suited to?"

"Oh, I dunno...no one ever really asked me that before. My papa always used to just force me to do the jobs he hated, and I guess I never had much chance to pick something I might be good at, you know? The only thing I ever really loved was reading. But I don't think that's a job," I laughed dismissively and Hastings smirked to himself.

"I think I may have the perfect idea," he said. "There's a new job starting up next week that could be just right. But I'll have to run it by Cain before confirming it."

We'd made it to the fourth floor where the cell blocks were located and I gave him an excited smile. "I'm sure whatever it is will beat sitting in my cell counting the bricks for the hundredth time. Thank you, ragazzo del coro."

A touch of a blush coloured Hastings' cheeks and I bit my lip before looking away from him again. As we walked down the corridor towards Cell Block D, we made small talk about Pitball and I made sure to point out how his broad shoulders must have made him almost unstoppable in defence, possibly implying that he could try his tackle out on me if we got the chance one day. Totally innocent – unless he wanted to interpret it differently for some reason.

Just as we reached the doors to my cell block, Cain reappeared in a blur of motion and dragged me away from Hastings.

"Don't forget your group therapy session tomorrow, Twelve," he growled as he herded me towards the cell block doors. "I'll be there to observe so make sure you're on your best behaviour."

"Please tell me it's just a bunch of inmates talking about shit and we don't have to actually read anything," I groaned as I let him tug me across the bridge and into my cell block.

"What's your problem with reading?" he asked with a frown and I shrugged like I didn't really want to say, but I answered him all the same.

"Nothing worse than sifting through a bunch of dusty old books," I muttered. "Are you sure there isn't a more physical correctional course I could do?"

"The whole point of correcting your behaviour is that we want to make changes to the things you do. So no, there isn't a more physical course you can take and if you question my opinion on what best benefits you again then I'll be writing you up for an infraction. And perhaps if you hate dusty old books so much, I should consider which courses involve the most of them? Unless of course you're looking to tell me more about what you were up to the night I threw you in the hole?" Cain asked, that angry vein in his temple coming to life just for me.

"No, sir," I replied sweetly.

"Good. Maybe you're finally learning your place."

He turned and shot away from me to ensure he got the last word and I watched as the bridge was retracted and the doors locked up tight with a smirk on my face.

If I wasn't very much mistaken, I'd just secured myself a job re-stocking the library. Point one to Rosalie and zero to Officer Stronzo.

ARIES. VAMPIRE. FIRE.
COMMANDING OFFICER
CAIN
DARKMORE
PENITENTIARY

Warden Pike had the great fucking idea to make my life even more hellish by deciding that I had to moderate Twelve in group therapy sessions so that I could gauge a deeper understanding of her for my report. I'd never had to spend this much time hounding an inmate before. But with all the new regulations she was bringing in, new inmates were getting extra special attention to try and set them on the path for rehabilitation back into society.

Personally, I didn't think monsters could be rehabilitated, they were born, bred or made just like I'd been. I could no sooner cut out the darkness in me than I could cut out my own heart and keep living. It was just who I was. And most of the criminals were in here for a good reason. If I was in charge, I'd be inclined to throw away the key on the lot of them too. But I guessed there were a few worth saving. And Rosalie Oscura happened to be among them. Maybe Pike could sense she wasn't some bloodthirsty creature who should be kept off the streets at all costs. Maybe she saw what I did; a girl who didn't belong here.

So I sat in the back of the therapy room where twenty inmates were gathered on chairs in a circle. Rosalie was amongst them, waiting while everyone took turns to speak about a difficult experience from their past. She'd spent most of the class listening to her fellow inmates with interest, seeming genuinely respectful about the shit some of them had been through.

Inmate number One-Twenty-One was currently on his feet

beside her, the huge Bear Shifter who people called Pudding. Though his name according to his record was Nigel Moonsythe. Everyone in the room was bored half to death over the story he was telling at nought point nought one miles per hour. It was fucking excruciating.

"-of course, that was back when I had my spoon collection. Four hundred and twenty-eight silver spoons made in the times of the Savage King. He didn't just have spoons made with his emblem on either. There were all kinds of knives too. Luncheon knives, steak knives, dinner knives, butter knives, fish knives, dessert knives-"

"And what was traumatising about this story, Nigel?" Mrs Gambol asked. She was the prison's therapist, a Rustian Sheep Shifter with tightly curling white hair and small features aside from her large eyes.

"Well, as I was saying," Pudding went on. "My silver spoon collection was my most prized hoard at the time, but my brother Theodore had had his eye on it for many years. He was always after my spoons. And one day...he got them." He sighed heavily. "And it was very, very, very...*very* traumatising."

He sat back down and one inmate clapped while everyone else remained stonily silent until they stopped.

"Well that sounds very baaad," Mrs Gambol said, her voice going sheep-like on the last word. "Thank you for sharing." She pointed to the next guy and I felt everyone in the room supress a groan - along with myself - as Twenty-Four stood up. Or Plunger as everyone called him.

"Well, I've got a bad story," Plunger announced.

"Oh my, is it really baaad?" Gambol asked, her eyes growing wider.

"Pretty bad, ma'am," Plunger agreed, adjusting the material around his crotch. "You see, my daddy was a mean kinda guy. He always said I was wrong-un, used to make me sleep in the barn. Polethius Moles emerge into their Order young and tend to disperse from their families even before their magic is Awakened. So I got used to being away from my family by staying in the barn most of the time. Anyways, this guy called Jimmy from my school used to come and bring friends over to the barn and drink moonshine. He didn't talk to me in class, but whenever he brought people over, he always let me watch them from the haystacks so long as I was quiet. One time, Jimmy brought this big ol' tub of chocolate ice cream to the barn that was already starting to melt in the balmy night air. I have a par-tic-u-lar fondness for chocolate ice cream," he purred and something about the way he said that made my skin crawl. "He placed the tub down while they all started messing around and I figured it was a good moment to make them like me at last. I'd been waiting for the prime time, thinking up how I could impress them. And I realised one way that would definitely win them round to me." He smiled and the sight made me shift uncomfortably in my seat. "No one ever paid me any par-tic-u-lar attention so when I slipped down from the haystacks and took off my clothes to show them my party trick, they didn't realise I was behind them until I hollered out."

"Did they laaaugh at you?" Gambol asked with a sad frown.

"No, ma'am," Plunger said, lifting his chin. "They watched in silence as I flipped the lid off Jimmy's ice cream tub and wet my dipping stick in the chilly goodness. Then I stood up with ice cream coating my plunger and bent over, licking off every bit of it – I'm very flexible see." He bent over, imitating what he'd done that day with added slurping noises that made bile rise in my throat.

"By the fucking moon," I muttered as Gambol made frantic notes on her Atlas and everyone stared at him in horrified disgust.

Twelve scooted her chair away from him which was a feat in itself as she'd already moved it as far from him as possible when they'd taken their seats, and she had to force the guy in the chair beside hers to scoot over too. The look of utter repulsion on her face mirrored my own thoughts on that story precisely and for half a moment as she met my eyes, it felt like we were sharing something. Of course, her lip curled back a second later, reminding me that she held me in just as much contempt as Twenty-Four and I cursed myself for the errant, pointless thought as she turned her gaze away like I meant less than nothing to her. Which was how I wanted it. Obviously.

"No one came to the barn anymore after that, so I guess I did it wrong," Plunger said sadly as he straightened. "I've perfected my party trick since though, so I won't ever get it wrong again. If there are any requests, I'm more than happy to oblige-"

"Thank you," Gambol said quickly. "For sharing. But we'll move onto Rosalie now." Everyone seemed thankful as Plunger sat down and I looked to Twelve whose nose was still wrinkled in disgust. She met my eye for a moment and my throat hardened as she got to her feet and turned to Gambol.

She twisted her fingers together, seeming nervous and that grabbed my attention like she'd just grabbed a fistful of my hair. I sat up straighter, frowning as she started her story.

"Well...when I was twelve, I had to move in with my stepmother for a while. My papa had married her on a whim and I'd never met her before, but I was excited to have a mother figure in my life. At first, my stepmother seemed nice. Things were okay. I used to help her out with chores. She lived on a farm so there was always work to be done and I wanted to pitch in. But she had two daughters who were a bit older than me and they used to laugh at my dirty clothes at the end of the day though I tried to laugh along, wanting them to love me as I tried to love them. After my papa died, my stepmother stopped making any effort with me. She never gave me the money to buy anything new and after a few months...my clothes were just rags. And when she started making me sleep in the attic...things got worse."

My gut twisted sharply and the curse mark on my wrist started to throb as I gazed at her eyes and she blinked back the wetness gilding them.

"It was so cold up there," Twelve murmured, eyeing her fingers as they knotted tighter together. "And there were mice living in the walls. They were really my only friends for a while – I used to talk to them and make them clothes out of scraps I found which seems so silly now. The longer I was there, the meaner my stepsisters got, and my stepmother just worked me harder. I'd have to be up before dawn and clean the pigs and the horses out before making breakfast for the three of them. In the winter, the snow was so deep and even though my step-mother had fire magic, she never leant me any to keep warm. There were holes in my shoes and the snow used to get in until I couldn't feel my feet at all."

"Oh that's very saaad," Gambol said and Twelve shrugged, making my heart bunch up in my throat.

I wanted to throttle the people who'd done that to her, tear them limb from limb. My blood was heating just thinking about it and I felt my fangs prick my tongue.

"After a few years, I guess I got used to it," Twelve went on. "I was always alone...but I'd sing sometimes just to keep myself company."

I didn't know she could sing...

"Sometimes I swear the mice used to sing back," she laughed, but there was a sadness to it that made me ache. "Anyway, this one day we got this letter in the mail inviting us all to a party. It specifically mentioned that every member of the house-hold was supposed to attend and I'd dreamed for years what it would be like to go to something like that. To meet other people...make friends. I managed to get a dress together using the material we had in the sewing room and though it wasn't perfect, it was good enough that I knew I'd pass for respectable. On the night of the party, I was so excited, I went downstairs to leave with my stepmother and sisters, but they..." She teared up and I swear I'd been holding my breath for a full minute. "They told me I couldn't go. And that I looked hideous in the dress I'd made. I was so humiliated..." She dabbed at her eyes and Mrs Gambol made a note on her clipboard with a sad shake of her head. "But after they left, out of nowhere, my godmother knocked on the door with a pumpkin in her arms and-"

"Hang the fuck on," I boomed, the penny dropping in my head like it was a damn slot machine. *I am such a fucking idiot.*

I rose from my seat, the legs squeaking as they were pushed across the wooden floor behind me, earning me the attention of everyone in the room. "You're telling the Cinderella story." I pointed an accusing finger at Twelve and she parted her lips, looking offended.

"I am not!" she gasped, turning to Mrs Gambol. "Does he normally come in here accusing us of telling lies?" She held a hand to her heart like she was so fucking aghast at me calling her out on her bullshit. But I was not gonna let this fly.

"Oh w-well he's normally not in attendance. It's for his report," Mrs Gambol stuttered, shrinking under my furious gaze.

"She's having you on, Barbara," I told the idiot therapist who was lapping this up. "That's what she does." I rounded on Rosalie, baring my fangs. "I see right through you, Twelve. If you don't cooperate in this class, I'll write you up to Pike. Last warning."

Twelve had the audacity to continue looking mortified, shrinking back down into her seat and poking her bottom lip out a little. Then she released a sob that made even Plunger frown sympathetically.

"*Really*, Officer," Gambol said sternly, raising her eyes to mine as she tried not to lose her nerve. "This is a safe space for the inmates. You cannot interrupt them or accuse them or anything of the sort. I will mention it to the warden if you have another outburst."

My teeth snapped together and she flinched as my predatory gaze bored into her. Mrs Gambol would do it though. I could see it in her eyes. So I had to hope Twelve had gotten the message.

"Fine," I snarled, moving back to my seat and dropping into it with a growl.

The curse mark on my wrist itched and burned and fire was starting to snake its way into my limbs. I stole a surreptitious glance at the mark and fear trickled into me at the sight of it growing further up my arm. I tugged my sleeve back down and locked my jaw, trying to focus on anything else. But when the next inmate stood up and Twelve paused her fake crying long enough to toss me a mocking smirk, I lost my shit.

"Get out!" I barked, rising from my seat and directing her from the room.

"Officer Cain," Gambol gasped. "You can't just - just-"

"I'm her CO so I can do whatever the fuck I think is in her best interest." I marched toward Twelve, gripping her arm and dragging her across the room, practically kicking the door down as I pulled her into the hallway. I didn't stop there, towing her along and around the corner out of sight of the cameras before throwing her against the wall and slamming my hands down either side of her head.

She laughed wildly, throwing her head back and that sound got my dick rock solid before I could even try and control myself.

I dropped one hand to her throat, my anger as keen as my lust in that second, and pinned her back against the wall, squeezing just hard enough to get her attention. "I'm sick of your lies," I hissed. "I'm sick of your manipulation."

"So what are you gonna do about it?" she asked bitterly. "Choke me to death?"

I released her throat, my gaze falling to where her pulse was pounding against her flesh, my fangs aching for a bite. Her blood called to me like no other. I hadn't tasted anything so sweet since her. Every other blood source tasted like cardboard by comparison.

"Or bite me?" she asked, ice dripping through her tone. "Are you going to take what you want from me, Mason? Force me to give it to you even though I can't defend myself? That's very unFae of you..."

I growled at her and the mark on my wrist started to burn hotter. I wasn't going to hurt her. That was the last thing I wanted to do. I just wanted to – *fuck,* I didn't even know what I wanted to do. I was so angry at her for drawing me in again, making me swallow her lies. And the way she'd just smirked at me afterwards, knowing how much she was getting to me, it brought up the pain over her previous lies. How she'd made me think I meant something to her, how she'd used me for whatever the fuck it was she was after.

"What were you doing in Psych?" I snarled. "If you don't tell me, maybe I'll come up with some reason to put you back in the hole."

She glowered at me with a venomous kind of hate that made me seethe. "Fine, you wanna know what I was doing down there? I was finding out what your freaky little guard friends were doing to the inmates who are sent there. What they did to my *friend* who was sent there. And you know what I saw?"

My anger fell away as I gazed at her, hanging on her words. I'd been trying to dig up the dirt on Psych for a long time. Had she really gotten in there and seen what they were doing first hand?

"What?" I pressed, urgency to my tone.

"They're taking something from them. Something fucking vital in some fucked up operation where they cut out a piece of them. Something that's made of light and pure energy. Like they're cutting them off from their magic or – or-" She shook her head, looking sick and emotion blazed in her eyes. "And some of them die. Like my friend *died*." Her eyes filled with tears and every ounce of anger in me crumbled to nothing.

I brushed a tear from her cheek as it fell and she looked up at me in surprise, but she didn't push me away. So I moved closer, my chest touching hers as I pressed her back against the wall.

"Did anyone see you?" I rasped, fear clutching my chest. I didn't know what the fuck it was they were doing down there, but the image she painted made me fear that she could be targeted if they knew she'd witnessed their secret.

"No," she said thickly. "No one but you. Question is, why haven't you told Pike I was down there? Why are you covering for me?"

The answer to that was too complicated, even I didn't know how to piece it together. "Because I..."

She frowned, tilting her chin up and waiting for me to finish that sentence.

Because I'm a fucking idiot. Because I care for you far more than I'll ever dare admit. Because no matter how much I keep telling myself you used me, a part of me still hopes it was more than that.

But I didn't say any of those things. I swallowed them hard and let my gaze move to her mouth. I didn't want to lie though. So I gave her some of the truth. "Because I want to know what's going on in Psych. Pike is covering it up, I'm sure. So I want this information to stay between us."

She narrowed her eyes at me. "Do you really expect me to believe you don't know what's going on down there?"

"Well unlike you, I don't have a habit of lying to people's faces."

She tsked, her eyes dragging down me in disdain. "I don't lie to the people who matter to me."

Shit. Her words hit me like a punch to the chest and I growled darkly at her, earning me another wave of pain from the curse mark. Being this close to her meant her blood was calling to me on a visceral level. I could almost taste the sweetness of it on my tongue as I remembered drinking from her.

"That's right, I'm just another pawn in your game," I said in a gruff tone. "But whatever it is you want from me, Twelve, you won't get it."

"Even if I let you hunt me?" she asked in a sugary voice, tilting her head to one side like she was offering her blood to me.

My throat tightened and my fangs sharpened as I gazed down at the pulse at the base of her delicate neck.

My eyes darted down the corridor and back to her, my mind spinning and my thoughts blurring as my base needs took over. By the sun, she was tempting. Would it be so bad to take blood from her? But even if I did, I certainly wasn't going to give her whatever it was she wanted. Maybe I could draw her back into letting me hunt her again, let her think I was offering whatever information she wanted, let her believe I would help her. She'd fucked with me enough, I was owed a little payback.

But even as my mind worked over the idea, it moved onto what I really wanted even more than her blood. I wanted her mouth, her body, her fucking heart and soul. I wanted to make her mine. Despite all I knew about her, how deeply she'd fucking cut me. I still harboured feelings for her that wouldn't go away.

"We need to go somewhere else," I murmured then she laughed a cold and cruel laugh, her head snapping back up.

"As if I'd ever let you drink from me again," she spat. "Good to know how strong your will really is though, Officer." She ducked under my arm, dancing away from me in the direction we'd come and I turned, opening my mouth to bellow at her, considering dragging her back here by the hair and punishing her for what she'd done. My hand went to the baton on my hip and my thumb grazed over it, but even the thought of using it on her made me grimace. The curse mark apparently agreed as an injection of liquid fire tore up my arm and I cursed as I took a step after her with a growl, meaning to do something to put her in line. But what?

Hastings rounded the corner ahead of me and Twelve suddenly ran toward him, throwing her arms around his neck and loudly sobbing into his shoulder. What the fuck?

"Please, can you take me back to my group therapy session?" Twelve pleaded. "Officer Cain is so angry at me. He dragged me out of there after he refused to believe one of the experiences I told my therapist."

Oh here we fucking go. "Don't fall for that shit," I warned Jack, but he had the nerve to frown at me and pat her back.

"Sure, I'll take you to your session," he told her and she thanked him as he peeled her off of him, but let her clutch his arm as he led her down the corridor. He threw a stern frown over his shoulder at me and I swore under my breath. That girl. That fucking *girl*.

I paced the corridor while I waited for Hastings to send her back to her session, determined to set things straight. I hadn't done shit. I wasn't going to be painted out as an asshole to him. Since we'd shared a few beers in his room, it was actually becoming something of a habit and though I wouldn't exactly have called him a friend, I didn't want her turning him against me when he was the only guy in this place I even spoke to on a semi-regular basis outside of work.

When she'd headed back into the therapy room, Jack strode up to me, folding his arms. "What was that about?"

"Oh don't fucking look at me like that. That girl is trouble," I snarled.

"She seems kind of...sweet to me," he said with a shrug. "Maybe you're being too hard on her."

Fucking hell. She'd brainwashed him too. Had I gone around looking like that when she'd had my balls in a vice?

I strode forward and clapped a hand to his shoulder, making him look me directly in the eye. "She's getting in your head. Don't believe anything she says."

"Why would she lie?" He frowned and I bit my tongue on the truth. I couldn't tell him what I knew or I'd be admitting my own guilt in everything I'd done with Twelve.

"Just trust me," I pushed. "She's bad news."

He sighed as I stepped back, rubbing his chin. "Maybe she just needs something to occupy her."

"Like what?" I grunted.

"Like a new job maybe. Pike needs a team to renovate the library. It might be what she needs if you're concerned she's misbehaving, boss," he said and my ears perked up at that.

Twelve was soon going to be returning to work and I'd been worried about having to monitor her alone again down on the maintenance level. And I sure as shit didn't need any more time with her than I already had. Especially after I'd just suggested to her that we could start playing the hunting game again. Like a fucking weak-minded moron. I couldn't risk that happening a second time. I may have wanted to believe I was incapable of being tempted by her. But I'd just proved that wasn't fucking true. Not in the slightest. Besides, renovating the library sounded like a tedious as shit job that would drive her insane, especially since she'd told me how much she hated dusty old books. Seemed like a win-win situation to me.

"Good idea," I said with a nod. "I'll make sure she's signed up."

"Beers tonight?" Hastings asked and I found I was glad of him doing so.

I nodded, giving him a tight sort of smile because apparently building friendships was alien to me and turned me into a fucking robot.

"Yeah," I forced out. "See you then."

He grinned like I'd made his day and he walked off, heading down the stairs on his patrol. I sighed as I realised I'd better head back to the therapy session and finish taking notes. But I swore to the stars, if Twelve started up that Cinderella bullshit again, I was gonna lose it.

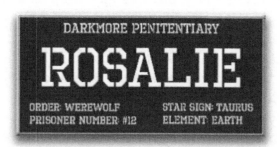

I arrived at the Mess Hall early after my thrilling group therapy session and strode in to the near empty room with my stomach grumbling and daydreams of pizza and burgers and chocolate cake. Of course, my reality was going to be some form of processed, low priced, high carb, low taste thing, but a girl could dream.

I headed for the counter to collect my food seeing as none of my Wolves were here to do it for me. Usually they fought over who got to bring it over for me anyway, so I was doing them a favour by taking that issue away for the day. That was just the kind of altruistic leader I was.

"Wait up, wild girl, I thought we had a date?"

I turned at the sound of Sin's voice, and found him striding towards me, tattooed arms on show where he'd tied his jumpsuit around his waist and his white Darkmore tank stretched tight over his broad chest.

"I didn't realise we'd set a time," I teased, waiting for him to approach me as I placed my tray down at the start of the line for food.

"I thought I'd surprise you," he said, moving to tower over me and leaning against the wall. We were effectively blocking off the access to the queue, but the few Fae who had shown up to eat weren't dumb enough to try and push past us. "I was going to bring you flowers, but you don't seem like the type to go in for cliches, so I got you something better."

"What?" I asked, a smile tugging at the corner of my lips. Only Sin Wilder could make me smile this easily after having to endure two hours of group therapy under Cain's watchful eye. Luckily the Vampire bastardo's shift had finished so we didn't have to worry about his bat ears listening in on us.

Sin dipped his mouth down to my ear, nipping the lobe playfully before he whispered my answer so that only I could hear. "I shoved a Sunstone Crystal up a Werewolf's ass for you yesterday, pretty girl."

Laughter burst from my lips and he growled playfully like he liked that, his hands curling around my waist as he tugged me closer.

"So is it still up the Werewolf's ass or has it moved house?" I asked and I was maybe taking one percent of glee at the idea of Ethan walking around the prison with a lumpy rock jammed up his butt for me. Although that really just proved the lengths he was willing to go to to hide his involvement with me which kinda soured my joy over it.

"It is currently keeping my manhood company in my boxers," he replied. "Feel free to retrieve it whenever you want."

"Really?" I asked, wondering if he was just trying to get me to feel around down there for it.

"Well, no, the Werewolf in question seemed to want to get the credit for stealing it even though I was the mastermind behind the operation. But there's another surprise hiding down there you might like to check out?"

My gaze dropped to his crotch and I grinned at him before shrugging and turning back to my tray.

"Maybe later," I said casually as I dragged the brown plastic along the little metal rails towards the food hatch where the Lunar Wolves had laid out tonight's offerings.

Before I could make my choices on what I wanted to eat, Sin leaned around me and started pointing out all of the different options so that the dude working behind the counter had to rush to plate everything up. When both mine and Sin's trays were piled high, we moved along to the end of the row where the drinks and puddings sat waiting for us to grab for ourselves.

I grabbed a cup and moved to fill it with water, but Sin snatched it from me and placed it on top of the serving counter instead. He whistled sharply to catch the attention of one of the guys working back in the kitchen then held two fingers up to him.

I frowned up at Sin curiously and he smirked at me. "Only the best for my wild girl. I may not be able to take you out on the town, but I sure as hell am gonna make sure you have something good to drink."

My confusion turned to excitement as the guy Sin had called over appeared with two cups of clear liquid that most definitely wasn't water and handed them over.

"Bottoms up, gorgeous," Sin commanded, tossing me a wink before downing the full cup.

The acrid scent of the alcohol almost burned my nose as I lifted my own cup to my mouth, but I sure as hell wasn't going to back down to his challenge.

The vodka burned all the way down before settling in my gut with enough weight to make me fairly certain I'd be feeling the effects of it before long.

"Again, garçon," Sin commanded and the provider of our beverages grumbled before re-filling our cups.

Sin placed them on our trays alongside four pots of pudding and four pots of fruit each and then grabbed both trays and led the way over to his usual table. If anyone had an issue with him taking way more than the allocated amount of food, then they definitely weren't saying anything about it and that was kinda hot in its own right. Who didn't like a guy who was so fucking terrifying that they just did whatever the fuck they wanted and no one dared complain?

"Look at you playing the gentleFae," I teased as I took a seat opposite him and he smirked at me.

"I can promise you I don't fuck like one," he growled in a tone that totally carried but I didn't care.

I smirked at him and peeled open my fruit pot as I started work on devouring my grapes.

"What would you eat if we weren't in here?" I asked him. "Like dream meal. Favourite thing in the world."

Sin made a low hum in the back of his throat as he considered it while shovelling his food into his mouth like he expected to run out at any moment. "I like chocolate brownies dipped in hot sauce."

"Seriously?" I asked with a laugh.

"Yeah. Don't knock it 'til you try it. I mean, I'd take hot sauce on just about anything at this point. Is it really so hard for them to put a few spices in the food?"

"Maybe it's just another form of torture. They want to deny us every small pleasure they can manage."

"Well, there's one form of pleasure they can't steal from us," Sin said, smirking suggestively. "And we can indulge in it whenever you want."

"I thought the deal was that you got a night with me once we escaped?" I teased.

"It is," he agreed. "But we never said that would be the *first time* we hooked up..."

I couldn't help but laugh at how freaking forward he was and if I was being totally honest, I was more than a little tempted to take him up on that offer. There was something about Sin Wilder that just drew me in, and I was starting to feel like I had the beginnings of an addiction to him taking root in me.

I made myself eat some of the tasteless pasta crap they'd given us today, knowing that I needed the carbs to help me gain back some of the weight I'd lost in the hole even though it tasted like shit.

When the rest of my pack showed up, they instantly started bickering within earshot about me screwing up some system they had in place for who got to bring me my food and sit opposite me for this meal. I hadn't realised they'd formed a schedule and maybe I should have felt a little guilty for ruining it, but honestly, sometimes dealing with their shit made me feel more like their mamma than their Alpha.

"Sonny?" I called and my Beta sauntered over to me with a smirk on his face for being singled out. "What in the ever-loving fuck are they arguing over now?"

"Well," he said dramatically. "Esme was supposed to be having her turn at getting your dinner and Brett was going to sit beside you and now they're saying that they should get to do breakfast instead, but of course Banjo and Laura are supposed to be having their turns at breakfast so they're pissed about the idea of changing it and-"

I stuck two fingers in my mouth and whistled. "Listen up!" I called and every member of my pack hurried over to surround our table while Sin watched me with interest.

"Let's not fuck with tomorrow's schedule, okay? Esme, Brett, have an extra pudding each." I tossed them both a pudding and they grinned widely at being offered some of my food. "And tonight, I think it's only fair if the rest of the pack make the two of you the focal point in the group sex plans. Obviously after Sonny gets his."

Sonny smirked as Brett licked his lips suggestively and I had to wonder if the two of them might be considering ditching the pack for some more one on one time soon because they were definitely into each other way more than anyone else in the pack.

"Do you want to join us, Alpha?" Esme asked hopefully, just like she did every night.

She started to shimmy out of her jumpsuit, pouting her lips as she thrust her tits out to tempt me and I had to suppress a laugh. Honestly, the poor girl was so desperate to prove herself between my thighs that I was half tempted to let her have at it for her birthday. An Omega like her wasn't really going to do much for me but I could fake an orgasm for her if it came to it and she really did have nice tits. I was actually kinda jealous. Mine definitely didn't bounce like hers did.

"I'm actually on a date right now," I said, pointing to the Incubus opposite me and a few of them flinched like they hadn't noticed Sin was there.

"Did you want *him* to join us?" Esme asked hopefully as a nipple slipped out.

I turned to look at Sin and raised an eyebrow at him, expecting him to jump at the chance to take part in a pack orgy, but his gaze was fixed on me.

"I think I'd rather you all scram and leave me with the only prize worth having at this table," he purred, not even shooting a look Esme's way as she started making out with Banjo.

"You heard the man," I said, flicking my fingers dismissively so that my pack scurried away.

Half of them didn't even bother returning to their table to eat, they just ran off towards the dorms, yipping and howling with excitement. From the corner of my eyes, I saw Esme's tits bouncing as she didn't even put them away and Officer Lucius started yelling at her to cover up.

"So..." I began, not sure where I was really heading with this, but I had to admit I was a little surprised that Sin had chosen a date with me over an orgy. "Are you all stocked up on sexual energy or something? Because that party seemed right up your alley to me."

"Nah, wild girl, I don't think so. I've done enough bad shit, good shit and damn outrageous shit in my lifetime to figure out that there's a difference between what's easy and what's worthwhile. And you, sweetheart, are the most worthwhile Fae I've met during my entire incarceration and maybe even before that too. I don't want a sex fest with a pack of Wolves, I want the undivided attention of the Alpha, and all the time you keep looking at me like that, I'm not taking my gaze off of you."

"You're such a fucking flirt," I teased.

"Yeah. But right now, I'm being deadly serious," he purred and I liked that. I liked it a whole hell of a lot.

We made our way through our food and our home brewed vodka and Sin was more than happy to help me finish up my oversized meal as we discussed all kinds of shit from the real world and I found myself grinning the whole damn time.

"Well, that was fun," I said as I licked the last of my pudding from my spoon.

"Don't go thinking this date is over, kitten," Sin said as I glanced at the door.

We still had a few hours of free time left before we had to head back to our cell blocks for the night, but it wasn't like there was a whole lot that we could do. I often spent the evenings in the gym when I wasn't working on anything to do with my escape plans and I knew Sin did too, but that didn't sound all that date-like to me.

"What else is there then?" I asked, wondering if he really had any plans or not.

"It's a surprise." Sin got to his feet, holding a hand out to me and I smiled indulgently as I let him pull me from my chair.

He instantly tugged me close, throwing one of his huge arms around my shoulders as he guided me towards the door. I glanced back and my gaze caught on Ethan where he sat amongst his pack, his eyes narrowed on me like I was doing something wrong. But screw him. I wasn't the one shacking up with a fake mate at night. And I wasn't the one too afraid to face the music by just owning what the moon had decided we should be to each other. Besides, I still planned on having words with that celestial being about that.

We headed downstairs and I held my tongue on any questions as he led me down to level seven and turned me towards the dark, silent corridor which led to the Belorian's cage.

"Sin..." I began but he just tightened his grip on me and tugged me along more firmly.

"Come on, wild girl. I wanted some time alone with you and there's only one place in this whole prison which won't be crawling with Fae. Besides, the beastie likes me. I let him have that little run around and all of those tasty snacks. He won't mind us coming for a visit. And it's not like he can get out of his cage again is it?"

I groaned in mild protest, but I knew he was right. The Belorian might have been terrifying, but while it was locked away it couldn't do a damn thing about us being out here. But due to the creepy feeling that the monster gave out alongside the fact that if the doors did happen to open while we were down here we'd be eaten first, no one ever chose to hang out down in this dark corner of the prison.

The corridor was dimly lit so that we could see where we were going, but the overhead lights were never turned on as there was no reason for any inmates or guards to come down here.

"If the Belorian eats any Fae it comes across, how does anyone look after it?" I mused as we closed in on the huge door at the end of the corridor where it lived.

"Maybe Officer Cain has tamed it by boring it to death with his lack of personality and can just stroll on in there?" Sin suggested with a chuckle.

"I saw it trying damn hard to eat Cain, so that's not it."

"Oh yeah. Let's not talk about you saving that motherfucker's life though, kitten, or I'm going to have to go kill someone to make up for my disappointment over him not dying."

I rolled my eyes but dropped the subject of Officer Stronzo. "I guess someone has to feed the Belorian though. What does it eat when it can't get its teeth into Fae anyway? And does it poop? I mean, it has to poop so who's cleaning that poop? Is there an automatic poop chute that cleans it all out when the thing is running loose around the prison at night?"

"Maybe they just leave food out for it in Mess Hall and it goes up there and sits at a table all proper like? And then it goes and takes a shit on the toilet when it's done," Sin suggested and he sounded so serious that I wasn't sure if he was joking or not.

As we drew closer to the Belorian's cage, that same sense of fear and dread I'd gotten from being close to it before began to seep into my limbs and I slowed my pace.

A shriek of rage echoed down the hall as it sensed us too and I gasped as I fell still, making Sin halt as well.

"Maybe we can just back up a bit?" I suggested. "Not to sound like a pussy or anything, but that thing almost ate me the last time I got this close to it and I would rather not rush into a re-union with it."

"I've got this, kitten, don't worry about it," Sin said confidently, releasing his hold on me and pulling a lemon from his pocket.

"You gave me one of those the night you let it out," I accused, wondering if he really was as insane as everyone claimed and was about to set the fucking thing loose again.

"Of course I did, wild girl, I wasn't going to just let it out without giving you something to defend yourself with."

"So you gave me sour fruit?" I asked, glancing back over my shoulder towards the exit and trying to decide if I should just make a run for it before he did anything crazy.

"Well, yeah," he said, moving right up to the door before ripping into the lemon with his teeth.

I watched in confusion as he spat a lump of the skin from his mouth before squeezing the lemon in his fist so that juice squirted all over the door to the Belorian's cage. The creature inside shrieked in what I could have sworn was pain and the sound of its rattling claws thumping across the floor moved away from us until the foul feeling that accompanied its presence was gone too.

"Did you just...scare it off with a lemon?" I asked.

"Yeah. Why did you think I gave you the lemon before I set it free?" Sin asked, looking around at me like I was the one who was a few pennies short of an aura here.

"I had no fucking idea. You didn't mention your reasons," I spluttered as I tried to figure out whether or not I should be mad that he hadn't made that clearer or pleased that he'd at least given me something to protect myself with before setting a monster loose in the halls.

"It just seemed so obvious." Sin shrugged. It absolutely wasn't obvious though, just like it had not been obvious to me that he really did intend to set the Belorian free after I'd specifically told him not to. "Now close your eyes for a minute, sugar tits, and give me a second to set this up."

"Close my eyes?" I asked, spotting a box which was sitting beside the door to the Belorian's cage just before Sin placed a hand over my eyes.

"Please, sex pot?" he purred and I couldn't help the stupid smirk that took over my lips as I obediently closed my eyes.

"This had better be worth it," I warned him and he chuckled as he set about pulling things from his box of mysteries.

"Erm, shit, I think they died," he muttered.

"What died?"

"Well... I might have taken a few old honey jars up to the Order Yard and caught myself a bunch of Faeflies so that I could make it all cute and girly down here for you."

"Seriously?" I asked, cracking my eyes open to see if he was bullshitting me or not and finding him lining up a bunch of the little jars we were given at breakfast on the ground, each of them holding a small, dead looking bug. "Wow, this is so...romantic," I said, bursting into laughter as Sin tipped a dead Faefly out onto his palm and scowled at it.

With a curse, Sin leaned down and blew on the little bug like he was trying to give it mouth to mouth or something and my laughter got louder as that thought occurred to me.

Sin suddenly hurled the bug and jar away from him so that it shattered against the wall and got to his feet, scowling at me before striding away like he was going to leave.

"Wait!" I called, hurrying to catch his arm and forcing him to look back at me.

"Forget it, wild girl, I'm not built for dating. I don't know how to do it and I've never attempted to before. Just let me know when you're ready to fuck me and let's forget all of this bullshit until then."

"Don't go," I begged as he yanked his arm out of my grip and stalked away. "I don't know how to date either!"

Sin hesitated as he looked over his shoulder at me like he didn't believe that, and I hurried to go on.

"When I was fourteen, something happened to me and I...well let's just say I didn't have any interest in dating or anything like that for a few years because of it. And by the time I felt ready to explore that part of my life, I was surrounded by other Wolves who had been taking part in orgies and gang bangs and every kind of physical exchange you can imagine for so long that I just kinda fell into the physical side of things without ever trying the dating thing."

"You seriously expect me to believe that no one has ever asked you on a date, kitten?" Sin asked disbelievingly.

"Well, Colin Bishop did once, but when I got to the restaurant his mom was there to chaperone us and she kept talking about kids and marriage and it was really fucking weird because I was eighteen and had just started to explore my own sexuality and had less than zero interest in any of that shit, so I faked a bathroom break and jumped out of a window to escape."

Sin smirked, turning to face me fully as he folded his arms and considered my story. "I had someone bring her mom to meet me too once," he said. "But it got really weird because it turned out they both had a thing for Johnny Depp and wanted me to take turns with them in his form."

"What did you do?" I asked, wrinkling my nose.

"I told the daughter to wait in the next room then showed her mom my best swashbuckling skills while doing a Jack Sparrow impression, tied her to the bed, fucked her in the ass and robbed them blind before leaving the daughter wanting. I mean, I'm all for double dipping if the situation calls for it, but why waste time when there's money to be made?"

I couldn't help but laugh and the tension in his posture relaxed as I smiled at him.

"I really do appreciate the dead bugs in the jars," I said, dipping my voice an octave as I moved towards him. "And I'm sorry I made you feel shitty about them, you know, *dying*."

Sin's lips quirked and he moved closer. "I'll forgive you," he said slowly. "*If...*"

"If?" I asked, raising a brow.

"You tell me about your ideal fantasy. Because I still haven't gotten a read on you, kitten, and it's driving me insane."

I rolled my eyes at him. "I told you, it's not about looks for me. I like a bit of everything."

"Bullshit," he growled. "There has to be something that gets you hot unlike any other. There just has to be."

I wanted to brush him off, but I realised that wasn't going to work here so I paused and forced myself to really consider his question. And after a while, I came up with an answer.

"Okay, so hear me out. When I was at Aurora Academy, it was the first time in my life that I'd been away from home for any real length of time and one of the first times where I'd had access to lots of different Fae who I wasn't actually related to - because my family is stupid big. So, I finally had all of these options of all these hot guys and girls who I could hook up with and I kinda...ran with that. I mean, that's just the way Wolves are so it wasn't exactly odd for me to be a bit promiscuous," I said with a shrug and Sin grinned like he was loving this story. "Anyway, the point is that after a while, I started to get the impression that I wasn't doing sex right because every guy and girl I'd been with couldn't even get me off as well as I could manage on my own if you know what I mean. Like, I'd be all excited to hook up with someone and then once we started going at it, I'd start thinking about my homework or what time dinner was or just generally hoping it would be over soon, you know?"

"No, but go on," Sin said with a filthy smirk.

"Okay, so one night me and my pack were out partying in town at this club and this guy walks in and I swear, the moment I caught sight of him, my heart fucking leapt. He had this aura of power about him that just screamed keep the fuck away but drew me in. He wasn't even that hot in the way that most people would appreciate, but he just had that grit to him that so few Fae have. Long story short, we barely made it to his car before he was inside me and I had *never* felt anything like it in my fucking life. I swear I came like six times in the space of an hour. I mean, it turned out he really was an asshole and I had to call stuff off with him after a few weeks, but he was the ticket to me realising what it was that I needed in a partner - an Alpha."

"Well, I hate to break it to you, kitten, but I'm no Wolf," Sin said in a low voice as he seemed to be mulling over my words.

"Not an Alpha *Wolf*, stronzo," I replied, moving closer to him. "Just an Alpha. You know, the kind of stronzo who's bigger and badder than every other fucker in the room and gives no shits about offending anyone. The type who sees something they want and just fucking takes it because no one is even capable of stopping them if they wanted to."

"Sounds familiar," Sin replied with a dark grin.

"Really?" I asked innocently, my gaze sliding down his body slowly before moving back up to meet his eyes.

Sin chuckled in that utterly heated way of his that made me bite into my lip and want to rip his clothes off.

"Your turn," I said, backing up as he hounded forward.

"My turn for what?" he asked, following me until my back bumped against the door to the Belorian's cage and he was leaning over me. He pressed a palm to the metal door either side of my head and looked down at me as he held me captive in the cage of his arms without actually touching me.

"Tell me *your* ideal fantasy," I said, raising my chin as I waited for his answer.

"No one has ever asked me that before," he said, tilting his head like he was trying to gauge whether or not I really wanted to hear the answer to that.

"*I'm* asking," I said.

"Well...I have a bit of a thing for hair long enough to pull and dark enough to match my soul," he murmured, reaching out and taking a lock of my black hair between his fingers before twisting it through them and tugging on it just enough to make my scalp tingle. "I like big eyes full of mischief and dirty promises which can see straight through bullshit and assess a man for who he is in the beat of a drum," he added, looking into my eyes so deeply that I felt a blush rising in my cheeks. "I like lips used to smiling and suited to kissing which can speak pretty words in a language I don't understand." His thumb traced my lips and I parted them for him, biting down on his flesh just enough to remind him that I wasn't some plaything he could wrap around his little finger.

Sin laughed darkly and released his hold on my hair as he withdrew his thumb from my teeth. His hands landed on my shoulders and he slowly pushed my jumpsuit down them and I let him, my heart leaping as he stepped closer to me, but he still didn't press his body to mine.

"I like a girl who can pack a punch and put mean mother-fuckers in their place," he continued, his hands caressing my biceps before trailing down my arms and raising gooseflesh all the way down to my hands which he curled into fists within his own. "And who isn't afraid of the devil in me."

"I think you said something along these lines the first time we met," I reminded him. "And you also mentioned that my tits weren't big enough."

"I think we agreed I needed a closer look to be sure of that," he protested, smirking at me like he expected me to tell him to back off again like I had every other time we'd flirted along this line, but this time I didn't want to. I was looking into the eyes of a monster unlike any I'd ever met and I wanted to know what it felt like to give in to his call.

"Did you mean it when you said I was the only one you were interested in?" I asked him, because as insane as it seemed that an Incubus might really feel that way about a single person, I was actually starting to believe it. He'd waited three months while I was in the hole and he could have had anyone he wanted, but he hadn't taken the chance to have them. And the idea of him wanting me like that made me feel a little less alone in this place. A little less expendable.

"Only you, wild girl. If I didn't know any better, I'd have said you were a Siren sent to lure me in, but instead I'm beginning to think you might be something far more dangerous than that."

"Like what?" I asked breathily.

"My own, personal obsession. My drug of choice, the answer to all of my desires rolled up into one little, Faetalian ball of danger. I think you might be my downfall, wild girl. But I think I like the idea of that too."

My heart pounded at his words and the idea that someone could really feel like that about me despite my many flaws and I pushed up onto my tiptoes, wrapping my arms around his neck so that my mouth could find his.

Sin groaned as I kissed him, his hands dropping to my ass so that he could hoist me up into his arms and I could kiss him more easily.

My lips parted for his tongue and a moan escaped me as he moved it against mine in a way that had me panting for him. I swear I could taste the heat of his fire magic in that kiss and I could feel this desperate kind of worship in it too.

As our kiss deepened, the swell of Sin's thick cock pressed between my thighs which had me aching for more of him. But he didn't seem in any hurry to get there, instead kissing me like he was marking me, memorising each and every moment that he held me in his arms and drinking it in like he was trying to lock it away and keep hold of it forever.

I caught hold of the back of his tank in my fist and dragged it off of him, breaking our kiss as he pinned me to the wall so that he could raise his arms to toss it aside.

"Don't tease me, wild girl," he growled. "I've been aching for you for a long time and we're reaching the point of no return here. If you don't want me then tell me to stop now or I'm gonna lose my damn mind if you push me away in a moment."

"You told me you can sense desire just like I can sense the light of the moon on my flesh, so you already know what I want," I said to him, my voice rough with need. "So stop making me wait, stronzo, and show me why everyone is desperate to fuck you."

Sin laughed this deep, dirty sound which promised me all the bad things and made my toes curl as his mouth fell to my neck and started moving up.

When his lips found mine again, his kiss was possessive and demanding, his huge body grinding me back against the cold metal door which was our only defence against a monster which would kill us if it could, but somehow that seemed right. Sin was danger embodied, this wild, unpredictable beast who didn't care about rules or laws or anything that might try to contain him. And I wanted to feel every bit of that, I wanted him to remind me that I wasn't in a cage. I was as unstoppable as him, as fearsome and just as wild.

I crossed my ankles behind his back and rolled my hips so that I was grinding against his hard cock as I drowned in the taste of his tongue against mine.

Sin pulled away suddenly, leaning back so that he could tug my tank and fugly bra off and freeing my breasts for him. The cold air of the corridor was enough to make my nipples pebble even if they hadn't already been hard for him and Sin groaned in appreciation as he dropped his mouth to capture my left nipple as his hand found my right.

I gasped as he did something with his tongue that I could only describe as French kissing and my head fell back as a moan of pure ecstasy escaped me.

My hands curled around his huge shoulders and my fingernails bit into the skin as he continued to play my nipples in a way that had me so wet for him that I wasn't sure I could take much more waiting.

"Less clothes," I growled in a clear command and Sin looked up at me with fire in his eyes.

"Your wish is my command, kitten."

He lowered me to the floor and stepped back, looking me right in the eye as he untied the arms of his jumpsuit from his waist and kicked his boots off.

I leaned back against the cold door and watched as he put on a show of sliding out of his clothes for me, pushing my hand into my panties and moaning as I dipped my fingers into the wet heat between my thighs.

"You're a sight to behold, wild girl," Sin purred as my eyes raked over the ink coating his dark skin. His tattoos flowed together and yet still left plenty of bare flesh for me to drool over too. He had violent representations of every star sign inked on his body and I moaned as I spotted the charging bull on his upper thigh which was for my own.

"Stop teasing me, Sin, I want to see all of you," I moaned as I circled my clit in just the way I liked and my body shuddered beneath my touch for him.

Sin kicked his jumpsuit aside with his boots and socks and then looked me in the eye as he peeled his boxers off so fucking slowly that it could only be meant as torture specifically for me.

I moaned as I watched him, dipping my fingers lower and teasing them inside myself before returning them to my throbbing clit.

When he finally pushed his black boxers down, I gasped at the sight of his long, hard cock springing free. Silver piercings glinted in the low light and spiralling ink wrapped its way between them. I should have known an Incubus would have a cock to remember, but this thing was a work of art. An absolutely *enormous* work of art which I wanted to inspect a hell of a lot closer.

Sin took a step forward but I shook my head to halt him, pulling my hand back out of my panties as I slowly shimmied out of my own jumpsuit and boots before stepping closer to him in nothing but my panties with my eyes on his dick.

"Okay, I was expecting your cock to be impressive, but this is like something you should hang on the wall," I murmured, licking my lips as I looked over the silver studs which adorned the head of it. There were four of them on show, presumably connected by bars on the inside and another pair of studs at the very top of his shaft where it met with the base of his abs. I reached out to touch it and Sin growled as I got so close to his cock without making contact.

"You'll like that one even better in a moment, kitten," he promised. "But if you keep me waiting much longer, I'm not going to be able to stay a gentleman."

"Well that's good to know," I replied with a smirk before wrapping my hand around the smooth, inked perfection of his length. "Because I'm no lady."

I dropped down to my knees before him and instantly brought the head of his dick to my lips, running my tongue over it before exploring the unfamiliar shape of the studs as the ache between my thighs grew unbearable.

Sin's hands fell to my head, but instead of knotting in my hair like I expected them to, he just pushed his fingers into the silken black strands and began slowly massaging my scalp.

"Look at me," he growled and I raised my eyes to his as I slid his cock between my lips and moaned my excitement for him.

Sin groaned, his fingers circling against my scalp in a way that felt seriously fucking good as I drew back again, exploring those piercings with my tongue once more and then took him in again. And this time I took him right in to the back of my throat, loving the curse that escaped him as my lack of gag reflex paid off yet again. I seriously wanted to thank the moon for that skill because I'd seen a lot of cocks getting sucked in my day and I knew for a fact that there weren't many Fae who could take it as deep as me, so I had to assume it was a gift from the horniest celestial being in the sky which just so happened to be the one I was linked to the closest.

As I drew back, I reached up to caress Sin's balls before pushing my other hand into my panties to relieve some of the need in my own body.

"Fuck, wild girl, you were so worth the wait," Sin cursed as I began to increase the pace of my movements, taking complete control of him and loving every second of it.

His hands slid through my hair and his fingers found the mate mark behind my ear, which seemed to tingle at his touch. He groaned like he could feel it too and kept stroking it, caressing it, like he actually liked the fact that I was marked for another man.

Sin kept his gaze on mine as I sucked and licked him, moaning my own pleasure as I played with myself and he swore as he began to pump his hips, demanding more from me. And I didn't disappoint.

I kept pace with him, sucking harder as I felt his balls tightening in my grip, his dick as hard as steel as he drove it into my mouth and with a groan of pleasure, he was coming hot and hard down the back of my throat, the salty taste of his cum flooding my senses for a moment before I swallowed it down.

I didn't even care that he'd finished already, loving the fact that I'd brought a creature built for sex to ruin on my own terms.

My own orgasm was building as I continued to circle my fingers on my clit and I tipped my head back as I felt it in every inch of my flesh. But before I could finish, Sin was hauling me to my feet and pulling my hand back out of my panties.

"Rule number one about Incubuses, wild girl," he murmured as his hands curled around my hips with a strong and commanding firmness and he walked me backwards until I was pressed against the steel door again. "We don't require a recovery period."

My eyes widened as I dropped my gaze to his dick which was still very much rock hard and I gasped as he gripped my panties and pushed them down my thighs.

"Don't go easy on me," I insisted and he licked his lips at the challenge in my tone.

Sin's hand dipped between my thighs and I moaned as he slicked two fingers straight down over my clit before pushing them inside me. He groaned in appreciation as he positioned his thumb on my clit and the moment he began to move his hand, a cry of surprised pleasure burst from my lips.

His hands were big and his long fingers curved inside me as he ground them against my G spot in this perfect, torturous rhythm that made me grasp his biceps with another moan, my fingernails gouging crescent moons into his skin.

Sin leaned forward and kissed me and I could feel the smile on his lips as instead of pumping his fingers, he began circling

211

his wrist, making his thumb on my clit and the two fingers deep inside of me rotate in this utterly fucking new and unusual way. I gasped as he kept up the motion, the pressure of his fingers demanding and controlling.

I came so hard and fast that I could only cling to him as my pussy clamped tight around his fingers and his tongue pushed into my mouth like he was trying to devour the sounds I was making.

Sin gave me no time to recover from the pleasure shuddering through my limbs before gripping the backs of my thighs and hoisting me up into his arms.

I fisted my hands in his hair as his cock seemed to find its own way to my opening and he eased the head inside slowly, making sure I felt the way those four studs rubbed inside of me just right.

"Sin," I gasped, my fists so tight in his hair that it was a wonder he wasn't snarling at me. Instead, he just pulled back enough to look me in the eye and then drove his cock into me so hard and fast that my breath caught in my throat and an unearthly moan of pleasure escaped me.

The moment he was fully sheathed inside me, that pubic piercing of his made a whole lot of sense as the two metal balls nestled either side of my clit perfectly and Sin rolled his hips to show me exactly what it could do. And oh *fuck,* I really had been missing out on having any metalwork in the cocks I'd been riding up until that moment because I was in heaven right about now.

Sin's grip on my ass tightened as he began to move, drawing back and slamming into me again, making me curse in Faetalian at the combination of his pierced cock filling me so fucking deeply and those studs working their own magic on my aching clit.

He was rough and possessive, his mouth stamping to mine as he thrust into me harder and harder and I worked to meet him by pushing off of the door at my back.

Before I knew it, I was close to coming again, my fingernails tearing into his back as he continued to fuck me hard and fast.

I was calling his name and cursing him and loving every single second of it.

I swear it was like he knew my body better than I did. Every time I felt an ache for something more, he was already doing it, tilting my hips so that his cock could sink into me just right, sucking on my nipple in the perfect way to make me scream, even kissing me with the perfect mix of heat and passion to have me panting for him at every turn.

Sin made sex into something magical. Not like some romantic bullshit where our souls merged or anything like that, but like our bodies had become vessels for pleasure which only we could satisfy. We fit together like two pieces of a puzzle, made just fucking right and I couldn't get enough of the feeling of his thick, hard length driving in and out of me.

Just as my body tightened with the desperate need for release again, his hand slid further behind me until he was toying with my ass, his finger pressing down harder with each thrust.

I gasped as each brush of his finger against that sensitive spot had me clenching tighter around him while aching for him to just do it already at the same time.

The moment he pushed it in, I came so hard I saw stars, my pussy clamping tight on his thick length so that within another three punishing thrusts, he was groaning his own orgasm and spilling his seed deep inside me.

Even then he didn't pull back, kissing me hard as he circled his hips so that his pelvis ground against mine and his pubic piercing had me shivering with need where it held my clit in its grasp. His finger was still in my ass and as he pushed it deeper, I came apart for him once more, panting and gasping as I bit down on his lip hard enough to draw blood.

Sin growled his approval, kissing me again as he slowly withdrew his hand and set me down on shaky legs before him.

"You really are perfect, aren't you wild girl?" he asked, his hand sliding down the tattoo which covered my left side as he

213

spoke, and I had to wonder if he was including my scars in that statement. Because despite the fact that they were almost impossible to see within my ink, you could definitely feel them and Sin's hands had been all over every single inch of my body.

"I'm going to set you free, Sin," I whispered in reply. "Not because it's a job for me. But because you deserve it. You deserve to be free again."

I kissed away the protests I could see forming in his eyes and if the bell warning us to return to our cell blocks for the night hadn't sounded, I probably would have insisted on having him again.

As it was, I had no desire to be anywhere near this door when they set the Belorian loose for the night, so I quickly grabbed my clothes from the floor and started pulling them back on.

Sin followed suit more reluctantly and the moment we were dressed, I took his hand and made him run with me back to the stairs. We jogged up them and through the crowd of inmates who were heading back too, but when we reached Sin's cell block, he didn't stop, instead leading me on towards mine.

"You do know you aren't allowed in my cell block, right?" I teased as he kept hold of my hand and I made no effort to reclaim it. It felt too damn good in his for that.

"I'm walking you home," he replied with a twitch of his lips that made me smile too. "That's what all good dates do."

"I've never had anyone walk me home before," I admitted with a grin. "Possibly because there's always a good chance that a psychotic Storm Dragon would be there to chase them off if they tried, but still."

"I'm not afraid of your cousin, kitten," Sin teased. "I'm sure he'll love me when he gets to know me. Besides, this is how dates are supposed to go and I'm doing it right up until the very last moment."

We'd arrived outside Cell Block D and I turned to look up at him with a raised brow. "Is that so? What other date things am I unclear on then?"

"Well, if it went well, this is the part where I'd kiss you," he purred, tugging me closer and cupping my jaw in his hands. "But we'd better be quick, because your grumpy old dad is watching."

"What?" I asked, glancing at the open doors and meeting Cain's pissed off expression half a second before Sin's mouth met mine and I forgot all about him.

Well, *practically* forgot anyway, because my little bitch heart still stung over him. But now Sin had given me new aches to focus on and his were so much more delicious that I was happy to comply.

When my unconventional date pulled back, I was more than a little breathless and my needy body was cursing the fact that I couldn't drag him back to my cell for more.

"Goodnight, wild girl," he purred before turning and walking away and I shamelessly checked out his ass as I watched him go.

I headed on into my cell block with a grin on my face and managed to not even glance in Officer Stronzo's direction.

And I was pretty sure that was another point to me. Go team Rosalie.

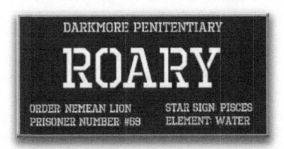

I was lying in my cell when Rosa came prancing in with a leaflet clutched in her hand, her smile bright and making me all warm inside.

"Hey, little pup, what've you got there?" I sat up, but she dove on me, scruffing my hair and tussling with me like a Wolf.

I growled as I wrestled her back. She didn't realise what this kind of shit did to me. I should have stopped it like a decent Fae would have, but apparently I was a sordid piece of shit because I rolled us over and pinned her down with her arms above her head on my pillow, pressing my hips down on hers as I snatched the leaflet out of her grip. As my gaze fell to it, she took the opportunity to throw me off of her and I gasped as I tumbled off of the bed and my ass hit the floor. She laughed, jumping up and pressing a foot down on my chest with a grin, her hair wild around her shoulders.

"I win," she announced and she looked too damn cute so I just nodded, knocking her foot off of me and lifting the leaflet up to read.

Warden Pike wants to help YOU!
Are you worried about how you'll fit back into society
after your release?
Do you have concerns about one or more of your
correctional programs and their efficiency?
Do you feel the opportunities in Darkmore Penitentiary
could be broadened to cater to your needs?
Do you think that your behaviour could be improved further

to help you return to a normal life once your sentence is up?
Then just make a request to one of the guards to come
and complete a feedback survey that will be read by
Warden Pike. She'll take into consideration all of your
Fae requests to correct and improve your nature.
It's time to go back to the way of the Fae and discover
who you truly are.

I scowled, dropping the leaflet onto my chest and looking up at Rosa. "What's this bullshit?

"It's not bullshit, Roar, it's a fucking dream come true." She plucked it out of my grip again.

I stole a moment to take in her figure, her curves starting to flesh out again since her time in the hole. My dick liked that for filthy reasons as much as I liked it for platonic ones. I was definitely going to hell.

"What do you mean?" I asked as I got up and she leaned in close, whispering to me, her breath feathering across my neck.

"The survey is held up in the guards' quarters." She pointed out the small print on the leaflet and my brows arched as I read it.

"Well, holy shit," I laughed, beaming at her. I grabbed her waist, picking her up and spinning her around before I could stop myself. She squealed excitedly, wrapping her legs around my waist as she clung on. "You're a genius."

"Yup," she agreed with a grin as I planted her down. "So let's go. We'll suss it out when we're up there." She grabbed my hand and I smiled stupidly at the back of her head as she tugged me out of my cell and started down the stairs.

We'd been trying to figure out a way to get into the guards' quarters for days but kept coming up short. Now the warden herself had handed us the answer. Everything about Rosa's escape plan was coming together and with us starting the library job tomorrow, I was now seriously excited about getting out of here. I let myself dream for once and Rosa joined me in it too, both of us painting pretty pictures of the life that awaited us beyond here. The fantasy that excited me most was meeting my nephew and niece at last. I just hoped they liked me. I'd spent a bunch of time around kids growing up, seeing as my family was so close with Rosa's. The Oscuras popped out babies like freaking kittens. I wouldn't be surprised if Dante produced a litter of more kiddies I could spoil soon enough.

We jogged toward the void in front of the closed bridge on the bottom level and Rosa waved at one of the cameras to get the guards' attention. After a few moments, the bridge lowered and Hastings walked across it, glancing between the two of us curiously. Rosa dropped my hand and hurried toward him.

"Is everything alright, Twelve?" he asked, looking to me again with what I swear was a hint of jealousy. Poor kid was so hooked on Rosa, he'd probably get withdrawals when she got out of here. But if this guy's heart was the only casualty of us breaking out, it would be a small price to pay. *Sorry dude.*

"Yep, me and Roary were just hoping to do this inmate survey thing." She held the leaflet out to Hastings and his eyes widened.

"Really?" he asked, seeming dumbfounded.

"Yeah, we have a few requests," she purred, fluttering her lashes. "Is there a problem?"

"No problem," he said with a small laugh, leaning a little closer to her as he dropped his voice. "It's just that literally no one has taken up the offer of this survey."

"Well, now they have," Rosa said with a grin. "So can we go?"

"Er yeah, sure," Hastings said, seeming slightly baffled still, but he turned and jerked his head at us to follow him over the bridge. "So, what requests do you have for this place?" he asked curiously as Rosa fell in to step beside him and I trailed along behind, my heart thumping with adrenaline at the thought of using my thieving skills again. The petty theft I conducted in here was nothing compared to this. This shit had serious consequences and that was the sort of job I'd always loved in the past. The longer the jail time, the more I wanted to pull it off and prove myself.

I'd had a decent chunk of my confidence knocked after I'd been caught for the first time ever though. Rosa had been in trouble and I'd helped her instead of running from the FIB. I'd known what I was doing. Known what I was risking. But, cocky asshole that I was, I hadn't believed I'd really be going to prison even when they'd slapped the cuffs on me. Rosa had gotten away at least. And that was the only thing that I'd had to hold onto in here. Now...she was stuck in here with me. And I'd pay any price to ensure she got out.

"I just feel like there could be a few more course options available," Rosa told Hastings without missing a beat. The girl could lie as a profession, I swear. She was as good of a liar as I was a thief. "It would be helpful if there was training too, for jobs we might apply for once we're out of here. I always fancied myself as a landscaper. I love wielding the earth, but a little training in construction would be amazing."

"Well I doubt Pike's gonna allow more magic time for something like that," Hastings said.

"I wanna try anyway," she said keenly. "Roary wants to put in a request about doing a crystal identification course too, don't you Roar?"

"Yeah," I agreed easily and Hastings glanced back at me.

"I guess it doesn't hurt to ask," Hastings said with a shrug and Rosa nodded with a bright smile.

We arrived at the elevator that led up into the guards' quarters and Hastings pressed his hand to the scanner before it opened and we followed him inside. My heart thumped unevenly as we rose through the complex and I flexed my fingers as I readied myself for this.

I shared a look with Rosa behind Hastings' back and more adrenaline flooded my veins which had nothing to do with this job and everything to do with her smile. I seriously needed to get a grip. I was just some washed up fucking thief who had literally nothing to offer her outside of these walls. Everything I'd ever stolen, I'd left in the care of my pride. And there was no way in hell my father would be giving it back. He saw me going to prison as me giving up any ownership I had over the things I'd stolen, the cash made from any stolen goods too. Which meant on the other side of these walls I was bum broke and potentially even more of a loser than I was in here. At least in Darkmore, I was *someone*. I had earned my position, fought for it with tooth and claw. But it meant nothing away from here. *I* meant nothing.

I pushed the bleak thoughts away as the doors ahead of me opened and I took a breath, readying myself for this. I followed after Hastings and Rosa moved to my side as we walked along the brightly lit corridor, the sound of chatter carrying from up ahead. I glanced around me, hunting for the antidote dispenser. Rosa knew it was here since she'd seen it before.

Just past a group of sofas and chairs where a couple of guards were drinking coffee, I saw it. The dispenser was embedded in the wall and a guard was standing before it, pressing a button so a plastic-wrapped syringe dropped out into his palm through a shoot. He walked past us, nodding to Hastings and as we headed by, I shot it a surreptitious look to my right, checking out that button. There didn't seem to be any need for a magical signature, no scanner, nothing. Up here, there weren't even cameras because why the fuck would they worry about an inmate getting into trouble here when the place was teeming with guards? Maybe they should have been more concerned.

Before we reached Warden Pike's office further down the hall, Hastings opened a door to his right and led us into a room. A few tables were laid out so it kind of resembled a classroom and there were posters on the wall with the same branding that the leaflet had had.

Become a better Fae today!

A brighter future is waiting for you.

Your sentence is a time to shine, not a time to turn to crime.

I fought the urge to roll my eyes at the words. Everyone knew getting out of Darkmore didn't mean you could just slip right back into society like it was nothing. Half the inmates in here had been power shamed, meaning no matter how power-ful they were, they were no longer allowed to fight for position in society. That meant ninety-nine point nine percent of jobs wouldn't even let them apply. Beyond that, there were plenty of Orders like mine who were shamed by their own kind for casting a shadow over them. So no, a brighter future was not waiting for me beyond my sentence. It might just be waiting for me outside of here with Rosa though.

The fantasies we'd come up with about claiming some far-away island and making a place of our own was alluring as shit. But did I really believe she'd stay with me permanently? My brother Leon could visit with stardust, as could Dante and the rest of Rosa's family. We didn't exactly need anyone else. But Rosa could also be hidden by the Oscura Clan easily enough if she wanted to live among her people. And why would she really choose me over them?

My brother had his own life, so it wasn't like I could go and live with him or put stress on his family for harbouring a fugi-tive. I wasn't going to be a burden to anyone. But I didn't want to end up alone somewhere either. I just didn't know if a future with Rosa was really that likely. It wasn't like we had any kind of romantic relationship waiting for us. So why would she stay with me? And why did I ache at the thought of not having her around every day, living beside her, laughing with her, being with her? I hated the idea of losing that despite how much I wanted to be free. I didn't want the price of that freedom meaning I had to go back to a life without her. Now she was here, it felt so natural to have her close. How was I going to give her up?

I focused back on the task at hand again, cursing myself for overthinking. It didn't matter what happened to me beyond this prison so long as Rosa was free. It was as simple as that. And I wasn't going to waste time contemplating the what ifs of my future. Anywhere I ended up had to be better than Dark-more.

We sat down side by side and I glanced over at the windows

that looked back into the corridor, veiled by open blinds.

Hastings placed down two surveys in front of us which were several pages long and gave us a couple of plastic pens too.

"I'm gonna grab some coffee," Hastings said and Rosa released a groan of longing, making him pause before he left. "You want some?"

"Can I?" she asked hopefully, her eyes so wide and innocent, I could have laughed.

I may have called her little pup and teased her for being a kid, but I knew she wasn't that really. And that girl had never been innocent of anything. If things went missing or got broken or dirty in her Aunt Bianca's house back in the day, it was invariably Rosa's doing. She was trouble with a capital T. And I fucking loved it.

"Sure." Hastings shrugged like it was no big deal and headed out the door. The second it swung shut, Rosa turned to me, lowering her voice.

"In ten minutes, I'll ask him to take me to the bathroom," she breathed and I nodded. "I'll buy you as much time as I can."

"I'll manage it even if I have just ten seconds," I said with a smirk and she arched an eyebrow.

"Cocky little bastardo," she taunted, picking up her pen and sucking on the end of it, making a retort die on my tongue.

Ho-ly fuck, that was hot. Electricity shot through my body and jump-started my fucking dick. I couldn't take my eyes off of her mouth, a mouth I had tasted and then yearned for ever since. When I felt like this, it was hard to remember why I kept friend-zoning her. She was an adult, so was I. The rest of the world would get over it if I claimed her. Maybe Dante would accept it too...

But then I remembered the promise I'd made him to always protect her, and I recalled her looking up to me when she was fourteen, seeing me as this king of beasts. I wasn't that anymore and I sure as shit didn't intend on breaking my promise to her cousin. I also knew I could offer her fuck all. So why even consider it?

I broke her gaze, nodding firmly just as Hastings returned to the room with a tray of coffees. I was surprised he'd gotten me one too and thanked him as he placed it down in front of me.

"These are made with ground coffee beans from Turembia," he said. "Proper coffee. Nothing like the crap they give you down in the Mess Hall." He was looking at Rosa, his eyes all glimmery and shit as he watched her sip from her cup.

"*Mmm,*" she moaned, the sound so sexual it gave my dick even more ammo in its argument against me not wanting her.

Hastings' jaw dropped a little as he watched her throat bob as she swallowed. Then she made a show of licking her lips that we were both glued to and I had a perfectly inappropriate vision of her licking the tip of my cock with that tongue, tasting me, wanting me. *Fuck.* I really had to get my head straight. I was in the middle of a seriously important job. I could not screw this up because I was getting hard for my friend's little cousin. By the stars, I was pathetic over her sometimes.

I looked away and Hastings cleared his throat, blushing slightly as he raised his cup to us and headed for the door again. "I'll leave you to fill in the forms."

He closed the door behind him and Rosa grinned at me while I started picturing Plunger's hairy ass in the shower this morning to soften my boner. It worked like a ship hitting a rock and sank it good.

Rosa started filling out the survey and I turned to face mine, starting with the first question.

Do you feel confident that your behaviour is improving since you first came to Darkmore Penitentiary?

I scribbled out some bullshit answer, moving through the questions slowly to make sure we had plenty of time. After ten minutes, Rosa got up from her seat, shooting me a grin before heading to the door and opening it. Hastings immediately stepped into her way, clearly having been standing sentinel outside the door.

"Can you show me to the bathroom?" she whispered.

Hastings glanced in at me and I dropped my eyes to the page, working on my next answer.

"I think that coffee went right through me," she laughed and in my periphery I saw her lean into him, her hand brushing his. I swallowed a growl, the tug of jealousy I felt over that totally fucking irrational. *She's working him over. And even if she wasn't, she's not yours, idiot.*

"Alright, come on," he murmured and the door snapped shut a second later.

I counted to ten in my head, my heart hammering like crazy as I fought down the wild smile pulling at my lips.

Game time.

I pushed to my feet, moving to the windows and glancing through the blinds to make sure the corridor was empty. It was. So I moved to the door, twisting the handle silently and gently tugging the door open a crack. I cocked my head, listening for any sound of guards approaching, but there was just the noise of the television coming from the little rec space further down the hall. I took a breath and stepped out into the corridor, hurrying down it on silent feet.

Laughter came from an office across the hallway and I froze as the door opened opposite me and a guard started backing out of it, still talking to whoever was inside.

"-swear if I have to report one more statistic to Pike, my head's gonna explode," he laughed.

"You're telling me," an answer came from inside the room.

I moved across the corridor at speed, flattening myself to the wall beside the room he was leaving, taking a gamble on which way he was going to turn when he came out. I was to his right, so I needed him to go left.

My throat was tight, my lungs full of a breath I refused to release.

Come on, asshole, go left.

He twisted around, closing the door and went left. Relief tumbled through me as he headed down the corridor and swerved past the wall to where the couches were.

I hurried back to the other side of the corridor, creeping

along the wall, my gaze pinned on the dispenser that was just ten feet away.

Nine, eight, seven, six, five-

Rosa stepped out of a room further down the corridor and Hastings appeared from around the corner a heartbeat later, walking toward Rosa so his back was to me. I pressed against the wall, swallowing a curse and Rosa's eyes widened ever so slightly as she spotted me over his shoulder then shifted onto Hastings as he approached her.

"All good?" he asked, moving to turn towards me, but she grabbed his arm.

"No, actually," she gasped. "I don't feel so good."

I inched along, my heart lurching at the sound of a guard's loud laughter just beyond the wall as I reached the dispenser.

"What's wrong?" Hastings asked, concern filling his tone.

"My head hurts."

"Bad?" he asked, reaching out to touch her forehead. "I can heal you."

I jammed my finger on the button to the dispenser, thrusting my other hand under the shoot just as a mechanical noise sounded within the device. *Shit. Shit. Shit.*

Hastings turned to look and suddenly Rosa gasped and dropped to the floor at his feet, as limp as a fucking doll.

"Holy shit," he cursed, kneeling down and three other guards darted into sight to help her.

The antidote syringe landed in my hand and I jammed my finger on the button another few times to make sure we had plenty. Two more syringes fell from the shoot then a whirring noise sounded as a message flashed up on the screen with a ding that Rosa tried to cover with a dramatic wail.

"Sto morendo, sto morendo e siete tutti così fottutamente stupidi!"

I read the message on the screen, cursing in my head. *Refill needed.*

This was going to have to be enough.

I started jogging away, my heart in my throat as I made it

back to the office with three syringes stuffed in my pocket, my hand landing on the handle.

"Hey!"

I turned my head at the voice, fear crashing through me. If I was caught, we'd never get this chance again. Plunger wouldn't be able to shift and dig us a tunnel. We'd never get out.

Cain stepped out of the elevator at the far end of the hall, his eyes pinned on Rosa on the floor. "What the fuck's going on here?"

He shot toward her and I swallowed a manic laugh as I pushed back into the room, dove over the table to my seat and dropped into it.

I wanted to whoop and cheer, but I just patted my pocket where the syringes lay hidden and took slow breaths to get my heart back to a normal rate.

"She needs to see the medic," Hastings said frantically. "I healed her and she's still not waking."

I snorted a laugh as I heard Cain's growl all the way from here. "Fine. I'll take her."

I chuckled as I finished up my survey. Rosa had told me about how suspicious Cain was of her, but she wasn't the one he needed to be frisking right now. And I had no doubt she'd be getting a pat down from him. But the contraband wasn't with Rosa. It was right in my pocket. And he didn't even know I was here.

By the time I finished my survey half an hour later and Hastings had taken me back to my cell block, it was almost impossible to wipe the grin from my face.

I ran up to my cell and Rosa leapt at me the second I stepped inside.

"Did you get it?" she asked, her eyes wide and hopeful.

I wound my arms around her, nodding as I finally let myself celebrate, laughing and hugging her.

"Fuck yes," she gasped in my ear as I crushed her against me.

"We're getting out of here, baby," I growled, not sure where that word had come from, but screw it.

She beamed, her smile so fucking beautiful that it drew all of my attention. "I can taste the sea air already, Roar."

***

While my Shades fetched my breakfast in the Mess Hall the next day, I pressed my back to the wall and took in the mass of inmates before me. I couldn't wait to pull off this fucking job and get out of here. It was bringing the old me back to life and that was one hell of a tempting feeling to fall into. If I did this, really did this, maybe it would be a start towards rebuilding my dignity as a Night.

Officer Lyle nodded to me as he approached and he moved to stand beside me, looking out at the inmates too. "Morning, Roary. Got any more funnies for me? I told my partner your last one and he almost busted a lung laughing."

I smirked, shrugging and he nudged me with his elbow.

"Go on, I'll throw in a few commissary tokens for you if you make it a good one."

I grinned at that. "Alright. But it's not as filthy as the last one."

Lyle laughed. "They're always good."

"So...a Werewolf knocks on the door of his old school bully's house, noticing the place is small and run-down, in need of a lot of repairs. On the rickety porch, the bully's wife is sleeping there in a rocking chair and a little dog is curled up at her feet. The bully answers the door and doesn't recognise the man standing before him. So the Werewolf says, 'Hello there, I noticed your house is in disrepair and thought I'd offer you a wager to make some money.'"

Lyle smiled broadly, already chuckling before I'd even gotten close to the punchline.

"The bully nods keenly so the Werewolf says, 'I bet you a hundred dollars I can get your dog to run down there and get into my friend's car.' The bully laughs and replies, 'You'll never get him do anything. It's easy money.' So the Werewolf walks over to the little dog and uses an Alpha command on him and the pup runs off and jumps into the car into his friend's lap. 'Well that's amazing!' cried the bully, but then frowns and says he doesn't have the money to pay up, but he'll owe him one. So the Werewolf says, 'Alright, well I'll give you another shot at winning to cancel out your debt. I bet you two hundred dollars I can kiss your wife without waking her up.' The bully laughs, shaking his head. 'You'll never manage that, it's easy money!' he cries."

"What happened next?" Lyle asked, hanging on my every word.

"So the Werewolf saunters over to his wife, leaning down and kisses her soft and seductively, giving her mouth a real dirty go over, and sure enough, she doesn't wake. The bully sighs at losing the game again and says, 'I'm sorry I don't have the money to pay, but I'll owe you one.' Then the Werewolf says, 'Alright, I'll give you one more shot, and this time I'll give you three hundred dollars if I fail.' The bully agrees and the Werewolf says, 'I bet I can piss in that pot beside you without spilling one single drop.' The bully looks down at the pot which is pretty far from the Werewolf so it seems unlikely he'll be able to manage it. So he agrees enthusiastically and the Werewolf takes out his dick and starts pissing. He pisses all over the man's shoes and legs, over the house walls, the porch, even all over his sleeping wife and the bully laughs loudly while he does it."

Lyle snorted laughed and I grinned as I went on.

"'You didn't get a single drop in the pot!' The bully laughs, clutching his belly. "Pay up!' The Werewolf laughs too and hands over the cash. 'Why aren't you upset?' asks the bully as he continues to laugh. The Werewolf heads down the steps towards his friend's car with a skip in his step. "Because my friend bet me a thousand dollars I couldn't steal your dog, kiss your wife and piss all over you and your house and leave you laughing about it.'"

Lyle roared a laugh and smacked me on the shoulder. "Good

one!" he chuckled heavily as Cain strode past us, shooting us a glare.

Claud beckoned me over to my table and I waved goodbye to Lyle as he wiped tears from his eyes and I dropped down in front of the feast laid out for me. Alright the word feast was a stretch, but I did have a mountain of oatmeal, a bowl of fruit and three honey pots. And that was about as close to a feast as things got in here.

Claud ate his own meal beside me and I noticed he had a picture of his wife and kids sitting beside his tray.

"I can't wait to see them again," he said with a sigh and I smiled sadly.

"You will one day soon," I promised and his eyes brightened as he shared a look with me. We couldn't say more than that in case Cain turned his Vampire hearing our way, but I could sense the anticipation on Claud as fiercely as my own. We were going to see our families soon enough. I couldn't wait to hold my niece and nephew in my arms. I'd pull off some jobs on the outside to get enough cash to spoil their asses until they were grey and old. I had years of making up to do on that account, and I planned on getting started as soon as possible.

"Ooh watch out, Miss Rosa is looking pretty today," Claud teased, jerking his chin in her direction.

I glanced over at her where she was sitting with her Wolves. Her new pack mate, Laura, was braiding her hair while she laughed at something Sonny was saying and her whole face lit up.

"Why is that something I need to watch out for?" I muttered, sounding uninterested, but my eyes were still latched onto her. He was right. She did look pretty today. She always did anyway, but there was a glow about her this morning and I wondered if it had to do with hope. We were starting the library job today and that meant we were closing in on the day we'd get out of here. I couldn't wait to see the sun beyond that damn Order Yard dome, I needed to feel it while I was free and stretched out in my Lion form, taking a nap on some faraway beach. But more than that, I dreamed of seeing the sun light up Rosa's skin, watching her smile somewhere miles from here and knowing that she would never be caged again.

"Because you luuuurve her," Claud mocked and I shoved him, nearly knocking him out of his seat with the force I used.

He continued to laugh as he righted himself, purring as he nuzzled against my arm. *Damn house cat.*

Claud may have been a Lion, but he wasn't cut from the Alpha cloth. It was unusual for male Lions to fulfil what were typically Lioness roles, but he was a people pleaser and him becoming my second had just felt natural in here. He led the Shades superbly and I wouldn't have survived my time in here without him.

"No, no, no, NO!" a girl screaming caught my attention and I twisted around, spotting her in the queue for breakfast. I recognised her as Bullseye, with her small frame and bright pink hair. She was grabbing handfuls of oatmeal and throwing it on the floor, seeming possessed as she dug through it. "It's not here! It's gone. Where are my diamonds? I left them right here!" She whirled on the guy behind her, snatching a handful of his jumpsuit in her fist. "You took them! You took them from Lady Jasinta, didn't you? *Didn't* you?" she growled and Officer Rind ran over, pulling her away from him.

"Get off of me, Colonel Mustard!" she wailed. "Oh now I see! You did it, didn't you? You killed her in the library with the candlestick and took her diamonds!"

"Stop fighting," Rind snarled, trying to stop her thrashing.

The other meathead guard, Nichols, ran over to help him and the two of them locked her cuffs behind her back as they escorted her toward the exit. Her voice carried back to us they dragged her through the door and her wild, crazed eyes seemed to lock on me for a moment. "Help me Professor Plum!"

She disappeared with them and my throat constricted, my eyes moving across the hall to lock with Rosa's, a frown pulling at her brow. Now I knew what Rosa had seen down in Psych, I was more afraid of going crazy in this place than anything else.

It was fucked up. And no one deserved that fate, not even a bunch of psychotic criminals.

Chatter broke out in the Mess Hall again and I sighed as I turned my attention back to my food. There was nothing we could do for the girl. It was just shit luck. Or maybe...

I looked over to Rosa again, jerking my head to get her attention and she frowned as she got up and walked over to sit opposite me.

"I'll see you in a bit, Claud," I told him and he nodded, getting the hint and hurrying off to sit with some of the Shades.

"What's up?" she asked, her eyes glittering a little and I reached out on instinct and gripped her hand. I squeezed gently and her mask slid hard into place before she took her hand back and I withdrew my own. She would never admit that seeing Bullseye taken away had upset her, not in front of so many watchful eyes anyway. If you showed weakness in here, the vultures would circle.

"I just had a thought..." I murmured, casting a look over at Cain, but he was busy breaking up a scuffle between two Harpies so I knew I could talk in private. "If they're taking people to Psych for some sort of experiment, then they must be orchestrating it."

"You think they're picking who goes crazy?" she breathed in horror and I nodded.

"Makes sense, don't you think?"

"But how?" she whispered.

"I don't know." I looked down at my food, thoroughly put off it at the idea of it being drugged. But our meals were all made in large batches, how could one person possibly be targeted? I checked that Cain was still busy then lowered my voice even further. "But the sooner we get out of here the better."

She nodded firmly and my excitement started to return again.

"Soon," I said, grinning and she smiled too, her eyes lighting up a little.

"Well good heavens, you look like you need some ass-istance with all that food you've got there, big boy," Plunger's voice made me turn my head and I noticed him walking close beside a huge Cerberus with a shaved head and a grimace on his face. I was fairly sure he was called Fred and he'd only been in Darkmore a few weeks.

"Back off, freak," Fred snarled as Plunger's hand sailed down his back.

Plunger's hand kept going, falling down to squeeze his ass. "You and me could be *real* good friends."

"Get your fucking hands off of me." Fred dropped his tray down on a table, turning sharply toward Plunger and shoving him so hard in the chest that he staggered backwards and slammed down onto his ass. No one laughed. Because everyone who'd been here long enough knew that Plunger may have looked like some weak Polethius Mole Shifter, but he was far from that.

Fred sat down in front of his food, tucking into it while Plunger got to his feet behind him, rubbing his bruised ass then reaching into his pocket and circling around Fred's table.

"Oh my, how rude of me," Plunger purred, grabbing Fred's attention again. "I have not offered you the kind services of my wish jar."

"What?" Fred grunted, spooning a mouthful of oatmeal into his mouth and a trickle of apprehension ran down my spine as Plunger sat opposite him. "Fuck off, you creepy ass weirdo."

"Oh I shall, but not before you make your wish, good sir." Plunger opened the little glass jar in his hand, sprinkling something into his palm and bile rose in my throat as I realised it was a tuft of grey pubes. He blew them at Fred and they stuck to his face and landed all over his meal.

"What the fuck is that?" Fred swiped at his face then Plunger stood up, grabbing his head and slamming it down into his oatmeal, rubbing it in then releasing him and spooning several mouthfuls into his parted lips just before the guards looked his way.

Cain shot over as Plunger's ass hit his seat and Fred roared in outrage, spitting out the oatmeal and swiping at his face to try and get the pubes off of his sticky skin.

"What the fuck is going on over here?" Cain demanded and Plunger smiled innocently.

"I was just making a new friend, sir," he said. "Wasn't I, Freddy bear? We were just playing a game."

Fred's nose was bleeding and he seemed to have caught on to what was in his food as he practically clawed at his skin to get rid of the pubes.

"Is that true, Three-oh-two?" Cain demanded of Fred and he looked up at him then nodded quickly.

"Yes, sir," Fred said in a far weaker tone than he'd used before.

Plunger got up, moving around and whispering something in Fred's ear who paled before he bowed his head. Plunger sailed away with a smug smile on his face and I turned to Rosa who shuddered.

"Remind me never to piss that guy off," she muttered.

"Only if you remind me too," I replied.

The bell rang to signal the end of breakfast and all thoughts of Plunger's pubes went out of my head. It was time to start our library job. Everyone filed out of the hall and Rosa beamed as she jumped up from her seat.

We followed the other inmates side by side, letting the flow of bodies pull us along toward the exit. Cain had a smug ass look on his face as he waited for the new team to gather out in the corridor beyond the Mess Hall, but I had no idea why.

"Something you wanna say?" Rosa asked him, tossing her hair.

"I hope you like your new job, Twelve," he said with a smirk.

"Well anything's better than the last one, right?" she threw at him and his eyes narrowed.

Claud, Sonny, Brett and Esme all joined us and Gustard arrived shortly after them. Plunger smiled widely as he took us all in, rubbing his hands together.

"Are ya'll ready to put your hineys to work?" he asked, eyeing up the tattoos on Gustard's neck which were peeking out above his perfectly ironed uniform. He had some fucking gall to look at a serial killer like that. But even Gustard wouldn't do anything to him in front of the guards. Especially after Plunger had just reminded all of us what happened to people who riled him.

Sin arrived next, stretching his arms above his head and smirking around at all of us. "Hey team."

"That's all of us, right?" Rosa said. "Let's go."

"We're waiting on two more," Cain said dryly.

"Officer Hastings said it was a team of nine," I blurted and Cain shifted his eyes to me, his gaze full of dislike.

"Well, he was wrong. There's eleven on this work detail," he growled. "You got a problem with that, Sixty Nine?"

"No, sir," I muttered, but shared a brief look with Rosa. Whoever showed up was going to have to be trusted with our secret. And who knew which motherfucker was about to exit the Mess Hall?

Shit, this is not good.

Ethan Shadowbrook appeared, striding over to Cain then glancing at Rosa with his jaw flexing.

"Oh fuck no," Rosa growled, her spine straightening. "I'm not working with *him*." Fear flashed through her eyes because this was much more than that. If he was on this job, she was going to have to trust him, let him come with us. And though I'd feared what it would mean for her leaving her mate behind in this place, that didn't mean I wanted the decision taken out of her hands.

"If you refuse to work with him, then you can go back to cleaning on the maintenance level, Twelve," Cain said, looking amused as fuck over her glaring at Ethan.

By the stars, this is not how this is supposed to go. And who is the last fucking member?

I glanced at the Mess Hall, the rest of the inmates already taken to their jobs or back to their cells. Who the fuck were we waiting for then?

"I can't wait to get renovating," Sin said, tossing Rosa an obvious wink when Cain wasn't looking. She kicked him in the shin and he bit his lip like he liked that. *Asshole.*

The door eventually pushed open and Pudding lumbered out, strolling toward us at a casual as fuck pace before slowing to a halt in front of Cain. "Reporting for duty."

Rosa looked surprised, her eyes darting from Pudding back to Ethan as another snarl built in her throat. I mean, Pudding wasn't exactly a threat, but he was slow as shit and I didn't know if he was gonna be of any help in this situation. What if he didn't want to escape? I had no idea how long the guy's sentence was or really anything about him beyond this prison, but he was a good guy. He wouldn't snitch on us at least.

"Pick another job," Rosa demanded of Shadowbrook who gave her a cold smile.

"No," he said simply, folding his arms. "This is the only one they'll give me since my privileges were revoked for stealing a cuff key." He said those last words with venom, his glare fixed on her and the accusation beneath it was clear. A growl rose in my throat and Ethan shot me a look which was as sharp as a knife.

"Follow me," Cain barked, striding off down the stairs, clearly done watching this conversation play out.

I kept to Rosa's side as she turned her back on Ethan and we hurried down the stairs together, keeping up with Cain's fierce pace. She gave me a look that said *what the fuck are we going to do?* and I tossed her one back that said *we can't do anything.* She growled again, descending into a fiery fury as we reached level six and walked along the corridor to the frosted glass doors of the library.

Cain held one of the doors open, gesturing for us to head in. "You'll be locked in until lunchtime. Eyes will be on you through the cameras. Any infractions and you'll risk losing your job privileges altogether. Any questions? Good. Get started." He shoved a piece of paper into my hands and waited for us to walk inside.

I looked down at it as we filed in, finding a checklist of all the jobs that needed doing. Inside were piles and piles of boxes which I assumed were filled with the new books, and beside them were buckets of paint and brushes, sheets, plaster, and all kinds of things for the renovation. Cain swung the door shut and a clunk sounded it locking before his shadow shot away beyond the frosted glass.

Everyone but me and Rosa moved forward to pick up tools and Plunger started running his fingers up and down the furry length of a paint roller.

"There's nothing we can do," I murmured to Rosa who looked ready to lose it.

I took her hand and she met my gaze, her breaths coming heavily. "He can't come."

"He has to," I whispered urgently. "We don't have a choice. Everyone in this room is coming or we're not going to be able to do this."

"Who's coming?" Plunger purred as he stepped closer, still stroking that damn brush. I snatched it from his grip with a growl and he raised his grey eyebrows in surprise.

"Listen up! Grab that renovation shit and follow me!" Rosa hollered, gaining all of their attention and surprising me as she strode away. I guess she'd made her decision.

Her gaze roamed over all of them except Ethan who she pointedly ignored. She beckoned them after her and I growled at anyone who didn't immediately move, including Shadow-brook who was frowning in confusion. Eventually, he followed her too and we walked into one of the many CCTV blind spots towards the back of the cavernous library.

Rosa climbed up onto a table, planting her hands on her hips as she stared down at us all and I found myself standing beside Ethan as we watched her.

"What the fuck is this about, love? You're not taking charge of the fucking library renovation crew," Ethan mocked and Sonny and Esme growled dangerously.

"It's real good, kitten, so hear her out," Sin said excitedly, bouncing on the balls of his feet.

"Listen to her, Wolf," Gustard put in. "You're lucky you're here. All of you fucking are."

"What exactly *are* we doing over here in the reference section?" Pudding asked in his slow tone, gazing around the aisles, holding a step ladder in one hand like it weighed nothing.

"Maybe the Wolf girl wants a different kind of pack to please her down here in the dark," Plunger murmured hungrily from behind me and I grimaced.

"We're here…because we're escaping Darkmore," Rosa cut to the chase, her voice low and serious. "Every one of us in this room and no one else."

"What?" Ethan blurted, taking a step toward her, but I threw out an arm to bar his way.

"Listen to her," I said in a warning tone. "She's offering you your life back."

"We're escaping?" Plunger asked excitedly as Esme, Brett and Sonny howled and hugged one another. "And how are we gonna get outta here, sweet pup? Do you know of a tight little passage we can wriggle into and crawl our way out of?"

"Not yet," Rosa said, grimacing a little at the way he phrased that question. "But you're going to dig one in your Order form, Plunger. Because you'll be able to sense the magical detectors in the ground and avoid them." She took a syringe of Order Suppressant antidote from her pocket, showing it to him and everyone else.

Claud gasped, looking to me with his eyes shining and I gave him a smile. He was going to see his kids again. I'd made that promise and I planned on keeping it. He looked up at Rosa with gratitude in his gaze. "Thank you, Miss Rosa."

She waved him off, but smiled all the same and I clapped Claud on the back with a smirk.

"Oh my sweet, hairy grandmamma's balls," Plunger said excitedly. "I will most definitely dig your hole, ma'am. I'll dig it deep and wide so we'll all fit snuggly in it together."

I grinned, ignoring the fact that Plunger was a total creep

because who cared when he was the creep who'd be tunnelling us out of this place?

"Did you hand-pick all of us, hound?" Pudding asked Rosa, his eyes bright.

"Um, yes, sort of," she said awkwardly and Pudding smiled while Ethan frowned deeply.

"Well I've never been hand-picked for anything before," Pudding said. "And I would like to accept your invite to take me to the surface and escape from this prison. Yes, I would like that, hound."

"Good," Rosa said with a tight smile. "So, we have work to do. Is everyone in?"

Ethan looked shellshocked as everyone agreed quickly and I turned to him with my sternest glare.

"You're either in or you make an enemy out of everyone in this room. You sell us out, Shadowbrook, and I'll kill you myself. No one is fucking this up. We've put far too much effort into it already."

Ethan looked at me, seeming so surprised that he didn't even appear angry over me talking to him like that.

"You're saying I get to go home?" he asked, desperation flaring in his eyes and for some reason I rested a hand on his shoulder.

"If you help us get out of here, you can go wherever the fuck you like, Shadowbrook."

I glanced at Rosa, finding her gaze now glued to Ethan and some deep emotion was peeking out from behind her eyes as she waited for his answer.

"I'm in," Ethan growled with a firm nod. "What do you want me to do?"

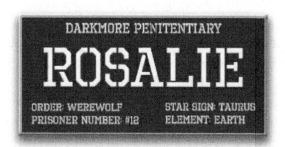

My heart was pounding and adrenaline was crashing through my limbs. This was it. No going back. The people in this room were officially my new best friends even if I did happen to hate three of them. It didn't matter, because from now until we were breathing the fresh air of the free, the ten of us were bound together like glue.

Sonny, Esme and Brett were all giggling excitedly as they began stripping books from the designated shelves for today and using the checklist we'd been given to box up the redundant stock. I'd already sworn them to secrecy in the Magic Compound when I'd made my choice for them to come with us, making them promise not to reveal the secret I gave up in here to anyone so I'd know if they betrayed us, but I wasn't really concerned about that at all.

Roary planned on making a similar oath with Claud the next time they were in the compound, and the two of them were talking in low tones as they started the job of hauling the newly emptying shelves away from the walls so that they could begin on the paint work. We'd be making Plunger, Ethan and Pudding swear to that the next time we were up there too. And Gustard if we could manage it, though I was willing to bet that slippery eel would find a way not to comply.

We'd spent the last half hour designating jobs with most of the team taking on the actual renovation work to cover the reality of what we were up to. I'd been seriously relieved when Pudding had told me he'd assumed he'd made the list because of his talent for building communication devices out of the chips in the old pudding pots, and now realised he totally should have anyway.

He'd agreed to get his brother to deliver receivers to the family members of our team so that everyone could make arrangements for when they got out of here without having to risk talking to anyone over the phone or in visitation where the guards would be paying attention. He was going to get one to Jerome too, the Fae who had paid me to get Sin out of here and who was vital to the final stages of my plan coming together so that we could hold off the FIB for as long as possible. All I had to do was make sure my Wolves kept getting him the chips and he'd be able to make enough transmitters for us to talk to everyone on the outside often enough to be sure their end of the plan was coming together too. Ethan had even agreed to get his Wolves gathering chips the moment Roary said he would get the Shades doing it, and Gustard reluctantly said he would get the Watchers on the case as well. With that many chips, Pudding would be all set to make as many transmitters as we needed so long as we all remained subtle about bringing them to him.

We'd selected a darkened corner of the library to start digging our tunnel, moving a bookshelf aside and giving Plunger a small dose of the antidote which would be enough to last him the two hours we had down here while saving the rest of the syringe for another day. We needed to ration it, but as the dose was enough to cover the guards for twenty-four hours we should have plenty with the three Roary had managed to steal.

Sin had volunteered to stay with Plunger in the tunnel and keep an eye on him and I was seriously grateful for that because Plunger on a normal day was too fucking much for me to handle, but Plunger in his shifted form was disturbing on a whole new level. I had literally never been one to Order shame before, but fuck me, Polethius Mole Shifters were fucking gross to look at. Or maybe it was just him. But couple that appearance with Plunger's less than wholesome personality and you had yourself a Fae who I did not want to be stuck in a small, dark space with for hours on end. No, Sin had saved my ass there for sure.

When Plunger had first shifted, I had honest to fuck thought he was having me on and had just done a half job to gross us all out, but no, I'd found a reference book and apparently they really did just kinda half shift. In his Order form, the grey hair which coated his body shrank away until he was smooth all over, but then his skin seemed to stretch until it was hanging in loose folds like one of those weird naked mole rat things, but his body stayed in its Fae shape so he looked kinda like a melting waxwork. Then his hands shifted into mole-like claws, his eyes shrank and his nose grew and turned all red and sprouted what looked like tentacles and *glowed* – honest to fuck, I'd never seen such a creepy looking Order in all my life.

And of course, because it was Plunger he insisted on stripping while he was shifted even though his actual body was similar enough in shape to his Fae form for him to have easily kept his clothes on. He kept bashing his ass against the sides of the tunnel as he dug, saying the words 'it's my method' enough times to drive me insane in the five minutes I'd spent with him while he began to dig.

Sin was seriously taking one for the team by overseeing that freakshow and I would happily pay him back in any way he liked to show my gratitude later.

Gustard was unsurprisingly not helping, taking a seat at one of the crappy tables and flipping a book open as he settled himself in to read.

"You have to help with the work, stronzo," I snarled at him, moving to stand over him and pressing my hands flat to the desk in front of him.

"I think you all have it in hand," he replied lazily, flipping a page and I growled as I reached out and slammed the book shut.

"We are two men down on this job while Sin and Plunger are in the tunnel," I hissed. "We can't afford to let it show that we're taking too long to do the work, or the guards might have questions for us. Or worse yet, they might decide to reassign the workers down here."

"Relax, my dear, the guards don't care how long this job takes or they would have hired magical professionals to do it. They just want to be sure that we hate every fucking second of it. So remove your greasy palm from my reading material and I'll go and take watch near the main door. No doubt you'd like fair warning if the guards return to check on us." Gustard tugged his book out from beneath my hand and yanked it back into his grasp, smiling dangerously before sauntering away toward the doors at the far end of the cavernous room.

Luckily for him, the CCTV covered his smarmy ass down there or I might be tempted to beat the shit out of him the way his fucking cronies had done to me in here once. I ground my teeth as I tried to force my anger at Gustard into a ball of hatred at the back of my mind. His time would come. I was already planning on the best way to get rid of him before we got out of here and I'd be getting revenge on his band of merry assholes if I got the chance too. Soon enough, all of my enemies would feel the iron fist of my wrath coming down on them.

A hand caught my elbow as I stood there seething and I whirled around to find Ethan glaring at me. He dragged me away from the rest of the group, into the stacks and through the maze of shelves with books dedicated to criminality and changing your life path.

I could have fought him off, but I didn't. We needed to have this out now that I was stuck with him on this team too and it made sense to do it sooner rather than later. Besides, the feeling of his hand on my flesh was too fucking good to deny, even if his grip was bruising and I could taste his rage on the air. I'd been avoiding him for too long and the mate bond had been aching to get me back in his arms for days. This was a good excuse to quiet its nonsense without me having to look like I'd caved.

When we reached the end of the row and were far enough from the others not to be overheard, he swung me around and shoved me back against the wall so hard that pain ricocheted through my spine for a moment. What was with all of these stronzos thinking they could manhandle me all of the damn time? And what was with me liking it so fucking much?

"Ciao, anima gemella," I purred, looking up at him with a taunting smirk as he growled in my face.

"What does that mean?" he spat.

"I called you my *soulmate*," I said in a tone that let him know exactly what I thought of that bullshit even though my heart was pounding at having him so close and some part of me just wanted him closer.

"Well you clearly don't think of me as your soulmate if you've been planning this entire thing and you didn't even tell me," Ethan snarled. "Did you even know I was going to be on this team? Were you even planning on bringing me with you?"

I licked my lips slowly as his gaze bored into mine, demanding that answer like he needed it more than breath.

"No," I said slowly, drawing out the word and watching it hit him in the chest like a bullet and I really hoped it fucking hurt.

Ethan just shook his head like he couldn't believe it, turning and striding away from me as if he just couldn't bear to look at me. But before he'd even reached the end of the aisle, he turned back and stormed towards me with fury in his blue eyes.

"Tell me you don't feel this," he demanded. "Tell me you aren't burning up with the need to see me, touch me, kiss me- it's driving me to the brink of insanity and yet you were willing to abandon me here and make us both suffer that ache for the rest of our lives? What the fuck, Rosalie?"

"Feel what?" I asked cruelly, the mask my papa had taught me to wear strapped tightly over my features. "The way you shunned me and the gift the moon offered us? The rejection of knowing my mate would rather let Sin make him into a little bitch and allow the entire prison to believe he mated a fucking *Beta* rather than stand up and claim me as his own? The hurt in my chest as you let that low ranking bitch paw at you and kiss you and fuck you and-"

"I'm not fucking her," he snarled like the idea actually disgusted him. "I'm not fucking anyone but you."

I laughed bitterly and tossed my hair even though relief spilled through me at his words. The idea of him choosing someone so much lower than himself over me had been driving me insane. If she was an Alpha then at least I could have understood it, but that bitch fucking simpered around him. *Simpered*. If I knew he got hard for that meek shit after having me then I wouldn't have ever been able to forgive it.

"Well it sounds a lot like you're not fucking anyone then, amore mio," I mocked. "Because you definitely aren't fucking me."

Ethan snarled, tilting his head to one side as he looked down at me. "You can't fight this forever love. We're fated, you and me, the moon wants us to be together-"

"But *you* don't," I sneered. "And I'm not going to be your dirty secret, Ethan. So choose me or leave me alone."

"I can't," he snarled, the Wolf in him seeming to flare in his eyes for a moment at the anguish he was feeling over this. But boohoo, he could cry me a fucking river. If he wanted to feel sorry for himself over this situation then he could go for it. This was supposed to be a gift, not a curse and I wasn't going to stand for being some regret he held.

"Then leave me alone. I don't need you anyway." I brushed him aside as I made a move to leave, but he caught me and pushed me back against the wall again.

I snarled at him and a soft whimper escaped him. "You were really going to leave me here, weren't you?" he breathed and the guilt I felt over that accusation burned up my throat like bile. Because yeah, that had been my intention. But as I stood captured in his bright blue eyes, I found myself wondering if I really would have done it, because standing here with him felt too fucking good even while I was so angry I could punch his lying face in.

"You don't want me anyway," I murmured.

"I want you," he said fiercely. "You're all I fucking want."

"Liar. You want your precious gang more." *Fuck*, it hurt to say that, to lay out the facts like that and wait for him to deny it, even though I knew he wouldn't.

"When we get out of here, it can be different," he began, though he didn't even sound convinced of that himself. "I know the gangs aren't at war in Alestria the way they are in here. I just need time, I need-"

"I'm not waiting around for you to decide you want me," I hissed. "I don't have to. You're not the only Alpha who wants to claim me for his own and I don't want someone who's ashamed of me."

A roar of rage escaped Ethan's lips and he turned, ripping the entire contents of books from the shelf beside us so that they tumbled to the floor.

"Who is it?" he demanded, forgetting to even keep his voice low as jealousy flashed in his eyes and he looked half tempted to shake the answer out of me. "Is it that fucking Lion? I'll rip his fucking mane off and make a throw rug out of it!"

"No. It's not Roary. I'm not good enough for him, either," I tossed the words out casually, but they fucking hurt all the same. How was it that I'd let three separate alpha-holes get close enough to hurt me with their rejection like this? Fuck all of them and their bullshit. I was sick of feeling like I couldn't meet their expectations.

Ethan's rage shifted into anguish as he took in the pain in me and he whined low in the back of his throat before moving into my personal space and nuzzling against me.

It felt so fucking good that I didn't even shove him off. And I hated to admit it, but I was relieved that he was coming with us now because I couldn't even begin to fathom the idea of being unable to see him ever again.

"I got you this," he muttered, finding my hand and pressing something warm between my fingers.

I drew in a deep breath as he nuzzled against me, trying not to love the way that felt while aching in the most beautifully painful way for him. I looked down and found the yellow

Sunstone Crystal Sin had told me they'd stolen together in my grasp.

"I hope you washed this," I muttered, though my anger at him was loosening just a little because he'd done this for me without even knowing it would benefit him too. He'd risked the guards catching him just to bring it to me and even though it had been days since he'd taken it, he'd clearly been carrying it around, risking getting caught every time he passed a guard. For me. That had to mean something even if I didn't want to admit it.

"I hate that fucking Incubus," Ethan growled, his lips moving up my neck and making a moan rise up in my throat with it, but I forced it back, not wanting him to know how much I was enjoying this.

"Sin is an acquired taste," I breathed.

"I'll take your word on that, love."

Ethan's big hands wrapped around my waist and he turned his head, seeking out my lips with a groan of longing.

But I wouldn't give them to him. I couldn't. So I turned my cheek and his hot mouth fell against my flesh instead of my lips, making sparks ignite beneath my skin.

Ethan refused to be put off, his mouth moving over my jaw and onto my neck until a moan slid from my lips like a traitorous bitch. Fuck, I needed to feel his flesh against mine. I needed to have him worshipping my body and satisfying this ache in my soul for him. Because he was mine and I was his. The moon had decided it even if we didn't want to agree.

He started tugging at the buttons of my jumpsuit and I growled as my hands slid up his back. "I'm not fucking you, Ethan," I insisted.

"Just let me make you feel good," he begged, his hands pushing inside my jumpsuit and teasing the top edge of my panties.

I growled again, wanting to tell him no and aching to tell him yes.

With a groan of frustration that I knew wouldn't be satisfied unless I gave in to him, I gripped his hair and exerted pressure as I pushed him lower.

Ethan growled a little as I urged him to give in to my control but when I snarled back, he dutifully dropped to his knees, seeming to realise this was going to happen my way or not at all.

He unbuttoned my jumpsuit until it was hanging all the way open and he was leaning forward to kiss at my wet heat through the barrier of my panties.

His fingers curled around the sides of them and I moaned a soft encouragement as he tore them clean off of me, baring my pussy for him as he pushed the ruined material into his pocket.

He moved his mouth to my inner thigh as I widened my legs to give him access, but that wasn't where I wanted him. My grip on his hair tightened as he tried to take charge of this and I forced his mouth where I wanted it.

Ethan growled as his lips landed on my clit and the vibrations of that sound had another moan escaping me.

He might not have liked me taking control, but his hot tongue began to tease me all the same and I shifted my hips into the movement, grinding against his mouth as pleasure skittered through my body.

Ethan raised a hand, pushing two fingers into me to add to the torture and I rode his hand shamelessly as I demanded more.

He began to slow his pace, toying with me as he devoured me and I snarled in frustration.

"Harder," I commanded in my Alpha tone, making him growl even more as I tried to force him to bend to my will.

That growl felt so fucking good against my clit that I moaned again, rocking my hips even more as I rode his face and fucked his hand and he gave in to what I wanted, licking and biting and thrusting his fingers in and out until I was coming hard and choking his name back. Because I refused to praise him for this. It wasn't about him. It was about our bond. And even as he sucked on my clit to prolong my pleasure, I refused to admit that I wanted him more than this.

He drew back and I began buttoning my jumpsuit again, meeting his gaze as he knelt before me.

"I'm sorry I hurt you, love," he said and I could feel how much he meant that as my throat thickened and my heart pounded.

"How sorry?" I breathed.

"I can't tell everyone about us," he said sadly.

"Then I guess there's nothing else to say." I stepped around him and walked away before he could see me crack. The mate bond might have made me hunger for him, but I didn't have to give him any more than my flesh and I'd fight that as often as I could too.

I was Rosalie Oscura and no one made me their bitch.

⁎

We spent a few days perfecting our routine in the library and as much as it killed me to hold off on progressing our plans, I knew it was important to get this right. While Plunger carefully used his gifts to create the two tunnels we needed - one leading down to the maintenance level and the other up towards the surface - the rest of us got to work at completing the task of painting the walls and removing the outdated books from the shelves. The cataloguing really was boring as fuck, so I'd been painting with Roary for the most part, slicking the grotty beige walls with a nice new lick of white.

"We need to figure out how long our window of opportunity is to use the tunnels once we execute the plan," I murmured thoughtfully as I worked so close to Roary that our arms kept brushing. It was totally a Wolf thing though, not some desire to be close to *him* in particular. And I'd keep telling myself that until I was blue in the damn face.

"Aren't you planning to start a riot on the night we escape?" he asked in a low tone, glancing around even though we knew there was no one near enough to overhear us.

"Yeah. But I need to know how long the guards will spend

trying to contain a riot themselves before they give up and release the Belorian. The last thing I want is that fucking thing stalking us through the tunnels and eating us all." I shuddered at the thought and Roary grimaced.

"No, let's not let that happen. So what do we need to do?"

"We need a test run so that I can time it. We need to get the inmates rioting and then make sure that all of us can escape the carnage and get down here fast enough to make our escape into the tunnels. We want to know that we'll be long gone before that monster is set loose to chase us or we're going to need to think up some way to neutralise it."

"I don't think there is a way to neutralise it," he muttered. "That monster was built to be unstoppable."

"All the more reason to have a practice riot then."

"Did I hear someone say party?" Sin purred from behind us and I turned towards him with a grin as he moved forward to inspect our work. Plunger was getting dressed beyond him as Sonny and the other Wolves made sure the bookcases were stacked against the wall to hide the tunnel again, so it must have been coming close to the end of our session. "You missed a spot, kitten."

I turned back to the wall with a frown and Sin plucked the paintbrush from my hand while I was distracted before swiping it straight down the side of my cheek.

I sucked in a breath of surprise and turned to him with a playful growl. "You did *not* just do that."

"Do what?" he asked, grinning as he slowly dipped the brush back into the tin of paint.

Gustard whistled sharply from somewhere over near the door to let us know the guards were coming, but I didn't care. This was war.

I caught sight of Ethan watching us through narrowed eyes from the side of the room, but I ignored him. It wasn't like he could complain anyway - not unless he wanted to Fae up and admit I was his to the whole prison. Even then, I wouldn't stop just because he told me to.

I grabbed another brush and loaded it up with paint just as Sin lunged for me again. He hooked an arm around my waist and would have had me off my feet if Roary hadn't caught my arm to stop my fall.

Sin looked up at him in surprise and Roary took the opportunity to swipe the white paint right down the centre of Sin's face.

I burst out laughing as Roary darted away from Sin's retaliation and I managed to slap my brush down firmly against the Lion's ass as he made his escape.

"Hey - I was on your side, little pup! What gives?" Roary demanded with a laugh.

"I don't need anyone on my side," I taunted, dipping my brush again as I moved to avoid Sin who was circling around behind me. "I can take you both down on my own."

"You hear that, kitten?" Sin asked Roary in that sultry tone of his. "The girl thinks she could handle the two of us at once. That sounds like the best proposition I've had in a while if you're up for it."

"Yeah," Roary replied, smirking at me and making me blush, much to my dismay. "I'm up for it."

He lunged at me and I shrieked with laughter as I leapt away from him, vaulting the tin of paint and managing to run two paces before Sin caught me and slapped the paintbrush against my other cheek.

I tried to back up, but Roary's strong arms coiled around me and he tugged me back against his chest as I squealed and slapped him with my brush as much as I could, coating his arms but not making him loosen his grip at all.

Sin grinned widely as Roary presented me to him and I fought somewhat half-heartedly as Sin quickly painted giant tits over my breasts complete with nipples and then painted an enormous dick over my crotch which hung down my right leg to my knee.

"I knew you wished my tits were bigger, but I didn't know you lamented my lack of cock," I teased as he laughed in triumph.

"Everyone enjoys a bit of sausage in their sandwich from time to time, wild girl," Sin teased and I bit my lip as I considered that. Not that I could grow a cock for him or anything, but the thought that he liked the idea made me kinda hot in all the right ways.

"Eighty-Eight, Sixty-Nine, release Twelve this instant!" Cain's voice boomed out, killing the fun like it was his own personal mission in life to suck the joy from every occasion. He was a Vampire who sucked happy from people just as much as blood. A happy sucker if you will.

Sin tossed his brush down and Roary let me go just as Cain caught my hand and yanked me away from them.

"If I catch the two of you trying to assault her again-" he began and I sighed dramatically.

"*Actually*, we were just discussing the three way we plan on having up in the Order Yard on our next trip there and figuring out what position was going to work best for us this time," I said, tugging my hand out of Officer Dickwad's grip and refusing to acknowledge the way my fingers were warming from his touch. "So no need to go making any false accusations. I assure you, anything either of them does to my body is entirely consensual."

Sin threw his arm around Roary's neck and grinned so excitedly that I was pretty sure he was taking me seriously and Roary shrugged him off with a growl. Roary would certainly bring some extra sausage to the sandwich if he didn't have that stick so far up his ass, but seeing as he did, I wasn't going to let myself get carried away with that particular fantasy no matter how salivating it was. But the idea of being pinned between Sin and Roary was definitely going on my bucket list.

Cain narrowed his eyes as he glared between all of us and then took in the work we'd been doing. "Is there a reason this is taking so damn long?" he asked. "Because you're down here to work, not flirt like a bunch of teenagers."

"It's hard work, sir," Plunger said, licking his lips as he

251

walked over to join us. "So long and hard. I guess we could push harder though if that's what you want? Do you want me to push even harder? Dig deeper? Thrust myself right into the-"

"You're not wandering the prison covered in paint, Twelve," Cain growled, turning away from Plunger and his gross insinuations. For once I was actually glad of them because they'd distracted Cain from his line of questioning. "You can come with me for a shower before lunch."

I opened my mouth to protest, but he grabbed my wrist and started tugging, forcing me to march along after him as the other guards appeared to get the rest of the group moving.

Ethan scowled at me as I passed him and I blew him a kiss, tossing in a wink just to add a layer of obnoxiousness to the move. He could stick his jealousy where the sun didn't shine for all I cared.

"What's the matter, boss man?" I asked sweetly as Cain tugged me along the corridor outside the library. "Don't you like my new cock? Or were you hoping for a closer look at my tits?"

Cain growled but said nothing as he just pulled me along faster.

I trotted along beside him like a good girl and even made the effort to shift closer to him. He was still holding onto my wrist so I twisted my arm in his grip, making my hand slip into his instead, before winding my fingers through his.

He frowned at me, growling and tugging his hand free, giving me the freedom I'd been aiming for.

"I'm starting to get the feeling you don't like me anymore, sir," I said with a pout.

"I never liked you, Twelve. I don't like anyone. And you in particular are extremely unlikable."

I laughed loudly as he led me up to the fourth floor where the cell blocks were located and took me directly to the shower block.

Cain pointed towards the showers and I gave him an insolent look as I folded my arms.

"So this was really about getting me naked and wet for you then, was it?" I asked.

Cain's upper lip pulled back in a growl and my pulse leapt as I spotted his lengthening fangs. "I have zero interest in your body or how wet you might get for me, Twelve," he said in a deadly tone that was almost believable. "Just strip off and wash that fucking paint off of your face and out of your hair and I'll go get you a clean uniform."

He shot away from me without another word and I released a string of colourful curses about him, hoping he was still listening in with his bat ears as I did as I'd been told.

The water was hot as I switched it on, and I couldn't help but sigh as it washed over my body, realising I was having the first private shower I'd been gifted in months. It was bliss.

I took my time washing myself, making sure I got all of the paint out of my hair as I enjoyed the small luxury and I *maybe* made some overtly sexual noises while I did so like I was on a Herbal Essences commercial from back in the day. But if people were nosing in on me while I was washing then they only had themselves to blame if they didn't like what they heard. Or if they did.

I shut the water off somewhat reluctantly and stepped out of the showers, but as I hadn't known I was coming here, I didn't have a towel so I was just left to stand there dripping wet and waiting.

When Cain didn't return and goosebumps began to rise all over my flesh, I rolled my eyes and looked around the room. There was a bench beside the lockers next to the showers, so I strolled over to it and kicked it over, cursing loudly as it crashed to the ground.

Cain shot into the room in a blur of motion and came up short right in front of me. "What happened?" he demanded, "I thought you hurt yourself."

"I'm alright, thank you Officer," I replied sweetly. "I was just trying to find a towel."

Cain clenched his jaw as he fought not to drop his gaze from my face and I licked my lips slowly.

"Do you want to look?" I asked, stepping closer to him as I let my gaze travel down his muscular frame and remembered how it had felt when he'd bitten me. I hated him, but I could admit to myself that I hadn't hated that. I'd quite liked being at his mercy if I was totally honest with myself. It was hot.

"You need to get dressed, Twelve," Cain bit out, but he didn't leave so I stepped up right in front of him and placed my hands on his chest.

"Do I haunt your dreams, Officer?" I whispered, sliding my fingers down over his black shirt as he watched me like he was waiting for me to pounce. "Do you like to think about chasing me? Hunting me? Biting me?"

"I like to think about putting you in your place and seeing you reform your character."

I laughed flirtatiously and tiptoed up so that my lips were pressed to his ear as I whispered my reply. "Liar, liar."

He snarled at me and I stepped back fluidly, laughing as I tugged his shock baton from the holster at his hip and spun it in my hand tauntingly.

Cain shot forward with a snarl of rage, snatching the baton back from me and wrapping his other hand around my throat as he pinned me back against the lockers. He jammed the shock baton against my left side and rested his thumb over the button to switch it on.

I raised my chin and looked him dead in the eye as I smirked at him, daring him. "Do it, boss man. Teach me another lesson."

For a long moment he just gritted his teeth and let the threat hang between us, his grip tightening on my throat as he searched my expression for something, but I had no idea what.

"Do you take anything seriously?" he demanded. "Or is everything just a game to you?"

"Like the way you played with me and then tossed me away when you got bored?" I challenged. "You might have the power to ruin me, Mason, but you don't have the power to make me bow to you."

"I did a bit of research about you, you know," he said in a low tone.

"Oh yeah? If you found the pictures I did for that naked photoshoot you should know that I regret them now. I had a lightning bolt design on my pubic hair and in hindsight I think it might have been a bit tacky."

"I know what your father did to you to give you those scars," he breathed, refusing to be baited and every muscle in my body locked up tight as the smile fell from my face. "What's wrong, Twelve, as soon as something gets too real, you don't want to face it anymore?"

"Go on then," I hissed. "Tell me I deserved it, that he should have done worse, that you wish he hadn't run out of time before he got a chance to start on my face."

Cain's brow furrowed and I shoved him back, surprised when he actually released me and stepped away.

"I just want you to be straight with me," he said. "And you weren't, so I looked into you myself. It's not that surprising. If you'd rather I didn't do it again then you could just drop the bullshit."

"Why would I do that, boss man?" I asked innocently, moving to grab the fresh uniform he'd dropped on his way into the room and tugging it on. I'd rather be damp than stay in his company any longer than absolutely necessary anyway. "It sounds to me like you know all about me without me needing to say a single word. So why don't you keep digging? Knock yourself out. Unfortunately, you won't find any other medical reports though, I'm afraid. The rest of my scars were healed away as if they'd never even been there in the first place and I have to admit I lost count of how many I should have had. Nice and neat and tidy."

"Tell me then," he commanded.

"No," I replied simply, and I didn't even know how to interpret the way he looked at me, but for a moment I could have sworn I saw pity in his eyes...or worse than that - understanding.

I kicked my boots on and headed out of the room without waiting for permission. The rest of the inmates would be in the Mess Hall for lunch now, so I knew where to go and by the look on Cain's face as I walked out on him, I was willing to bet he had no intention of following.

Every great group of convicts had a name which went down in history forevermore. And as we were going to be pulling off the biggest escape of all fucking time, we needed a *fan-fucking-tastic* team name. I'd made a list of all kinds of names from The Brave Jackals, The Mean Manatees, The Grim Squirrels. All of them were good but not nearly good enough. Not until I remembered the scariest motherfucking animal on the planet. And the sexiest one too. It was perfect. Fucking genius. It represented my dick, Rosalie's heart, Plunger's naked grossness. It needed all kinds of merchandise to go with it once our names were splashed through the news and every Fae in Solaria would want to be one of us...

The Daring Anacondas.

Fuck. Yes.

I needed to okay it with Team Captain Rosalie Oscura though and as she swept past me in the Mess Hall, I caught her arm so hard that she nearly dropped the tray in her hands.

"*Sin,*" she hissed. "Not now." It had been a few days since we'd started working in the library and every time I went in there, I was fucking pumped. Especially when she set me tasks. It legit gave me the shivers right down to my cock. I'd never been much of a submissive, but for her, I'd pull my pants down like a good boy, shove a ball gag in my mouth and hand her the whip to do her worst while bending over a bale of hay – because of course this fantasy took place in a stable where she made comments about me being hung like a horse and I begged her to ride me like a cowgirl.

"I just need a word, kitten," I said urgently.

Her eyes darted around the room then back to me. We were about to kick off the riot in T-minus-who-fucking-knows seconds, but this was important. Fucking vital. We *had* to have a name. What were we without a name? Just a bunch of inmates with no purpose. This gave us *purpose*.

"Is something wrong?" she asked, lowering her tone.

"Yeah something's wrong, sex pot, really fucking wrong." I dropped down onto my seat and tugged her into my lap, taking her tray from her hands and planting it on the table. I arranged her legs so she was straddling me, looking me directly in the eyes as I gripped her ass and rocked her over my cock with a smirk. I started singing Pony by Ginuwine, getting carried away with my little stable fantasy again. *I wonder where I can purchase a saddle when I get out of here...and what can I use to cut a hole in it for my dick?*

Her eyes widened and she suddenly locked her hands around my throat. "You'd better not be fucking with me right now, Sin Wilder. This is not the time."

"Mmm say my name again, sugar," I encouraged. I would have thought fucking her would end my blue ball misery, but apparently my blue balls were starting a dynasty. And they'd be around for a long fucking time while my little wild girl was in sight. Just looking at her made me ache for more. That was all I wanted since we'd fucked. More more more. My balls still throbbed like I'd never had her at all. But I had. Oh I fucking had. She'd felt like starlight wrapping around my cock and I swear it had shone afterwards for a good ten minutes, granting wishes to anyone who looked its way.

Rosalie wasn't just a good lay, not even a decent one. She was an epic fucking lay. One I wanted again and again and again. I had so many positions lined up in my mind to try with her, I knew it was going to take fifty fucks to even start making a dent in the list.

"*Sin*," she scolded, squeezing my throat while I grew hard between her thighs. "What do you want? You've got three sec-

258

onds to answer me. Three, two-"

I kissed her and her back arched as I sank my tongue into her mouth, murmuring the name of our team as I was lost to her.

"Did you just say anaconda?" She pulled back with a frown and I nodded keenly, my gaze wandering down her body to the material between her thighs. *I wonder if my plastic knife will poke a hole through there?* If it could, maybe I'd be able to get her off before the guards pulled me away from her. I'd have about fifteen seconds I reckoned. Less if Officer Cain saw us and shot over here with his Vampy speed. Could I make her come that fast? *Challenge accepted.*

"I need to be with my pack." She got up, swinging her leg over me, but I caught her ankle before she escaped, causing her to hop on one foot then try to kick me with the one I had hold of.

"The Daring Anacondas," I announced proudly.

"What?" she balked as I released her foot and she kicked me in the chest anyway, making my chair nearly topple over.

I caught myself before it did, smirking at her. "It's our team name. Do you like it?"

"Ahhhhhhhhhhhhhh!"

I swung around at the lengthy shout, finding Pudding with a chair hefted up above his head, towering over the Pegasus herd leader, Sparkle, so she was cast in his enormous shadow. She looked around just as he slammed it down on her and she whinnied in pain, falling flat on her back among the pieces of the shattered chair, glitter puffing up around her in a cloud.

Holy fuck tits!!! It's on!!

Pudding looked up, a slow smile spreading across his face, then all fucking hell broke loose.

The Pegasus herd descended on Pudding and Roary's Shades dove to his aid out of nowhere. Rosalie ran away from me just as her pack started shit with Ethan's and the two groups clashed hard. My wild girl leapt up onto a table, springing off of it onto Ethan's back and punching him in the head, not holding back despite the fact that he was in on this whole plan.

259

I sat there laughing my head off while chaos broke out all around me. This was my favourite kind of weather. Raining carnage.

Plunger got his dick out, running around and slapping anyone in the face with it who was unfortunate enough to still be sitting down and the guards flew into the crowd, crying out and trying to get everything under control.

I spotted Gustard and his guys pounding on a bunch of Sirens and I was so entranced by the mayhem that I wasn't remotely prepared when a thick, muscular arm locked around my throat and wrenched me out of my seat. I choked, clutching onto it as I looked up to find that Roary Night had hold of me, glaring down at me with venom in his eyes. He looked way too invested in making me hurt for real and I had to laugh because I realised why. I'd tasted the lust on him a thousand times around my wild girl. He wanted her, and he didn't like her wanting *me*. And he'd finally gotten his perfect opportunity to make me pay for it.

"Need – to – talk – to - you," I managed to rasp out as the strong motherfucker tightened his grip and didn't seem to give a damn about how hard I threw my elbows back into his gut.

When I was seeing stars and wondered if it was worth quickly jerking off to at least enjoy the rush of asphyxiation before I went, Roary released me.

I hit the ground and laughed wildly, whooping from the exhilaration of almost dying.

"Next time we do that, let's make sure Rosalie is sucking my cock." I got to my feet, but Roary's fist connected with my jaw and I staggered back into the table, laughing again as I tasted blood.

"You keep your hands off of her," he demanded and I stood up straighter, my smile becoming dark and twisted as a hunger for violence grew in me. It was one of my favourite things in the world. The freedom of drawing blood was like no other. And I was slipping into the darkest place inside me where no morals lived.

"She wants you too, kitten," I purred, striding toward him and raising my fists. "I've tasted her lust just like I've tasted her pussy. And both are so *sweet*."

He came at me with rage in his eyes and I ducked his next punch, throwing my shoulder into his gut as I tried to upend him. He stumbled back, locking one arm around my shoulders and pounding my kidney with his free fist. Torturous, glorious pain blossomed under my flesh and my laughs came harder.

I turned my head and bit into his abdomen, making him yell in surprise. I kept biting, tasting blood and he growled, throwing me off of him. But I came at him again, going full savage as I launched my whole body at him. I managed to knock him off of his feet and we hit the ground in a clash of fists and furious growls. My dick was getting hard because I was as hot for violence almost as hot as I was for my wild girl.

I clutched the Lion's head, slamming it against the linoleum floor as he threw punches that knocked the wind from my lungs.

"Why are you hard?" he asked in alarm as I crushed him to the floor and I grinned at him, my teeth still wet with his blood.

"Violence is a beautiful mistress, Roary," I growled. "Don't you like the way she caresses you from the inside?"

I punched him in the chest and he snarled, reaching up and latching his hand around my throat. I answered by locking my own hand around his in return, still smiling, having the time of my damn life.

"The two of us could make a beautiful mess of Rosalie," I rasped as he fought to block off my air supply. "Think how good she'd look between us, gasping our names."

"Are you actually propositioning me right now?" Roary choked out and I nodded keenly.

I loosened my grip on his throat a little, sitting back on his hips. "By the way I've come up with a team name for us."

He reared up, throwing a hard punch to my side which sent me flying off of him. I landed on my back and I cupped my hands behind my head as he stalked toward me. Fuck me, he was hot. All that long, dark hair cascaded around his huge, powerful shoulders as he leaned down to murder me. I could think of worse ways to die.

"The name has got to be good, as we're gonna be famous." I beamed just before his fist smashed into my gut and my muscles bunched up as I heaved out a cough and pain tore through me. He lowered over me to press his advantage, but I threw up my knee and slammed it right into his balls. A low blow, but he really wasn't listening to me. He fell to his knees, cupping his junk with a guttural groan and I was glad I finally had his full attention.

I squashed his cheeks between my hands as I leaned up beneath him, making him lock eyes with me. "It's The Daring Anacondas," I said dramatically. "What do you think?"

"Fuck...you," he groaned, then tried to headbutt me, but I jerked backwards before he landed his target, then darted back toward him again, smacking a wet kiss on his lips before crawling out from under him and running away. *Did he like the name? He didn't even comment. Nah, he must have liked it. It's the best name I've ever come up with. Ever.*

Pudding lumbered past me, wielding a whole table as a weapon as the Pegasus herd sprinted away from him with frightened whinnies. It was always the quiet ones who were secretly psychotic. And the extra loud ones. I swung between those two camps. Loud, quiet, scary, cute. I was your average friendly murderer. And it sure made life interesting.

I rubbed my jaw where Roary had hit me then sought out my wild girl in the crowd. She was still fighting with Ethan, but they were wrestling like two pups now, not really going that hard at one another and I licked my lips as I tasted their lust for one another. There was only one other Fae in the room right now who was oozing lust and that was Plunger who was still dick-slapping anyone he could get close to. If I tried that shit, I'd take someone's eye out. *Wait...is that a turtle head tattooed on his piece?*

Someone collided with me before I could figure it out and I spun around to find one of Gustard's guys there. He was a huge Minotaur called Tim and he was fighting with a couple of Siren girls like a raging beast and groping one of them in the process. I grinned evilly then kicked out his knees so he crashed to the ground beneath me. I reached into my pocket, taking out the plastic fork I'd used to eat my dinner and dropped down, jamming it right into his eye. He screamed like a baby and I pounded his large gut while he tried to deal with the fork sticking out of his face with shaking fingers.

Nasty, nasty shit that. Eye forks were no laughing matter. Except to me. Because I was laughing my ass off.

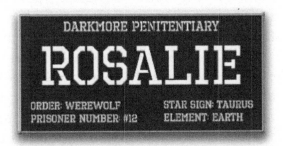

Ethan pinned me beneath him with a growl which wasn't even vaguely aggressive as he ground himself against me and I rolled my eyes at him before shoving him in the chest to knock him off of me. I mean, sure, all this rolling around with him was getting me all kinds of turned on too, but it wasn't the time.

"We need to go," I hissed and he growled again in frustration this time before letting me get to my feet and move away from him.

My lip was bleeding and I pushed my tongue against it as I leapt up onto a table to assess the carnage.

I cupped my hands around my mouth and howled to encourage my pack to keep going as the guards raced around, trying to catch people and using their shock batons in an attempt to force order.

A laugh burst from my lips as I spotted Sparkle and her gang of asshole Pegasuses huddled together in a corner, trying to defend their dinner table while looking like they didn't know if they should try and rush back into the fray or not.

For the first time since Gustard had found out about our plan and blackmailed his way into being included in it, I was actually pleased. With all four of the major players getting their gangs to riot, the entire prison had been thrust into chaos with hardly any work at all.

Sin's deep laughter drew my attention and I grinned at him as he leapt between the tables, shaking his ass at any guards who drew close enough to try and restrain him before leaping away again.

But despite the fact that this may well have been fun as all hell, we needed to get to our rendezvous point outside the fate room down on level eight. We had to see how fast the ten of us could make it down there without being followed and then figure out how long we had until the Belorian was set free. I couldn't spot Roary anywhere, so I was guessing he'd already headed down there.

I howled again to rile my pack up then made a run for the door.

Between the food throwing, all out brawling and general anarchy taking part in the Mess Hall, most of the guards had their full attention occupied with trying to restrain as many of the inmates as possible, so once I made it to the corridor I was hoping the way on would be clearer.

A huge net of vines was suddenly launched over my head and I threw myself aside to avoid getting tangled in it, but instead found myself colliding with Pudding as he lumbered towards the door.

I slammed into him and his eyes met mine just as the net fell over us and the magic was yanked tight.

"Fuck!' I yelled as I was crushed against the enormous Bear Shifter and the guard in control of the magic dragged us across the room before securing the net to the ceiling and hanging us up in a line alongside a bunch of other captured rioters.

I cursed the fact that I didn't have access to my magic as I fought to find a weak spot in the net while simultaneously being crushed beneath Pudding's ass.

"Pull harder, hound," he said in that totally chilled out, unaffected tone of his as the vines which made up the net cut into my fingers while I tugged as hard as I damn well could.

Pudding sighed like I was being dramatic or something and then rolled over, smooshing my face to the net and crushing me as I cursed him. But then he lifted his huge hands to the vines, grabbed hold of them and tugged them apart like they were made of nothing at all.

I didn't get a moment to be impressed though because the second I saw him do it, the whole net fell apart and the two of us fell straight out of it and down onto the hard floor beneath us.

By some miracle, I managed to roll aside before an enormous Bear could fall on top of me and I found myself beneath one of the tables as another guard threw a torrent of water our way.

I cursed and rolled further beneath the table, getting to my feet on the other side of it and spotting Pudding just as he strolled out the door like this was any other day.

A hand closed around my wrist and I whirled around with a snarl bursting from my lips, finding myself face to face with none other than my least favourite CO.

Cain smirked triumphantly and hoisted me over his shoulder before shooting from the room and down the stairs, the world blurring around me until we found ourselves outside my cell block where he dropped me on my feet.

"Let's see how long this goes on for without the ring leaders in play," he taunted, giving me a shove towards the doors where Officer Rind was shouting at all of the inmates to return to their cells or sleeping places in the coop for lockdown.

"Thank you, boss man," I said sweetly as I looked up at Cain. "For saving me the walk down the stairs."

He growled at me and gave me another shove towards the cell block before shooting away to help out with the rest of the rioters.

"Get your ass inside, Twelve!" Officer Rind boomed, but he was all alone and clearly had orders to man the door.

I glanced between him and the corridor to my right and then grinned widely as I darted away. His angry yells chased me down the corridor but there were hundreds of inmates running this way already, looking to get back to their cells for lockdown before the guards upped the game in an effort to regain control of us.

I tore down the corridor past the other cell blocks, ignoring the yells of the guards when they caught my ear and using the flood of inmates to hide my passage as much as I could manage.

When I reached the central staircase, I headed straight down, whooping with excitement as I bounded down step after step until I made it to level five where the gymnasium was housed. There weren't any other Fae down here right now, most of them racing back to their cell blocks or living their best lives causing havoc up in the Mess Hall and the silence surrounding me was almost eerie.

As I rounded the corner and prepared to leap down the next flight of steps, a prickle of warning ran down my spine and I whipped around half a second before a force of air magic slammed into me and lifted me clean off of my feet.

I was hurled into the gym, rolling across the tiled floor between the silent machinery before coming to a halt in front of a pair of boots.

I pushed onto my hands and knees, looking up to find Officer Nixon smirking down at me with a dark glint in his eyes that put me on edge.

"Looks like I caught a runway," he purred, a smile widening on his face that sent a shiver of disgust dancing along my skin.

"Sorry, sir, I was just-" I began, but with a flick of his fingers, he stole the air from my lungs and I choked on the next words I'd been going to say.

My eyes widened and I made a move to stand up, but Nixon reached out and pressed a hand to the top of my head to hold me down.

"I think you're alright where you are, sweet thing," he said roughly, licking his lips in that gross toady way that I hoped was because of his Order. "Get on your knees like a good girl. You are a good girl, aren't you?"

Nixon looked down at me with a superior kind of triumph on his face and I glared up at him as my lungs began to burn and I had to fight the urge to start convulsing on the floor and gasping for breath.

"Say, 'yes Nixy'," he prompted before allowing me to suck in a deep breath.

"What do you want?" I snarled and his gaze darkened as he snatched my air away again, wetting his lips slowly before he spoke.

"You may have heard about me from a few of the other inmates and heard that I'm a real good friend to have around here," he said in a slow drawl which made it clear he had no intention of hurrying himself along for the sake of letting me breathe. "I can get you treats and help keep you out of trouble when the need arises. For example, I imagine, you don't want me to have to drag you down to the hole for attacking an officer during the riot tonight?"

I shook my head, unable to speak while he held my oxygen hostage and he smiled wider.

"Mmmmm, well, sweet thing, then how about we become special friends? I like making friends and I like doing things to help them out. So how's about you scratch my back and I'll scratch yours?" He raised a hand to slick his eyebrows down with his finger and thumb then licked his lips again as he surveyed me on my knees before him.

Pinpricks of darkness were closing in around the edges of my vision and when he finally returned my oxygen to me, I had to spend a few moments sucking down air before I could reply.

"You want some kind of exchange?" I asked him, not bothering to hide the sneer of disgust on my face as I refused to look at the bulge of his cock which was pressing against his fly just a few inches from my face. "Spell it out plainly, sacco di merda, what do you want me to do to stay out of the hole?"

Nixon licked his lips again, his chest heaving with deep breaths as his eyes lit with excitement.

"Mmmmm, I think I'd like those pretty lips of yours wrapped around my cock, sweet thing," he purred with such casual confidence that it was clear to me this wasn't the first time he'd forced this bargain on an inmate in here. "Just show me a good time and I'll make sure that you get back to your cell block safe and sound. Then we'll both be happy, won't we?"

"Pensi di poter costringere la regina dell'Clan Oscura a succhiarti it cazzo come una puttana da branco?" I asked him in my most seductive voice and he groaned as he licked his lips again. *You think you can force the Queen of the Oscura Clan to suck your dick like a pack whore?*

"Mmmmm, I think you and me are going to have a real special friendship," he said, reaching down to unbuckle his belt so that his radio and shock baton hung loose in their holsters either side of his hips.

"Okay, stupratore, I'll give you what you're asking for," I agreed, looking up at him with a promise in my eyes, but not the one he was hoping for.

Nixon made that gross 'Mmmmm' sound again and slid his fly open, shoving his pants and boxers down so his hard and unsurprisingly small dick sprung free right in front of my fucking face.

The bastardo directed air magic at the back of my head, pushing me towards him as he gripped my head in his greasy hands and tugged me closer to his crotch.

But there was no way in hell that I was letting this stronzo's dirty cock touch me.

I reached out with a flash of motion and snatched his shock baton from its holster, twisting it in my grasp and flicking the switch to power it up. The baton needed his magical signature to activate which meant it had to connect with his skin while he was casting to read it. Nixon lifted his hand to defend himself with magic so the moment I slammed it against his dick, a thousand volts of electricity burst from the thing in a heartbeat.

Nixon was thrown back into a weight rack where his head slammed against one of the weights before he fell screaming and convulsing on the floor. That thing was strong enough to put him on his ass for several minutes and I wasn't going to waste a single one of them hanging around and waiting for him to wake up.

I slammed my boot into his face as I raced by, breaking

something with a loud crack as he twitched and screamed while the electricity continued to pour though him.

I tossed the baton on the floor and ran. The thing wouldn't work without his magic to activate it anyway and I definitely didn't want to be caught with a guard's weapon.

I tore out of the gym and down the stairs again, racing down flight after flight until I reached the eighth floor where I leapt into the corridor and ran for the doors to the Fate Room. The doors were locked up tight aside from when they allowed inmates in for sessions, so our group of escaping convicts were gathered in the corridor outside it, looking somewhat pissed as they spotted me.

"For someone who is supposed to be in charge of this plan, you sure took your time in getting down here," Gustard drawled and I scowled at him as I took a quick head count and realised that we'd all made it.

"I ran into a few asshole guards who held me up," I growled back, refusing to seem even the least bit rattled by what had just happened. And to be honest, I wasn't really. Nixon wasn't the first perverted scumbag I'd come across in my life, but he was the first I'd known to be abusing his power like that. I was more concerned about the Fae he had managed to force into his disgusting little tit for tat friendship arrangement than I was for myself. "Point is, we're all here and they haven't resorted to letting the Belorian out yet."

"That was fun," Sin grinned broadly, moving forward to grab me and hoist me into his arms. He whirled me around and I laughed as Sonny, Brett and Esme howled with excitement too and I spotted Roary and Claud grinning.

"I'm leaving before we get found down here," Gustard said icily, turning and walking away at a fast pace. "Let me know how long it takes for the monster to come looking for you."

Sin set me back on my feet and I rolled my eyes at Gustard's retreating form, but he did have a point. "He's right, everyone should head back up to their cells now. We know that we can get away undetected and I can keep timing to see how long it

270

takes for them to release the Belorian. We don't need to wait here for it to show up."

"Can we head back to the riot?" Sonny asked me hopefully and I laughed as I agreed, the group hurrying towards the stairs ahead of me as Sin tugged on my hand to hold me back.

Plunger danced away after my Wolves, rolling his hips to some music in his own head and Pudding headed off too with Claud walking at his side as the two of them fell into a conversation, leaving me with Sin, Roary and Ethan.

"Any chance you're going to be cluing me in on some more information any time soon, love?" Ethan asked, his gaze moving to the point where Sin was still holding my hand and his eyes narrowed. "Maybe we can talk while we have a moment alone down here?" He gave Roary and Sin a pointed *fuck off* look and my jaw tightened.

"What he means, kitten," Sin said, moving up close behind me and sweeping my hair back over my shoulder so that he could speak into my ear. "Is that he wants to fuck you down here in the dark."

"Of course he does," I replied scathingly. "Ethan only wants me where no one can see. I'm his greatest shame."

"You know it's not like that," Ethan protested as Roary growled and stepped between us.

"Then why are you acting like you're ashamed of her?" he snapped. "Rosalie deserves a mate who will stand up and tell the whole world how much he loves her, not a cowering creature like *you*."

"Why are you so interested in what me and my mate do?" Ethan snarled at him and Roary stepped forward like he would happily take him on. "Is it because you want her too, by any chance? Because I've seen the way you trail around after her like some desperate little snake-"

"I'm her *friend*," Roary growled. "And I won't let you treat her like shit."

I wasn't sure whether to be hurt or touched by that one, so I just held my tongue.

"A friend who wants to bone her," Sin chuckled, using my hand to spin me beneath his arm before tugging me close again and I smirked at him as I placed my hand on his chest and looked up into his mischievous eyes.

"You don't know what you're talking about," Roary snapped at him and Sin just laughed.

"Oh, I think I do. My magic reserves are currently being fed up nicely by the way the two of you are panting for our girl. Why don't you just stop wasting time on fighting and let's have a competition to find out which one of us can turn her on the most - which I will be able to judge accurately by the way."

"Get your fucking hands off of my mate, Incubus," Ethan snarled, trying to shove Roary aside so that he could get to Sin, but Roary shoved him right back again and the two of them bared their teeth at each other like they were about to throw down.

"I would if she wanted me to," Sin taunted, lifting my hand to his mouth and placing a kiss on the inside of my wrist that made a gasp escape me as heat spread along my flesh.

"You're such a shit stirrer," I accused and he just smirked at me like that title pleased him.

"I mean it!" Ethan yelled, lurching towards me again as Sin failed to release me and I made no move to escape him. He managed to push Roary aside so that he could grab me by the arm and I growled at him in a protest which he utterly ignored.

Ethan tugged me away from Sin and pushed me behind him before snarling at the other guys and baring his teeth. I had no doubt that if he could shift right now there would be a big ass black Wolf standing before me, guarding his property. And as much as I wanted to protest the idea of him claiming me without my agreement, I did kinda like the idea of the three of them fighting over me.

"Wait," I said, stepping forward and placing my hand on Ethan's arm and the three of them looked my way like they thought I was about to choose between them or something. "Can the three of you take your shirts off before you start fighting? And if anyone happens to have some baby oil with them..." I bit my lip at that idea and Sin offered up a dirty laugh before tearing his tank off and tossing it to the ground. Oh yes, this idea had some serious fucking merit to it.

"Anything for you, wild girl, just tell me the winner gets the first turn between your thighs and I'll lay these two fuckers out for you in five minutes flat."

"Unlikely," Roary growled, flexing his muscles as he glared at Sin but sadly kept his shirt on.

"Deal," I countered, tugging at Ethan's shirt in an attempt to drag it off of him and smirking at him as he turned to scowl at me.

"This isn't a joke," he growled, all alpha male and angry and my thighs clenched together at his tone.

"Then why don't you win and show them all who owns me, anima gemella?" I purred.

"I'm down for watching that," Sin agreed and I grinned.

"I'm not looking to fuck her or watch anyone else fucking her," Roary snapped and Sin just burst out laughing.

"Then you and your cock are in serious disagreement. Maybe the two of you need some couples counselling with that old Sheep Shifter in group therapy?"

Roary growled and I couldn't help but look his way, wondering why he was so determined to deny Sin's suggestions. I swear sometimes I felt the air burning between us with all the things I wished he'd do to me, and he was clearly feeling the lust aspect of that attraction. Of course, that really just meant the problem was with *me* specifically.

"It feels like this is ending in a four way whatever way we look at it and seeing as the Belorian might be on his way, we could just skip to the good bit," Sin suggested, winking at me.

"I'm okay with that," I agreed and Ethan snarled at me as Roary just kinda stared like I'd lost my damn mind.

"What?" I demanded because they were looking at me like they'd never had group sex before but I wasn't buying it. I mean, maybe none of them had had this ratio of girls to guys involved and I had to admit I hadn't either, but I was definitely okay with figuring out how best that could work. Especially as these three were my exact form of temptation. Was I down for an Alpha four way with all of that warring testosterone and rough treatment, the competition and rivalry and fighting for dominance? Well, duh, who wouldn't be?

"Stop fucking around, Rosalie, if you're trying to make me angry then congratulations - it's working. But I know I'm the only one you want. I feel the effects of this bond the same way you do," Ethan snapped.

"Erm, apparently not," I scoffed and Ethan turned to glare at me, forgetting the others for a moment.

"You're not seriously trying to say you want them, are you?" he demanded like it made no sense to him and I just shrugged.

"Look, this might surprise you, stronzo, but I'm not a precious little flower sitting around and crying because my moon chosen mate decided to reject me. You don't want me? Fine. But there are plenty more fish in the sea and I don't owe you shit after the way you've treated me."

Ethan opened his mouth like he wanted to argue against that, but Sin got there first. "What did you think would happen? That she would just sit around and pine for you? Grow the fuck up, asshole, it's like the girl said. There's plenty more dick in the sea."

"She said *fish*," Roary muttered like this whole conversation was pissing him off.

"She meant dick, though, I can tell - I'm an Incubus. Plus, I got the message loud and clear when she was sucking my-"

"What the fuck are you four doing down here?!" Cain bellowed and I snapped around as he skidded to a halt before us, whipping his shock baton from its holster and snarling at us.

"We were about to get naked," Sin explained. "So either strip down or fuck off, yeah?"

Wow, Sin was on point with the good ideas today. I mean, Cain could definitely still go take a long walk off a short pier as far as I was concerned, but if he wanted to make this party into a five way with a healthy dose of hate sex included, I might be convinced...

Cain's eyes flashed with rage and he struck Sin in the gut with a fierce blow from his baton, but at least he didn't power it up.

"I specifically took you back to your cell block, Twelve," he snarled, his gaze fixing on me. "And now I find you down here colluding with two of the prison's other gang leaders and *this* delinquent." He pointed at Sin who puffed his chest up like that was a compliment.

"Like Sin said, we met here for a hook up. It can be kinda hard to find somewhere appropriate seeing as we aren't all in the same cell block," I said with a shrug and his murderous gaze fell on me.

"Get back upstairs right now," he commanded the four of us. "The Belorian is about to be set loose to gather any stragglers, so unless you want to try your chances with it, you need to move."

Ethan growled angrily, glaring between me and Sin like he couldn't decide if he believed what Sin had just been saying or not and I offered him a smirk just to piss him off. Why the hell shouldn't I be hooking up with Sin anyway? Just because the moon said I was *his*? Please, if I spent my life letting fate decide my life for me, I'd be dead and buried a long time ago. And it certainly wasn't like I loved Ethan – I barely even knew him, so he was just going to have to suck it up if he didn't like it. Or make a play to lock me down if he wanted me to stop. He stalked away without another word and Sin sighed dramatically as the rest of us turned to follow.

Cain stayed close on our heels like a snarling bulldog, making sure that first Ethan and then Sin headed into their cell blocks before marching me and Roary back to ours. But as Roary crossed the bridge to head inside, Cain caught my arm and tugged me back.

"We need to have a word, Twelve," he growled, his fingers

digging in as he nodded to Officer Rind to make sure that Roary didn't attempt to follow us.

"I really have no interest in-" Cain whipped me off of my feet for the second time tonight and I cursed as he raced away through the prison.

When he reached the door to the isolation unit, I sucked in a breath of dread and began kicking and yelling, trying to fight my way out of his arms as he unlocked the heavy door and stepped inside.

Cain shot through the space between the cells and all the way along to the stairs which led down to the maintenance level below. When he finally set me back down on my feet again, I was trembling with rage and fear and I backed up a step before spitting on the floor at his feet.

"Pezzo di merda," I snarled. *Piece of shit.*

Cain arched a brow at me and then lifted his radio from his belt and called the warden.

"The prison is clear, release the Belorian," he said calmly and I shot a look at his watch, seeing as there wasn't a clock down here for me to check, taking note of the time. An hour. Almost exactly. That was how long we would have from the beginning of the riot until they set the beast loose to hunt down stragglers.

"Have you even taken the count?" I asked as he hung the radio back on his belt and surveyed me cautiously.

"No. In the event of a riot, we disband the troublemakers and send them all back to their cell blocks and then we lock the doors and set the Belorian loose while we do the count," he said with a dark smile. "Anyone foolish enough to have hidden from the guards will find themselves prey to the monster that roams the halls."

"Nice to know you're so concerned about that," I snipped.

"I don't know how many times this needs to be made clear to you, Twelve, but no one cares about you down here. We don't care if you kill each other, we don't care if the Belorian eats you, we don't care if you kill yourselves. You're nothing but a

276

burden on society and it's up to you to Fae up and survive this place until your term is over, not ours to babysit you. We are here to make sure none of you escape, not to worry ourselves about whether or not you live full and happy lives. You lost that right the moment you were sentenced."

"Fine. So why do I now have the displeasure of your company while the Belorian roams the halls?" I drawled, folding my arms.

"Because I know you were up to something tonight. I don't believe the story about the four of you meeting up to fuck in a corridor. And I'm getting really fucking sick of your lies. So I want the truth. Why were you down there after I specifically told you to go back to your cell?"

I pursed my lips, wanting to tell him that he could shove his questions up his ass, but he was taking far too much interest in me all the damn time and I needed to give him something. Something real, too, because I knew I'd already passed his threshold for my bullshit.

"Come here," I said, holding my hand out to him and he eyed it like it was laced with poison.

"Why?"

"Because I need to show you, or you won't believe me." I tilted my head so that my hair fell forward over my shoulder and he reluctantly moved into my personal space.

I smirked at him as I took his hand and lifted it to my face before tracing his fingers over the moon mark behind my ear.

"What is that?" he asked.

"If two equally matched Wolves fuck beneath a full moon, then the moon can choose to mate them," I breathed, looking up at him as he stood so close to me that I couldn't see anything else aside from him. "A few months ago, I made a mistake with Ethan Shadowbrook..."

"*What?*" Cain snatched his hand back like the mark had burned him. "No. How? You hate each other."

"Funny how often hate and lust can keep company," I purred.

"So you were meeting One?" he asked, a look of disgust passing over his features. "Then why were the others down there too?"

I sighed, not really wanting to risk a lie so I changed tack instead. "If I tell you about something that happened to me on my way down to meet him, can I trust you to keep it secret?" I asked.

"Why would you trust me? I thought you hated me?" he grunted.

"Oh, I do," I agreed icily. "But I can't ask anyone else to help me with this."

"Help you?" Cain took a step back, shaking his head. "I'm not falling for one of your games."

"Fine. I'll deal with it myself," I spat, turning my back on him and stalking away through the machinery that filled the space down here.

He didn't follow me at first and I made it all the way to the doorway that led into the storage area before he shot to my side and caught my arm to halt me.

"Spit it out then," he growled, looking suspicious as fuck.

"On one condition," I countered, raising my chin and trying not to smirk, because if he agreed to this then I knew I still had him.

"What?"

"You have to bite me," I said simply.

Cain flinched like I'd struck him, shaking his head as he took a step back. "No." But the hungry look in his eyes gave away his desire to do it.

"What's the matter, boss man, don't you want me anymore?" I asked him in a mocking tone.

"Why would you want me to bite you now?" he growled.

"Maybe I enjoy it," I replied, my lips twitching because that was actually true.

"And what else?" he asked, seeing straight through me. I liked it when he did that even if it was irritating as fuck sometimes too.

"And...I don't want you to be able to share this memory with

278

anyone. I'm not a snitch so I'm going to tell you this in confidence and I don't want any chance of you trying to make it official or anything like that. If you want the truth from my lips then you'll have to wet yours with my blood. Come on, boss man, be bad for me, you know I won't tell."

Cain narrowed his eyes on me and I flashed him a challenging smirk before turning and running.

I darted into the storeroom, turned the corner and he was on me before I could take another step, gripping my wrist and spinning me back around to face him. He caught my other wrist in his grip too and pinned them to the wall above my head before leaning in and sinking his fangs into my neck.

The groan that escaped him sent a flood of heat rushing down my spine and my fingers curled into fists as his body pressed to mine and my back arched against him. There must have been something in his venom that turned me on because I absolutely refused to believe I was hot for this asshole. But I swear, I'd actually missed the feeling of his fangs sinking into my flesh, the rush I got from trying to escape him and the exhilaration of knowing I was at his mercy once he had me. I'd even had dreams about it that woke me up aching and panting, not that I'd ever admit it to him.

He didn't hold back, drinking deeply until I felt like my knees might buckle and a soft moan escaped me as the strength began to leave my body.

Cain's grip on my wrists slid up to my hands and his fingers wound through mine as he held me there and as he slowly withdrew his fangs from my neck, I sighed in relief, like a weight had just been lifted from me.

His tongue swept across the wound as he devoured the final drops of blood, but as he pulled back, he didn't release me, instead looking into my eyes like he was searching for something as he slowly drew our clasped hands back down to my sides.

I held his gaze, all the hate and contempt I felt for him shining clearly for him to see, but there was something else, too, that hurt he'd left me with when he'd thrown me down into the dark and forgotten all about me.

He looked like he had something to say to me, but I found I didn't want to hear it.

"Out of interest, do all of the guards demand sexual favours in return for protection in here, or is that just Nixon?" I asked, cutting to the point of this little exchange as I tugged my hands back out of his to try and put some distance between us.

"What?" Cain demanded, taking a step closer to me so that we were almost pressed together again.

"It's just that you spout such shit about everyone in orange being worthless scumbags, so it seems a little hypocritical to me if that's common practice amongst the Fae in uniform."

"Tell me what he did to you," Cain snarled and there was a wild kind of fury in his gaze that made my heart race as he looked at me, like he would tear the fucking world down for me and would kill that son of a bitch if I said he'd laid a hand on me. But that didn't make any sense. Cain hated me. He'd more than proven it. So why did I feel like I owned him in that moment?

"Nothing," I breathed. "Though not for lack of trying. He caught me heading downstairs and used his magic to haul me into the gym. Then he forced me to my knees and gave me the choice of going to the hole or sucking his filthy, little cock."

"So why aren't you in the hole?" Cain demanded furiously.

"Because I stole his shock baton and delivered a thousand volts directly to his dick in answer to his proposition," I replied with a twisted smile. I hoped it had fried the thing so thoroughly that it couldn't be healed, but I doubted I'd gotten that lucky. "I'm only telling you because I want to know if you'll make sure he doesn't throw me back down in the dark in retaliation and as my CO, I'm guessing you can make sure he can't."

Cain gripped my jaw between his hands, looking me right in the eye as he spoke. "He won't come near you again. I swear it to you. He won't so much as dare to fucking look at you after I'm through with him."

My lips parted in surprise at the heat in his words and the

utter rage in his eyes. I didn't know what to make of it or how I was supposed to feel about it, but my gaze fell to his mouth and for a moment of complete and utter insanity, I almost wanted to-

"The Belorian has returned to its cage. All officers, please complete the count asap so that we can do a casualty assessment and write up the incident report," Warden Pike's voice came over the radio at Cain's hip and he jerked away from me like he'd been burned as he pulled it from his belt.

"Copy that," Cain replied, before shoving the radio away again and quickly healing the bite on my neck.

He hoisted me into his arms without another word and shot back out of the maintenance area before heading up to isolation, passing through the security doors and then speeding all the way back to my cell block. Once we were inside, he ran me up to my cell, barking into the radio to get the door open for me before placing me down inside.

Cain held my gaze as the barred door slid closed between us again and a frown pinched at my brow as I tried to figure out what the hell had just happened between us. He shot away, leaving me to wonder and Roary's voice pulled me out of my thoughts.

"You okay, little pup?" he called from his cell.

"Never better," I agreed, flopping down onto my bed and banishing thoughts of Vampires with dark eyes and deep secrets. I had bigger fish to fry anyway. "One hour, Roar," I added, talking about how long we would have before the Belorian came hunting.

"Will it be enough?" he asked.

"Let's hope so."

ARIES. VAMPIRE. FIRE.
COMMANDING OFFICER
CAIN
DARKMORE
PENITENTIARY

Blood was pounding hard and fast through my veins. I could still taste Rosalie on my tongue and feel the magic I'd taken from her fizzling through me. I was high on her. But I was also angry as all hell.

My fangs were still sharp in my mouth as I shot along the corridors, racing downstairs to the gymnasium. It was quiet as I slowed outside the door and I cracked my neck before shoving it open, hearing groans and whimpers from somewhere close by.

I hit a solid air shield barring my way forward and cursed, slamming a hand against it.

"Hey, Nixon! You in here?" I snarled, fighting to keep the rage from my tone.

The changing room door pushed open and Nixon hobbled out, his pants burned off around his crotch and his hands cupped over his fried junk.

"H-help me," he stammered and the air shield fell away in front of me. "The Belorian showed up and I-I had to fight it off. I could only h-half heal myself and now I'm out of magic."

"What happened?" I strode toward him at a slow pace, my voice dropping an octave as I savoured his pain. I wanted to see if he'd own up to what he'd done, to see if I needed to add lying to the list of crimes I was going to punish him for.

"That little whore assigned to you – the Wolf girl, Twelve – she fucking attacked me," he said passionately, anger in his eyes. "We need to punish her, Cain. Fucking *destroy* her for this."

The last of my resolve vanished in the blink of an eye and I shot towards him in a blur, knocking him back through the door forcefully so he crashed onto his ass in the changing room while I stalked after him and kicked the door shut.

He gasped in alarm, throwing up his hands to hold me back, but no magic came out. His charred junk came into view and I lifted my foot, slamming my boot down on his crotch and crushing his cock and balls beneath my heel, making him scream like a fucking baby. I flicked my fingers, raising a silencing bubble so the rest of his screams remained contained as I pressed my weight down harder, my upper lip pulled back in a sneer.

"Lie to me again," I growled, the monster in me taking over. "I dare you to."

"Mason, *stop*," he croaked like the toad he was. The guy rarely spoke a word to me or I to him. We weren't friends. I wasn't going to pity him. And if he was appealing to my better nature, he was about to discover that I didn't have one.

I twisted my ankle, crushing his junk harder as I thought of him trying to abuse Rosalie.

"What are you doing?!" he wailed, clutching my leg as he tried to fight me off. But with his magic tapped out and my Vampire strength thrumming powerfully in my veins, he could do fuck all to stop me. Except shift into his Order form. But shifting into a Toad wouldn't stop me from choking the motherfucker and I could do even more damage if I stomped on him in that form.

I grabbed his neck, taking my foot off of his groin and lifting him up, slamming him against the wall above me with one hand so his feet kicked and jerked off the ground. I punched him solidly in the face, then again to drive the message home, relishing the feeling of my knuckles splitting with the blow.

"You ever touch Rosalie Oscura again, and I'll kill you. And if you wanna go to the warden about my threat, then I'll request a Cyclops interrogation to prove what you did to her and what you tried to do to her. Do you understand me?"

He was turning blue as my hand locked tighter around his thick neck and the scent of his zapped dick was making my nose wrinkle in disgust.

His skin started to seep with a thick, green gloop, one of his Order gifts releasing the pungent sludge that could poison me if it got on my skin. I let him go before it touched me, and he crashed to the floor in a crumpled heap at my feet. He curled up in a ball, croaking feebly as the slime coated his bald head in an effort to protect him better. He was fucking pathetic.

"Why do you care about h-her?" he stammered, and I noted he hadn't answered me.

Fire blazed to life in my hands and I leaned down, grabbing his face in my palms which was currently still clean of the toad slime and forcing him to look at me while he screamed once more, thrashing and fighting as my power seared the flesh from his skin.

"Answer me!" I bellowed, desperate to kill this rat, this *scum*. He'd laid his hands on her, forced her to her knees beneath him like she was some common street whore. She was a goddess, a fucking queen. I didn't know when I'd realised that, but I knew it in the depths of my soul and I wouldn't let this piece of shit get away with disrespecting her.

I kicked him forcefully in the side and he was thrown across the floor, curling in on himself as he hit a row of lockers. "I w-won't touch her."

"She doesn't exist to you," I said icily. "You don't see her, you don't touch her, you don't even fucking think about her."

He nodded, clutching his bloody face as he whimpered in pain and I snatched his arm, keeping my hand clamped over his sleeve as I hauled him to the sink and rinsed his hand of the slime before taking hold of it in an iron grip.

"Swear on the stars not to speak of this," I demanded.

"I won't tell anyone," he rasped fearfully and magic rang between us.

I dropped his hand and let him suffer for a few moments

longer, savouring his agony as I thought of what he'd tried to make my girl do. Fuck, *my* girl? Since when was she my girl? She wasn't my anything. She hated me. She'd cursed me. She was mated to fucking Shadowbrook.

I noticed the curse mark was thrumming in time with my pulse, warmth spreading out from it that felt like liquid sunshine in my veins. It felt like her. It felt like everything I'd been missing my entire life. But it couldn't be that. Because she didn't belong to me and she never would.

I lowered down to a crouch before the pathetic creature beneath me, my fangs bared. The scent of his blood was like piss in comparison to Twelve's. There was zero desire in me to taste it. I wanted to spill more of it though. All of it. Paint this whole room red with his death and make him hurt so deeply that he'd be in pain even beyond the veil.

I drew in a long breath, watching him squirm with no ounce of pity in me. I felt nothing but disgust and rage, the two emotions coiling into a storm inside me. But I couldn't let myself fall too deeply into it. I had to keep my head. Killing him wasn't an option. And I couldn't hand him over to Pike either. She'd question Rosalie, get a Cyclops to check the truth of her words and if they saw her memories, they could also see me in them too. See all the rules I'd broken, see the way I'd touched her, bitten her.

Bile flooded my tongue as I wondered if I was as revolting as the cretin cowering before me. Did I also deserve his fate for touching her myself? She'd encouraged it though, it wasn't like I'd taken anything from her she hadn't wanted. But I was in a position of power. I was supposed to be better. But I'd also never claimed to be. I'd been biting strong inmates for years before she'd arrived. Only with her it never felt like I was doing it just to take her blood and punish her. I'd ached for the press of her body against mine too. I'd let my hands roam, I'd longed for her mouth, yearned to feel my cock inside her. It was wrong. And it made me like *him*.

I reached out, pressing the very tips of my fingers to a clean space on the back of Nixon's neck, allowing healing magic to flow into him. I had to hide the evidence now, even though healing him made me sick. But there was no other way.

I stood up when it was done and he gazed at me, panting heavily, his eyes wide. I turned my back on him, striding over to the sink and rinsing my hands of his blood, the insult of a Vampire washing it away enough to make him gasp. Then I turned my back on him and strode from the room, letting the door swing shut behind me and disbanding the silencing bubble as I went.

I wasn't done drawing blood today. My monster was unleashed now, so it was time to put it to good use.

***

Midnight came and went and I left the guards' quarters in my uniform. It wasn't my shift, but I'd worn it to cover my ass if anyone saw me. No one ever questioned me taking on extra hours. It was a habit most people expected of me. Besides, the only one who gave a damn about what I got up to was Hastings and he was currently tucked up in his bed for the night.

I'd spent the evening alone after my shift had ended, my rage not having dulled even a little bit. I kept thinking of Nixon touching Rosalie and anger would burn through every inch of me all over again. I wanted to annihilate him for that single act. The possessiveness I felt over her was a headfuck of its own. I didn't know what to do with all of these *feelings*.

I was used to being angry, but not jealous. When I'd seen her down by the Fate Room with Shadowbrook, Night and fucking Wilder, I'd wanted to tear her away from them all and never let her near them again. But this had to stop. I didn't own her. I didn't have a right to stop her being with whoever she wanted. Especially someone she was fucking mated to. By the stars, how could the moon have mated those two? They were sworn enemies and not only that, but fuck Ethan Shadowbrook. I despised him. Envied him. Wanted to cut out his heart and hold it up to the moon to show her what I thought of her fucking mate bond. But I couldn't do that. Rosalie wasn't mine and never would be.

So why did I ache for her to want me too? Why couldn't I stop thinking about ways to get her alone, to try and make amends for all the bad shit between us? Make her see that I was capable of being good to her. That I painfully regretted leaving her in the hole all that time.

But maybe she was just getting back in my head again. Maybe this was just another game she was playing. Maybe I really was just a fucking idiot who was pussy whipped over a pussy I'd never even had. Maybe she'd snuck under my skin again and was puppeteering everything I did, everything I *felt*.

But when I'd spoken with her down on the maintenance level, I'd been sure she'd told the truth for once. I could sense the difference, I'd been certain this time. Then again, maybe I really was just a fucking moron living on a damn dream.

I rubbed my eyes as I headed down in the elevator to level eight. Violence would help settle this untamed creature in me tonight. Then tomorrow, I'd wake and I'd be back in control. I'd be able to fight away these strange emotions and bury them deep. Twelve wasn't for me. But for now, we had one particular goal we shared and I wanted to dig deeper into it. For me, for her. For every inmate who was dragged down into Psych and ended up burning in the incinerator for it after. Burned by *me*.

I'd played a part in whatever was going on down here. Done my duty. Burned the bodies who were laid out to be destroyed each week. It wasn't a pretty job, but Fae corpses had to be burned or else their power remained in their bones and that magic could be stolen if it got into the wrong hands. Part of me had always thought of it as the only way a lot of the unfortunate assholes in this place ever got free, pumped out of a chimney into the sky.

I could accept burning the bodies of those who died because of another inmate or a magical accident, but I'd never signed up to destroy the evidence of those killed by the workers here. And I wasn't going to keep blindly following orders and covering up whatever dark shit they were up to.

I strode down the empty corridor toward Psych, checking my watch before moving into an alcove and shrinking back into the shadows. I was a predator waiting for his prey, my breaths coming faster as the thrill of the hunt made my pulse race. It was just a few more minutes before a door opened at the end of the corridor and I waited for my mark to walk by.

Janice Cunning was one of the lead doctors in Psych and if anyone was sure to know everything about what was going on in there, it was her. I knew her schedule by heart. I'd come down here plenty of times, trying to get in, trying to find out more information. And tonight I wasn't going to hold back. It was time I unveiled the truth.

The sound of her heels clicking along the floor made my fingers tingle with magic and my fangs lengthen. I wouldn't be biting her though. I'd had a feed today which no other could match. And Janice Cunning didn't appeal.

She walked past me in her white doctor's coat and I sped out of my hiding place, as silent as the wind as I raced up behind her, cupped my hand over her mouth and lifted her off the ground. I ran with her as she thrashed and kicked, her scream muffled against my palm. Her wings burst from her back and tore through her coat as she tried to shift into her Harpy form. I cursed as I adjusted my arm around her, locking her wings down as she fought furiously. She was strong, but I was stronger. Angrier. More determined. She wouldn't fight me off.

I reached the ninth level and kicked open the door to Quentin's little torture room, throwing her to the floor. He pounced on her with a squeal of glee, jamming a gas mask over her face as she thrashed and I leapt forward to help hold her still. Her wings dissolved to nothing as she cursed and kicked, the Order Suppressant stealing away her ability to shift and as Quentin locked two magic blocking cuffs on her wrists, she was totally incapacitated. He'd known I was coming; I'd bought his silence.

I lifted her up, dumping her on the hospital bed at the heart of the room as she screamed.

"What are you doing?!" she begged, her blue eyes wide as she stared at me in recognition, confusion and fear. I helped Quentin strap her in place on the bed, tightening the chains until she yelped.

Quentin cast a silencing bubble, chuckling demonically to himself as he moved to lock the door. He looked to me, wetting his lips as his eyes gleamed with excitement. He was nearly half my height, his back was hunched, his eyes bright red and his teeth sharpened to points, all features he'd altered himself by magic. Because he liked being a scary motherfucker, I guessed. And it worked. The guy creeped the fucking shit out of me, but I'd needed his help and he'd agreed. I knew he wouldn't be able to pass up the chance to torture someone. That was just the kind of twisted little freak he was.

"The money?" he purred and I reached into my pocket, taking out a roll of auras and tossing it to him.

He licked his lips again as he placed it down on the side then moved up onto a step beside the bed so he was looking down at Janice.

"You're going to spill all your little secrets, Janice," he sing-songed in his too-high, nasally voice.

I moved to lean against a counter which was teeming with all kinds of magical torture devices, and some non-magical ones too like drills, blades and bone saws. I wasn't squeamish, but I had paid Quentin for specific services here. I wasn't looking to attend one of his horror shows. This was purely business. Of course, that didn't mean he wasn't going to hurt her.

I took my Atlas from my pocket, setting it up to record as Quentin cast a spell over Janice's lips and sealed them together, silencing her screams.

"Shhh, young Janice," he whispered and she blinked back tears, looking to me in fear and accusation.

But maybe she shouldn't have been such a shady psycho

bitch and I wouldn't have had to resort to this. She'd refused to talk to me plenty of times and now that Twelve had seen what was going on in her funhouse, I wasn't going to feel bad about handing her over to Quentin. It took a lot to make me feel bad about anything, and this did not make the list.

"You're going to stop screaming now," Quentin said. "Aren't you?"

Janice nodded as a tear ran down into her hair and I gritted my jaw, hungry for the truth to spill from her lips. Quentin unsealed her mouth and she sucked in a shaky breath.

"W-what do you want?" she stuttered as Quentin's long fingers caressed her neck.

"We want to know what exactly it is you're doing down in Psych," he said almost soothingly and she tensed up.

"I-I can't," she rasped. "I'm not allowed to-"

"You will talk, baby bird," Quentin cut her off. "You will give me all your secrets."

"*No*," she growled, yanking against her restraints as Quentin got down off his step and hummed under his breath as he moved to a trolley full of tools closer to the bed. He reached down for something, picking up a small metal pot and I frowned. *What the fuck is that?*

Janice looked to me in desperation. "You can't do this to me. Please, *help* me."

I remained silent, saying absolutely nothing that would incriminate me on this video. I wasn't stupid enough to think this shit couldn't get me thrown into prison with the inmates I guarded all day. But I was going to get my fucking admission from her no matter what it took.

Quentin moved back onto his step, opening her coat and pulling her shirt up before placing the pot down on her bare stomach. I frowned as he twisted the lid off, unsure what to expect. Then heaps of thin, black Fire Acid Slugs crawled out and immediately started burrowing into her flesh like they were starved. Janice screamed as they slithered all over her body and I clenched my jaw as I watched, waiting for her screams to turn to words and for her to start telling us everything. Because fuck. That. Shit.

"No – please – stop!" she begged as the monstrous little creatures started eating her with sharp teeth.

"Tell us what you do down there, Janice," Quentin asked, looking like he was getting high off of her pain as he watched her writhe and scream.

Little pools of blood were forming all over her where some of the creatures had disappeared into her body and she looked close to blacking out as she stared at them too.

"I won't," she panted then screamed again, tipping her head back. "I'll never tell you!"

Quentin smiled like it pleased him that she was refusing and I pursed my lips impatiently. He tapped the pot with his finger and a dark blue light shone from it before all the slugs started slithering back into it. They crawled out of her flesh and returned to the pot then Quentin screwed the lid on and put them back on his trolley of torture devices.

I watched as he tried method after method to make her talk, healing her after he'd made her bleed again and again. A sheen of sweat formed on her brow as she was hurt in unspeakable ways, but still she didn't give up the answer.

"Well then," Quentin purred at last, looking to me. "It seems Cyclops interrogation is the only way, Officer."

It may have seemed like the torture was unnecessary when all he really needed to do to search inside her mind for the answers was to use his Order gifts, but in fact for most Cyclopses, they couldn't just break through another Fae's mental shields and steal all of their secrets. There were a few particularly strong Cyclopses like that scumbag Gustard who could do that, but for most of their kind like Quentin, they needed to weaken the victim's mind before entering it if they wanted to get to the information that was being hidden.

We really could have done with a stronger Cyclops working here, but they were few and far between and none of them would settle for the low pay and long hours down here in the dark so we'd had to put up with Quentin instead. At least he was creative in his torture methods, so I was fairly certain that he was able to break down the mental shields of most Fae before entering their minds with his gifts. There was always the chance that the strongest inmates might still be able to withhold information from him, but it was the best we could do.

I switched the camera off, placing my Atlas down with a snarl. "She needs to say it out loud."

"Perhaps once we see the truth in her mind, she will speak more freely," Quentin suggested and I sighed, scraping a hand over my hair. I needed this video as evidence. If she didn't admit the truth out loud, I would have nothing to send the FIB to investigate this. Quentin was using a concealment spell that meant he couldn't be identified in the video; if she would just admit it, I could expose Darkmore's dirty secret and be done with it. But there was more at play here stopping her from saying the words. And I needed to confirm my suspicions.

I strode toward Quentin, offering him my hand so he could show me the memories while he used his Order gifts on her. I didn't like the creep touching me, but it was the least of the sacrifices I was making to get answers.

His slim fingers clutched mine and his eyes slowly slid together until they were one, large entity at the centre of his face. Then he reached toward Janice whose eyes were full of fear as she jerked against her restraints once more. But it was no good. And as Quentin's hand pressed to her forehead, she fell still a moment before my mind went dark.

I was no longer standing in that room, but hanging in an abyss while disjointed memories tore through my head. I tried to make sense of them and I felt Quentin's power slowly mould them into order, playing them out in my head like they were my own memories. I only had to urge my mind towards one and I could view it as if I was there, seeing it through Janice's eyes.

She was shaking hands with the warden, magic sparking between their palms before she signed a contract on her desk.

Then the memory changed and she was pulling on scrubs, walking into a surgery among other doctors and nurses.

She was looking down at a man strapped to a table as he jerked against his binds, his chest carved open as light poured out of him and into a large glass jar, channelled there by some strange metal object that was glittering with a dark and ominous magic. Sickness clutched my gut as that light was torn free from the man's body by the scalpel as Janice cut through it, carving away the strange, ethereal matter that connected it to him. To his soul. To his very being. Then as soon as the jar was sealed, he started convulsing and everyone in the room ran forward to heal him, his chest stitching back together, but he was still jerking and his eyes were rolling back into his head as he screamed. And finally, he fell deathly still.

Janice drew her hands away from him with a curse, turning to note down the loss on a clipboard. A number struck out. Three hundred and eight.

Then she waved her hand and the man was wheeled from the room before another one was brought in.

The memory faded once more and I was drawn into another one as Quentin guided me into it. I was looking through Janice's eyes into a glass chamber where a girl with pink hair was strapped to a chair. My gut tightened as I recognised her as one of the inmates who'd lost their minds in this place recently. But she didn't seem crazy now, she just seemed...absent. Her eyes were hollow and I could tell that a vital part of her was missing. Whatever that light was that had been taken from the man who'd died, it had been taken from her too. She may have survived, but it didn't look like her soul had been left intact.

A fierce anger filled me as I watched a nurse stride into the room with a jar of light clasped in her hands. Janice followed her into the room and moved to stand in front of the pink haired girl, gazing down into her dead eyes.

"What was she before?" Janice asked the nurse who checked an Atlas in her palm.

"A Vampire," she replied and my jaw tightened.

Janice nodded and took a scalpel from a trolley beside the inmate and started slicing slim, shallow cuts across her wrists, the crook of her elbows, her neck, her temples, her ankles. Then she took the jar from the nurse and laid it in the girl's lap, firmly twisting it to open the lid. The light immediately filtered out like it was a living thing with a mind of its own; it shifted and writhed and seemed to search for something as it drifted across the girl's body. As it reached her cuts, it slowly slipped inside her and the girl gasped, her eyes brightening as her head snapped back.

"That's it," Janice urged hopefully. "Accept the new sensation. You're a Werewolf now. Can you feel the change?"

The girl just gargled and shock rippled through me as I realised what was happening. What those jars were. What had been done to this girl.

Fur spread across her skin and she screamed as her mouth and nose extended into a snout and razor sharp teeth filled her jaw. The shift was slow and looked tortuous as she fought against it, the fur drawing in again as she shook her head and sobbed.

"That's not me. It's not me," she begged. "Please take it away."

"Accept it, stop fighting," Janice growled, taking a handful of her hair and yanking her head back. I could feel her anticipation, her hope, her thoughts racing through my head. Their experiments had never gotten this far before. It had always failed until now.

The girl started screaming in a way that made my heart bunch up in my chest. She shook her head, convulsing and going limp in the chair.

"Stabilise her!" Janice commanded and the nurse rushed forward with a syringe, injecting it into the girl's neck.

But she didn't stop jerking, her hands shifted into paws, her eyes bulging, then blood spilled from her nose and she stopped convulsing. Her eyes stared lifelessly up at Janice. And the bitch just tutted.

"We'll try again tomorrow," she growled then the visions faded altogether and suddenly I was standing back in that room, my eyes locking with Quentin's. Janice was unconscious as Quentin kept her under his spell and the usually unshakeable guy looked at me with the colour draining from his face.

"They're...taking the inmates' Orders away?" he rasped and I nodded stiffly, my throat burning, my stomach knotting. I released his hand, backing away, swiping a palm over my face as I tried to process what I'd seen.

Pike was responsible for this. She'd organised the whole thing. Hired Janice. She must have known what was happening down there this whole time. That they were ripping out people's Orders and trying to force them to accept another that wasn't theirs. It defied the stars. Defied all Fae laws. It was repugnant, vile.

Quentin heaved and I looked over at him in surprise. For all the sick things he did in this room, this was the first one I'd ever seen him unable to stomach.

"What are you gonna do?" he asked me as my breaths came unevenly. My mind snagged on Rosalie as fear carved a path through my chest. She'd gone down there, risked being caught. What if they'd found her? What if they'd done that to her? Cut out her Wolf? Forced it on another Fae and tried to make her something...else. I snarled ferociously, pacing back and forth, fighting the base urge to tear Janice's head off. But I had to keep calm. Had to figure this out.

"She won't say this on camera," I finally said in realisation. Janice had made a star deal with Pike. If she spoke the truth out loud, she'd be cursed with seven years of bad luck. Pike would feel the deal breaking. And I had the feeling that my boss was far more dangerous than I had ever realised. Crossing her would not end well. Janice's resilience to Quentin's torture proved that. She'd rather bleed in here than end up at Pike's mercy.

I drew in a deep breath through my nose then strode over to the medicine cabinet across the room where Quentin kept his poisons.

"What are you doing?" he asked as I found what I wanted, taking the memory erasing potion into my grasp. I opened it, walking over to Janice and prising her lips apart to pour it in.

"Wait," Quentin said urgently, catching my arm and I growled in warning. "She'll vomit when she wakes."

I nodded, grunting irritably and standing back so he could release her from his power, his eyes sliding back into one for a moment as he did so. She reared up, vomiting onto the floor and Quentin grabbed a hose, washing it down the drain that sat beneath the bed, eerily quiet as he worked.

Janice blinked a few times, glancing between us in horror as she realised what we knew.

I strode toward her, fisting her dark blonde hair in my hand and yanking her head back hard.

"Please!" she begged. "Don't kill me."

"You deserve the worst death I can dream up," I growled in her face, my upper lip peeled back to reveal my fangs. "I'd cut off every one of your limbs and toss you to the psychos in this place to finish the job."

"B-but you won't, right?" she asked shakily and I could practically taste her fear.

I let a long pause stretch between us to draw out that terror in her then shook my head.

"No," I agreed. "Not today. But your death is coming. I promise you that."

I ripped her head back harder and brought the memory erasing potion to her lips, pouring a healthy measure down her throat which would destroy a few hours of memory, enough that she would have no recollection of me bringing her here.

Her eyes became dazed and Quentin appeared, ready with a sedative as he slipped the needle into her neck. She cursed me as she passed out and I let her slump back onto the bed, having the urge to wipe my hands off after touching this vile bitch. Quentin unlocked the magic cuffs on her wrists, his breaths coming heavily.

I turned to him and he backed up as he saw the decision in my eyes, shaking his head.

"I've served you well!" he protested, knocking over his trolley as he tried to escape. But I shot at him with my speed, locking my hand around his throat and forcing his head back before pouring the potion down his throat too. His eyes went blank and I shoved him across the room, shooting away from him and unlocking Janice from the bed, throwing her over my shoulder.

I snatched my Atlas and the money I'd paid Quentin as I left the room and raced back upstairs to Psych. I left her in the corridor where she was already stirring, the dose of sedative obviously low enough that it hadn't completely knocked her out. I was gone before she opened her eyes, all evidence of what I'd done destroyed apart from the video on my Atlas. I promptly deleted it as I made it upstairs. It didn't serve me. Only the truth locked in her head did. But unless I could convince the FIB to investigate her or one of the other assholes who worked down there, even that knowledge was useless.

As I pushed into my bedroom and stripped off my uniform to take a shower, I was filled with the unshakeable urge to go to Rosalie. To see that she was alright, still sleeping soundly in her bed. And by the time I'd done washing, the curse mark on my arm was throbbing as if begging me to follow through on that need. But I had no good reason to go marching down to her cell block and charging in there. The other guards would think I'd lost my damn mind and I didn't need to draw attention to myself.

I sighed, drying myself off and pulling on a pair of boxers as I stepped back into my room. It was cold and bare and felt like the last place I wanted to be in the world. But I always felt this way here. And the problem wasn't the room. It was being alone with myself.

As I fell into bed, trying to fight away the sickness over what I'd learned tonight, the curse turned on me once more. And I was dragged down into a sleep full of my past, returning to face

the man who'd raised me as a monster. My personal nightmare.
Benjamin Acrux.

I sat in group therapy, bored to fucking tears as Sparkle stood on the far side of the circle telling her story while holding the Stick of Truth. Mrs Gambol had produced it with a flourish at the start of today's session, claiming it was a branch from a pixie tree and had been blessed with a truth spell by Faerial the Great. Seeing as I was like eighty percent certain that Faerial the Great was nothing more than a bedtime story for kids, I had my doubts. If he had been real, I also firmly believed he was an idiota because the story of his death had always annoyed the hell out of me even if a bunch of the other stuff he was supposed to have done was pretty impressive.

Long story short, Faerial the Great was a Phoenix Shifter who had lived a few hundred years ago and during his lifetime he'd been responsible for coming up with all sorts of spells and creating countless magical artefacts. He'd supposedly used his Phoenix fire in never before tried ways as well as using his Elemental magic for things no one had ever considered before either. The man was a genius – assuming he really was responsible for the discovery of half of the things he'd been credited with – but as happened with a lot of great Fae, he'd clearly begun to believe in himself too much.

I'd read several books on him, gaining something of an obsession with him after I'd discovered that I was a Moon Wolf because Phoenixes had a lot of strange gifts too and I couldn't find much on my own kind to study. But Faerial had done something so stupid that I seriously had to question the sanity of the people who still hailed him as one of the greatest Fae of all time. He'd taken a trip to the mortal world using stardust and had travelled around, seeking out the myths and legends that the mortals believed were true about Phoenixes before coming back to the Fae realm and trying to find evidence of them being correct.

He'd dedicated ten years of his life to trying to prove that Phoenix tears could heal anything, especially wounds that no other healing magic could combat or fatal Fae illnesses no healer could fix. But he was wrong. Fuck knows how much crying he did and how many desperate fuckers had to drink his tears/have them sprinkled over them/dance in them and countless other nonsense he attempted, but eventually he had to admit that they were just tears. No miracles included. At which point I would have assumed that he'd have just accepted that mortals really had no fucking idea what they were talking about when it came to Fae powers, but of course he didn't.

He became obsessed with the idea that he could become immortal, believing wholeheartedly that he could be reborn in flames. So, after years of study and theories and tests, Faerial the Great summoned a court of over five hundred people to come and watch him die and be reborn. He cast a huge pyre of Phoenix flames and then stood beside them and thrust a sun steel blade straight into his own heart. Well, he died alright. And then he fell back into the flames which he had been certain would give him life again...and they burned his body to a crisp. Turns out dead Phoenixes could burn and everything. It was lamented as this tragic loss in the name of science, but all it said to me was that he had been fruit loop crazy and wanted to believe in fairy tales way too much. There wasn't some magic cure to death even in a world with magic and even if you happened to be a badass Phoenix. It sucked, but life was a bitch and there were no easy ways out, I'd learned that the hard way.

That said, so far the Stick of Truth had been getting some truly tedious truths out of my fellow inmates so perhaps there was some merit to the magic it held regardless of its dubious history. I guessed he did get some stuff right before he went off his rocker.

"It just really put me back to how I felt as a kid, you know?" Sparkle said, her eyes welling with glittery tears as she looked Mrs Gambol dead in the eye.

It was hot in this room and Sparkle had opted to tie her jumpsuit arms around her waist, revealing her colourful arm tattoos to the room at large and I snorted a laugh as I spotted one of a naked dude with curly blonde hair, bending over while a pink Pegasus drove its horn up his asshole and he gripped his hard cock with a look of ecstasy on his face. The words *Horny for the Horn* were painted beneath it in rainbow coloured lettering and I had to wonder what Caleb Altair would have thought of it if he'd seen it and laughed louder before I could stop myself.

All eyes in the room swivelled to me and it took me a moment to realise that I'd clearly laughed at a bad moment in Sparkle's story.

"What?" I asked, glancing at Mrs Gambol.

"Bed wetting is a perfectly normal thing to experience in stressful conditions. And these sessions are supposed to be a safe space for our members to speak freely about their experiences," she chastised.

"Sparkle's wetting the bed?" I asked, choking back another laugh as I turned my eyes on the Pegasus in question.

"I was relaying a story about my *childhood*," she snapped, chomping her teeth at me. "Not discussing how I wet the bed *now*."

"Were you building up to discussing that then?" I asked, raising my brows as I less than subtly cast a look at her crotch to check for wet patches. "Because I didn't mean to interrupt."

"That was one time!" Sparkle yelled, stomping her foot before gasping in horror at what she'd said and slapping a hand over her mouth as I burst out laughing alongside half the rest of the members of the group.

"Oh dear, this is baaaad," Mrs Gambol muttered.

Sparkle glared at the Stick of Truth in her hand before

launching it at me with a shriek of rage. I managed to catch it despite the tears sliding down my cheeks and I almost didn't realise Sparkle was charging at me with her head lowered as I howled with laughter.

I pushed to my feet, but a moment before she could collide with me, Cain shot into the centre of the circle, caught Sparkle by the back of her collar and hauled her away.

"You need a time out, Thirty-Two," he growled as she whinnied in protest, trying to grab me as I smirked at her and leaned out of her reach. Cain dragged her to the door and passed her over to Officer Nichols who was standing outside. "Take her back to her cell block, and can you make sure there's a plastic sheet protecting the mattress on her bed too?"

Sparkle started screaming death threats and I fell apart as I dropped back into my chair, the ridiculous Truth Stick held loose in my grasp with its colourful ribbons trailing down my leg.

"I don't know why you look so happy, Twelve," Cain said loudly, forcing the rest of the group to settle down as he pinned me in his gaze, but I swear he actually looked amused for half a second too. "Because it looks like it's your turn with that stick next."

Instead of returning to his little seat in the corner, Cain took Sparkle's spot directly opposite me and pinned me in his gaze with a look that said *got ya*. But fuck that. I wasn't letting some damn stick force the truth from my lips, though I was beginning to have my suspicions about just who had managed to find this magical artefact for Mrs Gambol to use. *Dickweed.*

"Oh yes, that's not a baaaad idea," Mrs Gambol piped up and I pursed my lips as I looked down at the stupid stick which was thrumming with a soft power in my hands.

"Great," I agreed, giving them my cherry pie smile as I twisted the stick between my fingers and wondered how it worked.

"Let's have something from your childhood," Cain prompted. "Something that lets us get to know more about what it was like to grow up in the lap of the Oscura Clan and the big bad Wolves."

I opened my mouth to try and feed him some bullshit, but my tongue felt heavy in my mouth and seemed to fight the words until I was choking them back. *Fuck.*

Cain gave me the hint of a smirk and all the other inmates eyed me hungrily, like they expected me to offer up some piece of my soul to them here.

I gritted my teeth as Mrs Gambol began to make notes despite the fact that I hadn't said a damn word.

"This is going to be baaaad," she murmured beneath her breath and I grunted in frustration.

I don't want to give them my truth. I mentally begged the universe to save me from this shit and just as I was about to open my mouth again, warmth seemed to radiate through my fingertips and I glanced down to find that soft, shimmering light that appeared when I harnessed my Moon Wolf gifts sliding along my fingers for a moment before the call of the truth stick left me entirely. No one else seemed to notice the ethereal glow and suddenly I was just a girl, sitting in a room full of stronzos, holding a stick with ribbons tied onto it.

"Okay..." I said slowly, ducking my head as I fought to hide my smile. *Nice one, moony.* "So, when I was about eight or nine, my grandmother got sick," I said, twisting the Stick of Truth between my fingers like I was lost to the horrors of my past.

"Go on," Mrs Gambol breathed and I nodded, lifting my gaze to hers and biting down on my bottom lip as honest to stars tears welled in my eyes. Damn, I loved playing this part, reeling them in and making them bite at the big, juicy worm of lies I was offering.

"So, my family is really large, but a lot of us live fairly close to each other, all within proximity of this huge patch of forest," I explained. "And my grandmother's house was on the far side of the forest to ours, so my mamma made up a basket of ingredients for a potion to help make her better and asked me to run them over to her. The only problem was that at this time, the gang wars were raging in Alestria-"

Several murmurs around the group said that people remembered those dark times well and I nodded while Cain stared at me like he was drinking this all in and a thrill raced down my spine as I tossed him a scowl, like I was mad about him making me share this before I went on.

"So, my mamma warned me that there had been sightings of an unfamiliar Wolf on the outskirts of our land who she was pretty sure was a Lunar spy. She told me to keep an eye out for the Wolf and to make sure I ran to my grandmother's house as fast as I could just in case. It was winter, so I grabbed my gloves and cloak and I did as she asked and ran down the path into the forest. Before long, I started to get the creeping feeling that someone was watching me, so I upped my pace and ran on. An unfamiliar howl sounded in the trees somewhere behind me and of course I totally freaked-"

"This is baaaad," Gambol murmured and I nodded as I blew out a breath like I was building up to telling them something awful.

"I was so scared that I shifted, bursting through my clothes and grabbing the basket of ingredients between my teeth as I sped away in my Wolf form, though luckily, my red cloak stayed tied around my neck as I ran. The unfamiliar howls chased me through the trees until I was certain a whole pack was closing in on me and I swear, I'd never felt fear like it. Somehow, I made it to my grandmother's house, but the magical wards protecting it were down and as I burst inside, I found the place in darkness. I shifted back into my Fae form, shoving the door closed behind me and rushing upstairs as I called out to my grandma, wrapping the cloak tight around me as I went."

"Ohhh, it's baaaad," Gambol breathed.

"Her room was dark, but when I saw the outline of her body in the bed and the deep sound of her breaths filling the room reached me, I relaxed, assuming I'd just found her sleeping off her illness. But as she sat up and beckoned me closer, I screamed-"

"What was it?" Gambol urged, typing furiously. "Was it baaaaad?"

"I just couldn't believe..." My gaze moved to meet Cain's and I dropped the terrified mask as my lips hooked up in a smirk. "What big eyes she had."

"What?" Cain barked, the penny finally dropping.

"And what big ears she had," I added, my taunting smile growing even wider. "And what big teeth-"

Cain's arms wrapped around my waist and he was hoisting me out of my chair and shooting out of the door before I even realised what was going on. We shot down the hallway and into a little office with two armchairs and a small table in it. He shoved me up against the door and snarled in my face, throwing a silencing bubble over us.

"Tell me how you did that?" he growled. "How did you overcome the Truth Stick's magic?"

"Does it make you angry when I lie, boss man?" I taunted, shifting the Truth Stick in my fingers until I was pressing it to the back of his hand where he was fisting a handful of my jumpsuit in his grip.

"You know it does," he growled.

"And does it turn you on too?" I teased.

"More than I would ever admit," he said in a deep voice which had heat rushing between my thighs before I could stop myself from reacting.

It took him a moment to realise what he'd said, and he looked down at the Truth Stick which I was still pressing to his hand before bellowing in rage and ripping it from my hands then smashing it against the wall.

The Stick of Truth broke into two pieces which bounced down on the carpet and I smirked at him in triumph.

"How did you manage to lie like that while you were holding it?" he demanded, still pinning me to the door.

"Maybe I wasn't lying. Maybe my life just happens to draw parallels to fairy tales a lot of the time. When I pricked my finger on a spinning wheel it actually hurt like a bitch though. And I have to say, there was nothing charming about that prince who kissed me awake - he finger fucked me so hard I could still feel it a week later."

"Stop," Cain commanded.

"Also, if we're being honest here, I really shouldn't have been afraid of the big bad Wolf when he told me his mouth was all the better to eat me with. I recently let a big bad Wolf eat me and it was so fucking good that I don't even have words for it."

Cain just stared at me like he didn't know whether to lose his shit or laugh and I grinned at him as I waited to find out which he would land on.

"You're impossible," he murmured, his lips twitching the tiniest amount.

"I think the word you're looking for is insatiable," I replied.

Cain groaned and I raised an eyebrow at him as he tipped his head back. "We might as well start our one on one session now. Take a seat," he muttered, releasing me and stepping back.

It was so...un-Cain that I couldn't help but narrow my eyes in suspicion.

"That's it?" I asked, slowly moving to take the chair opposite him with the table dividing us.

"Will you tell me how you stopped that Truth Stick from working?" Cain asked, but in a way that said he knew I wouldn't.

"I don't know," I replied which was actually the truth. My Moon Wolf gifts seemed to just show up when I was most desperate for them to, I didn't even know what they were going to do half the time, much less understand how I accessed them, despite the fact that I was under the influence of the Order Suppressant.

Cain regarded me for a long moment and then nodded in acceptance.

"I dealt with Nixon. He won't bother you again," he said, his fist closing at the memory and revealing his cracked knuckles to me. There was no reason why he wouldn't have healed that shit away, but one look in his eyes told me why he hadn't. He relished the pain of those injuries because the memory of gaining them was too fucking good and he didn't want to let it go yet.

"What did you do to him?" I asked, licking my lips as I imagined Cain beating the shit out of that scumbag. But would he really have done that for me? It was probably more about the principle of the thing, but either way, it was really fucking hot. Even if he was a total assbag.

"Let's just say that if I hadn't healed him, he wouldn't be breathing anymore. Point is, he won't come near you again. But if he does, then you tell me and I'll finish him."

My heart pounded at the sincerity in that statement and I just stared at this man I hated so much, trying to figure out why he cared so damn much. Then my mind wandered to him drinking my blood and I wondered if that was my answer. Cain hadn't officially claimed me as his Source, but it was something that powerful Vampires often did when they liked the taste of a particular Fae's blood. And in that case, they would protect their Source with a furious kind of ownership to defend what they saw as theirs. That must have been it, because I knew for a fact that Cain didn't like me, certainly not enough to go to bat for me if there was nothing in it for him.

When I didn't say anything else, Cain swiped a hand over his dark hair and pinned me in his gaze.

"I also found out what they're taking from those Fae down in Psych," he said in a low voice, the frown on his face saying he wasn't sure if he should be telling me this and I perked right up.

"Oh?"

"But before you go getting all excited, you should know there isn't anything I can do about it unless we can somehow get evidence of what I found out of here. The warden is in on it and my source won't talk again willingly. We don't even have enough to make the FIB start up an investigation, but I think you might be the only person around here who gives a shit about it, so..."

"You're going to tell me?" I asked in surprise.

Cain eyed me for a long moment then took his shock baton from his hip holster and laid it on the table, pointing at me. With his other hand, he reached up and clasped the remote at his neck, eying me for a long moment before using it to deactivate my cuffs.

I gasped as magic rushed to my fingertips and the urge to use it spilled through me in a wave. Before I could, Cain's hand landed in mine and he drew my attention back to him.

"I swear to tell you the truth of this if you swear to keep this secret among people we can trust with it," he growled.

"I swear," I replied in agreement, the look in his eyes urging me to comply. Magic clapped between our palms as the deal was struck and in a blur of motion, he'd released me and switched my cuffs back on before taking his seat again.

I pouted at the fact that I hadn't been able to use my magic more than that, but as Cain started talking, I forgot about being annoyed.

"They're stealing people's Orders from them," he growled, glancing at the door even though it was locked and his silencing bubble still enveloped us. "They've figured out how to remove it surgically - though the whole process takes hours and is utter agony for the subject. A lot of Fae die from the shock of having it stolen though, which is what happened to your Mole friend."

"She had a name," I growled. "Sook was a good person."

"Well she's a dead person now. And by the sounds of it that's for the best. The Fae who survive the process live a shell of a life, half crazed, totally fucked up and left to rot in cages. So far they can't figure out how to place the Orders into someone else though. Their goal is clearly to figure out how to give Fae multiple Orders."

"But if that became possible...they'd start doing this more and more. Stealing Orders from Fae and selling them to rich stronzos who want to be something more powerful than they were born," I gasped.

"There are plenty of rich, evil fuckers who will always want more than they've got in life no matter how much they already have. Just look at Lionel Acrux," Cain muttered but I just shook my head, not wanting to get distracted by talking about that evil bastardo.

"What can we do?" I breathed, leaning forward so that I was resting my arms on the table.

"I'll keep trying to get solid evidence that I can turn over to the FIB. In the meantime, just avoid anyone acting crazy. Like Eighty-Eight for example. You don't wanna get dragged down by association."

"What's the matter, boss man? You don't like me hanging around with the sexy Incubus?" I teased and Cain's jaw ticked.

"I'm just trying to give you some advice."

"Noted. So, are you going to tell me why you decided to open up to me about all of this?" I asked.

Cain clenched his jaw and rubbed at the wrist of his left arm where the curse mark I'd placed on him sat.

"I figured if I expect honesty from you then I could offer you the same," he gritted out.

I pursed my lips as I considered that then got to my feet, hopping up on the table and sliding over it before swinging my legs down on the other side and sitting in front of him.

"Let me see it," I said, placing my feet on the chair either side of his legs and holding my hand out for his arm.

"Why? Are you going to curse me again?" he asked icily and I smirked at him.

"Let me see and I'll give you something real," I said. "Giuro," I added in a low tone, painting a cross over my heart. *I swear.*

Cain's lip pulled back like he didn't really believe me, but he unbuttoned his sleeve and rolled it back to reveal his muscular forearm before presenting it to me all the same.

His skin was hot with the presence of his fire magic beneath his skin as I took his arm between my hands, turning it to inspect the curse mark which now extended up to his elbow and disappeared beneath the rolled sleeve of his black shirt.

"Maledizione della luna," I breathed as I reached out to run my fingers over the mark. His flesh shivered beneath my touch and the mark seemed to glow with that same ethereal shine that it had when I'd channelled my gift into creating it.

"What would it take for you to remove this curse from me?" Cain growled and I looked up at him, my fingers stilling in their movement over the mark.

"I'm a Moon Wolf," I replied, holding his gaze. "The moon offers up use of these gifts as and when it sees fit. I don't understand them any better than you do, I just follow what the moon pushes me to do. I couldn't remove the curse even if I wanted to."

"And you don't want to?" he asked, his tone deadly as his fist clenched.

I tilted my head to the side as I regarded him and decided to give him a truth about me that might give him some small sense of understanding.

"The man who gave me my scars spent years trying to force me to become a ruthless creature of his design," I murmured. "And when I failed the tests he set me, he would punish me in all kinds of ways. One of which involved him locking me alone in the dark for days on end. He had a pit in the back yard, a crawl space under the front steps and a tiny closet which were his favourite places for me, and I never knew how long I would be trapped there once he threw me in. The walls would seem to close in on me and the darkness would whisper all kinds of horrors in my ears."

Something dark flashed in Cain's eyes at my words like they caused him real fury on my behalf and I scoffed at him as I pressed my thumb down on the first curse mark I'd given him.

"When I saved your life, you punished me in just the same way, locking me up in the dark for far longer than he ever had with nothing but my memories of him to keep me company. And if you haven't figured it out yet, my memories aren't somewhere I like to reside," I said, my gaze hardening as I remembered exactly how his betrayal had hurt me. "So no, boss man, I don't want to remove the curse. And if I could give you another one, I'd do it in a heartbeat."

Cain's eyes darkened but it didn't seem to be with anger at me for once. In fact, if I had to guess, I would have said it was regret. But it was far too late for that to make any kind of difference. He could have come and gotten me out of that hell any time he liked but he chose to let me rot.

Well, payback really was a bitch. And she had nothing on Rosalie Oscura.

I got to my feet as the bell sounded the start of the dinner hour and I headed to the door without another word. Cain got up and unlocked it for me, catching my arm to stop me from pulling it open at the last second.

I looked up and waited to hear what he had to say but he just gritted his jaw and pulled the door wide, letting me go. And I walked away without a backwards glance.

DARKMORE PENITENTIARY

ETHAN

ORDER: WEREWOLF
PRISONER NUMBER: #1

STAR SIGN: CANCER
ELEMENT: WATER

I showered a few feet away from my pack, letting Harper stand close to me, but I couldn't have her wash me. I couldn't stand her hands on my flesh for too long and I'd end up snapping at her if she even attempted it and then give away the truth. She scrubbed at her dark dreadlocks and my gaze hooked on the silvery crescent tattooed behind her ear. It made even me angry to see it, let alone what it was doing to Rosalie. Fuck I hated this. Hated having to hide her away, hated fighting with her all the time. A guy like me needed his beauty sleep and I was scraping by on sub-par ugly-as-a-pig's-asshole sleep. I swear at this rate I was gonna get wrinkles before I was thirty. And that would just be a travesty for my perfect face.

My pack finished washing and I sent Harper after them as I stole a few moments alone under the stream of water. The showers were emptying out and I wanted to just stay there and not have to return to my cell block where a night sharing my cell with Harper awaited me. I made her sleep in another bunk, the weight of guilt of sharing my bed with a woman other than my mate too much for me. I swear the mate bond was getting stronger, begging me to go to Rosalie, to make it up to her. And I wanted to, I really fucking did. I just knew there was no way she was going to accept me into her life unless I proclaimed her as my mate to my pack, to the whole fucking prison too. She needed that from me, and I couldn't provide it.

But how could she expect that? In Darkmore, our gangs were so fiercely divided. I'd be mocked, outcasted. I may even be killed for such a betrayal to the Lunar Brotherhood. *Maybe that's what she wants...*

I growled, stepping out of the water and my jaw dropped as I found Rosalie standing beside the lockers with a towel wrapped around her body, her hair dripping wet, her eyes full and round and hungry as they dropped to take in my cock. I got hard for her instantly and she laughed softly, curling a finger to beckon me over. I shot a glance at the door, but everyone was gone and there were no guards in here. I had no reason not to go over there and claim my breath-taking mate.

I strode toward her as she bit down on her full bottom lip and I growled, looking forward to doing that myself. But then I blinked out of my stupor, my eyes narrowing with suspicion. She hated me. Why was she here tempting me in? Especially when she'd made it clear she had her pick of Alpha males to fuck. Though I swear to the fucking stars, if she was serious about screwing them, I was gonna make them bleed. I just needed some hard evidence before I made my move.

I slowed, picking up my towel off the bench and hooking it around my waist, which didn't do much to hide my boner, considering the material was now tenting out around it.

I scowled at her, folding my arms hard across my chest as I fought the allure of her body. Of the water droplets sliding over her perfect skin, tempting me to move in close and lick them off.

"Hey big boy," she purred, a smile playing around her mouth. "Aren't you going to come closer?"

"Don't we hate each other again? I can't keep up, love," I said, keeping my voice level and cold.

"Your cock says you like me," she teased, batting those long lashes of hers and I found myself stepping closer.

Far be it from me to reject Rosalie when she was in the mood to fuck me. I knew it wouldn't make her hate and rage go away, but if I was honest, it only made the sex hotter anyway. And I was aching for her. Day after day, I had to go without her, while watching her flirt with other men and act as if I didn't exist. It was excruciating. So why shouldn't I claim her and sate this need in me? Just for a little while…

I reached out to cup her cheek and she leaned into my touch, making me growl in approval. I slid my fingers into her wet hair, gripping it in my fist as I closed the distance between us and my cock pressed to her toned stomach through her towel.

I hated all the tension between us and I was so sick of bottling up everything I felt, the burning emotions that plagued me day in and day out desperate to be spilled. I just needed to say it. Even if it didn't change anything. She had to know. "I miss you every day. I think the pain of being away from you is going to kill me."

"Then you know what to do, shadow man," she breathed and I didn't question that strange ass nickname because I kinda liked it.

"I can't tell my pack, you know that. But love, I can't keep away from you anymore. There's got to be a compromise we can make?"

She said nothing and I feared I was losing her again, so I pressed my forehead to hers and a smile curled up her lips.

"I ache for you in the dark and pine for you in the light. There's no moment day or night that I don't want you. It's more than desire, I think it's even more than love. Fuck, Rosalie, if you weren't an Oscura, if there was some other way-"

"But I *am* an Oscura. Nothing's going to change that. So what are you going to do about it, pup?"

"I'm not a pup," I snarled and her smile only grew.

"Yes you are. You're a lost little pup who wants to go home, but you won't let yourself because it's not the place you thought it was. Just give in, Ethan. Who gives a fuck if your home isn't where it should be? It's still where you belong." She pressed a hand to my heart, her eyes serious. "I would give anything to belong somewhere."

"I thought you-"

She snaked a hand between my legs, gripping my cock through my towel with a smirk, making my words fall dead on my lips.

"What am I gonna do with you?" I growled, pulling her hair to make her tilt her head back. She was letting me take control for once and I really fucking liked that. It got me so hard that the head of my dick was throbbing needily and the way she was caressing it was making it hard to concentrate. *Man*, her fingers were skilled.

"First you're going to kiss me," she said seductively, tip-toeing up and locking me in her eyes, her mouth parting as she waited for me to close the distance. And yeah, I was hot on that.

I leaned in, sinking my tongue into her mouth and she kissed me back with languid, slow strokes like she was enjoying me. I knocked her hand away from my dick and yanked her firmly against me by the hips, grinding my hard on into her flesh and tearing her towel away so it dropped to the floor.

My hands roamed down her velvet smooth back and I clutched her ass tight, crushing her to me. I frowned at the feeling of something hard pressing into my thigh, but didn't question it too much as her hand slipped between us, pulling my own towel away so our flesh met everywhere. I jerked backwards as that hard thing on my leg felt most definitely like a-

"What the fuck?!" I shouted as I looked down and spotted a huge pierced dick standing proud and fucking hard between her thighs.

Rosalie grinned at me, then her hand locked around my throat while the other curled into a fist and slammed into my side. Pain sliced through me as she did it again and again and I spotted the sharpened end of a toothbrush in her hand as I staggered back, blood pouring down my skin as I took in what she'd done.

"*Why?*" I begged, panic running through me. Did she want me dead? Was this her way of dealing with a mate she'd never asked for? How could she even hurt me with our bond in place? It shouldn't have been possible.

She suddenly shifted before me and it was no longer my mate I was looking at. It was Sin, naked as hell and covered in ink with a huge ass grin on his face. *What? How is that possible??*

"*Motherfucker,*" I rasped as I clutched the deep wounds, my back hitting the lockers as I grew woozy, the blood pouring hot and fast out of me and pooling at my feet. How had he shifted? How could this be fucking happening?

Sin casually turned the bloody shank around in his hand and slammed it into his own gut, then again and again, barely even wincing as he did so. This asshole was fucking crazy. He was gonna kill us both, and for what?

"Guard!" I managed to yell, my mind sharpening for a second and Sin tossed the toothbrush onto the floor, wailing with me.

"Guard!" he begged and I didn't know what the fuck was happening, only that I was most definitely bleeding out and now he was too. He shot me a look, pressing his finger to his lips. "Trust me, shadow man. You'll be fine."

But I wasn't fine, I was sliding down to the ground, blood spreading out further and further. And anger tore through me that I was going to die here naked at the feet of Sin Wilder. A heaviness dragged at my very soul and as two large shadows raced into the room, my eyes closed and I thought of Rosalie. And how I'd never get to make things right between us.

***

My mind slowly slid towards consciousness and Sin's voice filled my ears somewhere nearby.

"-I dunno Brenda, all I saw was a mad man running into the showers and stabbing Shadowbrook. I tried to help, because he was really screaming like a girl. Just screaming and screaming for his mommy, it was really sad. And then the guy came at me as I tried to save him and I managed to punch him even though I never got a proper look at his face. He stabbed me a few times, but I obviously scared him off. Dunno who it was, I guess the adrenaline had me thinking of only Shadowbrook. I wouldn't say I'm a hero or anything, but..."

"Baps on a bagel," Mother Brenda breathed and I opened my eyes, doing a mental sweep of my body which felt fine thankfully. I should've known I'd be okay. Ethan Shadowbrook didn't die bleeding out on the floor of a fucking shower room. "That must have frightened the rabbits out of you."

"Yes, ma'am," Sin agreed seriously and I turned my head, spotting him sitting on a hospital bed across from mine, his legs folded up beneath him and a lolly pop in his mouth. *Is he kidding me right now?* "I shat out at least three bunnies."

Mother Brenda laughed, straightening her nurse's uniform as she patted his arm like they were on friendly terms.

I cleared my throat, drawing their attention and Brenda's eyes widened as she hurried over. "How are you feeling? I had to give you a blood regeneration potion, it can cause a little nausea on account of the eckle worms in it."

I wrinkled my nose. "I'm fine." My eyes shot to Sin again, accusation pouring from me. But I was no snitch, I wasn't going to tell the truth even though the asshole had almost killed me.

"Lucky Sin was there to fight off that dastardly Daniel who attacked you," Mother Brenda said, throwing a warm smile at Sin like he was my fucking saviour.

"Yeah," I gritted out. "Real lucky."

"I think he needs a lollipop, Brenda," Sin said firmly and she chuckled, nodding her agreement before hurrying over to her desk and opening the top drawer.

"Strawberry or cola?" she asked me and I peeled my eyes away from Brenda who was waving one of each at me. Why the fuck did she even keep those here? There weren't any kids in Darkmore. Except the two hundred pound psychotic, tattooed bastard sitting across from me apparently.

"Strawberry," I chose, because turning down a rare treat like that in prison was moronic. I was still angry when she passed it to me, but I unwrapped it and stuck it in my mouth all the same. *Oh fuck balls that's good.*

I worked over what had happened up in the showers and my rage sharpened again. How the fuck had he shifted into my girl? How had he used his Order? Why the fuck had he attacked me? Then himself??

"You boys can have a little winkle time." Brenda winked. "I need to go fill a report in for the warden."

"Winkle time?" I muttered as she stepped out of the door and locked it.

"She means rest time obviously," Sin said like he spoke fluent crazy. And oh yeah, he did.

"Why the fuck did you do this? And *how* did you do it?" I growled, speaking around my lollipop as I slid off the bed and realised I was in a hospital gown which billowed open at the back, letting a cool breeze chill my bare ass. Sin was dressed in a fresh jumpsuit and there was another one waiting for me at the end of my bed with some underwear.

"I did it for Rosalie," he said unhelpfully. "And I just stole a dose of the Order Suppressant antidote Plunger's been using so I could shift. It wasn't that hard. The effects have already worn off. Did you like what you saw?"

"You should be in Psych, I dunno why they let crazies like you stay in gen pop." I pulled on the socks then picked up the boxers just as Sin came up behind me and spoke in my ear, the scent of a cola lollipop reaching me from his mouth.

"I wouldn't go putting those boxers on just yet, kitten," he purred and I threw my elbow back to make him move the fuck away from me. There was no camera in here, but it would be pretty fucking obvious who'd attacked Sin if I laid into him. But by the stars, he was marked. He wasn't going to get away with what he'd done to me.

"What the hell are you planning?" I growled.

"Well, I wasn't planning on taking a field trip to see the moon from the top of Buttcrack Canyon," he said. "But the moon is definitely out and looking rather peachy tonight." He slapped my ass and I wheeled around, throwing my palms into his chest with a furious snarl.

"You're dead," I hissed. "You think you can just stab the leader of the Lunar Brotherhood and get away with it? You should have cut deeper, Wilder, because I'm still alive and that means your death is written."

"Calm down, Lassie," he said, smirking as he used his tongue to roll the lolly from side to side in his mouth. "It's not like I pushed little Timmy down a well."

"What the fuck are you on about?" I snapped, snatching up my boxers again but Sin lunged forward, grabbing them from my hands and stuffing them inside his jumpsuit.

"You fucking-"

He spoke over me, "I didn't try to kill you. I just needed to get us down here so we can help Rosalie."

I ground my teeth, waiting for him to expand on that, but he just turned and strode over to a medicine cabinet and swiped a key card over a panel beside it, making the cabinet spring open.

"Where'd you get that?" I gasped.

"I stole it off of Brenda. She'll just think she left it here." He tossed the card onto the counter then knelt down and started rummaging through the cupboard like he had all the time in the world.

I glanced at the door anxiously then moved across the room to help him. "What are you looking for?"

Sin opened a little linen bag and took out a Nevercot Plum, the bright purple skin shimmering a little in the light. He looked up at me with a serious expression on his face. "You need to put this up your butt."

My jaw went slack and anger pulsed through me. "*That's* why you brought me here?" I snarled as he stood up, locked the cupboard and started tossing the plum up and down in his hand.

He threw it higher, bouncing it off his elbow and catching it again. "Yup. Want a hand, kitten? Turn around."

"No," I hissed furiously. "Rosalie didn't even give a damn about me getting her that crystal. Why the fuck would I bring her anything else?"

"What do you think all these items are for, sugar?" he purred, arching a brow. "The escape of course. She needs the ingredients to neutralise the Order Suppressant tank."

My lips parted and my heart pounded harder. Fuck, she really did need this.

"Then *you* do it," I insisted. "I'm hardly needed here."

"I can't, kitten, they always strip search me."

"Bullshit," I snapped, getting up in his face as I sucked furiously on my lolly. "You didn't get searched when we left the Fate Room and I've been watching you since. They don't strip search you any more than they do me."

He chuckled low in his throat. "Busted."

The lock clicked open on the door and Sin snatched my boxers from his jumpsuit, wrapped the plum up in them and shoved them into my hand just as Brenda stepped back into the room.

"I'm so glad you're okay," Sin purred, running his thumb over my lips to cover why we were standing here together and I drew away from him, nodding stiffly as I tried to mask my rage.

"Thanks," I muttered, moving back to my bed.

Brenda hurried over to the counter, fishing up her key card and glancing between us while we acted nonchalant. When Brenda wasn't watching, Sin made an O with his finger and thumb then shoved his other index finger into it, giving me a pointed look.

I swallowed a growl, pulling my boxers on under the gown and keeping the plum in my fist.

"Any chance of another lollipop, Brenda?" Sin asked, turning to her. "One for the road?" He flicked the stick of the one he'd finished into the trash can and she waggled her finger at him.

"Naughty boy, you're as cheeky as a whale on vacation," she chastised. "Just this once." She turned to her desk, pulling the drawer open and Sin looked to me, furiously thrusting his finger into that O again like I hadn't understood him the first time. I glared at him, a growl building in my throat.

I really fucking hate Sin Wilder.

I pushed the plum between my cheeks, bending forward a little and working it up my ass because apparently I would

320

put anything in there for Rosalie. Or maybe it was because I wanted to escape more than anything now. Either way, this had better be the last fucking thing that went up there. Or I was going to fucking lose it.

When it was done, I moved with awkward, slow steps to try and get used to the hard flesh of the plum in a place it should never fucking see in its life then pulled off the gown and tugged on my tank top and jumpsuit. When I was dressed and Sin had another lollipop sticking out the corner of his mouth, Brenda ushered us to the door.

Officer Hastings stood outside and he patted us down before eyeing the lolly in Sin's mouth.

"Give it here," he instructed, holding out his palm and Sin growled like a dog. "Here. Now."

Sin took hold of the stick and tugged sharply before a loud crunch came as he crushed the lolly between his teeth then deposited the stick in Hastings' palm.

"Spoil sport," Sin muttered and Hastings pursed his lips as he directed us ahead of him.

"Why are you walking like that?" he clipped at me and I immediately straightened, sharing a look with Sin.

"I crushed his balls a minute ago," Sin said casually.

"Why?" Hastings balked.

"He likes it," Sin answered, smooth as fucking butter and I chewed the inside of my cheek to bite back my irritation.

"Why would you like something like that?" Hastings asked me in alarm.

"I just...do," I said, feigning enthusiasm. "Nothing like a knee to the balls or a fist squeezing them until I nearly black out."

"By the stars," Hastings muttered, wrinkling his nose at me and I added that to the list of reasons I despised Sin Wilder.

Alongside the fact that he was potentially fucking my moon bound mate, and all the items he'd encouraged me to put up my ass. I just wished there was something in this prison that someone could come up with as leverage against him. But maybe I didn't need that anyway. If we got out of here soon, nothing would protect him from my wrath. And he'd find out what happened to people who crossed me. Because no matter how long it took, they *never* got away with it.

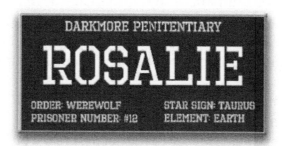

I sat in the Mess Hall, twisting my spoon through my oatmeal as I pouted down at it, wishing it was pancakes, or French toast, or chocolate. Yeah, I could really have gone for some chocolate covered chocolate right about now. But the only chocolate they had in commissary was gross. Like honest to shit, I was pretty much certain they had actually done something to it to make it taste like someone had dipped it in detergent or something. It had this gross kind of floral after taste that left you feeling like you'd been chomping down on some soap after eating it and totally wasn't worth the tokens it cost. I was going to have to beg Roary to get his brother to sneak me some in past the guards the next time he came for a visit.

I was so caught up in my pouting that the only reason I even noticed Gustard approaching was because all of my Wolves started growling and pushing to their feet around me.

Sonny bared his teeth and rose to his full, towering height at my side as Gustard paused before me and I quirked an irritated brow at the tattoo-faced psychopath.

"We need a word, runt," Gustard purred and within a heartbeat, every Wolf at the table was on their feet, teeth bared and snarling as they lunged between me and this piece of shit.

My gut dropped at the sound of that old nickname on his lips though and with a lurch of vulnerability, I realised that he'd gone further than just finding out about me and Ethan and our escape plans when he'd pillaged my brain for information. He'd probed into the darkest corners of my psyche and torn the memories of my papa into the light too. He knew. Every deep, dark, fear-filled moment of my childhood was in his grasp and the smirk he gave me as I barked an order at my Wolves to stand down said he thought he owned me for it. I would seriously kill this motherfucker before I'd let him come with us when we escaped.

"I can't imagine it's all that important," I said to Gustard, fronting him out with a withering look.

He may have held the key to my deepest fears, but I'd learned a long time ago how to segment my emotions and file all of those things away, never to look at it dead on. It didn't matter if he knew the fear I'd felt at my papa's hands as a pup or the neglect I'd felt at my mamma's. Those things didn't define me. I'd escaped them and that life. I'd risen from the ashes of it and built myself up into someone feared and respected throughout the whole of Alestria and the rest of Solaria beyond.

Fear knew my name and whispered it on the breeze. I wasn't going to become the toy of some pathetic little worm like him.

"Speak to me like that again and I may find my tongue loosening at an inopportune moment," Gustard said in a sly voice that had Sonny growling as he reluctantly lowered himself into the chair at my side.

"Just say the word and I'll fold this motherfucker up like a pretzel and stick a cocktail stick up his ass for good measure," Sonny offered and I didn't bother to hide my amusement as the rest of my Wolves all tittered around me, making Gustard's eyes flash with rage.

I took my time swirling my spoon through my oatmeal before lifting it to my lips and taking a huge bite of it. I moaned loudly and obnoxiously, making Gustard wait as I finished off the bowl and then very slowly rose to my feet.

"Walk with me then, stronzo, let's hear what you've got to say," I said, sounding more than a little uninterested as Gustard's eyes narrowed and Esme fastened the top buttons of her jumpsuit like she was trying to defend her tits from him. Good on her, those tits were too fabulous for the likes of him.

I headed for the door without waiting to see if Gustard was

following and strode out into the corridor before he fell into step beside me.

"I won't tolerate your attitude with me in public like that again," he snarled as we started walking towards the mail collection point where there weren't many inmates lurking around seeing as it wasn't currently open.

"Well, I won't simper like a little bitch for you, stronzo, so try intimidating someone weaker next time. It would look strange as fuck to my pack if I did and I'm not raising suspicions for anyone. Besides, I'll never bow to you or be intimidated into doing anything by anyone. I'm Rosalie Oscura, not some bottom feeding bitch ready to drop down and suck your cock just so that you won't hurt me. Find some other way to get yourself off."

Gustard chuckled like I amused him and then leaned close as if we were two besties sharing a secret. "I wouldn't want your filthy runt mouth anywhere near my cock, you jumped up little street whore. If I wanted to get myself off over you, I'd find myself a sun steel blade and strap you to a table while I finished the job of carving you up like your daddy started." His hand brushed my side where my scars lay beneath my jumpsuit and I whirled on him, my hand snapping closed around his throat as I threw my weight into him and slammed him up against the wall.

Gustard bared his teeth at me in the mockery of a smile and dropped his voice so that there was no chance of his words carrying despite the fact that we were alone here.

"I'm bringing someone else with us when we leave this place," he said, not seeming to care as I crushed his windpipe harder and snarled at him with death promised in my eyes.

"Over my dead body," I growled. "You don't call the shots around here, stronzo. And if you seriously think you can tell me what to do then you must be fucking deluded."

"Please, papa," he said in a pathetic little voice which I knew was a mockery of me. "Not the den. It's snowing and I'm so cold, please don't throw me out there."

325

I flinched the smallest amount as he threw that memory in my face and it was clearly the opening he'd been waiting for as he thrust his hand between us and something slammed into my stomach with a punch of pain so deep that a scream of agony escaped me.

I shoved myself back away from him and he twisted the weapon in his hand, ripping it sideways before wrenching it free and blood poured from the wound in a flood.

I clamped my hands against it, stumbling further away from him as I fought against the agony in my body and way too much blood tried to escape the confines of my flesh.

Gustard watched me with a deep and potent heat in his gaze, licking his bottom lip slowly as I snarled at him in fury, keeping one eye on the weapon in his hand as I prepared to try and fight him off if he came at me again. He knew my plan. Was he trying to get rid of me so that he could implement it himself? But if he knew it then he knew I was relying on Jerome and Dante too and there was no way he could get either of them involved without me, let alone try and replace their skills.

Somehow, his jumpsuit didn't have a speck of blood on it, despite how much of mine was pulsing from my body, pooling on the floor.

"Don't forget who's in charge now," he said, his eyes glinting hungrily as he looked to my stomach and the blood oozing between my fingers where I clamped them down against the wound. I couldn't even try to fight him while I was bleeding this bad or I was likely to bleed out the moment I stopped exerting pressure on it.

"A morte e ritorno," I snarled at him, spitting my family motto in his face and promising him death by my hands one day soon.

One of Gustard's lackeys appeared around the corner, his eyebrows lifting like he hadn't expected to see this when he'd come here, but he had clearly been invited all the same as he made no comment and just waited to one side of the space like he was expecting something.

"You're my girl," Gustard said, taking a step closer to me, his eyes wild with excitement and my heart beating out of rhythm because that sounded a hell of a lot like the words my papa had spoken to me right before he drove that sun steel blade into my side and began to carve me apart with it. "My pup," Gustard went on, confirming my fears as he quoted the man I hated most in all the world like he fucking admired him or something. "*My bitch*. And you'll always be that no matter what else happens."

With a growl of fury, I gritted my teeth, blocked out the pain in my body and launched myself at him with nothing but tooth and claw to defend myself.

The hot, wet flood of my blood spilling down my stomach inside my jumpsuit drew an inch of my attention, but I ignored it in favour of ripping this motherfucker's head from his fucking body.

Gustard's eyes widened half a second before his little stooge slammed into me, knocking me away from his boss and I crashed down onto the floor beneath him with a cry of agony. He punched me in the gut and I screamed before rearing up and head butting him clear in the nose.

The moment he fell back, clutching his battered face, I managed to get my legs between us and kicked him as hard as I could, launching him away from me towards Gustard.

I rolled over, pushing up onto my hands and knees, my fingers slipping through the puddle of blood beneath me just as I saw Gustard hand the shank over to the little nobody and turn away from me.

I struggled to my feet, one hand to my gut as I expected the guy to come at me again, but he just stood there, smirking at me until the sound of pounding feet drew my attention to the corridor beyond him.

Hastings and Officer Rind burst around the corner and I sagged in relief as my little choir boy ran forward with a curse and managed to catch me before my legs gave out.

Rind slammed Gustard's man up against the wall as he

shouted out, "I did it! I hate the bitch and I wanted her dead!" and I snarled at the conniving son of a bitch. That mother-fucker would be going to the hole in Gustard's place with a confession like that and no one would even bother to double check his story. I wondered what Gustard had promised him to take the fall, but it didn't matter. Point was, the wrong man was going down. He held a weapon which was covered in my blood and had been found here alone with me before making a confession. The only way that I could change that was if I rat-ted Gustard out and I'd die before I snitched.

Hastings was saying something to me and it took me a mo-ment to realise it, blinking through the fog of my brain as he lowered me down to sit against the wall and yanked my jump-suit open.

"I can fix it," he said, his eyes wild with concern and I couldn't help but smile at my poor, sweet choir boy.

He was so innocent looking with that floppy blonde hair and bright blue eyes. I swear he probably thought there was a lot of good in this fucked up world if you knew where to look for it. Probably believed there was some good in me too.

The warm flow of healing magic swept beneath my skin and he made quick, neat work of healing the damage to my flesh as I just lay back and let him do his thing.

I was panting from the adrenaline rush and more than a little dizzy from blood loss, but one psychotic Cyclops wasn't going to rattle me.

I was pretty sure I'd just gotten a clear look at Gustard though, the meticulous psychopath who tortured young girls to death. I'd seen that hunger in his eyes and I knew that he was gaining more pleasure from taunting me with my own worst memories than he was from the wound he'd inflicted. He liked to cut people deep in both ways and watch them bleed. It excited him, got him off. He wanted to put me back into my nightmares and use them as a torture device just as thor-oughly as any weapon.

Fuck him.

He wasn't getting out of this prison alive. I didn't give a shit about the evidence he had ready to drown me. It didn't mean fuck all once we were out of here. Gustard would breathe in one, single breath of fresh air outside of this place before I stuck him full of so many holes that he could win a competition for being a Swiss cheese look alike.

Officer Rind dragged the nobody piece of shit away from me with promises of time in the hole and I sighed in relief as Hastings stole the pain from my body with his healing magic.

"Shit, Rosalie," Hastings murmured and I tore my mind away from all the deliciously dark paths it had been heading down and raised my eyes to his. "All that blood...for a moment I was afraid I was too late-"

"Even the devil knows not to mess with me, ragazzo del coro," I purred, reaching up to cup his cheek in my hand. "You don't need to worry about me."

"If I'd lost you, I... " He cut himself off but as his gaze flickered to my mouth, I realised where his mind was going and the faintest twist of guilt tugged at me.

Hastings was sweet and naive in the most weirdly cute kind of way. I even liked the guy, I liked his optimism and his stalwart belief in what was right and wrong. I just hoped that wouldn't be shaken too firmly when I broke out of here and he realised I'd been playing him all along.

"Nothing to lose," I assured him, offering up a smile much sweeter than I was and getting to my feet.

"I need to take you to medical," Hastings insisted, but I waved him off.

"I'm fine, honestly," I assured him. "I'm used to Vampire bites, so a little blood loss doesn't worry me."

"Seriously?" he asked with a frown and I realised my mistake.

Damn, maybe I did need a medical. But we had work assignments up next and I couldn't miss out on the hour in the library for the sake of a bout of blood regeneration. Gustard would be there and I needed to make sure he wasn't up to anything else.

"Umm, yeah," I said, chewing on my bottom lip and playing up the innocent thing I did so well. I mean, really, you'd think that him knowing I was in here for a massive heist coupled with a murder charge would be enough to make him see through me, but my little choir boy just wanted to see the positives in people. "Before I came here I had a Vampire boyfriend and he liked to bite me when we were...you know." I blushed. Honest to the stars, I didn't know where I found the blood to make heat rise to my cheeks, but with more than a few filthy thoughts about the things Sin had done to me down by the Belorian's cage, I managed it.

"Oh," Hastings breathed, blinking a few too many times as he took a step back. "I...didn't mean to pry. I didn't know you had a boyfriend."

"I don't," I said all coy and charming as fuck. Honestly, I would have been falling for me if I didn't know what Pegasus shit was currently falling from my lips. "We broke up before I came here. I really like anal and he didn't, so..."

Bless his little cotton socks, Hastings' eyes almost bugged out of his damn face. It was too cute. I wished I could take a picture.

"Can I go get changed before my work detail starts?" I asked when words just didn't seem to want to come to him and he shook his head like he'd just remembered where we were and what was going on.

"No need," he said, stepping forward and taking hold of my bloodstained jumpsuit between his fingers and using his water magic to draw all of my blood out of it and into a globe with what had spilled onto the floor.

"Are you going to put that in a cup and give it to Officer Cain?" I teased and Hastings snorted a laugh.

"Maybe I should," he agreed though I didn't think he meant it. I wished he did though, the look on that stronzo's face when he got a takeaway delivery straight from his vein of choice would have been priceless.

"Waste not want not," I purred and Hastings shrugged, glancing at the swirling globe of my blood like he was actually considering delivering a takeaway service to the boss man and I really hoped he was. "Thank you for saving me, ragazzo del coro," I said softly, moving into Hastings' personal space and tiptoeing up to place a kiss on his cheek.

I was gone again before he could chastise me or lean in or whatever a choir boy would do in a compromising position, and the heat in his cheeks said that he didn't even know what to do with me.

Before he could figure it out, I turned and walked away, swaying my hips as I went and striding off towards the library.

The Mess Hall was emptying out as I reached it and I moved into the crowd as everyone headed for the stairs, letting them sweep me towards it.

But as I took the first step down, the dizziness swept through my mind like a wave again and I stumbled, almost falling. And if it hadn't been for the hand which clamped around my arm to stop me, I probably would have gone ass over tit all the way down to floor seven where the Belorian could laugh at me for being a silly twat.

"What the fuck just happened to you, love?" Ethan growled in a low voice and as I turned my head to look up into his eyes, I found them wild with panic.

"Shit, baby, do you care now?" I asked, wide eyed and innocent as the flood of inmates continued to pour past us and we drew more than a few curious looks. The Lunar King and Oscura Queen should never be seen together after all – the poor common folk would shit their britches. Couldn't be having that.

"Don't dick around with me on this," he hissed, yanking me along until we reached the next floor down and he tugged me a little way along the corridor to gain some small level of privacy. "I was having the joy of a random cavity search because *someone* tipped the guards off to say I'd been smuggling a shank up my ass when I felt your pain like a punch to the fucking gut. I clenched down on Nichols' fingers so hard that I'm surprised I didn't break them."

I couldn't help but laugh at that visual and Ethan actually smiled back. For one, fleeting heartbeat it was like we didn't hate each other. Like we actually could be what the moon had wanted us to be for each other.

But that must have just been the blood loss talking, because the shine faded fast and his brows pulled together as if he'd seen me slamming the door to my heart closed in his face.

"Rosalie, please, I-"

"What's going on?" Roary's deep voice drew my attention over Ethan's shoulder and my heart twisted in this almost guilty, definitely painful way as I glanced between these two men I'd sworn not to ache for and felt as though I was bleeding all over the floor for them even more than I had been upstairs.

My lips parted on the truth, but I held it back. If they knew what Gustard had done then they'd run right on down there and beat the living shit out of him, maybe even kill him, and we couldn't afford that. They might end up in the hole if they were caught and if not, that memory crystal would be handed over to the FIB and everything we were doing here would be for nothing. I could deal with Gustard alone. I didn't need either of them risking anything for me.

"It's no big deal," I said dismissively, moving around Ethan and heading to Roary's side. He tugged me under his arm and I let him even though I knew in my heart that I shouldn't. But I needed the reassuring contact from a member of my pack...not that Roary really was my pack, but sometimes it felt like he was. He reminded me of home, and he made me feel safe in a way that had nothing to do with protecting me from murderous psychopaths.

Ethan growled as he moved to my other side, keeping pace with us as we headed down the stairs, but he stopped with the questions, clearly realising he wasn't going to get any answers.

With Roary's arm around me, I didn't stumble again, but I definitely didn't feel like I was on top form.

We headed into the library and found the boss man waiting for us, his hair still wet from a shower and his uniform crisp and fresh. I guessed he'd just started his shift but as his eyes fell on me and lit with a fiery rage, I also guessed he'd heard about my little incident upstairs.

My gaze fixed on him for so long that it took me a while to notice the new addition to our crew, but when I did, I sucked in a breath of horror.

"Two-Hundred has just returned from his stint in the hole," Cain said, flicking a look my way that said he wasn't best pleased about landing me in a room with that Dragon Shifter motherfucker either. So why the fuck was he? "The warden thinks it would be good for him to work alongside Eighty-Eight so that the two of you can get past your issues and the prison can be a happy place again."

"I went to the hole for a murder he committed," Sin growled ferociously, pointing at Christopher in accusation. "You can't seriously think we are going to just work through shit like that?"

Damn, he was hot when he growled and even hotter when he lied. Shit, I almost believed him, and I was the one who had planted the murder weapon on Christopher the pervy Dragon to get Sin off the hook. Well, technically Roary had, but I'd been the one to go get his secret shank so that we could plant it on the bastardo and let him rot in the hole. Though I didn't personally feel like he'd rotted for nearly long enough. I got three months because Cain threw a bitch fit and he got five for murder. How the fuck did that work out?

"I don't give a shit if you work it out or not," Cain drawled. "Frankly, I hope you try to kill each other and I come back here to find a body waiting at the end of your shift. Then I can get rid of one of you for good and send the other to rot in the hole again. It's win-win for me and the world as a whole."

Sin smirked like he'd just been given a free pass and I bit my lip as I eye fucked him so hard, I was surprised he hadn't come in his pants. The filthy look he gave me said he could sure as hell tell what I was thinking though and I was seriously hoping he'd follow through on that promise in his eyes soon.

"I need a word, Twelve," Cain barked, drawing my gaze back to him and in my slightly excitable state, I may have had to check him out too. Yeah, Cain would totally get it if he wasn't such a stronzo.

"Of course you do," Roary muttered as Cain strode towards me and he threw the Lion a dark look filled with hatred before taking my arm and tugging me towards the stacks at the side of the room.

"The rest of you get to work," Cain barked and the others all headed off towards the back of the library as commanded, though I could feel eyes on me as I walked away.

We kept walking until the cameras couldn't see us anymore and Cain threw a silencing bubble over us too.

"Hastings just told me what happened," Cain growled, looking down at me with darkness in his eyes and a promise I really hoped he would keep.

"I'm not sure what you're talking about," I said casually.

"I'll kill that little worm, Fifty-Three for touching you."

"Will you now?" I purred, arching a brow at him. "Why do you care so much, boss man?"

Cain's nostrils flared and he leaned down to speak into my ear. "What makes you think I *care?* I'm your CO. It's my job to look after you."

I laughed, tossing my hair over my shoulder and starting back towards the central part of the library, turning my back on him without giving a shit that it was a huge insult.

"Whatever you wanna tell yourself. But maybe you should make sure you're going after the right Fae before you start out on a mission of vengeance," I purred as I moved to leave, but he shot around in front of me, making me flinch, which in turn made my head spin and I stumbled back against a bookshelf with a curse.

Cain caught my waist and tugged me upright with a growl, digging his hand into his pocket and offering me a small bottle of blue potion.

"What's that?" I grunted, trying to shake him off but he wouldn't let go.

"It's a regeneration potion," he said. "It will help your blood get back to normal levels."

"So sweet," I cooed, taking it and eyeing it suspiciously. My family had a lot of enemies and we were always careful about accepting drinks from strangers, but in this place it wasn't like I could really be picky. "I guess you're concerned there won't be enough blood for you to drink if I don't get back to normal quickly."

I unscrewed the bottle, ignoring the frown Cain offered me that said he was mildly offended by that suggestion. But what did he expect me to think? That he'd gotten me this potion for no other reason than his unyielding care for my health? Please. I'd believe that when he managed to keep his teeth out of me for a month. He'd certainly caved fast enough when I'd offered it to him. And even if he did manage not to bite me again, I'd probably still have doubts.

I downed the contents of the little bottle and then smiled sweetly at him.

"If Fifty-Three isn't the one who attacked you then why was he found with the weapon and why would he confess?" Cain asked and I rolled my eyes at him.

"Use your noggin, Stronzo. I'm not telling you shit, so figure it out or stop wasting my time."

Cain narrowed his eyes on me. "Which gang is Fifty-Three in?" he asked.

"Before today, I didn't even know that stronzo existed," I replied in distaste.

Cain looked like he wanted to shake the answer out of me and then his eyes lit up like he'd figured something out. "You're friendly with the Lion and One is your mate. The only other gang leader to come after you and not be dead yet for it is Gustard."

I shrugged like I had no idea what he was talking about, but

I winked as he frowned and that gave him pause. I guessed he was wondering why I was letting Gustard get away with that shit, but I seriously doubted he'd ever be able to figure it out.

"Come on then, boss man, tell me what it is you want me to do to pay for that kindness," I asked, handing him the little potion bottle to distract his inquisitive mind from the issue at hand.

"Fuck off, Twelve," he snapped. "Don't ever make me out to be like that motherfucker, Nixon. That's the last time I'll do you a favour."

I scoffed but he was already shooting away, leaving me with a sour taste in my mouth like I owed *him* something now. But fuck that. I'd just call this payment for one of the days he'd left me down in the hole. Eighty-nine more little favours like that and we'd be square. Until then, Officer Stronzo could go suck on a rotten egg.

By the time I reached the rest of our crew of escapees, I found Ethan looking like he was about to rip Christopher's head off while Roary and Sin closed in behind him like they wanted a turn too.

"How did Gustard even tell him about our plans?" Ethan snarled, his gaze swinging to me like maybe I wanted the scumbag rapist on the team with us. I guessed in my absence, Gustard had made it clear he intended to bring the Dragon stronzo with us. "You made everyone swear an oath not to tell, didn't you?"

"Forget it," I snapped, flicking a disgusted look between Gustard and Christopher. I could hardly explain the whole black-mail situation I had going with Gustard right now and I didn't owe him any answers anyway. That stronzo had refused to make a star bond, promising not to share our secret when we'd tried to get him to and clearly it was because he'd been planning this shit. "We have work to do."

"Oooooh yeah." Plunger started stripping out of his jump-suit and I shuddered before I had to see him shift. If I never saw that wrinkly ball-bag looking shifted flesh of his ever again then it would still be too soon.

Everyone headed away to their assigned work places and I relaxed a little as Christopher and Gustard strolled away towards the front of the room to 'keep watch' and sit on their damn asses while we worked.

"Pudding, I need to make a call," I said in a low tone, moving towards him and hoping that he had what I needed on hand.

"I need more pudding pots, hound," he warned as he handed over a transmitter. He constructed them inside the old pots and as the other things he used to make them could easily be considered trash, he could just carry them around without the guards even noticing them. If he got stopped for a search, he just crushed the pot in his fist and it looked like trash. And no one ever questioned him for carrying pudding pots around because that was his whole thing. It was pretty genius really. "Can't keep making them without the magical chips. And the magical chips are in the pudding pots."

Now that he'd had to make transmitters for each member of the team as well as a few for me to keep Dante updated on our plans, we were struggling to keep up with the demand for chips, but I'd make it happen.

"Got it," I agreed, making a mental note to remind the pack about that and accepting the pudding pot which held the transmitter from him before catching Roary's eye and heading off into the stacks while everyone else got to work.

We wound our way through the shelves and I tried to figure out how the hell I was going to deal with this Gustard issue. He was already pushing me beyond my limits, but while he had that fucking memory crystal in the grip of his lawyer, there wasn't a whole lot I could do except lie back and take whatever the fuck he wanted to give me. But that just wasn't in my nature and I was getting seriously close to just killing the freak and hoping he was full of shit.

"Calm down, little pup," Roary said in a low voice, wrapping an arm around my waist which I immediately shrugged off before whirling on him.

"You know, when you call me that, I don't fucking like it," I snapped. "And I feel like you just do it to remind yourself that I'm younger than you, but I don't really care about your reasons. I'm twenty-four years old - the same age you were when you got locked up here. Tell me, did you think of yourself as a child then?"

"That doesn't really have anything to do with anything," Roary said, meeting my gaze with his golden eyes and refusing to flinch from my anger.

But I wasn't in the mood for his shit right now and maybe I was just looking for an outlet for my anger, but he needed to stop with this kid bullshit.

"Do you think I'm sweet and innocent, Roar? Are you worried you might corrupt me or something?"

"Rosa..." Roary frowned at me then growled beneath his breath like he didn't want to have this conversation.

"Whatever," I huffed, turning my attention to the transmitter and connecting the dental floss to the chunk of blueberry gum like Pudding had shown me to get it to call out. "But I hope you realise I've fucked guys older than you before. Dirtier too. So don't go thinking I'm some sweet little virgin or anything crazy like that."

The growl he released following that statement sent a shiver running down my spine and my heart pounded at the look in his eyes as I lifted my gaze back to his.

"Rosalie? Is that you?" Dante's voice came through the receiver and I lifted the pudding pot to my ear as tension hung in the air between me and the Lion stronzo who was looking at me like he either wanted to bite my head off or possibly do something much more interesting.

"Yeah. Did you manage to find the other crystal yet?" I asked, holding Roary's gaze with my best resting bitch face and loving the way his eyes flared with anger which made heat prickle along my skin.

"I'm sorry cugina, I don't know how this stronzo is doing it, but he's gone to ground better than a rat in a nest. I can't find so much as a trace of him let alone get on with torturing the information about that crystal's whereabouts from him. Is the bastardo who sent it causing you problems?"

"He half gutted me in the corridor a little while ago," I grunted, fiddling with the hole that shank had put in the front of my jumpsuit and Roary's lips parted in confusion, his gaze shifting to my stomach as he tried to piece that together for himself. He tugged my hand aside and snarled as he spotted the hole, but I just continued with my conversation. "Don't worry about it. I'll come up with a plan to get him out of my hair. If I can get him sent to the hole for the date in question then we won't even need to worry about him tagging along."

Dante chuckled darkly and I closed my eyes so that I could listen to that sound as children started shouting in the background.

"Papa, papa! You have to come and see what he's doing now! He climbed up in the apple tree and says he won't come down unless Mommy gives him a special gift, but we don't know what he wants."

"Is that RJ?" I asked, smiling as I opened my eyes again and found Roary's gaze softening at the mention of my niece. I beckoned him closer and he leaned in as I held the transmitter so that he could listen too and the kids started laughing while Dante told them off for interrupting him in the least convincing voice known to man. If his enemies knew that the king of the Oscura Clan was as soft as butter for his babies then they would probably be a whole lot less terrified of him.

"Say hello to your cugina," Dante called and the kids started shouting hello at the top of their lungs as I laughed.

"Are you little pups being good for your papa?" I asked them, smiling as I remembered their chubby little cheeks and aching to see them for real as soon as possible.

"I'm not a pup," RJ announced loudly. "I'm going to be a Lion and roar louder than anyone else in the entire kingdom."

"Well I'm going to be a ninja," Luca replied in a superior tone. "Who also can turn into a Dragon and a Basilisk and a Tiberian

Rat."

"I don't think that's how it works," I laughed.

"Is too. I saw it on Late Night Weird and Wonky with daddy the other night," he protested.

"I feel like that show is inappropriate," I replied. "I'm sure I saw a Fae on there who was a Medusa but had managed to make snakes form in their...not head hair for...unmentionable reasons."

RJ and Luca fell about laughing as Dante protested that he wouldn't let them watch that show ever again and I found myself grinning at Roary as we escaped this underground prison for a little while in their laughter.

"Is it sunny today?" Roary asked in his deep, rumbling tone.

"Zio Roary, is that you?" RJ asked in excitement.

"How could you tell?" he asked in reply.

"Because you *always* ask if it's sunny." She started laughing again and I smirked at him as he rolled his eyes.

"Ha ha, let's all laugh at the silly old Lion locked underground," he joked and the kids laughed even louder like that really was funny.

"I'll keep you updated on that memory crystal, Rosa," Dante interrupted and I guessed our time was about to run out. The magic only lasted a few minutes and a hundred of them wouldn't have been enough.

"It's okay," I replied with a sigh. It had been a long shot anyway. "I can take Gustard out of the picture. I have no intention of letting him ever escape this place."

"Addio, Rosa. Ti amo."

"Ti amo, Dante. Ti amo, kids," I called but as they started to yell a reply back to me, the magic died and their voices were cut off.

I sighed, letting my eyes fall closed as I crushed the pudding pot in my fist, turning it back into the trash it was made from as I tried to cling to the final notes of their laughter and tie them up tight around my heart.

Roary's arms closed around me and I sighed as I let him pull me close to his chest, inhaling the rich sandalwood scent of him as I listened to the beat of his heart beneath my ear and tried to convince myself I didn't want anything else from him.

"When I see you, I don't see a little pup, Rosa," Roary said in a low voice, returning to the argument we'd been having before that call. "I see a Fae worth respecting, fearing, following. I see one of the only good things in here and a piece of home I never dared to believe I'd have again. I don't think you're some stupid pup. I think you're the one thing I needed more than anything in this place. Hope."

I didn't know what to say to that so I just curled my arms around his waist and held him close for as long as my aching heart could take it without breaking for him.

When I pulled back, I gave him a tight smile and headed back towards the main part of the library where the work was underway.

As we stepped out of the aisle we'd been in, I almost bumped straight into Gustard and I flinched minutely, narrowing my eyes at him as he smiled almost pleasantly.

"Problem?" I challenged, taking in that smug glint in his eyes like he held all of my secrets close and was just waiting for the right moment to reveal them.

Gustard gave Roary an assessing look, his mouth hooking up at the corner like he was tempted to reveal my feelings for him but instead, he just shrugged innocently.

"No problem I can't deal with, pup," he said and a shiver of warning ran down my spine as my gifts pricked up at the threat in his voice.

He walked away from us and I narrowed my eyes at him.

"You don't think he was listening to us, do you?" I murmured once I was sure he was out of earshot.

Roary frowned as he considered it then shrugged. "If he was, I think he would have said something, reminded us of his leverage."

"Yeah," I agreed, letting him turn me away from Gustard as a frown pinched my brow.

That unsettled feeling wouldn't go away though. But if Gustard thought he could take me on and win, he had another thing coming.

"But if you don't kill him when we get out of here, I'll do it myself, Rosa. No one hurts you and gets away with it while I still draw breath," Roary growled and despite all the reasons I had to be worrying, I couldn't help but smirk to myself at that declaration.

ARIES. VAMPIRE. FIRE.
COMMANDING OFFICER
CAIN
DARKMORE PENITENTIARY

I exited the processing room, healing the scratches on my arm from the new inmate I'd just sent into Darkmore. My shift was ending and I wasn't looking forward to the hours alone in my room. I nodded to Lyle who was sitting in the security office, parted from me by a wall of glass.

"Ombrian Tiger Shifter, eh? Don't get many of those anymore," he commented and I shrugged.

"Guess not," I said, tucking my Atlas into my pocket, about to leave, but he kept talking.

"My great uncle Neville was a white Nemean Lion," he said thoughtfully. "I've got a nice red coat, but it's not that rare. Are there rare types of Vampires?"

"I don't know," I said, stepping toward the door.

"I suppose there's not much to be rare about a Vampire, fangs that glow maybe," he chuckled.

"Yeah, maybe," I grunted, then wondered if this was why I had no friends.

It wasn't like most of the guards here weren't decent Fae. It was that I wasn't. And that I'd lost the desire to bond with people a long time ago. After the only person I ever cared about was ripped from this world, I decided not to make a habit out of caring for people again. That kind of wound didn't heal right. It would always be there and the moon curse I was under liked to remind me of that even more often than before.

My gaze slipped to the CCTV screens behind Lyle's head as he started talking about his uncle Nigel or whatever the fuck his name was, and my eyes hooked on the back of a girl's head as she pushed into the gym. Most people probably wouldn't have been able to tell who she was, but I knew it was Twelve just from that one glance and I found I couldn't drag my eyes away from her, watching as she passed by the single camera in the gymnasium which only showed a small section just past the entranceway. She disappeared beyond the range of the camera and a flare of annoyance prickled through me followed by a wave of pain running up my arm from the curse mark. The silver rose vine had reached my shoulder now, wrapping around it and binding me even more tightly to her. To my oncoming fucking death.

I'd read the book on moon magic back to back and there had been no more information about how to break this damn curse. At the rate it was spreading, I didn't know how long it would be before I'd succumb to it entirely. My anger at Rosalie over cursing me hadn't lessened, but unfortunately I understood why she'd done it now. After I'd found out what her father had done to her, I felt like a prime asshole. I'd fucked up on so many levels when I'd put her in the hole. I'd done the unspeakable to her. Something she could never forgive. And now I was paying the price for my selfishness of wanting to keep her out of sight, out of mind. I should've known she'd find a way to punish me for it.

"So are you finishing up for the day?" Lyle asked, cutting through my thoughts as the pain needled deeper into my arm.

I grunted, checking my watch. I had ten minutes left. I could call it a day...or I could head down to the gym and see Twelve. Not that I'd talk to her or anything. It's not like I wanted to go fucking perving on her while she worked out either, though I wasn't exactly denying to myself how hot that would get me. Mostly I just wanted to see her. Check on her. And the curse on my arm seemed to agree with that, the pain ebbing away until the magic hummed keenly against my flesh instead. *Fuck the moon and its ways.*

"Yeah, soon. Night Lyle," I muttered and he waved to me as I headed out the door.

I took the elevator downstairs and arrived on the fifth floor, shooting along it to the gym. It was almost time for lockdown and as I sped inside, I found the place empty. I frowned as I paused by the boxing ring, straining my ears as the sound of a shower running carried from the locker rooms. Maybe she'd realised there wasn't enough time for a workout and headed back to her block. And maybe I was a fucking moron for caring about where she was anyway. But I was still pissed that I'd missed her.

I turned to leave, but a muffled yell made me swing around. It was barely more than a peep, but I knew it had come from her in the depths of my soul. I tore across the room as fast as I could, shoving the locker room door open and flying through it into the showers at the end. An orange jumpsuit was soaked in the water filling the space before me, the number twelve staring up at me on it, stained red with blood. My gut clenched into a tight ball.

The locker rooms were built in a U shape so I shot down to one end and around the corner, my heart hammering, fear making every muscle in my body coil in anticipation. *What if I'm too late? What if someone's hurt her? Killed her?*

My eyes fell on the ten inmates surrounding my girl as she fought for her fucking life. They tried to pin her down, blood pouring from a busted lip and a deep gash sliced along her right arm. Two Hundred was naked, his hairy back aimed my way as he barked orders at the others to hold her against the wall while his moving arm told me he was stroking his cock.

I took this all in within three seconds and in that time, I became nothing but a vicious, bloodthirsty animal with no boundaries, no rules holding me back, nothing but the primal need to protect the girl they wanted to hurt.

I didn't see red. I saw the fires of hell blazing everywhere, flaring through every corner of my mind. My fangs lengthened and I dove toward my enemies with the full strength of my order, breaking two necks before the rest of them even realised I was there. I ripped out one girl's throat who was holding Rosalie's arm and my girl's eyes widened for a moment before she wrenched her other arm free and leapt into the fray with me. Some of them were trying to escape. But none of them would. I couldn't let a single one of them leave this place. I'd destroy them all, make the water run red for what they'd tried to do.

I was blinded by my need to kill them, tearing Ninety Four's throat out before punching a hole in Four Hundred and Ten's chest. Blood poured, mixing with the rush of heated water tumbling from the showers above so a whirlpool of it twisted around my feet. I wasn't satisfied with that though. I wouldn't be until all of their screams were silenced forever.

I grabbed a fistful of one guy's hair as he made to leave, twisting him around fast and throwing him into the wall so hard his skull shattered.

Adrenaline mixed with the bloodlust inside me, my eyes razor sharp as I took in every movement around me.

Twelve was fighting Two Hundred as his huge fists thumped into her body and I roared my rage, racing towards them. One idiot tried to block my way and I ripped his throat out with my teeth before diving over him and wrenching Two Hundred away from Rosalie. The final girl still standing made a run for the exit and Rosalie charged her down, knocking her to the ground and twisting her head until a loud snap sounded.

I threw Two Hundred against the wall, the monster in me housing every piece of my flesh right then as I started throwing my fists into him repeatedly. And maybe this was who I really was anyway. Maybe it wasn't some part of me, but all of me was this dark, this evil. And so long as I was Rosalie's beast, I didn't want to hide it. I'd gladly spill the blood of her enemies again and again until there was no creature left on earth who'd dare touch her.

I didn't kill Two Hundred immediately, I stopped pounding into his flesh and pinned him back to the wall by the throat, my fangs bared as I paused and let him see his death in my eyes. He was shaking like a leaf and a tinkling noise at my feet told me he'd just pissed himself. I grimaced, disgusted by this foul thing who claimed to be Fae. He wasn't even close to that, he was nothing but a leech, sucking the life out of anyone he could. He lived in the shadows, surrounded by worthless rats just like him, and together they made themselves powerful. But alone, they were *nothing*. And I was happy to remind him of that.

"But you're supposed t-to protect us," he stammered out as my grip on his throat tightened.

"No," I said in a cold, detached voice. "Too many Fae in this place get that wrong, Two Hundred. We're here to make sure you don't escape. And to use necessary force against you if you break the rules."

"I didn't break a rule!" he gasped. "I haven't tried to escape."

"No," I said in a dark and hungry tone. "You haven't broken any rules. But you've made a mistake in thinking that *I* follow the rulebook."

"But y-you're a guard." he gasped.

"And you're a disgusting rapist. But mostly, Christopher," I whispered, leaning in close so my words were just for him as he trembled beneath my hold. "You're a dead man."

I felt nothing as I gripped his head between my hands, ripping and ripping and ripping while his screams of pain turned to ones of utter, excruciating fear, begging me, pleading with me. Rosalie's beautiful voice filled the room, speaking my name as I tore through muscle and bone and flesh and I thrived on the moment the light went out in his eyes. I wrenched his head clean off and his body crumpled beneath me like the sack of shit it was.

Blood coated me as I tossed his head aside, the shower not running at this end of the unit so I remained painted in his death, my shoulders rising and falling as I drew in slow breaths to bring my heart back to a normal beat.

The curse mark on my arm sent waves of heat through me. Heat that felt almost connected to my Wolf girl, like it was coming directly from her veins into mine. I soaked in that sensation, shutting my eyes as I absorbed the consuming closeness of her. It was intoxicating. *She* was intoxicating.

Her hand suddenly pressed to my back and I turned, finding her standing there in her underwear, gazing at me with her lip bleeding and the long wound on her arm dripping red into the water at her feet. I reached out, healing the gash away before reaching up to press my thumb against her split lip.

"Mason," she rasped, her eyes wide and unblinking. My name was the undoing of the raging, monstrous spell that held me in its grip. And I no longer hungered for death, I hungered for her. I was laid bare. What I'd done was admitting how I felt about her a thousand times louder than words ever could have.

"I-" Before I could get another word out, she leapt at me, winding her legs around my waist and her mouth clashed with mine. I hadn't healed the wound on her lip so her blood instantly ran over my tongue and I groaned, twisting around and driving her back against the wall.

I pushed my tongue into her mouth and she met my kiss with hungry movements of her own, a wolfish growl leaving her that made my cock harden to iron. Her nails tore down my back just as the bell sounded for the start of lockdown. I didn't care and I didn't fucking stop, kissing her deeper, tasting her honey sweetness and wetting her in Two Hundred's blood which was splattered across the wall. She groaned, her thighs tightening around my waist and drawing me flush to her body so I felt the heat between her thighs burning against my stomach.

I cursed as she gripped my hair, yanking hard to break our kiss. I took in the damp hair plastered to her cheeks, her panting mouth and heaving chest and I was lost. Ready to give up everything, lose my job, my home, fucking all of it to have this girl. I'd wanted her from the first moment I'd seen her and that want had grown to a need. A need that defied all rules, transcended every good reason I had to place her down now and walk away.

"Don't you dare run away," she hissed as the bell continued to ring. It was like fate chiming in, demanding I answer its call.

We were standing in a bloodbath of inmates I'd killed savagely. There was no disguising that and I didn't even dare let myself think about the world awaiting me beyond this chamber of death. Despite the terrifying reality of what I'd done, I was also standing in my darkest fucking fantasy. Rosalie wrapped around me, aching for me while the room ran red with blood around us. It was a Vampire's wet dream and not one I'd ever imagined would really happen. But fuck, here I was. And there was no chance of me turning away. I was surprised she couldn't see that decision in my eyes. But maybe that just proved how little she trusted me. And since when did I start trusting her either?

Her hand slid down between us and she fisted my achingly hard cock through my uniform trousers, drawing a desperate growl from my lips.

"I'm done running from my problems," I said and she sneered.

"Is that what I am to you? A *problem*?" She squeezed my dick hard enough to hurt and I bared my fangs at her, only growing harder at that.

"Yeah, sweetheart," I slammed her back against the wall hard enough to bruise, pushing my hand between us and shoving hers away as I felt her hot wetness waiting for me, soaking through those ugly prisoner panties. "You're my dirty -" I freed my cock from my pants, "-filthy-" I tore her panties aside "-*problem*." I lined myself up with her slick entrance and she gasped, locking her ankles behind my back as she tried to pull me forward, telling me she wanted this as much as I did. "And I think I've finally found a solution."

I shoved myself inside her and she tipped her head back with a cry of ecstasy that sent my ego shooting through the roof. I cast a silencing bubble, barely able to concentrate with the walls of her pussy squeezing my cock and making me forget everything but her. I pinned her to the wall, taking her hard

349

and fast with furious thrusts of my hips as her nails scraped down my neck. She pushed her hands under my guard jacket, forcing it off my shoulders before pulling my shirt over my head. I groaned at the feel of her hands on my bare flesh, her fingers roaming my muscles, taking in all of me like she'd dreamed about my body as much as I had hers.

I stole a kiss from her puffy lips and my cock thickened inside her as I tore her bra from her chest, needing to feel more of her skin on mine as our bodies ground together. The bell had stopped ringing and I knew what that meant, though it was seriously fucking hard to think of anything but how good her pussy felt clutching my solid length as I pumped it in and out of her. But we were running out of time before the count was finished and someone realised she was missing. So we had to be fast. And as a Vampire, that was my middle fucking name.

I stood back, lifting her off of me so she dropped to the floor. She gripped my throat with a snarl, trying to take control and I laughed darkly as I spun her around by the hips, using my Order strength to dominate her. She hissed like a bobcat as I tilted her hips back for me, taking a moment to appreciate the perfect roundness of her ass. Then I spanked her hard as I entered her again with a firm thrust and she braced her hands on the wall with a moan of pleasure as she gave in to my demands.

I pounded into her a few more times then gave her no warning as I started using my Vampire speed to claim her. Her escalating screams were music to my ears as she clenched around my pulsing cock and I fought not to blow inside her as I reached around her perfect body, clutching one of her full breasts in my hand hard enough to mark her while she reached back to tear her nails down along my arm and remind me how much of animal she was. And I liked that so fucking much.

I dropped my other hand to her clit and started circling my fingers over that sensitive spot with the speed of my Order, running my tongue over her shoulder in the exact place I was hungering to bite.

"Holy *fuck*," she gasped as she came within seconds and I

dragged her back against me, biting her hard, my fingers still working her clit in lightning fast movements, drawing out her orgasm. "*Mason*," she half whimpered as I kept stroking her, wanting to feel her pussy grip me again and she writhed like she could hardly take it, her skin over-sensitised as my rough fingers worked her up toward another explosion.

"Come for me, Twelve," I used her inmate name, making her snarl angrily and I smirked like an asshole as I enjoyed having her like this. She couldn't escape, all she could do was come on my cock and scream like a good girl when she really wanted to be a bad one.

I drank her blood in deep gulps, my mind dizzy as euphoria drowned all the concerns I should have been having about what I was doing. That I'd killed ten inmates. And what was going to happen after this was over. But fuck she felt too good. Her body was more soft, more wet, more fucking tight than my imagination could ever have conjured up. I'd jerked off over her too many times to count and I hadn't even come close to picturing the reality.

When she came again, she howled, tipping her head back and fuck that sound alone had me about to lose my mind. But I'd had enough fantasies of this moment to know how I wanted this to go. I gripped her hair, forcing her to look back at me over her shoulder, wanting to see how undone she was for me.

But as her eyes met mine, she smirked like *she* was in control, like she held all the cards of fate and would hand me mine however she pleased. And that was somehow hotter than me owning her, much fucking hotter. I came hard, my balls tightening as I got the release I'd been yearning for for months. Pleasure spiralled through me as I stared into the depths of her dark and secretive eyes, spilling myself deep inside her while she watched me fall apart for her. And fall *for* her at the same time. Because I was a goner. Fucking ruined by this girl. She'd tortured me, cursed me and now she'd claimed me too. And I didn't give a fuck anymore about trying to stop wanting her. I'd possibly just thrown away everything I'd ever owned for this girl. I could end up in a cell in Darkmore for what I'd done here today. And I found I didn't care about that nearly as much as I should have.

I pulled out of her and she turned around, that satisfied smile still on her face as she reached out and tucked my dick away for me.

The smile soon turned to concern though and her fingers ran down my cheek for a second before she caught my hand and tugged me into the flow of water still running from one of the showers. She tucked herself against me as the water washed over us and I just stared and stared at this naked goddess who now owned me. And who I still didn't own a piece of in return.

I healed the cut on her lip, the bite on her shoulder and the bruises I'd marked her with while she washed the blood from my body and started looking at me differently. Not with disgust or hate, with something close to gratitude. Maybe something close to like. But I was probably just getting my hopes up on that one. I was still the asshole who'd thrown her in the hole even if she did lust for me.

"You rescued me, boss man," she said, her lashes fluttering as she looked up at me in a way that seemed genuine for once. My throat just bobbed as I tried to respond to that. I apparently couldn't form any words though so I just grunted, not confirming it or denying it. "And now we're in trouble. Can you...get us out of it?" She bit her lip as she looked between the dead bodies surrounding us and I slid my arm around her waist, drawing her close so my lips grazed her ear.

"You don't have to worry about anything," I promised and I felt the mark of the curse thrumming happily and that shit actually started to glow, drawing her attention as it claimed me deeper. As *she* claimed me deeper.

Her fingers grazed over the silver vines reaching across my shoulder, but we didn't have time to discuss it. My mind was finally sharpening, coming down from the high of murdering ten Fae then losing myself to the most beautifully captivating girl I'd ever known. And there was one truth that rang clearer in my mind than anything else. *I am so fucked.*

I looked around at the carnage as Twelve gazed at her torn off underwear floating in the water with a worried frown. I put a plan together in my mind then shot away from her out of the locker room into the gym, snatching up some of the heaviest weights and a weight bar before shooting back into the showers with Rosalie. Her lips were parted and fear flashed in her eyes.

Fuck, did she think I'd actually abandoned her?

I shot toward her, resting my forehead to hers for half a second that I didn't have to waste. But for the sake of wiping that suspicion from her eyes, I would.

"I got you," I swore and she frowned at me in confusion before I sped away again, wetting the weights in blood and ramming one end of the bar into Two Hundred's back. Some of the stronger inmates could have caused this kind of massacre with weapons. It wouldn't seem too suspicious.

I burned the remains of her underwear then grabbed Rosalie's jumpsuit and my uniform. I used my fire magic to dry them quickly before throwing her over my shoulder while she gasped in surprise. I raced into the locker room, placing her down and using my fire magic to dry her body while she rested her hands against my bare shoulders. I dried myself off too then pulled her jumpsuit on, practically flipping her over my shoulder again as I didn't let her help, doing it in less than a second. When she stood before me, dry with a grin playing around her mouth, I pulled on my own clothes, hurriedly doing up the buttons of my shirt and healing away any marks she'd left on my skin. Rosalie stepped forward when I was finished, flattening my hair as she chewed on her bottom lip.

"Sure I'm not gonna get in trouble, boss man?"

"I'm sure," I growled. When bodies turned up dead in Darkmore, there weren't many questions asked if there were no obvious witnesses. And I sure as shit wasn't going to let her seem culpable. "So how are we going to get out of here without being caught on the CCTV?"

"I can move faster than the cameras can record," I said and a teasing smile pulled at her lips.

"I know just how fast you can move," she purred and my throat thickened. Was I an idiot to think she wouldn't tell the other guards about what I'd done? She could destroy my life with a few words to the warden. Everything about my future was held in her palms. And there was nothing I could do about it. But I wouldn't have taken back a single drop of the blood I'd spilled even if it were possible. Those monsters would never lay their hands on her again and that was something I would never be sorry for.

"The Oscuras will take credit for this," she said, glancing back over at the dead bodies. "Gustard has been coming at me publicly so it won't be a surprise that the gangs came to blows. There's over a hundred Wolves in my pack, so all I have to do is whisper in a few ears about the way we crushed these fuckers and they'll all just assume it was other members of the pack who actually struck the blow while they take credit for it as a group. They won't even realise the boast is a lie. Gustard will believe it too. So long as you swear not a single one of my Wolves will be punished for it."

For a moment I could only stare at her, surprised that she'd make me that offer after everything I'd done to her. It didn't even feel like she was offering to do it so that she could own me, though I supposed she could hold this secret over my head now. But she'd already been keeping secrets that could have seen me fired at the very least and hadn't even revealed them when I'd left her down in the hole. I didn't know why, but I trusted Rosalie Oscura.

"They won't be punished," I swore. "If any evidence happened to show up, I can easily get rid of it."

"Looks like I've got you too then, Mason," she purred and my throat thickened at that statement.

For all the hope that we could cover this up, there was still a massive chance this would all blow up in my face. Which

354

meant this could be my last moment alone with Rosalie for a long ass time. I caught the back of her neck and crushed her lips to mine, taking one final taste of her so that if my life went down the drain then at least I had good reminders of why I'd done it. She moaned against my mouth and that sound was a carnal sin that had blood pounding to my dick again. I'd fucked my queen in a sea of blood and I wanted nothing more than to keep worshipping her, slower next time, making her beg for more of me. I'd never wanted to kneel for any Fae. But she held more power over me than the stars themselves. And I wanted to surrender everything I was to her in that moment.

I broke our bittersweet goodbye and tossed her over my shoulder before she could say a word, tearing out of the room and going full speed, not holding back even a little as I sprinted through the prison faster than I'd ever moved in my life. I soon rounded into the corridor of cellblocks, shooting up in front of Block D just as Hastings was about to close the bridge.

I planted Rosalie down and his eyes filled with relief. "We were just about to release the Belorian," he said anxiously, looking at my girl with moony eyes that made me want to punch him straight in the face.

"I got trapped under a fallen bookcase in the library," Rosalie lied, twirling a lock of hair between her fingers as she played the innocent act. Why was seeing her lie to someone else so fucking hot? I had to turn away slightly so Hastings didn't get a view of how hard I was or figure out how furiously my heart was pounding. "Officer Cain found me."

"Isn't your shift over?" Hastings asked me and I shrugged. "You really need to take a break more often."

"Yeah, yeah," I muttered. "Lock her up tight," I barked then shot away towards the elevators, not looking back, because if I did, I'd want to turn around and find a way to spend a few more seconds with her.

I made it upstairs, speeding through the guards' quarters to my room and shutting the door as I stepped inside. A laugh fell from my lungs and I couldn't remember the last time I'd laughed like that as I just fell the fuck apart and pressed my head to the door.

My whole world could go to hell soon enough when those bodies were found. But I had to hope they'd be written off as a gang incident and it would be left at that. Time in Darkmore was known to be a possible death sentence anyway, it was what made this place so terrifying. And even the warden herself wouldn't clamp down on murders too hard because then Fae outside of this place would have less to fear, less deterrents to commit crimes.

And as crazy as it was, even if Pike did find out the truth, even if she ruined my life over Rosalie Oscura, at least there was no other Fae in Solaria I'd rather be ruined for.

DARKMORE PENITENTIARY

ROSALIE

ORDER· WEREWOLF
PRISONER NUMBER· #12

STAR SIGN· TAURUS
ELEMENT· EARTH

With that sick fuck Christopher dead and my pack sending whispers all over the prison about the way the Oscuras had dealt with the Watchers in a gang skirmish, the suspicion had been turned away from the boss man and I was back to not owing him a damn thing. Which was the only reason why I'd helped him of course. He might have said that he'd deal with it for me, but I knew the only thing that could really explain the mess he'd made of those corpses was a gang war, which meant the winners needed to be bragging. I wasn't going to risk any suspicion falling on him and it had been simple enough to get my Wolves in on the plan. They didn't even know it was bullshit – there were so many of them that they all just assumed it was other members of the pack who had done it. Though maybe I should have let Cain get caught in payment for throwing me in the hole, but unlike him, I took a life debt seriously and I wouldn't let him rot for saving me.

I could feel Cain's eyes on me as I crossed the Magic Compound and it made my skin prickle, like I was a mouse caught in the gaze of a hawk. But I was no mouse.

I stopped abruptly and turned to look right at my CO where he stood patrolling the outer edge of the fence that surrounded the compound. His grey eyes were fixed on me and his gaze was carefully blank, but there was something in the way he watched me that said something had changed between us now. I wouldn't have pegged him for the type to get all sentimental after sex, but there he was, watching me like I might just belong to him. *Unlikely, stronzo.*

With purposeful strides, I locked my gaze on his and headed across the compound, watching the way his pupils dilated as I drew near and the way his nostrils flared too. He didn't look particularly pleased to see me coming. Or perhaps he was too pleased. I wasn't sure yet.

"Is there a problem, boss man?" I purred, twisting my fingers through the air and wrapping a silencing bubble around myself from behind which ran up to the fence that divided us and remained open for him to hear me.

Cain flicked his own fingers to make a silencing bubble on his side of the fence too and I couldn't help but smirk at the hint of panic in his eyes as he folded his arms and his jaw ticked.

"No problem, Twelve," he grunted.

"Shit, I love it when you call me by my number. It gets me so hot to know that I'm nothing to you and you could just switch me out for another at any time," I said in a seductive voice that had that vein in his temple pulsing. Cain baiting really was my new favourite game.

"Did you have something to say to me?" he ground out, eyes darting left and right like he thought someone might see us and damn, I just realised I'd become someone else's dirty little secret. What the fuck was that about?

"Not me, boss man. But you were eye fucking me so hard I could practically feel your cock inside me again, so I assumed you wanted me to come over."

A strangled noise escaped him and I smiled wide as he fought against the urge to lay into me, try and put me in my place and maybe...laugh. Huh, who'd have thought that Cain had a sense of humour hiding away beneath all of that grouchiness.

"I...what's your plan then? You want to hold this over me? Use it to make me bend the rules for you? Was it all just some honey trap you've been laying out for me and waiting for me to stumble into?" he snarled.

"Rude," I commented, raising an eyebrow. "Do you always

assume people you fuck are after something or have you just been with too many hookers?"

That vein pulsed again and I could see a war taking place within his eyes.

"I'm not saying you're a... You have to understand that in my position, if this came out-"

"Please, stronzo, as if I'd want to brag about fucking you anyway. Although it would be funny to see Ethan sent to the hole for beating your head in if he found out." I ignored the little twist in my gut that said I didn't want Ethan going to the hole because that bitch was weak, and I twisted a lock of my hair around my finger.

"If you care about your mate so much, then why-"

"I gotta go," I said with a grin. "So unless you wanna pull your balls out of your purse and just spit out whatever it was you really wanted to say..." I started backing away and Cain took half a step closer before halting himself with a frustrated growl.

"I won't be around as much this week," he said and I cocked my head at him, wondering why he thought I'd care about that. "The warden is installing a new bio-detection forcefield surrounding the prison and I'm going to have to oversee the workforce when they come in to install it, so-"

"When?" I asked, sweet as pie and keeping that mask slapped tight over my face because holy mother of shit, we were fucked if that thing came online. I hadn't accounted for that. Who knew what it would be capable of doing? I had no way to research it or figure out how to circumnavigate it or anything. My pulse was suddenly thundering in my ears and panic was dancing to a merry tune in my chest. But I didn't let any of that show on my face.

"I'm not sure exactly. They're hoping to complete installation and get it working by Sunday week, but these things never stay on schedule. Point is, if Gustard's people come at you again, I might not be around to-"

I laughed darkly, tossing my hair. "Please tell me you aren't worried about me, boss man?" I taunted. "Do you think I can't handle myself in here without you? Or is this more about you being concerned that you won't be able to find time to bury your cock in me again any time soon? Because you really shouldn't be making presumptions about me or what I want from you."

Cain frowned and I felt like, one percent guilty about that low blow, but fuck him. A few orgasms weren't going to make me forget that he'd left me in the hole for months. And who cared if he'd saved my life? I saved his not so long ago and got no thanks for it.

"I just thought you should know," he grunted and I rolled my eyes.

"Noted."

I turned my back on him, striding away without another word and forcing myself to keep my pace slow as I sought out Roary amongst the huge crowd of inmates.

As if he'd felt my need for him, my beautiful Lion Shifter slipped out of the crowd and approached me, his brow pinching in the tiniest of ways which I doubted anyone but me would notice. But I always noticed everything about Roary Night. It was my curse. But I couldn't bring myself to wish myself free of it either.

"What's up, little...Rosa?" he asked, just about managing to swerve the pup jibe and earning himself a brownie point.

I tucked my silencing bubble in tight around us and took his hand as I led him around the wall dividing the centre of the Magic Compound and moved to lean back against it, tugging him close so he stood before me.

I was shaking, useless adrenaline surging through my veins as I ached to do something to fix this shit but was forced to remain here like nothing had happened and play nice. Cain would still be watching me, though I'd bought myself a little time by circling the wall so he would have to walk around the outer edge of the compound to get his eyes on me again. And as I was willing to bet he wouldn't shoot right around and risk drawing attention, I was going to have to make sure that was enough.

"Kiss me, Roar," I commanded, my heart leaping even though it was just for a cover, but the idea of Roary Night's mouth on mine was always going to exhilarate me.

He didn't question me, understanding that something was wrong as he stepped up to me, cupping my cheek in his hand and tipping my jaw up towards his.

I didn't touch him, instead twisting my fingers in complex patterns either side of us and encouraging tall grass to grow up through the concrete at our feet to create a barrier for us to hide within.

Roary dipped his mouth so close to mine that I couldn't help the soft moan which escaped me, begging him to stop playing with me, to just kiss me and make everything in the world okay again.

The grass grew and grew as I threw my power into it and within moments, we were hidden within it.

Roary's lips still hadn't found mine and now that there was no need for them to, he stopped drawing closer to me.

Fuck, why did it have to hurt so much when he did that? I would honestly rather take that shank to the gut again a hundred times than have to feel this fissure being torn wide inside my heart.

"Tell me what happened," he murmured, his forehead pressed to mine, his hands still wrapped around my waist.

I should have been pushing him back. I should have been telling him to get off of me. I should have been wrenching myself away. But I was caught in his spell, trapped in this unending need for him that I couldn't rid myself of no matter how hard I tried.

"Cain just told me they're installing a new bio-detection forcefield around the prison next week. We can't combat that, Roar. I haven't got any plans for it or any way to make any. If we don't get out of here before they install it-"

"What was it you promised me when you got here, Rosa?"

Roary growled, pinning me in his golden gaze and refusing to let me squirm away from the look of intent in his eyes.

"That I was going to set you free," I breathed.

"And I believe in you," he said firmly, with no room for negotiation. "We're going to get out of here and find that desert island to go live on and-"

I started laughing and he paused, his mouth hooking up at the corner as he squeezed my waist tight between his big hands.

"Won't you be sick of me by then?" I asked. "You won't really want to be cooped up somewhere all alone with me like that."

"You're the only person I could ever imagine being cooped up with alone like that and loving every single second of it."

My lips parted and I frowned up at him because I didn't understand that. He didn't want me. He didn't want to have me in all the ways that counted. So why the hell would he want to be alone with me for the rest of our lives?

I shook my head dismissively and tried not to flinch as I forced out my next words. "You'll go out there and find yourself a harem of beautiful Lionesses," I teased. "You'll forget all about the annoying Wolf pup who got you sent to prison and then came to bust your ass back out again."

"Don't be ridiculous," he snarled.

"As much as the idea of living out my days in your guest quarters appeals to me, I think it might make more sense for me to just return to my family," I went on.

"I thought we *were* family?" he demanded and I released a long breath.

"We are, Roar. The Nights and the Oscuras are as thick as thieves. Always." I dropped my gaze to his chest and a rumble of frustration thundered through him as he growled at me.

He didn't reply, but he shifted his hands beneath the hem of my shirt so that his flesh was pressed to mine and his magic bumped up against the barriers of my skin in a clear demand. I wasn't strong enough to deny him, so I dropped my own barriers and let his power flood into me with a moan of exhilaration.

I felt like a vessel being filled with the might of a storm as the raw and turbulent energy of his water magic crashed through my body and my heart leapt and pounded in a way that had me aching for more. Earth needed water in this deep, intrinsic way and my magic craved the touch of his like it ached to use it for creation.

Roary groaned as I moved my hands to his stomach and slid them beneath his tank, the magic growing more powerful as it found more places to pass between us.

He drew back suddenly and rain began to fall over us, the droplets fat and warm like that perfect spring shower where every drop of it feels revitalising and pure as it kisses your skin. He shrugged his arms out of his jumpsuit and tugged his tank over his head, dropping it to the floor beside us and moving to push my jumpsuit from my arms as well.

I was so shocked to find Roary Night tugging my clothes off that for a moment all I could do was stare at the perfection of his golden skin across those tight abs and broad shoulders.

The moment my arms were free, Roary moved closer to me again, his hands pushing up beneath the back of my tank top as I wound my arms around his neck and trailed my fingers all over his skin. His forehead pressed to mine again and with so many points of contact between us, our combined magic pulsed and thrummed to this heady, happy rhythm until it seemed to find this perfect balance and instead of pawing at each other, we fell still, bathing in the feeling of it flowing through our bodies.

The rain continued to fall on us and pink blossoms tumbled down over us too as the magic found an outlet and we created this tiny little corner of freedom within the walls of the prison.

"I have faith in you, Rosa," he breathed as the bell rang to signal the end of the session and I gritted my teeth as I forced away my stupid little wobble. He was right. This wasn't a bad thing - we just needed to move faster and get our asses out of here before that thing was installed.

"Okay," I agreed, pulling back to lean against the wall, my hands sliding down to rest against his chest as I looked up at him. "Then we're going to need to haul ass," I said firmly. "This has to happen this week or it's not happening at all. Plunger is getting close to the maintenance room with the first tunnel and Sin and Ethan have managed to get me what I need to neutralise the ipump so that the Order Suppressant will be out of action. I haven't been able to figure out a way around the cuffs unless we want to try and force a guard to release us from them, but I feel like that could be more risky than it's worth. We'll all have access to our Orders so we'll be able to move fast. Dante and Jerome have their own parts to play and I'm sure we'll be able to get out of here without needing our magic anyway. Then we just need to make sure Plunger and Gustard don't actually make it out, either by incapacitating or killing them then running for our fucking lives. We'll figure out a way to get the cuffs off once we're free. If I have to cut my hands off and have them re-attached I'll take that trade."

"Shit, you really are a badass, aren't you?" Roary teased. "Just casually talking about murder and dismemberment like it's any old Tuesday."

"You know me, Roar, been there, done that, got the t-shirt. Speaking of which, I'm going to burn these fucking jumpsuits once we're free. We can get Sin to build a pyre for us all to dance on top of."

He started laughing just as a real fire tore through the long grass surrounding us and my skin prickled as I straightened, pulling magic to my fingertips a moment before it was locked off and my cuffs glowed blue again.

I relaxed back against the wall as I realised who'd come to poop on our party and turned my gaze to Cain as he glowered between me and Roary, taking in every place where we were touching each other as well as Roary's bare chest.

I couldn't help but smirk at Cain as he looked like he was fighting the urge to blow his top and Roary growled beneath his breath at the interruption.

"If you two love birds don't get your asses out of here in the next thirty seconds, I'll be taking away your dinner privileges," Cain snarled, pointing towards the exit where most of the other inmates had already left the compound.

"Are we in love, Roar?" I asked, smiling up at him and fluttering my eyelashes dramatically

"Stranger things have happened," he purred in reply, reaching down to grab his tank and shrugging it back on while I smirked at Cain over his shoulder.

"Is there a reason why you don't like that idea, boss man?"

"Just get inside," Cain commanded. "The library won't renovate itself and if I find out the two of you have been spending your time in there fucking then I might have to start supervising you while you work."

Roary tensed up the smallest amount, but I just squeezed his hand reassuringly and slipped past him to walk beside Cain.

"Do you like me that much, sir?" I asked him in a low tone which definitely carried. "You want to spend hours down there with me, watching me stack shelves in all the dark and forgotten corners of that big old library?"

"Of course not," Cain snapped, his eyes flaring with warning, but there was a heat in them too. "Just make sure you're keeping the work up to scratch and we won't have an issue."

"Cross my heart," I swore seriously, moving close enough to him to brush my arm against his.

Roary watched me from the corner of his eyes as we walked and Cain growled another warning at me to back off. But I just wasn't the type to take no for an answer, so as we moved through the door to exit the compound and Cain made to follow me through, I stopped so abruptly that he bumped into me and with my hand behind my back, I caressed his cock through his pants.

A grunt of surprise escaped him, but I was already heading away, moving to walk at Roary's side and smirking over my shoulder at my CO as he glared at me and stayed behind.

Everyone was either heading to their work assignments or

back to their cell blocks now, so Roary and I headed on down to the library at the tail end of the crowd.

"What are you up to with Cain?" he murmured, once we were sure the Vampire in question had chosen not to follow us.

"Me?" I asked innocently, feigning shock. "What makes you think there's anything going on?"

"Because I know you, Rosa, and there's always something going on."

I laughed lightly, brushing him off while wondering what he'd think if I told him that Cain had fucked me in a shower full of corpses last night and I'd loved every second of it almost as much as I'd hated it. But with us about to be stuck in with Gustard for the next hour, it seemed like a bad call to tell him those details right now. I needed to try and contain this situation before it got out of hand.

When we stepped into the room, unsurprisingly, Gustard was waiting for me with a face like thunder.

"Where is Christopher?" he demanded, his eyes flaring with rage and accusation. It had been fun avoiding him all morning, but I'd known that this was coming.

"Who?" I asked sweetly, remembering the way that motherfucker's blood had stained the walls.

"You know who. Christopher. And the rest of my people. You saw them in the gym last night and now there are rumours flying that every last one of them have been killed and-"

"Shit, that sounds bad," I said, my eyes widening and my hand linking with Roary's. "But I'm not sure what you mean about me seeing them last night. I was barely even in the gym."

"Bullshit," Gustard hissed. "I know your routine down to the minute."

"Do you now?" I asked curiously, though that didn't surprise me in the least.

"Well last night, she didn't stick to her routine because she was with me," Roary said in a bored tone, covering my ass as easy as breathing.

"You expect me to believe that?" Gustard scoffed.

"I was there too," Sin put in as he hopped down from a shelf above us and made everyone jump. "We were down by the Belorian's cage having a good old fashioned spit roast. You gonna call me a liar too?"

Gustard scowled, looking seriously unconvinced and Roary threw a half disgusted, half grateful look Sin's way.

"True story," Sin said casually, folding his arms as he leaned back against a bookshelf. "I was telling Roary how our girl can deep throat like no one I've ever met and he couldn't believe that she could seriously take my monster cock all the way down to the base."

"He's right," I agreed with a smug little smirk as I mentally high fived myself. "I'm a Moon Wolf, so..."

"What does being a Moon Wolf have to do with it?" Roary asked in confusion, getting diverted from the point of this story.

"Oh come on, haven't you ever been out on the lunar eclipse fucking 'til dawn?" Sin asked with a scoff that said he definitely had and didn't believe for one second that Roary hadn't too.

"The moon is super horny, Roar. And I was born with Venus in my chart, so..."

"Right."

"That's why we're so good together, wild girl. Both born with a natural affinity for fucking like animals," Sin purred.

Gustard stepped forward suddenly, his dark eyes fixed on mine like he was wishing he could go all googly-eye and Cyclops the truth right out of my head. *Note to self - make sure this fucker stays well away from me in the Order Yard.*

"I don't know how you did it," he hissed. "But I'm going to make you pay for the blood you spilled last night. Christopher has been my friend for-"

"Listen up, stronzo," I snarled, dropping every hint of pretence that I was even vaguely amused right now, because it was time he got a few things straight about me. "I'm not some little pup for you to push around and threaten. I'm not someone you can intimidate or blackmail into submission. I'm a real

Alpha who earned my place at the top of the pecking order with blood, sweat and tears. So you'd better understand a few things. Your little memory crystal has bought you one thing with me and one thing only. A ticket out of this place. There's no free rides for your little stronzo friends. There's no special privileges for you, you're not the boss, you're not frightening me. This plan doesn't work without me. You may know everything that I'm going to need to do to get us out of here, but you can't get Jerome to do his part for you and if you think for a single second that you could convince the Storm Dragon, King of the Oscura Clan to show up without me right there, standing front and centre beyond these walls then you're looking to get barbecued with a lightning bolt. So I'm done listening to your shit. I'm done letting you think you can stab me or send your little group of mindless minions my way any time you think you might be able to catch me alone. I promised to get you out of here and that's it. So here's the deal. You shut the fuck up and play your part. The next time you or one of yours comes at me, I will declare war on your gang. And I'm pretty sure that Ethan and Roary will jump right in on my side of it too. How long do you think the Watchers will survive if the Oscuras, Lunar Brotherhood and the Shades all come for them at once? And when every last one of your people is dead at your feet, how tough do you think you'll be then? Will you come at me Fae on Fae? Or will you lay down in the corner like the little bitch you are?"

Gustard looked ready to flip the fuck out but I just turned my back on him and walked away. I was done playing nice. I didn't just happen to fall into my position at the top of my pack and I wasn't going to let this shit go on a second longer. No doubt he would be plotting my downfall just as surely as I was plotting his now. But he could go ahead and fantasise about strapping me down to a table and torturing me the way my papa did. At the end of the day, he'd be the one who found himself bleeding at my feet.

I strode through the library towards the back of the room

where Sonny and Brett and Esme were all busy painting walls and re-stocking shelves. I looked around at the work we'd completed so far and chewed on my bottom lip as I ran through the final things we needed to execute this plan.

"Who's in the tunnel with Plunger?" I asked, but as Ethan was the only one of us missing, it was pretty obvious.

"Your boy told me to have a rest today, kitten," Sin purred, moving up behind me and winding his arms around my waist. "He's getting to like tight, dark spaces, if you know what I mean."

I bit my lip on a laugh. When Sin had told me about tricking Ethan into thinking he was me in the showers, I swear I'd laughed for a solid day – after punching him for stabbing my mate and making me feel the pain of his wounds of course. I even woke up in the night chuckling over it. In fact, I quite like the idea of seeing what I looked like with a dick, I bet I could pull it off.

"You're an ass," I chastised, smacking his arm to make him release me while Roary narrowed his eyes on us. "Help out with moving some of the boxes while I go down and check out how everything is coming along. We need to be moving faster now and I wanna be sure Plunger isn't slacking off."

"Fine," Sin said, sighing dramatically as he released me. "But I want you to be real bossy with me the next time we're alone. I think I'd enjoy being dominated by you, wild girl."

I laughed, pushing away from him and heading to the bookshelf at the back of the room which concealed the tunnel. Just as I slipped behind it, Roary caught my hand and pulled me back around to look at him.

"Tell me that was just bullshit for Gustard's benefit," he said in a low voice, looking into my eyes like he was really hoping it was.

"What part?" I asked.

"The part about you and Sin."

"And my lack of gag reflex? No, Stronzo, I wouldn't lie about that. There are some things that are too sacred to bullshit about. Why do you care anyway?"

"I thought you were mated to Ethan?" he growled, his grip on my wrist tightening and I sighed.

"So? He doesn't own me. He doesn't even want me. Why should that mean I'm faithful to him? Besides, Wolves are polyamorous so it's not that hard to understand."

"Wolves are polyamorous until they find their true mate," Roary protested.

"Yeah, well, I'm a Moon Wolf which means the same rules don't apply to me. So maybe I plan on making a pack of mates. Lions do the same thing, so why would that be so shocking to you?"

"It's not," he said slowly, releasing my arm and actually seeming less pissed, though I didn't know what I could have said to make that the case. But I wasn't going to look a gift Pegasus in the mouth, so I just took the win and headed down into the tunnel.

I took a deep breath of the damp soil which surrounded me as I moved into the dark and placed my hands on the walls either side of me. There was something calming about being amongst the dirt and stone down here. Something which called to that base part of my soul where my Element was connected to me. Earth was my friend, my nature as a Taurus was linked to the solid and unmovable ways of the Element, but I was always willing to grow and change too. My star sign may have made me stubborn, possessive and uncompromising, but it also made me patient, practical and devoted to things I cared about which was why I was so certain that this plan would come together in the end.

It didn't take long before the dim light from the library was stolen and I was plunged into complete and utter darkness with nothing but the sound of my own breaths and footsteps filling the cold space around me. If I really thought about the weight of all the dirt up above us I guess I should have been freaking out, but I'd done more than my share of underground tunnelling with my magic, so it wasn't that unusual to me.

Though as I currently couldn't use my magic maybe it should have been because if the tunnel caved in on my head then there wasn't going to be anything I could do to save myself. Gah, I really wished we hadn't lost our damn cuff key and all the freaking cuffs hadn't been changed.

As I descended down the four floors towards the maintenance level, the sound of Plunger digging reached me and I upped my pace. The tunnel sloped hard and my boots slipped a little on the dirt beneath them, but I managed to keep my feet as I drew closer to them.

"How's it going?" I called when I was sure I must be right by them and as I rounded a corner, the red glow from Plunger's nose filled the space and I could just make his silhouette out ahead of me.

"There's a wall right ahead of me," Plunger replied, his voice all weird and nasally because of that gross star nose situation he had going on. "I can use an ultrasonic boom to loosen the mortar, but you'll probably want to move back a bit and cover your ears, sweetness. It'll be a big boom that really thrusts into everything – that's my method."

A hand found mine in the dark and my heart lurched as Ethan's scent surrounded me and his other hand curled around my waist. A deep, canine sound escaped his lips and he nuzzled into me in greeting, the barest scrape of stubble lining his jaw scratching against my neck as he buried his face against me. I couldn't help but give in to my instincts and nuzzle him back, my hand sliding up his back and pushing into his hair as I pulled him closer.

"I've missed you, love," he breathed so low that I could only hear him at all because his mouth was brushing my ear.

He started to walk me backwards, away from Plunger and I let him move me as I drew him closer, the ache in my chest loosening as I gave into the pull between us and let the mate bond have what it had been aching for.

"I've been dreaming of you," I murmured as we turned a corner and Ethan growled in a possessive, self-satisfied way as he threaded his fingers through mine and squeezed my hand tight.

"What kind of dreams?" he asked, his mouth moving to lay kisses along my throat and sending shivers through my skin.

"The kind where you stand up and tell the whole world you're mine," I replied breathily.

Ethan growled in frustration, shifting back an inch until I could feel the brush of his lips against mine.

A high-pitched noise started to build around us and I stuffed my fingers into my ears as Ethan did the same thing half a second before Plunger's ultrasonic boom took out the mortar.

Adrenaline rushed through me and my heart thundered with excitement. This was it. The plan was coming together and we'd be getting out of here really fucking soon.

Ethan kissed me and I let him sweep me up in the excitement of what we were doing, his tongue sliding between my lips in the most delicious way as he dominated the movements of our mouths together and I let him because it felt too good to protest. There were so many unspoken words in that kiss, longing and promises and heartache and grief and I didn't know if it hurt or if it was filling a void in me which I was desperate to see made whole again.

"Let me follow you when you run, Rosalie," Ethan murmured, making my heart thrum like the wings of a hummingbird. "Let's get out of here and figure out how to make this work. I can't keep being without you. It's tearing my heart to ribbons."

"You'd follow me back to my family?" I questioned, wishing I could see him to gauge something from his expression.

Ethan hesitated for a long moment and I knew he didn't want that.

"I think I'd follow you to the moon itself at this point," he sighed.

I tiptoed up to taste his lips once more then pulled away and hurried down the tunnel to meet back up with Plunger again. I didn't know what to make of Ethan's declarations. He always seemed to find it so much easier to make them in the dark where no one could see us. But what would really happen when we were standing beneath the light of the sun once more?

"The bricks are as loose as a leprechaun's g-string," plunger announced proudly and the sound of grating stone followed a moment before he tugged one of the large bricks out of the wall and the dim red lighting from the maintenance level spilled in to illuminate the darkness.

I kept my gaze firmly away from the loose, folding skin of the naked dude beside me and peered out with my heart pounding and a big ass grin on my face.

I could just make out the ipump over to the left of the hole we'd made and with the instructions Dante had sent me alongside the ingredients Sin and Ethan had gotten, I had everything I needed to contaminate the tank and neutralise the Order Suppressant for the riot when it was time for us to make our move.

This was really happening. In a few days, we'd be packing up and shipping out of Darkmore Penitentiary for good, and I for one was never going to look back.

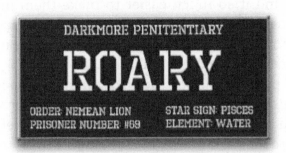

We'd made serious progress in the library this week. Plunger was working on the tunnel to the surface, gaining meter after meter and everyone's mood was sky high as we drew closer to the day of escape.

I was painting the wall near to the hole where Plunger was digging. A bookcase was blocking it from view, though I still got a rush every time we were in here. I was excited. Fucking ecstatic. I wanted out of Darkmore so bad and ever since Rosa had turned up here, I felt like I'd been given a new lease of life. I wasn't alone anymore. And now I had a real future waiting for me beyond that tunnel. I just knew there were a few loose ends to tie up. Particularly when it came to Gustard. We had to deal with him. There was no way we could walk out of here and set that fucking serial killer loose on the world. I couldn't let that happen. And me and Rosa had been discussing ways to deal with him late into the night. If we could make sure he didn't leave with us, that was even better. Because the riskier option was having to deal with him during the escape. And though I didn't like to wet my hands in blood again, I would do it to rid the world of Gustard, and to ensure that he paid for everything he'd done to Rosa too.

Either way, he wasn't getting out of here. But an intelligent psychopath like him could not be underestimated. There was a reason he had such a high body count beyond these walls and that was his meticulous planning. I wouldn't have been surprised if there were far more bodies in the ground than the ones he had been sentenced for, never to be discovered.

Ethan crawled out of the tunnel, stretching his back and catching my eye. The tunnel widened out further inside so we could walk out of here, but now we were on a time limit, Plunger was focusing on digging as far as he could before the night we escaped, so it wouldn't be as wide the further in we got. He'd still have to dig us a few hundred feet up to the surface when we ran but he'd have done the bulk of the work. His Order gifts would help him avoid the detectors in the ground so we could just sail on up to the free world. Now that the tunnel was completed down to maintenance, he was working as hard as he could to get as far as possible before it was show time.

"You wanna swap in for a while?" Ethan asked with a grimace. "I can't stand looking at that guy's hairy asshole any longer. Does he really need to be fucking naked while he works down there?"

My nose wrinkled and I shook my head. "Maybe we should get some boxers onto him, I saw a stapler by the front desk, we could make sure they stay in place."

Ethan chuckled darkly and I found myself smiling a little. Not that I liked the guy or anything. But for the sake of covering up Plunger's ball sack, I was willing to team up.

"I'll go." Rosa appeared around the corner, pulling her hair up and tying it into a knot to keep it out of the way. "You two can finish painting this wall together." She smiled sweetly, picking up a paintbrush and planting it in Ethan's hand before she disappeared into the tunnel.

Both of our eyes watched her round ass disappear into the tunnel and I cursed myself internally for never being able to stop staring.

Ethan shot me a sideways glance like he hadn't been planning on staying near me, but now she'd put a brush in his hand, he would have to admit he didn't want to be around me if he was going to leave. I sure as shit didn't want to be around him either, but I wasn't going to stop what I was doing. And I had the feeling Ethan wasn't going to lose face by letting me know my company bothered him enough to make him leave.

I ran the roller up the wall and Ethan sighed, dropping down to kneel on the sheeting on the floor and started painting along the skirting boards. It didn't matter if we got our jumpsuits splattered, they just gave us new ones once we got back to our cells anyway. And there wasn't much point in giving us work-men's clothes because that was essentially what we were wearing to begin with.

The silence stretched between me and Ethan for so long that it became deafening. I knew he meant something to Rosa, even if she'd never admit it to me. My brother's mate was his whole world, the pull he felt towards her was unrivalled by any other force on earth. So if Rosa was suffering like I suspected she was over Ethan, then he must have been in the same boat.

"So er...what's your plan when you get out of here?" I asked, deciding to make an effort for Rosa's sake. Not that I was sure why I wanted to do that exactly, especially when she wouldn't even admit that she liked him herself. But I had told myself I wanted the best for Rosa. A mate who cared for and protected her. So if she was stuck with this guy then maybe I'd better figure out if he was worthy of his moon-chosen place at her side.

I was from a family of Lions and had been surrounded by my three moms and my dad's influence my whole life. I knew the power of mate bonds. And it went deeper than just a celestial being forcing them together. On some level, they were made for one another. And as much I didn't like it, I was far more aware than Rosa was that Ethan wasn't going anywhere. She may have thought her moon gifts could break the bond between them, but I begged to differ.

Despite that, I'd spent far more time than I wanted to own up to envying Ethan for his bond to Rosa. I was still furious at him for not being Fae enough to claim her outright. Not that I wanted her attention stolen by another man or anything. But she'd said herself she wasn't like other Alpha Wolves. She didn't want one mate. *Great, so she can mate with a bunch of other Fae and you can be her supportive 'friend' whose balls turn so blue they fall off.*

"I'm going to go home and be with my sisters," Ethan said. "They've all had pups I've never met and most of them have married guys I've never vetted."

I released a breath of amusement then hooked on that one thing we had in common. "I haven't met my niece and nephew either. And the last time I saw my brother, he was hoping his wife was pregnant again. If they have another one before I get out of here, I'm going to lose it."

Ethan looked up at me from the floor with a frown. "It fucking sucks, doesn't it?"

"Yeah," I muttered. "But I guess we'll see them soon enough."

He smiled at that, hope shining in his eyes. "I was never even meant for prison," he sighed. "But I'd do anything for family."

"What did you do?" I asked offhandedly, but I knew the weight of that question in here. Most people didn't share their crimes unless they wielded it to scare people, it was big in the news, or you were just plain dumb.

"I didn't do anything," he admitted, surprising me. "I covered for someone I love."

My brows arched at that and though my instinct was to call bullshit, I could see the truth in his eyes and there was no reason why he'd lie. I turned back to face the wall as I painted it.

"I'm here because of someone I love too," I told him and when the word *love* slipped out, I hated the way my heart pounded wildly. Because I'd meant it as family, but I'd felt it as something far different to that. If I thought of Rosa as family, then apparently that meant I wanted to fuck my little brother and my parents too. But of course, I was just lying to myself as always. Rosa was family, but not like my blood were. She was the sort of family I wanted to make moan my name as I kissed every inch of her flesh. The type who I wanted to lose myself in every night, make a life with, a fucking home with. I never, ever wanted to lose her now I had her back. But she was also the type of family I could never touch because I was just some washed up Lion who used to be someone and now was no one, and I had absolutely zero to offer her. So yeah, whatever type of twisted family that was, she was it.

"I heard about your story," Ethan said with a smirk in his voice. "Everyone in Solaria fucking heard."

"Well you don't rob a High Councillor without the whole world hearing about it, I guess," I said, a grin pulling at my mouth. I still didn't regret the actual heist. Technically, I'd still pulled it off. Only my brother had gotten away with the goods and I'd gotten caught. Rosa had been with us, which was a stupid fucking idea on reflection. But we'd needed someone small who could get into a vent and pass through a magical detection spell. As her magic had been unAwakened at the time, she was the perfect fit for the job. It was only when we were trying to run that it had all gone to hell. I could have gotten away. But Rosa had been in trouble and I wouldn't have abandoned her for any stolen prize in Solaria. She was more valuable than anything I'd ever taken. And she always would be.

"Why'd you do it?" Ethan asked curiously. "Just for the thrill? Or were you after something specific?"

I shrugged, not giving him that answer. There was a reason we'd targeted Lionel Acrux, but it wasn't my secret to tell.

"Come on, man, I know the press twisted that story saying all of Lionel's possessions were returned to him. But your brother must have been on that job too, who else could have taken the haul when you were caught? You're not telling me Leon Night didn't pocket something," Ethan scoffed.

I looked down at him with a smirk dancing around my lips. "Yeah, I'm not saying that. But I'm not telling you what he got either." I winked and he scowled. But before he could push me for more details, the sound of Gustard whistling sharply reached me. My heart lurched at the signal of a guard coming and we had no time to prepare as the library door banged open and a wind swept through the room from the speed they were travelling at which told me a Vampire had just arrived. *Fuck.*

"Headcount!" Cain's voice echoed throughout the entire library and my blood turned to ice.

I dropped the paint roller, diving towards the hole and sticking my head into it, hunting for Rosa, but not daring to call for her in case Cain heard me and came running this way. She wasn't there. Not anywhere close. The tunnel was deep now and there was no chance of me getting her out fast enough.

I shared a look with Ethan who howled suddenly, tipping his head back so Rosa would hear then he grabbed hold of the bookcase and I hurried over to lift the other end. We moved it into place, covering the hole and a second later, Cain shot into view, coming to a halt right in front of us.

"What the fuck are you doing? I said, headcount. Get to the front of the library *now*," he snapped and my heart thudded furiously as I nodded and we walked past him down the aisle. I couldn't resist glancing back and saw the nosy fucker inspecting what we'd been doing. I shared an anxious look with Ethan as we rounded the corner, moving to join everyone else near the front doors.

Sin frowned at my expression as we approached and stepped right up next to me, leaning in and breathing into my ear so his words wouldn't be caught by Cain. "Where is she?"

"The tunnel," I mouthed and his eyes widened as he stepped back, a fearful glint in them.

Everyone else seemed to catch on and a ripple of anxiety ran through the group as we waited for the blade of fate to fall on our heads. Cain shot back in front of us, looking from face to face with a scowl etched into his brow.

"Where's Twelve and Twenty-Four?" he growled dangerously.

"They were working with us over in the far corner," Sonny said immediately, pointing towards the opposite end of the library to where the hole was.

"No, the hound was with me. Though that was perhaps a while before she joined you. Or perhaps it was after..." Pudding pointed to another corner of the room away from the tunnel and Cain's scowl deepened.

"Plunger was stacking books that way too," Claud said, nodding.

"Twelve! Twenty-Four!" Cain bellowed. "Come here, now! You have five seconds. Five - four - three-"

"It's very muffled over there, voices don't really carry," Sin cut him off and everyone nodded their agreement.

"Doesn't carry at all," Gustard said.

"Perhaps there is a muffling spell on that area of the library," Pudding said thoughtfully.

"There's no such thing," Cain hissed, glaring at us all but then he shot away toward the far corner.

I was running before I could stop myself and Ethan was at my side as we raced back to where we'd been before. Sin started singing Sex Bomb by Tom Jones at the top of his lungs, covering the noise of our footsteps as we raced toward the bookcase.

I nodded to Ethan as I took one end and he took the other and we swung it out half a foot. Rosalie and a very naked Plunger spilled out of it and we quickly shoved it back into place. Sin's singing grew even louder and the others started heckling him, telling him to shut up so their voices filled the whole library.

Plunger swiped up a paint brush, splashing some of it over his naked flesh, abandoning his jumpsuit which was folded beside the bookcase as we all sprinted back towards the front doors. I grabbed Rosa's hand in mine, squeezing firmly and she squeezed mine back before I released her again. We rounded the corner, coming to a halt just as Cain shot back in front of us and his brows lowered even further as he spotted Rosa and Plunger standing behind me and Ethan.

"Shut the fuck up Eighty-Eight!" Cain barked at Sin and he fell quiet, grinning wickedly.

Cain muscled his way through the group, his eyes raking over Rosa before shifting to Plunger's hairy naked flesh.

"Why the fuck are you naked?" he demanded.

"It's how I express my inner crea-tiv-it-ai," he said innocently. "I need to be free of clothes when I paint, it is my way, sir."

Cain grimaced then looked back to Rosa while fear pounded through my limbs. If he figured out something was up, we were so fucked.

"What were you doing? This lot said you were over there," he growled, pointing to the section of the library he'd just searched.

Rosa batted her lashes. "I went to see how Plunger was getting on. He's slowing down our work by trying to use his dick as a paintbrush."

Plunger shrugged like that wasn't unusual behaviour. "It is the way of my crea-tiv-it-ai."

"It's creativit-*tee*," Cain growled irritably as he looked between them then whirled around to face the rest of us. "You've had plenty of time to finish this job. Why is it taking so long?"

Rosa hurried forward and caught his arm, giving him a serious look. "Can I have a word with you? Me and Roary need to tell you something." She glanced at me and I frowned, but quickly schooled my features as Cain glanced my way and I nodded, matching her expression.

A muscle worked in Cain's jaw as he considered that then finally nodded, making relief spill through me even though I had no idea what she had planned. Rosa headed off into the stacks and I followed with Cain in tow until we were out of earshot of the others.

"What is it, Ro- Twelve?" he corrected himself last minute and I cocked an eyebrow at that. He shot me a glare that said he'd rip my tongue out if I mentioned it though.

"It's Plunger," she whispered, sharing a frown with me. "He takes his time with his work and has his own strange...methods that most people here aren't that comfortable with. So me and Roary agreed to keep an eye on him, and some of the others too. We don't let him work on his own, and when you got here I was busy arguing with him about him working while he's naked so I didn't hear you right away." She shrugged innocently and I could see that technically everything she'd said had probably been true.

I nodded to back up her story. "We basically take it in turns to make sure he's at least using the tools and not his dick to paint the walls."

Cain's nose wrinkled a little and he finally nodded. "Well if he's not suited to this work-"

"He's surprisingly good when he's kept in check," Rosa said quickly, giving him a sideways smile. "I think we'll have the job finished by the end of the week so long as he's pulling his weight."

My pulse pounded in my ears as I nodded my agreement. By the end of this week, we'd be finished the job alright. And hopefully lying on a beach somewhere with smug ass grins on our faces while the world talked about the convicts who'd managed to do the impossible. I was pretty excited to put my name on the map again. What would Father think if I managed that?

"Fine, but if this goes on longer than a week, you're done. I'll have you reassigned and a new team brought in here," Cain said firmly and we nodded.

He shot off back to the others and I heard him shouting at Plunger about wearing clothes while Rosa threw herself at me, hugging me tight. The sweet scent of her smelled better than freedom ever could and I held her close as the door banged and Cain left.

"Just a few more days, Rosa," I purred in her ear and she shivered in my arms. I didn't know if it was because of me or because of what I'd said, but the asshole in me hoped it was the former.

"I'm ready, Roar," she said excitedly, pulling back and looking up at me with the whole world staring back at me in her eyes. "It's almost time to follow through on that promise I made you."

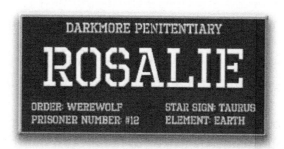

DARKMORE PENITENTIARY
ROSALIE
ORDER: WEREWOLF
PRISONER NUMBER: #12
STAR SIGN: TAURUS
ELEMENT: EARTH

Everything was coming together and I was beginning to feel like there was a live wire constantly sparking beneath my skin. I was this vibrant ball of energy, aching for an outlet and ready to explode.

We returned to the others and once I was certain Cain was long gone, I beckoned everybody close, hopped up onto one of the tables and sat there with my legs crossed beneath me.

"Listen up!" I called, my gaze sliding over each and every member of this unconventional team as I looked for any signs of weak links. "Plunger has the tunnel closing in on the surface and we need to be ready to move as soon as it's done. The plan is simple. In two days, a riot will break out again at dinner time and I'll head off to dose the Order Suppressant tank down on the maintenance level with the ingredients needed to switch the gas coming from the vents in the main prison into an antidote. So everyone up here just needs to get a few deep breaths of air from the vents and you'll be able to shift to your heart's content. That should be more than enough to cause carnage to cover our escape. Assuming they stick to what they did last time, we will have one hour from the riot breaking out until the Belorian is set loose."

"The poor beastie will be looking forward to getting another free run," Sin interrupted, winking at me and I paused, narrowing my eyes on him.

"To be clear, we absolutely don't want the Belorian to be set loose for as long as possible."

"Heard you loud and clear, wild girl," Sin said, tossing me

another wink and I growled, pushing to my feet and stalking towards him as everyone else watched with varying levels of confusion.

"Sin Wilder," I said in a low, warning voice, moving up close to him and pressing a finger to his chest. "Repeat after me: we do not want the Belorian set free."

"We do not want the Belorian set free," he purred, grabbing my wrist and lifting my finger to his mouth before nipping it playfully. "Got it." He winked again and I bristled.

"If you set that monster loose while we are trying to escape, I will personally beat the shit out of you and make you pay me triple the price Jerome is paying to orchestrate this whole thing. And believe me, that's a lot of auras."

"Wouldn't want that," he replied with a chuckle and I narrowed my eyes, waiting to make sure he didn't wink again. *Goddamn crazy Incubus.*

Instead of winking, Sin lunged at me, gripping my face between his hands and kissing me hard in front of the entire group.

Ethan let out a furious growl and I jerked back a second before he collided with Sin and the two of them went crashing to the floor.

Ethan landed on top, straddling the Incubus and throwing furious fists with abandon as Sin howled with laughter beneath him.

"It's okay, kitten, there's plenty of me to go around. I promise to put something in your ass again later," Sin said loudly before Ethan locked his hands around his throat and started choking him out.

"For the love of the moon," I growled as Sin tried to talk around his crushed windpipe and Ethan looked inclined to actually murder him.

I stalked forward and threw my weight into Ethan's side, knocking him off of Sin before pouncing on top of him and snarling down at him.

"Do you have an issue you want to share with the group,

stronzo?" I demanded loudly, glaring down at him as he bared his teeth, looking half tempted to lunge at me next.

Sonny, Brett and Esme began whooping and howling with excitement at the sight of me pinning the Lunar gang leader to the carpet and his gaze flicked their way as he seemed to realise that he was on the brink of revealing his bond to me in front of the whole group.

I tilted my head as I regarded him and I could practically see the cogs in his mind spinning as he tried to decide if his secret was worth more than his pride. He was an Alpha Wolf, seeing another Fae touch his mate would be enough to send any Alpha into a tailspin, all of his instincts were probably screaming at him to drag me back to his cave and screw me until I forgot anyone else even existed - right after killing Sin of course. And I found that I actually wanted him to follow those instincts. I mean, he wasn't going to kill Sin, but if he stood up now and told everyone that I was his and he was mine, I was pretty sure I would agree with him. And I didn't like the ache in my chest that said I wanted that so much because I knew it meant he had some power over me. Or at least over the way I felt.

"Forget it," Ethan grunted, moving to sit up and pushing me back.

I stood, locking my jaw and taking half a second to let the pain of those words twist through me, my eyes prickling for the briefest of seconds before I slapped a cherry pie grin on my face and turned my back on the stronzo.

"Anybody else need to get anything off of their chests?" I demanded just as I caught Roary's gaze.

His golden eyes were full of fury and he stepped towards Ethan, swinging at him so fast that I barely even saw the blow coming.

Ethan's head snapped aside as he took the heavy punch to the jaw and he made a move to lunge at Roary next but I inserted myself between them.

"Enough!" I demanded in my Alpha tone, shoving them both back and growling myself as I waited to see if they were going to fall into line or not. "I can end this easily if I have to."

For a second I thought a brawl was going to break out in full force and Sin started chanting, "Fight, fight, fight," beneath his breath. But as I turned my glare on Ethan, he huffed out a breath, seeming to realise I was about three seconds away from telling the room at large that we were mated and he turned and stalked away, his posture filled with fury.

"Don't leave," I called after him. "I haven't finished going over the plan."

Ethan growled but stopped his retreat and turned to look back at me, anger filling his eyes as he leaned against a book-shelf and folded his arms.

"Okay," I began, hopping back up to sit on the desk and acting like there hadn't been any interruptions as Sin dusted himself off and came to stand behind me. He started massaging my shoulders and it felt kinda nice so I allowed it as I went on. "So, once the riot is underway we all need to make our way down here. But don't be obvious about it and make sure the guards aren't watching you. Jerome is going to hack into the prison systems and set the guards' quarters onto lockdown. That means that the guards who aren't on shift won't be able to get out of there to come and help calm the carnage and it should mean the rioting will go on even longer. That's good, because we want to have as long as possible before they can take the count. Once that happens, they'll be on our asses so we need to be quick. We get here and we follow Plunger into the tunnel which he's digging to the surface."

"What if one of us is detained by the guards?" Brett asked and I shrugged.

"Not my problem. Anyone who doesn't show up gets left behind. The only ones we won't leave without are me, Sin and Roary."

"What makes you three so special?" Gustard sneered and I rolled my eyes at him.

"Jerome won't help lock the guards away and block the out-going calls to the FIB unless we get Sin out for him. Dante won't down the fence unless he sees me and Roary. And that's the final barrier. The outer fence is lethal to touch and burrows underground surrounding the entire prison in a dome. The one and only gate is too well guarded for us to try and escape through that, so instead we have a Storm Dragon on call to fry the fence."

"And what if he can't?" Gustard drawled. "What if we get all the way out there to the fence and find he can't bring it down?"

"If you doubt my cousin's power then feel free to stay behind, stronzo," I purred. "I really don't mind if you do."

"What do we do once the fence is down?" Sonny asked, his eyes glimmering with excitement.

"Shift and run," I said with a grin. "We need to get about a mile out so that it's safe for Dante to land and he will be waiting there for us with stardust. He'll take us to a secondary location and at that point, I will wish you all well and disappear out of your lives for good."

"We'll be on our own?" Esme asked nervously.

"It's safer that way," I said in a soft voice. "But if you head to Alestria and find the Oscuras I'm sure we will find our way back to each other one day. But initially I'm going to leave with my cousin, Sin and Roary." My gaze flicked to Ethan's and his brow pinched into a frown, but unsurprisingly, he didn't speak up in protest.

"Are you going to tell us where this secondary location is?" Gustard asked irritably. "Not all of us have Orders who can shift into a creature that can run a long distance."

"Well that's not my problem," I replied with a shrug. "I promised to get you out, not drag your one-eyed ass back to your mommy's house. I'm sure you'll figure it out."

He snarled at me but I ignored him. I didn't have any intention of taking him that far anyway. And I was going to tell all of the others exactly where the secondary location was in private so that they could arrange for people to meet them. Pudding had already made enough transmitters for them to make the calls to firm up the arrangements with no chance of the guards listening in.

"Okay, we've wasted enough time so get back to work," I commanded, pushing to my feet and making Sin release me.

I watched as Gustard strode away to take up a watch position by the door like the lazy bastardo he was, and Sin followed Plunger to the tunnel while the rest of the group continued with the renovations for our cover story.

Ethan headed away to get some boxes of books and I hurried after him, catching his hand and tugging him away from everyone else into the stacks. We had shit to sort out and I was done playing the waiting game with his fears.

"Are you fucking the Incubus?" he growled as I pulled him along and I snorted derisively before turning back to him.

"Do you still have that fake mate of yours sleeping in your cell?" I tossed back.

Ethan's grunt of frustration was answer enough and I growled in irritation before shoving him back against one of the shelves.

"Tell me, pretty boy, are you glad the moon chose me for you? Or do you want me to try and break this bond between us?" I asked in a deadly purr, not giving a single piece of my own feelings on the subject away.

"I want you," he growled instantly, no sign of any hesitation in his tone. I didn't want to admit how fucking good it felt to hear him say it so simply, so honestly, but shit, I think if he'd told me he wanted me to break the bond I would have just fallen apart over it.

"Okay. Then do you want to come with me when I go back to my family?"

Ethan flinched like that idea physically hurt him. "To the heart of the Oscura Clan? Shall I just spit on my family's graves while I'm at it?"

"Perhaps. Were they particularly nasty bastardos? If you have reason to hate them then spit away."

"You know that's not what I meant."

"Enlighten me then," I suggested.

Ethan worked his jaw, glaring at me as I pressed my hand over his thundering heart and looked into his blue eyes.

"You want me to just turn my back on my family?" he asked in a defeated sounding voice.

"No. I just want you to stop hating mine for no reason."

"The Storm Dragon hates me. You do know I was at Aurora Academy with him, don't you? I was there when Ryder..."

"This isn't about what happened to Ryder," I growled. "And believe me, Dante doesn't hate you. I doubt he even remembers you. Sorry, stronzo, but he's too busy to hold a grudge against some Lunar motherfucker who got himself carted off to Darkmore. You're not even a player on the board anymore. And even if you were, even if you were the worst of the worst, he loves me. If I tell him that you're mine and I'm yours then he won't stand in our way."

"You would tell him that? Just like that?" he asked in disbelief.

I scoffed at the way he was looking at me like he actually doubted the sway I had in my Clan.

"You've been out of the loop a long time, pretty boy. There isn't just one Alpha running the Oscura Clan anymore - there's two. Dante doesn't question me. He loves me. So that's my offer. Come with me when we run and tell the world I met my match in you. Or don't, and I'll make whatever bargain with the moon that I have to to cut the cord that binds us. Because an equal of mine is afraid of nothing and no one so if you want me, it's time for you to stand up and claim me."

I pushed away from him and left him there to think about that. I was done waiting around for him to figure out what he wanted. Time was ticking and we were either walking out of here together or I'd be leaving him somewhere in the wilderness and never looking back.

It was the day before the escape was going down and I was psyched. Like a polar bear with a ticket to nowhere, I was ready to ride. And as I sailed up in an elevator towards the Order Yard, I knew exactly what Order I was going to shift into first. I'd spent a few years in my youth actively picking up the desires of any and every Fae I could get close to. And when you headed to famous Orderality clubs like the Black Hole in Alestria, or the Dirty Venus in Daylight City, an Incubus could detect all kinds of weird and wonderful desires from anyone lusting over Fae in their Order forms. So nowadays, I could shift into pretty much any Order and a bunch of cross-Orders like fluffy Dragons, pocket sized Pegasuses and Basilisks that looked like giant cocks. All the family favourites.

But today I was going to embody that polar bear with a ticket to nowhere. I stepped out of the elevator and tore off my jump-suit as I went, tossing it behind me with a wild laugh before dropping my boxers, my dick slapping between my legs as I went. Then I leapt forward, the shift rippling through my flesh, my body doubling then tripling, quadrupling, five-doopling in size until I was a massive ass Polar Bear Shifter, roaring in the face of a tiny little Experian Deer. She squeaked, pooped herself then bounded away from me out into the forest waiting for us.

I breathed in the fresh air and raced out into the woods, tearing left and right between the trees as my huge paws pressed giant tracks into the ground. As I made it to a cliff with an enormous waterfall tumbling down it, I didn't stop, I leapt off of the edge and shifted into a shiny pink Butterfly Shifter, letting myself drop down toward the river below before twisting up on a breeze and laughing a tiny butterfly laugh.

I flexed my wings, making them grow as I shifted into a Caucasian Eagle, my huge wings beating hard as I flew up, up, up towards the tantalising sky far above. I nearly knocked a couple of Pegasuses out of the sky as I shot through their herd and they neighed indignantly at me as they righted themselves and flew towards the rainbow glistening in the sky. There were fake clouds in the dome today and rain started tumbling in thick, fat drops against my face. I flew up through the clouds, higher and higher until I broke into the odd space at the top of the dome above the clouds where magic fizzled about me in the air and the dome crackled ominously above. Beyond that, was what I'd flown here for. The real sky. Far beyond the energy field that housed us here was a beautiful bright blue day, the sun beating down on me, warming my back.

I released a mournful cry as I circled that space, noticing a few Griffins doing the same at the far end of the dome. Then a howl sounded far below me and if my beak could smile, it totally would right now. The howl was human, so she hadn't shifted yet.

I tucked my wings, falling like a stone as I nose-dived towards the earth. I saw her running out of the building by the elevators, her jumpsuit falling at her feet. I landed in front of her, shifting back into a naked ass man and smirking right in her face as she pulled her tank top off so she was left in her underwear.

I released a low whistle as my dick jumped to attention, my eyes drinking in her tight little body before she planted a hand on her hip and frowned at me.

"Outta my way, Sin, I'm about to go Wolf on you."

"Nah, kitten. It's time for another date," I said, showing too much teeth as I smiled so I probably looked like I wanted to eat her for lunch. And hey, that wasn't a bad idea.

Her eyebrows arched and a smile pulled at her luscious lips. "What did you have in mind?"

"How do you feel about riding a Dragon?" I asked, wiggling my brows at her. "I once met a girl who dug Lionel Acrux in his Dragon form."

"Shit, seriously?" Her lips parted.

I backed up a few steps, turning my back on her and leaping forward, shifting into a huge ass, jade green Dragon that was the size of a house. Several Fae ran screaming from the incarnation of Lionel Acrux showing up here, and that was saying something about my gifts. Unfortunately, the girl who'd been attracted to him had also liked the idea of him being able to blow bubbles instead of fire. So as I let out a roar, a stream of colourful bubbles poured from my lungs instead of Dragon Fire and Rosalie fell about laughing.

"This is what someone's attracted to?" she balked.

I cocked my leg to let her see the scaly green monster dick between my thighs which was still glittering with my piercings. I didn't often shift my dick away because my beautiful cock was the single perfect thing about me. But for the sake of Rosalie falling apart with laughter, it was totally worth it.

"Seriously? Where would someone put that? I'd need a kooch the size of a garbage truck to enjoy that."

I released a growl of laughter then lowered my wing to form a bridge up onto my back, jerking my head to beckon her onto me.

Her lips parted and she moved forward with a smile. "I miss riding Dante. You should see him in his Storm Dragon form. He's as big as this, his scales are the colour of the deepest ocean and when he casts a storm into the sky it's like...magia," she whispered and I cocked my head in a question. "Magic," she translated.

She moved forward, climbing up onto my back and settling herself in at the base of my neck. She ran her hands over my scales, a soft breath of amazement leaving her. "By the stars, the last time I was this close to Lionel's Dragon form, he was hunting me down for stealing from him. Roary's brother drew him away...it was, fuck... that night will always haunt me."

I released something close to a placating purr which was the best I could offer her right then and she caressed my neck in soothing strokes. Today, I was going to show her the extent of my powers. I was going to fulfil her desires at long last. I'd been watching her closely and had a few ideas of what she lusted for. So I was going to become her perfect wet dream and she was going to melt like a snowman in a microwave when I was through with pleasing her. But right now, it was time to scare the shit out of some people and give Rosalie the ride of her life before I gave her, well, the ride of her life.

I took off into the sky and Rosalie clung onto me with a whoop of excitement as I climbed higher before sailing across the forest, beating my wings as I hunted for some Fae to frighten. When I caught sight of Ethan and his pack, I grinned and dove towards them on silent wings as they sprinted across the meadow. My shadow surrounded them and Ethan looked over his shoulder, barking furiously to alert his pack. A bunch of them looked back at me, whimpering in alarm and picking up speed as I let out a roar that sent bubbles shooting all over them, popping on their fur. Ethan slowed, his eyes narrowing like he'd figured out exactly who I was and he snapped his jaws at me as his mate laughed on my back.

I started doing a whole lap of the whole Order Yard, from the cold tundra, to the heated desert where the Nemean Lions were lazing. Roary looked up at us in his golden Lion form, his dark mane and huge size making him stand out amongst the others. There were Lionesses grooming every Lion but him. He sat alone, curled up on a rock in the sun and when he watched us go by, I swear his little kitty face frowned.

I flew us around to the rocky hills where the Bears liked to hang out amongst the burrowing Orders like the Moles and the Rabbits then soared back towards the forest. I landed heavily on the cliff that overlooked the waterfall and Rosalie slipped down from my back. I shifted into a Harpy, the skin of my lower body coated in bronze armour so I wasn't totally naked and I folded my equally bronze wings behind my back. Apart from that, I was myself. But not for long.

"That was amazing," Rosalie said brightly, moving to sit on the rocky ledge which looked out over the frothing pool below. I sat beside her, taking her hand in my grip and bringing it to my mouth. I sucked each of her fingers then threaded mine between them and rested our hands on my knee.

She laughed lightly, looking to me. "Why'd you do that?"

"Because you taste like Christmas. And Halloween. And Easter. And New Year. All the holidays actually. But mostly Christmas. That's my favourite. Though...I've never really celebrated it. I mean, I have, but not in the traditional way. I was paid to break into a house on Christmas day once and kill the guy who lived there. The whole place was decked out like Santa's grotto and after I murdered the guy in his bed, I opened all his family's presents and imagined what it would be like to be a kid waking up on Christmas morning. It was a great day."

"By the sun, Sin," Rosalie gasped. "What about his family?"

"Well, by a happy coincidence, his wife had left him the night before and taken the kids with her. I knew that because I'd been waiting outside all night for the guards to swap shifts so I had a window of opportunity to get in. He was selling kiddies to dirty men in faraway kingdoms. So..." I shrugged.

"I like that you only killed bad Fae," she said and I smiled.

"Yeah, I mean Jerome picked them for me, but I know cruel beasts when I see them. I can recognise my own kind, kitten," I purred and she bit her lip, leaning closer to me. *Oh my little pudding likes that, does she?*

"Am I your kind?" she asked curiously and I frowned, shaking my head.

"No, sugar, you're better than my kind. Better than most kinds. You're the best type of kind there is actually."

She wet her lips, gazing down at the waterfall and oh fuck my moontits, was that a blush lining her cheeks? I reared forward, raking my tongue over her cheek to taste the heat on her flesh and she chuckled lightly.

When I pulled away, she turned towards me and ran the hot

pad of her tongue up my cheek too, then moved her mouth to my ear. "I like your brand of crazy. Do you like mine?"

"Yeah," I rasped, already rock hard for her, my dick as straight as an arrow sticking out a of dead man's eye. "Do you wanna make a crazy pie with me? The recipe includes two hot Fae, a waterfall and my finger in your ass."

"Sin," she snorted.

"What? You liked it last time." I grinned and she smirked, turning to look out at the view again and releasing a long sigh. Her expression got my heart all knotty like a too-tight shoelace and I frowned as I tried to figure out what she was feeling right then. I never usually cared what people were feeling. Didn't really affect me. But Rosalie affected me. I'd spent a lot of time watching her features, wondering what her moods were, why she was laughing or pouting or frowning. "Sometimes I wanna shift into a beetle and crawl in your ear all the way to your brain to find out what's going on in there," I murmured.

She blew out a breath of amusement. "You could just ask, you know."

I considered that, nodding my head. "Okay, I'm asking."

She didn't turn to look at me as she continued to have that contemplative little frown on her face that was piquing all of my interests. "I'm thinking that...this is probably the last time we'll come out here. Tomorrow, we'll be somewhere free. And I'm trying to decide where I want to go first. After I've seen my family that is. I'm not sure if I want to see the mountains or the beach first."

"I know a little place in Sunshine Bay where you can see the mountains *from* the beach," I offered and she smiled.

"That sounds perfect."

I got to my feet, stepping back a few feet as I figured now was a good time to do what I'd been planning. I'd practised this the last time I was in the Order Yard, drawing on the desires I'd already tasted on her to try and piece together the perfect Fae for her. I let my Harpy form fall away then let my hair grow long and thick down to my shoulders in a wavy mane. Next, I worked on my face, shifting my nose to match the sharp line of Ethan's and the golden eyes of the Lion, then I shifted my mouth into the flat an angry line of Cain's.

I made my body muscular, but not as thick as my own, landing somewhere between all three of those men I'd felt her lust for. And finally, I let my chest swell until her pack mate Esme's breasts sat sculpted and full on my chest. There was nothing left of me except my one, perfect feature. My cock stood long and thick and proud, hard as a lollipop for her as I waited for her to turn and see me. This had to work. This time, she was going to melt into a puddle and be lost to her perfect desire. Because I was sure I'd figured out what this girl was after at last. She lusted for more than one Fae in this prison. And I was now a balance of all of them, brought together and ready to make her scream.

She turned around, and she screamed alright. Though it wasn't the pleasure filled one I'd been hoping for.

She leapt to her feet, taking in my new form with bulging eyes and her jaw hanging open. I reached out with my gifts to feel for her lust, but it wasn't there and I growled irritably.

"It's the tits, isn't it?" I huffed, cupping them in my hands and jiggling them up and down. "They're too much. Dammit, turn around again and give me another shot."

"Sin," she gasped, shaking her head. Then she started doing the unthinkable. She laughed, falling apart, clutching her stomach as fucking tears ran down her cheeks.

It took a lot to get me angry, but when I snapped, I snapped fucking hard. I shifted back into myself, running forward and snatching her throat, shoving her out over the waterfall and baring my teeth in her face as she yelped in surprise. She clung to my arms as I choked her with both hands, fury racing through every inch of me. I despised being laughed at. I wasn't some fucking clown. I was a killer who struck fear in the hearts of every Fae who'd heard my name. Who'd known what I'd done.

She growled, clawing at my arm and I bared my teeth at her

before dragging her back up and tossing her onto the ground. Fuck this. I was done trying to be desirable to her. I was never going to find out what it was she wanted. Her Moon Wolf powers must have been blocking me out. And now my pride was wounded and I didn't want her looking at this imperfect version of me any longer. I leapt over the waterfall, hearing her call my name just before I hit the water and sank deep into its cool depths. The world became muffled as I sank into the dark, a stream of air leaving my lips as I bellowed my rage.

Another body tore through the water to my left as I started swimming up to the surface, kicking my legs until I breached it. Rosalie popped up beside me a second later, a furious scowl on her face.

"Don't you run away from me, Sin Wilder," she snapped, swimming toward me.

I went to turn away, but she got there first, winding her legs around me and cupping my cheeks in both her palms. "You fucking idiota," she snarled and I found myself wrapping my arms around her, unable to resist the temptation of her as I treaded water to keep us afloat.

She was my own version of perfection and I wanted her like I'd never wanted anyone or anything. I just wished I could give her everything she deserved. I wished she'd let me read what she needed from me, because without my gifts, I was nothing.

Something close to sickness filled my gut at what I'd done to her and I tried to turn away again. I was always going to be this dark creature who couldn't function like a normal Fae. I lived and breathed violence and sex. And those two things were all I'd ever be good for.

"I'm sorry, Rosalie," I said over the sound of the crashing waterfall that was sending frothy waves up around us.

"Sorry you choked me or sorry I liked it?" She arched a brow and a smirk pulled at my mouth.

"The first one," I said, grinning now, unable to help it when she looked at me like that. But then I remembered her laughing at me and my anger returned like a hot knife carving through my chest. "Tell me what you lust for, wild girl. Let me be your greatest desire. It's all I want. It's my nature. I *need* to be that for you."

A V formed between her eyes as she stroked her thumbs across my cheeks. "I've told you before, there isn't one ideal version of what I want. But there are a few, Sin. And you're one of them. Just as you are, no wings, no scales, no jumbo Dragon dick, no fucking tits." She dropped a hand to squeeze one of my pecs and I grinned again, falling under her spell. "Nothing but you. As you are. Like *this*." She moved that same hand over my shoulder, then down to my bicep, her nails raking lightly against my flesh.

"No modifications?" I frowned, trying to get my head around that.

"Not one," she swore, her eyes glimmering like moonlight for a moment. "This is how I want you." She gazed into my eyes and I saw a truth there I had never expected to see from any Fae. She wanted me. As I was. *Just* the way I was. She was Mr Darcying me right now and I was Bridget Jones in my granny panties, bared for her to see and she liked it. She fucking *liked* it.

She released me, diving under the water and her lips suddenly wrapped around the head of my cock. I groaned loudly as her tongue flicked my piercings and she licked her way up my shaft like a fucking expert, taking me all the way in, tightening her lips and sucking my dick like it was an oxygen lifeline down there.

Fuck. Me. I'd never been sucked like when she did it. I was usually the one handing out pleasure, not the one getting it in return. Most people were so caught up by the fantasy I presented them that they were solely focused on getting their kicks. I rarely got my kicks like this, like I was the centre of her desire and not the other way around. But Rosalie, *fuck*, my beautiful wild girl was kicking my libido repeatedly in the balls.

She released my shaft from her hot mouth before coming

up for air and I barely let her catch a breath before I drove my tongue into her mouth, guiding her backwards through the water toward the edge of the foamy pool. My feet hit gravel and I pushed my toes into it, dragging her with me until we reached the bank then lifting her up by the hips and planting her ass down to sit on it. I dragged her panties down her legs, tossing them onto the grass beyond the water and placing my hands on the insides of her thighs. I spread her wide for me and she bucked her hips, her fingers knotting in my hair demandingly.

I feasted on her like the best pudding of my life, dipping my tongue into her hot, creamy middle then licking my way up to the cherry on top which I devoured slowly with rakes of my teeth and sucks of my lips. She panted my name and I swear I was harder than the rocky cliff of the waterfall as I ate her slowly, my tongue flicking and twisting and driving into her tight hole as I devoured her. I spread her thighs even wider for me, my tongue sliding down to her ass then back to her pussy, making her shiver and pant and claw at me. I was one dirty motherfucker and she was so into it that she didn't realise how dirty she became for me in return.

"You taste like strawberry laces, Coca Cola and fucking ecstasy on my tongue."

"*Sin*," she growled needily as I buried my face in her again.

"Sorry, sex pot, but it needed to be said," I growled into her wet heat.

She was about to fall and I drove my tongue into her to feel her come apart, her body tightening around me as she came and I drew out her orgasm as I fucked her with my mouth better than most men could manage with their dicks.

Her body went limp as she released my hair and moaned her satisfaction, falling back against the bank as she caught her breath. I climbed out of the water, rearing over her and lining up my cock with her freshly eaten pussy. She caught my jaw in her grip before I entered her, squeezing hard to make me look at her. "Take me for your own pleasure, Sin," she commanded. "Use me like every Fae you've fucked has used you."

"No, sugar puff. Your pleasure *is* my pleasure." I smirked then thrust my hips and slammed myself fully inside her, making her whole body arch beneath me. I clawed my hands into the mud beside her head, rolling my hips and fucking her with everything I had.

I hooked one of her legs over my waist then wrapped my hand around her throat, squeezing until she moaned, her tight body clamping around my cock again as she came. My wild girl liked me being rough and that just so happened to be my favourite style of fucking. Maybe we were a match made by the stars after all.

I was on the verge of finishing, my pleasure held back by a dam about to burst in my body when she forced me to roll over so she was straddling me. Rosalie rode me like a true Alpha and I cupped my hands behind the back of my head, enjoying the view as her tits bounced and I tore her bra off so I could view the show in HD. She placed one hand to my chest, keeping me down as her pussy worked miracles on my cock. She lowered herself over me just enough that my pubic piercing ground against her clit and as she came again with a Wolf's howl, I gripped her hips to hold her in place, finished deep inside her and tipped my head back to howl with her.

My chest heaved with furious breaths as she sagged over me, melting across my body as she rested her head against my shoulder. I wrapped my hands around her, nuzzling into her neck in a way I hadn't done with any Fae before. She was a blueberry muffin dipped in hot sauce. My favourite Fae in Solaria. My perfect desire. And she liked me for who I was.

She turned her head to kiss me and I leaned into that kiss, stroking her tongue in slow movements as I felt a connection to her that shook the foundations of my being. I was going to be cast to pieces and remade by her. And I wanted to know the new version of me. Because I had a feeling he was going to be happier than the old one had ever been.

She eventually slid off of me into the water and I followed her into it, kissing her shoulder as I washed her body. Then I kissed her neck, her ear and had soon found her mouth again. I knew she was another man's mate, but he was either going to have to fight me to the death for her, or the moon was going to have to make room for another match in her life. Because I wasn't going to let my wild girl go. Even if every celestial being in the sky commanded it. I'd fight them all with teeth and fists and claws to keep her.

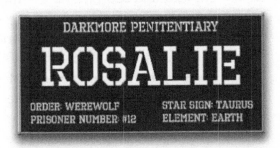

Tonight, we were going to escape Darkmore Penitentiary and never look back.

Those words were like a mantra playing on repeat over and over in my head as I checked and double checked every inch of the plan and tried to look for loopholes that weren't there. It was flawless. I was sure of it. The only things that could go wrong now would be unpredictable and I couldn't worry about that unless they happened. We just had to get through today. Which for right now meant enduring yet another thrilling group therapy session.

"This is baaaaad," Mrs Gambol said sheepishly - yeah like a sheep, because she was a Rustian Sheep Shifter I guessed, but it did seem like she played up to it a lot.

Although I guessed I was always growling and snarling and howling and shit, but something about her doing it just riled me up. Maybe it was because she was a Sheep and I was a Wolf and I just had a natural affinity to wanna hunt her down and eat her up. But as I looked at her knobbly elbows, I couldn't say I would enjoy that meal much either. So maybe she was just irritating as fuck.

I yawned without bothering to cover my mouth as Pudding told a story about getting lost in a china factory when he was a kid on the hunt for the perfect teapot. I mean, he clearly wasn't lost anymore, so I had to assume it all worked out in the end. Not exactly riveting stuff.

"There were blue teapots, red ones, yellow ones, three kinds of green. Olive green, forest green, mint green-"

I tuned Pudding out, fighting the urge to drop my head back and groan like a tired toddler.

My gaze slowly trailed over the circle of inmates surrounding me and then fell on the guard observing us.

Cain was already watching me as usual, his gaze hungry and penetrating. My skin flushed from the attention and I casually unhooked a few of my jumpsuit buttons before sliding it off of my arms and tying it at my waist.

I slowly drew my black hair over one shoulder, running my fingers down to the ends of it and caressing my breast as I held his gaze.

Cain's jaw tightened and I bit my lip to hold back a smile before looking away from him again.

"Rosalie?" Mrs Gambol prompted and I realised it was my turn to share.

I considered my options, giving merit to using Beauty and the Beast or Rapunzel or even Tarzan for my story of the day, but everyone was used to that by now and I was ready to play a more interesting game.

"Okay. I think I'd like to share the story of the first three-way I took part in that really pushed my limits," I said, a smile tugging at the corner of my lips as I remembered that. "I have a thing for Alphas and I'm wondering if that's a natural part of who I am or if it's really just some kind of symbol of the things that are broken in me."

"Oh, it could beee," Mrs Gambol agreed. "What was it about this particular foray that you feel is relevant to your life paaassage?"

"Well, I guess it was the first time I realised how good it could feel to ride two cocks at once. As a matter of fact, the two of them were pretty famous, though I probably shouldn't say who-"

"I'm on a tight schedule today and need to get Twelve's one on one done early, so I'm afraid this little story is going to have to wait for another day," Cain said loudly, getting to his feet and fixing me in a glare as he pointed me towards the door.

I sighed dramatically, pushing myself out of my seat and striding away ahead of him. There was a smirk tugging at the corner of my mouth as I put a little extra sway into my hips and headed down the corridor to our one on one room without bothering to wait for him.

Of course with his Vampire speed, he was breathing down my neck in no time, staying silent and raging and standing too close as he hounded me into the little room. Cain threw a silencing bubble over us, then locked the door as I moved away from him to take my chair.

"Was that particular story meant for my benefit?" he asked with a growl and I grinned up at him.

"Why? Does the idea of me fucking two guys at once turn you on?" I teased. "Or were you desperate to find out their identities so you could sell the story to the press?"

"How would a girl from the Oscura Clan end up in a situation where you were getting together with anyone famous?" he scoffed like he didn't believe me.

"I played Pitball for my Aurora Academy team and we went to Zodiac Academy to play against them," I replied easily. "It was actually two of the Celestial Heirs as you're so desperate to know."

"Bullshit," he growled but my smile only widened. A lot of my stories were bullshit, especially for him, but not this one. "Which Heirs?" he demanded after a few seconds and I laughed loudly, miming zipping my lips and tossing away the key.

"I signed an NDA," I said with a little shrug. Utter bullshit of course, I could sing to the rooftops about fucking the two of them and sell my story to the press for good measure if I wanted to. But I didn't want to. As strange as it would probably seem to Cain or anyone else in the place for that matter, I had actually counted the former Heirs as friends of mine. But still.

"Take a seat," Cain barked, dropping it even though I could see the curiosity in his eyes.

I did so, leaning back in my chair like I gave no fucks and the world was my oyster, which today I had to admit it felt like it was.

"Why so angry, boss man?" I asked with a pout. "Are you bored of me now you got what you wanted?"

Cain's eyes darted back towards the door again and he shook his head. "I don't think I could ever get bored of you, Rosalie."

My heart leapt at the sound of my name and the way he raised an eyebrow at me said he'd heard it, but I covered that with a laugh.

"So why aren't we doing it again instead of having this thrilling chat?" I taunted, my skin tingling with the idea of him claiming me on this tiny little table with all of those guards wandering up and down the corridor outside.

He held my gaze for a long moment, assessing the dare in my eyes as I licked my lips and waited him out. Cain pushed his chair back slowly, his dark gaze never leaving mine before he pounced.

A shriek of laughter and excitement left me as he vaulted the table in a blur of motion, swept me out of my chair, sending it crashing to the ground before shoving me back against the wall and kissing me so hard it stole my breath from my lungs.

I moaned against his lips, drawing out the beast inside him to come play with me as I reached for his waistband and pushed my hand beneath it.

My fingers found his hard cock as his tongue raked against mine, his fangs grazing my lips with the most delicious promise of what was to come.

I drew back with a moan as his hand moved beneath my tank and inside my bra, his fingers finding my nipple and tugging on it in the perfect fucking way to have me crying out for him.

The moment I tilted my head aside for him, his fangs drove into my neck and I moaned even louder as I began to work his thick cock in my hand and he groaned with need and longing.

I barely even noticed the sound of the door unlocking, but my eyes snapped open as the door was pushed wide and I found my gaze locked on Hastings.

"What the hell is going on here?" he asked, his innocent little eyes going all wide with shock as Cain froze, pulling his teeth out of me and shifting back enough to look into my eyes with horror filling his gaze.

"I may have punched this stronzo in the face," I lied, tugging my hand back out of Cain's pants and leaving his poor dick hard and wanting. "So the motherfucker bit me."

"You were out of control, Twelve," Cain growled, catching on fast enough and taking his hand back out from beneath my tank top while Hastings still couldn't see exactly what we were doing.

As he drew back, my view of Hastings was blocked and I smirked up at the boss man with the thrill of almost getting caught before shoving around him and hurrying over to Hastings.

"Is he allowed to do that to me?" I demanded, pouting as I looked up at my choir boy and damn, I bet it looked like I was almost crying.

"Well...yeah, if an inmate attacks one of us, we can use our Order gifts to defend ourselves," Hastings explained, giving me a sympathetic look. "So maybe don't punch him next time and he won't have to."

I huffed a sigh of acceptance and Hastings gave me a pitying look before reaching out to heal the bite for me.

"The warden thought it would be a good idea for me to sit in on these sessions," Hastings explained as Cain shot back around the desk to his seat and tucked himself beneath it with a growl of irritation. I was gonna bet his dick was still hard for me and the table was the only thing hiding the evidence right about now.

"Alright," Cain agreed. "Go grab a chair from another room. And knock next time instead of just unlocking a locked door. If you'd come in a few minutes earlier she would have been mid freak out and could have bolted."

"Yes, sir," Hastings agreed before heading back out of the room in search of a chair.

"Or a few minutes *later* and he might have found you balls deep inside me," I breathed, dropping down into my chair as I righted it again.

I reached out to catch a drop of my blood from the corner of Cain's mouth as he growled, pressing it between his lips with a teasing smile.

I drew back as the sound of Hastings' footsteps approached from the corridor, tucking myself in tight beneath the desk and kicking my boot off beneath the table.

"I was just about to finish running over Twelve's progress," Cain said, grabbing his Atlas from his pocket and switching it on. "And we need to assign her some areas to improve on."

"I could be more generous," I suggested, leaning forward and lifting my foot beneath the table to place it on Cain's knee. He flinched at the contact, but couldn't do anything to stop me as I slid my foot between his thighs and rested it on his chair with my toes caressing his dick.

"How so?" Hastings asked.

"I don't think I give enough blowjobs. I'm a pretty selfish lay, always just wanting to feel a cock deep inside me instead of messing around on foreplay, you know?"

Hastings cleared his throat and Cain growled.

"Lies," Cain said firmly.

"You think I'm lying?" I asked innocently. "You think I secretly love sucking-"

"I think that we need to work on your inclination to stretch the truth," Cain said loudly, cutting me off.

"But where's the fun in life without a little embellishment?" I teased. "Besides, everybody lies. I bet you have a few dirty secrets in your closet, don't you, boss man?" I flexed my toes over the hard ridge of his cock as I said that and he grunted.

Hastings didn't seem to notice though, sitting there and nodding his head like he was taking this all in and giving it real consideration.

"Maybe we could arrange for you to get a bit of reading material in your room? It might help to curb your appetite for entertainment. I know we don't generally allow the inmates to take more than one book from the library at once, but with your love for reading-"

"What love for reading?" Cain interrupted. "She told me she hates old books."

"Then why did you agree to set her work assignment for the library?" Hastings asked in confusion and I leaned back in my chair, laughing like this was all some big joke while Cain narrowed his suspicious gaze on me again. *Fuck it.*

"Some books in my room would be great, ragazzo del coro," I said with a warm smile for Hastings, circling my foot on Cain's junk so that he was thoroughly distracted from this point. One more day and I'd be long gone anyway.

"Did you just tell me you hated books because you wanted a job in the library?" Cain asked, his stare penetrating.

"If I'd told you I loved them you would have given me something else out of spite," I replied with a shrug, hoping he assumed my heart was racing because of what I was doing to him beneath the table rather than getting any real suspicions about why I'd wanted to be given work down in the library.

"That's because you're not here to enjoy yourself. You're here to be punished," Cain growled.

"Noted," I replied. "I'm a bad girl. I'll make an effort to remember that."

"Well...no harm done," Hastings chipped in, offering me a little smile that said he was on my side with this.

Cain grunted like he didn't agree, but he didn't push on with the subject either.

"Why don't you tell us something real now then?" Cain asked. "Prove that you're capable of it."

I pursed my lips as I considered that and a crazy, foolish, quite probably insane thought occurred to me. After today I was never going to see Mason Cain again. I'd cursed him with my gifts, and I was going to take off into the night and leave him to suffer whatever fate that entailed. But what if I didn't have to? What if I could tell him where he could find me once I was out of here so that he could come looking if he wanted to when I was gone? I mean, I still hated him, but I had to admit something had changed between us and as strange as it was, I didn't like the idea of never seeing him again.

"I miss spending the full moon with my family," I said honestly, sliding my foot back out of Cain's lap as I leaned back in my chair. I wanted him to hear every word of this just in case and he didn't need me distracting him. "Every single month we would all gather and race around the Oscura stronghold together. There's a mountain there called Mount Lupa and we would race up the steep paths in our Wolf forms with the Storm Dragon flying overhead and make it to this beautiful lake about half way up where the moonlight would reflect in a perfect sheet of silver across the surface of the water. When I get out of here, that will be the first thing I do as soon as the moon is full again. Race up that mountain with a thousand Oscura Wolves at my back while they all howl for the return of their queen."

I grinned as the two of them took my story in and Cain offered me something that was about as close to a smile as I'd ever gotten from him.

That was the best I could do for him. It wouldn't even matter if he told the FIB that story. That entire mountain and the land surrounding it for miles all around was owned by the Oscuras. They couldn't come onto the land without a warrant and if they got a warrant, our spies within their midst would warn us about it well before they ever got close to me.

So if Cain ever wanted to come find me there, he was going to have to come alone and offer himself up to the mercy of the Oscura Clan. But at least he knew where to look. That was all I could offer him and probably more than I should have.

The bell rang to mark the start of lunch and I pushed to my feet.

"Your shift is over now, isn't it?" Hastings asked Cain. "I can take her down if you wanna head off?"

Cain looked inclined to protest and my heart lurched uncomfortably as I realised this was it. Goodbye. And he didn't have the faintest idea.

"Thanks. I guess I'll see you when your shift finishes then." Cain gave me a look that sent my skin prickling with goosebumps and then he shot away.

I stared out into the corridor where he'd gone with my heart thrashing and this gut-wrenching sense of loss following him out of the room.

"I heard they got a new shipment of oranges in last night," Hastings said to me conspiratorially and I tried to muster a smile for him, but it fell flat on my features. "What's up?"

I was about to brush him off when I realised that this was actually the opportunity I'd been hoping for. We were breaking out today and I had absolutely no intention of bringing a pair of psychopaths with us when we did it. We needed Plunger to stay with us until we were above ground but Gustard was dead weight. And though I'd considered hunting down the motherfucker and making sure he met with a nasty end right before it was time for us to leave, on reflection I'd decided to leave him here to rot instead. Specifically, I wanted him to rot in the hole.

"It's nothing I can't handle," I muttered, giving Hastings a sad smile as we started walking down the corridor.

I counted down the seconds in my head until he cracked and asked for more information. "Are you worried about something?"

"I just... Sometimes it's hard being at the top of the pack, you know? There's just constant drama, especially in here with the rival gangs. There's always something to deal with from gang brawls to rumours and the death threats that come my way. But I'm sure it's nothing."

"You've been getting death threats?" Hastings asked with a growl that told me he didn't like the sound of that.

"Like I said, it's nothing I can't handle. I've already taken a shank to the gut, so what could be worse than that?"

"They could come at you harder this time," he said, catching my elbow as we made it to the top of the stairs and turning me to look at him while we were alone. "Just tell me who it is who's threatening you. Is it one of the other gang leaders?"

I chewed on my bottom lip but didn't say anything. I didn't deny it either and Hastings nodded like he'd expected that.

"I know you're close with Sixty-Nine, so who is it? Shadowbrook? Are the Brotherhood looking to start another war?"

"No, it's not Ethan," I said quickly then shook my head and hurried away from him. "I shouldn't be telling you anything at all. Just mentioning this could be enough to get me killed. Even my own pack wouldn't stand for me getting so close to a guard." I threw him a look like I was embarrassed I'd just admitted that and he grabbed my arm, tugging me around to face him once more.

"Is it Gustard?"

I said nothing but I sure looked guilty which was the closest anyone in here would get to admitting something to a guard and his eyes flashed with understanding.

"Maybe I should just skip lunch and then we don't have to worry about it." I tried to pull away but he drew me back.

"I won't let anyone hurt you, Rosalie," he growled, his blue eyes flaring with a promise that was so sweet it gave me toothache.

"I don't need anyone to protect me ragazzo del coro," I replied sadly, reaching up to brush my fingers down his cheek before pulling back like I knew I shouldn't have done that.

"Rosalie, I-" Hastings lunged at me, eyes closed, lips puckered, all in crazy gun-ho idiota. It would have been cute if it wasn't so ridiculous.

I shifted back with a gasp, placing my hands on his chest to stop him. "Hastings, we can't," I breathed like a real lady with morals and a sensitive constitution. "You could get into so much trouble and it would break me if that happened."

"I'm sorry," he spluttered, burning as red as the sun as he stepped back and let me go, swiping a hand down his face. "I don't know what came over me. Just the thought of something happening to you-"

"It's alright," I assured him, laying my hand on his arm. "But I should go. I'm sure I was worrying about nothing anyway."

I gave him a tight smile, tiptoed up to press a kiss to his cheek then turned and jogged away down the stairs smirking like an asshole. And I probably should have felt worse about toying with Hastings' feelings, but it was just so damn easy to get him dancing to my tune that I couldn't help it.

I headed into the Mess Hall for my lunch and spotted Gustard holding court in the rear corner of the room with his Watchers.

I grinned to myself and headed over to join my pack who all started howling and yipping with excitement as they spotted me, brushing their hands over every part of my body until I snapped at them to stop and they let me take a seat with my meal. As Hastings had promised, there was a nice, juicy orange waiting for me on the tray and I grinned at it as I got myself into a good position to watch the doors.

Banjo got all over excitable and started singing a song in my honour which I tolerated because he literally went around like a kicked puppy all day the last time I'd told him no and I couldn't take the guilt of it. Besides, this was the last time I'd be hearing any of his songs so he might as well unknowingly give me a send off.

"There was a girl so pretty that I wrote a little ditty and her name was Rosalieeee. She was strong and brave, liked to misbehave and one day she noticed meeee. It was a lonely place with my fall from grace but she made it all okayyyy. And I love her so, I need her to know, so she never goes awayyyyy."

I glanced at Sonny who shrugged at the choice of song lyrics but I guessed it was just what rhymed, not that Banjo had any idea what we were up to.

I probably should have been feeling bad about leaving so many of my pack mates here, but I knew what each and every one of them had done to earn their spot in Darkmore and it was an unfortunate fact that most of them deserved this. I was not Robin Hood sitting amongst the Merry Men. I was a gang leader surrounded by murderers and sick motherfuckers and I wasn't going to be setting a plague of them loose on the world.

I spotted Hastings the moment he entered the Mess Hall and his gaze fell to me for a brief moment as he gave me a firm nod before turning away and stalking towards Gustard's table.

I grabbed my orange and jumped up, moving around the room and catching Roary's eye before heading over to join him at his table where we would have a good view of the drama as it unfolded.

I hopped up to sit in front of him, pushing his tray of half eaten food aside and earning myself a growl for touching his meal. Lions didn't share food and all that jazz. I rolled my eyes and pushed a segment of my orange into his mouth to apologise and the noise that escaped him as he sucked my thumb between his lips was a wholly different kind of growl.

"I knew it," I hissed, pointing at him in accusation. "You like it when people do shit for you. Even though you claim not to want to use your Charisma to earn yourself a bunch of slaves to hand feed you, you like it when I do it!"

"Maybe that's just because it's *you*, Rosa," he said in a playful tone as he leaned towards me and parted his lips for more.

I giggled like a fucking idiota and then tossed my hair because I'd already gone that far, offering him another segment before snatching it back and eating it myself.

Roary growled again, grabbing my knees and yanking me closer to the edge of the table so my legs hung either side of him as he opened his mouth for more.

But before I could oblige him, a shout went up from Gustard's table and I looked up in time to see Hastings pushing him against the wall as he searched him.

Roary turned to look too, his hand sliding from my knee up my thigh as he did so and making my pulse skip as I tried not to think about that too much.

Officer Nixon prowled over to help Hastings and I didn't bother to hide my sneer at the pervertito as Hastings started checking Gustard's pockets.

"Did you do it?" I breathed, reaching out to run my fingers through Roary's luscious hair and he groaned as he leaned into the contact.

"Of course I fucking did it," he said cockily, like it was an insult for me to even ask.

"Why the fuck are you carrying this around?" Hastings asked loudly, tossing Nixon a shiny blue butt plug with a look of disgust. Nixon raised an eyebrow and then pocketed it, making me shudder as I got the feeling he planned on keeping it.

"That's not mine!" Gustard roared and Roary chuckled.

"It's surprisingly easy to smuggle sex toys in," Roary explained, snorting a laugh.

"Is it now?" I asked, tussling his hair in a mixture of annoyance and playfulness as I wondered when he'd first found that out.

"Well, only the boring, non-magical variety, but yeah. I asked and Leon delivered."

The next thing to appear from Gustard's pockets was a pair of nipple clamps followed by a pair of lacy panties.

"Hey," I hissed, dropping my mouth down to Roary's ear to make sure we weren't overheard. "If you could have gotten me nice panties then why the hell have I been wearing these fugly ass-bags for months?"

"You wanted me to smuggle you in nice panties?" he asked, drawing his gaze from the show and giving me a look that made me blush as his golden eyes seemed to burn like molten metal.

"Well, duh," I replied, refusing to back down. "And bras. The things they provide here should be illegal. In fact, maybe they are and they're serving a sentence down here too."

"They don't look that bad on you," he tsked and my blush deepened.

"Well...you haven't seen me in something red and transparent, so you have nothing to compare it to," I said and he growled again, the noise making everything south of the border clench deliciously. *Shit, I was hopeless for this man.*

414

Luckily we were saved from continuing that conversation by Hastings finally finding a shank in Gustard's pocket which was enough to see our plan come together.

"Come on Four-Oh-Six, you're going to the hole," Hastings snarled and Gustard started cursing as he was hauled towards the door.

His eyes fell on me and I couldn't help but smirk like a smug bastarda, loving the fury in his gaze as he realised exactly who had just set him up.

"I need to make a call!" he bellowed but Hastings ignored him and I knew there was no chance of that.

I started laughing, tipping my head back and howling with excitement, setting off a chain reaction from my pack which got my blood pumping.

To my surprise, Ethan tipped his head back and howled too, his pack joining in right after and our eyes meeting across the crowded room in solidarity for a moment.

"I'm gonna go and check on Claud, make sure there's no whispers of anything going on that we need to know about," Roary said, pushing to his feet and I pouted in disappointment.

"Are you ditching me, Roar?"

"Never," he disagreed, but he walked out on me anyway.

I huffed to myself as I finished off my orange, wondering what I should do with myself for the next hour before we had to head to the Magic Compound. We'd all agreed to avoid the library today because we didn't want to risk drawing attention to it now that we were ready to move. We weren't going to take any chances today. Everything had to go by the book.

As I sat procrastinating over my last orange segment, Ethan got up from his table and met my gaze as he left his pack behind and started walking towards the door. I popped the slice of orange into my mouth and frowned after him as I chewed.

The mate bond had been itching at me incessantly again the last few days and the heat in his eyes made it clear that he had been suffering with it too. I'd been dreaming of him all night and I was aching to just get up and run to him, scream at the world to go fuck themselves and kiss him until I was breathless.

Of course, I wasn't going to do that, so I just stole another orange from a Fae who was walking past me with his tray of food and then glared at him when he tried to protest.

He backed off quick enough and I peeled my prize with a smug little smile as I started chomping down on the delicious fruit.

My gaze was drawn to Ethan again as he headed through the doors and the moment he was out in the empty corridor, he turned and beckoned me. *Beckoned.* Like a cocky bastardo who thought I'd just come running. Who the fuck did he think I was?

He smirked at me and I swear I could practically hear him saying, *come on love, submit.*

Fuck him. He was the one who would be submitting.

Ethan turned left and strolled away and I continued to eat my orange angrily as the stupid mark behind my ear began to burn and a knot of sexual frustration tightened in my gut whispering things like, *just make use of him* and *you can put him in his place.*

I ate the last segment of my orange and got to my feet with a growl as I stalked out of the room to find him. *Gah. He was such an ass.*

I turned left and headed down the visitation corridor. The rooms used for the visits with our loved ones were all locked now so there was no one here, but as I found Ethan leaning against a door at the end of the long hallway, he threw me a grin and opened it.

"How?" I demanded, stalking towards him and wondering who he'd bribed to get use of this place and what it had cost him.

"Veiled Wall job, love," he purred. "I paid up a shit load of commissary tokens, but I figured I'm not going to need them now anyway. And what I *do* need, is you."

"Is that so?" I asked, cocking my head at him. "Because I don't like being summoned."

"Well I can't exactly call you, love, I don't have your number." He smirked at me, beckoning again as he leaned his ass back and sat on the edge of the table, waiting for me like he was so sure I'd come.

I was tempted to climb him like a tree and force him beneath me before riding him until he couldn't take anymore to prove which one of us was in charge here, but I got the strange feeling that he wanted that. Damn him and his alpha-male controlling bullshit. I needed to win here, but I was already in his space, at his beck and call and practically panting with need for him. Maybe it would have just been easier to give in and let him have what he wanted. But it grated against my nature so much that I couldn't make myself do it.

"Any room for a little one?" Sin's deep voice interrupted us as he rapped his knuckles against the door and grinned in at us.

"There's nothing little about you, Sin," I scoffed, but I was smiling too, because this looked like my ticket right back to power again.

"Fuck off," Ethan snarled. "I need some alone time with my mate."

"That sounds kinda lame though," Sin said with a shrug, stepping inside and closing the door behind him as he moved to stand at my back. "Are you threatened by the competition? Worried you can't keep up with a creature made for sex?"

Ethan snarled in outrage, his eyes flashing with hatred and Sin just chuckled as he dropped his mouth to my neck and started kissing me.

Ethan leapt to his feet, stalking towards Sin like he intended to throw him out by force, but before he could get to him, Sin caught my waist and pushed me into his path instead.

I knew exactly what Sin wanted me to do and I was more than happy to play his game. I caught Ethan's face between my hands and kissed him hard, taking that fury he was feeling and making him use it on me.

"I'll just watch," Sin said with a chuckle from behind us. "And maybe give you some pointers."

I believed that about as much as I would have believed that Sin was a virgin, but I wasn't going to call him out on it because this was a game I was hungry to play.

Ethan broke our kiss and growled angrily. "You want him watching us?" he asked me, the fire burning in his eyes saying that he wasn't totally against the idea no matter how much he might want to cave Sin's head in for being this close to his mate.

"You want to show him how loud you can make me scream?" I asked in return, biting my lip as I began to unbutton my jumpsuit.

"Fuck yeah," Ethan said just as Sin groaned.

"Oh, wild girl, I think I've found my match in you," Sin purred.

Ethan kissed me again before I could reply and I wound my arms around his neck as his tongue pressed between my lips and I moaned with need. Kissing him felt like stitching my soul back together, righting a terrible wrong and feeding all the empty parts of me with something I'd been hungering for more than I liked to admit.

Sin moved right up behind me, his hard cock pressing against my ass as he reached around me and unfastened the rest of my jumpsuit buttons, allowing Ethan to slide his hands inside it and beneath the hem of my tank. Sin tugged the arms of my jumpsuit down and I released my hold on Ethan to let him slide it off of me.

Sin tugged the jumpsuit right down to my ankles and then dropped down to unlace my boots for me.

Ethan dragged my tank top up and over my head, swiftly followed by my bra before dropping his mouth to take my nipple into it and sucking hard enough to make me moan.

I had no idea how Sin managed to get my boots off as fast as he did, but I found myself standing there in nothing but the ugly prison panties which I quickly shoved off too.

Sin ran his tongue up the back of my leg, over the curve of

my ass and then straight up the centre of my spine as he stood, and a shiver chased his movements as the cold air in the room found my naked flesh.

Ethan pushed a hand between my thighs, growling possessively as he caressed my pussy, his fingers sliding through the wetness he found waiting for him before he began circling my opening with slow, teasing movements that had my hands fisting in his hair as I ached for more.

I dragged him up to kiss me again and Sin pressed close behind me once more, the heat of his bare chest finding me and letting me know he'd stripped his tank off too.

As Ethan toyed with my clit in one hand and my nipple in the other, Sin's arms wound around my waist and he reached between me and Ethan, untying the arms of Ethan's jumpsuit where it was knotted around his waist.

I moaned into Ethan's mouth as I fisted a hand in the back of his tank and dragged it up, forcing him to stop teasing me as I yanked it over his head and revealed his gorgeous, tattooed flesh to me.

My hands roamed down his body as Sin's mouth started kissing my neck once more and Ethan reclaimed my lips with a possessive growl.

As my hand found the waistband of Ethan's boxers, Sin's fingers met mine and he chuckled against my neck as he helped me peel Ethan's underwear down to reveal the thick length of his hard cock.

I took his dick in my hand and Sin's fingers closed around mine as he started guiding the movements I was making up and down Ethan's shaft. My mate growled at the Incubus in a half-hearted way, but as Sin encouraged me to start moving my hand in a corkscrew motion, the groan that escaped Ethan seemed to counter any protests he might have been harbouring.

Once I had that motion down, Sin's hand slid from mine until he was caressing Ethan's balls and the moment he gave them a soft squeeze, my Wolf thrust his fingers deep inside me.

I moaned loudly, hungrily, my pussy clamping tight on his fingers as he began to pump them in and out and Sin thrust his hips against my ass, making me move on Ethan's hand to the most delicious rhythm. I could feel his dick pressing keenly through his jumpsuit, but he was keeping it on, denying me the feeling of his naked flesh against mine.

Ethan kept pumping his fingers in and out of me, adding a third as Sin's free hand found my clit and I gasped at the feeling of the two of them working together to destroy me.

With a cry of pleasure, I came for them, tipping my head back and breaking my kiss with Ethan as Sin urged me forwards, making all of us move towards the table in the centre of the room.

Ethan pushed his pants the rest of the way off of his ass and dropped back to perch on the table, pulling his fingers out of me with a needy groan as I continued to play with his cock and Sin moved his hand to the base of his shaft. Sin caught Ethan's hand and lifted it to his mouth, sucking on the fingers that had just been inside me and growling like a feral beast as he released him.

Ethan seemed caught between being pissed about Sin's involvement and liking his contribution too much to complain about it as we both worked his cock for him and he groaned in pleasure. He shifted back on the table and Sin moved to grasp my hips, lifting me up easily and moving me to straddle my mate.

I released my hold on Ethan's cock, gripping his shoulders and looking into his eyes as he took hold of my ass and pulled me down towards him.

Sin stepped in close behind me again, his arousal clear through the material of his pants as he reached around me, took hold of Ethan's dick again, making him curse as he gave it a few firm pumps before guiding it to my opening.

Ethan tugged me down hard and I cried out as his thick cock filled me in one hard thrust. I was so wet that he slid in easily and the full feeling of him possessing my body had my heart squeezing with pleasure as the mate bond hummed happily like a string being pulled tight between us.

I started to ride him and he used his grip on my hips to make me go faster, harder, take every inch of him all the way in over and over as he drove up and into me.

Sin caught my chin and turned my face to his, kissing me deep and slow and making Ethan fuck me even harder as he growled in anger and jealousy.

"Come on, big boy, make her scream," Sin commanded as he watched us with hunger in his eyes and my cries filled the small room, but apparently that wasn't good enough for him.

I started moving faster, riding Ethan as I fought to take command and pressing my hands down against his chest to give me a better position to control him.

Sin stood back to watch us, the feeling of his eyes on my skin making me even hotter as I moved my hips up and down so that I could feel the whole length of Ethan's cock driving in and out of me and he groaned as I pushed him closer to the edge.

Sin grabbed my shoulders and tugged me back, making me lean back so far that I could only maintain the position because he was holding me there. But as Ethan drove his dick up into me again, he hit my g spot so hard that I saw stars.

Sin laughed in the dirtiest way known to man as he held me in that position, making me take the punishing thrusts of Ethan's cock as I screamed for them, panting both of their names between the curses leaving my lips. When I came again, I almost blacked out as I forgot to fucking breathe and my whole body went rigid with tension as I pressed back into Sin's arms. Ethan came with me, my pussy tightening around his shaft and making him growl as he thrust in deep and spilled himself inside me, his fingers digging into my ass so hard I knew I'd have bruises.

Sin kissed me in a way that was almost tender as he shifted me back upright again, his hands sliding through my hair and Ethan sagged back against the table beneath us.

Sin released my lips and Ethan pulled me down to kiss him

instead, fisting a hand in my hair possessively as his tongue tangled with mine.

"Tell me you're mine, mate," he demanded, the heat and need in his blue eyes undeniable.

"I'm yours," I agreed, because it was true. No matter what shit we might have had between us, no matter how angry he might make me or how frustrated he left me, this bond between us was real. And it wasn't just some magic trying to force us to be together. I really believed he was my destiny. The moon wouldn't have just mated us because we happened to fuck under it. It knew as well as we both did that we were a perfect match and that this was always inevitable no matter how hard it might be.

Ethan brushed my hair from my face and kissed me again as he sat up, lifting me off of him and setting me back on my feet. His gaze slid to Sin and I turned to look at him too, his chest bare and cock straining against his pants with the desperate need to be fulfilled.

"Do you want him too?" Ethan asked me, his voice hard but the smallest thread of lust in there as well.

"Yes," I breathed, because I couldn't deny it. My body was tingling with satisfaction and I was achy in all the right ways, but looking at Sin had me wanting more. I wanted to please him too and feel him bow to my desire the way that Ethan had.

"Well it's my job to keep my mate happy," Ethan said and I turned to look at him in surprise, wondering if he really meant that or not. But he could have made Sin leave the moment he'd arrived and instead he'd let him stay, watch, even join in a little.

"Do you really mean that?" I asked, arching a brow at him.

"Only one way to find out," Ethan replied darkly, pushing himself to his feet and jerking his chin to beckon Sin closer.

The Incubus didn't need any more encouragement than that and he grabbed me, pushing me against the wall as he kissed me again and I moaned for him, my hands running down his bare chest until I found his waistband.

Ethan moved up beside us, tugging my chin to break my kiss with Sin before stealing my lips for himself.

Sin turned his head and kissed Ethan's jaw before moving his mouth to his neck and I moaned as I watched them, my heart pounding with excitement.

Sin lifted my leg and curled it around his hip, his cock pressing against my opening in the most arousing way before he drove it in deep and slow, making sure I felt the passage of his piercings all the way in.

Ethan growled as he drew back to look at us and I reached out to take his hardening cock in my hand, wanting him to be a part of this. Sin began to roll his hips, making his pubic piercing grind against my clit and I gasped as pleasure skittered through my over sensitised skin.

Sin gripped Ethan's jaw and tugged him close, kissing him as he fucked me while I began to work my hand up and down his shaft. It was so fucking hot. I didn't think I'd ever been so turned on in all my life.

Ethan broke his kiss with Sin in favour of me and my lips parted for his tongue as I was overloaded with sensations.

Sin's hand moved over mine, helping me work Ethan and the three of us started thrusting and grinding together in this perfect synchronicity which was most definitely being helped by the Incubus's natural affinity for sex.

His piercing rubbed against my clit and had me moaning and begging and rocking my hips against him harder and harder until my whole body was worked up into this frenzy of want and need.

With a deep thrust of his hips, Sin forced another orgasm on me, slamming his dick into me as I rode the wave of it over and over again until he was coming too and we forced Ethan to join us in our ecstasy and he bit down on my lip as he growled out a curse.

We sagged back against the wall in a tangle of panting, sweaty limbs and I couldn't help but laugh as I pressed back against the cold stone wall behind me.

"Well that certainly helped me out with the tension I was feeling," I teased.

"There had to be a good reason for me to be on the escape team, wild girl," Sin chuckled and Ethan released a breath of laughter too.

"I'm pretty sure I'm supposed to be pissed about this," Ethan muttered, a smirk playing around his lips.

"Says who, stronzo?" I teased. "The moon chose me for you and she knew full well that I'm not the type to be tamed easily. Maybe she sent us Sin too."

"Yeah, I felt the moon alright," Sin agreed. "She was shining on my cock and whispering your names to it. I'd say the bitch knows what she's up to."

"Fuck off," Ethan cursed, rolling his eyes, but when his gaze met mine, the heat in them said he wasn't in the least bit annoyed. He'd enjoyed that just as much as I had.

We moved apart and located our clothes, tugging them on in silence that was thick with the memories of what we'd just done and I bit my lip to stop myself from grinning like a dick-struck stronzo.

"Well, thanks for topping up my magic with all of that delicious lust," Sin teased as he headed for the door first and grabbed the handle. "I'll see you two later on in the library. And maybe the next time we do that it'll be right where the moon can watch us and enjoy the show."

I laughed at him and he strode away, whistling happily with a spring in his step. He might as well have been shouting out for the whole prison to hear that he'd just gotten laid, but I didn't have it in me to care. There was a darkness in Sin Wilder which swum beneath the surface of his eyes far too often and I was just pleased to have put a smile on his face.

The door swung closed behind him and Ethan moved around me, reaching out to fasten my jumpsuit buttons for me as I combed my fingers through my hair.

"I'll come with you, love," he said in a rough voice. "I'll dive right into the depths of the Oscura Clan and trust you to make sure I don't fall flat on my face when we get there. It doesn't even matter if I do though. I've tried to go without you, I've tried to deny my own heart, but I can't anymore. I don't want to. The only thing I want is you, love. So if you want me too then why don't we just run off into the fucking sunset and try to forget this place ever existed?"

"I like the sound of that," I agreed, leaning up to kiss him one last time. "So I guess we'd better make sure we don't fuck this up then."

"The plan is perfect, love. *You're* perfect. What could possibly go wrong?"

The tension in my muscles at dinner could have powered a Fae bomb. My eyes flicked between the faces of my pack who I was leaving behind with a twist of guilt in my gut. Harper had been a good Beta, and my other Wolves had served me well. But I still couldn't feel entirely terrible about leaving behind them, knowing I hadn't committed the crime that had landed me in here and they had. And I wasn't willing to spend another fifteen years in this place.

If I was caught, then what was another ten or more years on my sentence at this rate? I'd risk any price for freedom. But more than that, I'd risk any price for freedom with my mate. I planned on claiming Rosalie fully once we got beyond these walls. Fuck everything else. I could announce her as mine to the world beyond Darkmore. And then I'd face whatever came after that, take it in my stride for her.

It was different in here. There were more consequences for betraying my gang. Like having my body cut into ten pieces for becoming a traitor to the Lunar Brotherhood. The thing I'd sworn above all else when I'd been dragged into Darkmore was that I wasn't going to die in this place. Enough of my life had been pissed down the drain, I sure as shit wasn't going to end up burned in the incinerator because of one foolish decision. If Rosalie could only see that, then we could've worked things out a long time ago, seeing each other in secret. But with us getting out of here anyway, I had to just hold onto the dream that beyond this prison, she would claim me back so long as I claimed her openly and told the world that she was mine. Mated to me by the moon. And that was exactly what I planned to do.

I hugged Harper, knowing it was goodbye but she would be out of here in a few months so it wasn't goodbye forever. My gaze trailed over to Rosalie across the room who was in the midst of a dog pile of her own. Her eyes locked with mine and I swear I could feel her want for me as keenly as my want for her. The connection I had with her was unlike anything I'd ever known and I planned on honouring it properly in a few short hours, when there was no longer a reason to keep away from her.

Sin was eating alone, a smile pulling at his mouth as he shovelled stew down his throat like it was his favourite candy. I was still kind of shell-shocked from the three-way he'd sprung on me. I wasn't supposed to desire any other Fae, but somehow with him there, it had felt good. I'd enjoyed his hands on me, even more so because Rosa had looked so turned on by it. Pleasing my mate was ingrained in me by the moon, and if Sin pleased her then maybe I was going to have to get used to the occasional orgy with my mate. So long as she was mine at the end of the day, I guessed could handle that.

Sin had two more bowls lined up as if he was eating for a marathon tonight. I'd filled my belly well too, unsure where the next meal would come from. I knew it would be a while before I could go to my baby sister and eat the delights of her kitchen again. Once the alert was raised, the FIB would head straight to the homes of anyone connected to us, and unlike Rosalie, my family wouldn't be capable of hiding me, but I had ways of reaching them. Contacts the FIB could never link to me.

I didn't plan on becoming a leader amongst the Lunars when I left here. No, after too much time in Darkmore, my priorities had changed. I wanted to move somewhere far away from the cities and find a pack of my own to rule alongside my mate. I just had to convince her to join me in that dream once we escaped. And I hadn't figured out quite how I'd manage it just yet.

Pudding and Claud were talking together across the room

and excitement rippled down my spine as I looked to Rosalie again and she tossed her hair, the signal clear. It was time.

But before I could open my mouth, the Mess Hall doors opened and Officer Nichols escorted Gustard into the room, making my gut drop like a fucking stone. I looked back to Rosalie whose face paled as he was released into the masses, straightening his sleeve where the guard had been holding him before throwing a broad smile at my mate. That fucker. That piece of shit. He'd found a way out. I should have known that shady asshole would find a way to be here tonight. He moved to sit down amongst his gang and I swallowed the lump in my throat, sharing an intent look with Rosalie. She gritted her jaw then shrugged infinitesimally at me. And I knew there wasn't a single thing we could do about Gustard, because it was time to fucking go.

I howled furiously, diving out of my seat just as Rosalie dove out of hers, the two of us rushing together and drawing our packs after us. I took Rosalie to the ground as our Wolves collided either side of us, not questioning our reasons, just following us blindly into war. The shrieks and whinnies, cries and squeals breaking out around the room told me that the rest of our team were starting their own fights and the guards roared orders at us to stop.

I lowered my mouth to Rosalie's ear as she punched my sides more fiercely than was really necessary and I crushed her to the floor. "See you soon, love."

She smiled for half a second and a moronic part of me considered claiming a kiss from her, afraid it might be our last if this all went to hell. But I couldn't risk it. I had to hold myself in check even now. *Just a little longer.*

I scrambled away through the mess of bodies, subtly carving a path for Rosalie to get through so she could make it to the door. Her fingers clasped mine for the briefest moment then she was gone, slipping through the riot like a ghost.

I smiled, howling before throwing my fist into one of her packmate's faces then diving over him as he fell at my feet. The crush of bodies was cover enough and it helped that the fight was already spilling out into the hallway.

Sparkle charged through the crowd with her Pegasus herd at her back, whinnying furiously as she knocked people down beneath her and they were trampled underfoot. I raced past her, kicking out the backs of her knees as I went and she neighed angrily as she went down.

I fled past Pudding who was throwing chairs at a herd of Griffins, knocking them out one at a time with frightening accuracy. I slapped him on the back as I sprinted past him, tossing one last look at my brawling pack over my shoulder and saying a silent goodbye. My mate was waiting for me. And my whole life was too. I was going to see my family, meet my nieces and nephews, exert my Alpha status over my brother-in-laws and become the most infamous male Werewolf in Alestria.

I slammed into a solid body and crashed to the floor on top of Officer Nichols. His eyes were wide as he snatched the baton from his hip and I didn't hesitate, grabbing his wrist and breaking his arm with a furious twist of my hand. He roared in pain as I leapt up and kicked him in the jaw before I raced away. *Sorry bro.*

Sin flew through the doors ahead of me with something yellow bundled in his arms, but I couldn't tell what it was as he disappeared into the fray. Roary released a Lion's roar close to me and I glanced over to see him and his Shades ripping through a group of Medusas.

Gustard was standing back as his bastard unFae fuckers cut down Fae ten on one. Plunger was gone already, though as I passed my unconscious tattoo artist Alvin with a turd on his face, I had the feeling he was responsible. Only Plunger was that gross.

I made it beyond the doors, turning into the stairwell, avoiding heavy punches thrown my way as I ducked and dived and weaved my way through the riot. I was knocked left and right and took elbows to the gut, but never slowed, forging a path to the stairs and suddenly I broke free of the crowd and was sprinting down the steps, taking them three at a time as I raced toward level six.

I was panting and full of adrenaline as I made it to the frosted doors and pushed my way inside.

Esme, Sonny and Brett were there, patting each other on the back as they rounded into the aisle heading in the direction of the tunnel. I jogged on, brushing past them and taking in the group standing there. Rosalie was counting heads, her eyes flitting from one person to the next and relief filled her eyes as she spotted me. Plunger stood beside her, peeling off his jumpsuit readying to go into the tunnel. I was among the first here and I hoped to shit everyone else would hurry up.

I turned as footsteps sounded behind me and Gustard arrived with three of his men in tow who were all huge and built of pure muscle. One had a tattoo over his lips that looked like stitches and another had his eyebrows tattooed together like they were one, for who knew what reason.

"Who the fuck are they?" Rosalie snapped and Gustard smiled, smoothing out a crease in his jumpsuit.

"I am hardly going to leave here alone, pup. I have hand-picked my strongest men to assist us in getting out of here. And I will need a ride once we are at the surface, so I have chosen Orders who can carry me."

Rosalie bared her teeth in fury then shook her head. "Fine, do whatever the fuck you want," she hissed.

As angry as it made me seeing him here with his little *pals*, it was too late to do anything about it now; we had to just stick to the plan and take this opportunity because another one wouldn't be coming if we fucked this up.

Roary jogged in with Claud behind him and Rosalie sighed in relief, smiling at him. That just left Pudding and Sin to arrive.

"Are we leaving or what?" Gustard demanded, stepping toward the tunnel and Rosa straightened her back, blocking his way.

"We need Sin or we're not leaving," she growled.

"He was ahead of me." I frowned. "He should be here by now."

Worry rippled through the group and Sonny whined as he looked to Rosalie for direction. Her eyes locked with Roary's as they communicated some silent fear and I felt that terror in her as sharply as if it was my own.

"I'll go find him," I announced as worried chatter broke out and everyone looked to me.

Rosalie's eyebrows lifted as she turned her gaze on me, moving forward with hope in her eyes. "You'd do that?"

"You need to get down to maintenance and Plunger needs to get digging the rest of the tunnel," I said firmly. "I'll make sure Sin is here by the time you get back from neutralising the Order Suppressant."

A smile split across her cheeks and warmth spread through my chest.

"Thank you," she said seriously and I nodded, turning away from her and jogging toward the exit just as Pudding plodded through the door with a line of blood on his cheek, but a smile on his face.

"Get moving, Pud!" I called to him and he chuckled.

"I am well on the move, hound," he called after me and I pushed through the doors, hearing screams and shouts from the guards upstairs.

If Sin was in trouble, I had to find him and make sure he got the fuck back here in time to make it out. There was nothing I wouldn't do to make that happen for Rosalie. Even if I was putting my own freedom on the line. And I wondered when the mate bond had become far more than just a force beyond my control and turned into a deep kind of love that would surpass the bond even if it no longer existed. For her, I'd do anything. So by the fucking moon, where the hell was Sin Wilder?

My heart pounded with fear as I watched Ethan leave and I tried to convince myself that everything was okay. I'd told everyone that the only people I wouldn't leave here without were Sin and Roary, but as he left me behind, I knew that wasn't true. Me and Ethan had issues, but I wasn't going to be leaving him in this place. He was mine. My soulmate. La mia anima gemella. The one the moon had chosen for me. And as much as that particular celestial being liked to choose strange paths of fate for me to follow, I truly believed that she'd never set me wrong before. Which meant I needed my mate to come with us when we escaped this place or I wouldn't be leaving either.

I swallowed thickly as I admitted that to myself and tried to figure out when the fuck that shift in attitude had occurred. But maybe I'd been feeling like this for a long time and I just hadn't wanted to accept it because I was a stubborn stronzo and a Taurus never faltered from their path. But I was starting to think I needed to learn to compromise at least a little. Just this once. I needed to because I was aching for Ethan Shadow-brook to be mine for now and always and I wasn't going to let anything stop us from claiming that fate.

"Everyone needs to start heading into the tunnels," I barked, turning my back on the door and raising my chin as I used my Alpha tone with all of them. "I'm going to put the call in to Jerome and make sure that he locks off the guards' quarters. Cain is up there, so we don't have to worry about a Vampire sneaking up on us. Just follow Plunger, stay together and wait for me, Sin and Ethan to catch up to you before you breach the surface."

Gustard caught my eye with a wicked smirk and I cursed beneath my breath, wondering if the moon might wanna give me the gift of smiting so I could smite him good. *Come on, just a little smite for a nasty bastardo. Please?*

The moon didn't seem to be in a giving mood, so I gave up on that idea and forced myself to forget it for now. Roary followed me as I accepted two transmitters from Pudding and used the first to connect a call to Jerome.

"Hello, beautiful, do you have my cargo ready to go?" Jerome's silken voice came across the transmitter as I lifted it to my ear and I blew out a relieved breath to hear that he was there and waiting.

"You know Sin, he's keeping us on our toes," I admitted.

"Well don't go making the mistake of leaving that place without him," he replied in a deadly tone. "He might be a fuck up and real piece of work to deal with, but he's my brother and I want him out of there. If you leave him behind, I don't think you need me to spell out what that would mean for you."

"No need to threaten me, stronzo, I've been working this job for months. I'm hardly going to execute the plan without the main player in tow. You still haven't paid me my fee after all."

Jerome chuckled and once again we were the best of friends. He was a nasty bastardo to anyone fool enough to cross him, but he was also a Fae of his word and I trusted him to keep to his part in this.

"Have you locked down the guards' quarters?" I asked urgently.

"Don't get your panties in a twist, beautiful. It will all be done as requested and the magic will be put in place to block any lines of communication from making it out of Darkmore within the next five minutes. So if you have any other calls to make then you'd better do it now. After that there won't be a peep heard from Darkmore for the next three hours by phone, transmitter, email or even carrier pigeon."

"Three?" I growled. "You promised me six!"

"Well, it turns out their overrides are going to be a lot harder to block than I anticipated. I'll give you all the time I can, but I don't want to promise more than three hours. Once you get to your cousin and the stardust, you won't need to worry about the FIB being on your asses anyway. And I'll up your fee to cover the extra risk involved."

"Gee, thanks," I said sarcastically and he laughed like this was all some big joke. Which I guessed when you were sitting up in your penthouse hacking a few systems it probably seemed like it was. Never mind us little folk trapped in a hole in the ground and left down here to rot forevermore if it all went to shit.

"See you on the outside, beautiful. Try not to get caught." The line went dead and I cursed, crumpling the pudding pot in my hand as the magic ran out and tossing it aside.

I turned and found that almost everyone had headed into the tunnel already behind Plunger, but Roary was waiting for me, his arms folded and his mouth set in a firm line.

"All good?" he asked.

"Pretty much," I agreed. "I've just been given a firm reminder that if I don't get Sin out of here then all of our heads will be on the chopping block. Oh, and the six hours we were supposed to be getting with no interference from the FIB just became three. Which means we need to hurry the fuck up."

"You've got this, Rosa," he said firmly, holding my gaze as he waited for me to confirm I believed that too.

"Damn straight I do, Roar," I replied firmly. "I just need to call Dante before the external communications are all blocked off."

He nodded and I pulled the second pudding pot transmitter from my pocket, connecting the dental floss to the blueberry gum to start up the magic and then lifting it to my ear.

"Is that you Rosa?" a voice called excitedly and it took me a moment to recognise Roary's brother as a load of interference messed up the sound.

"Leon?" I asked with a frown. "Are you with Dante? Is something wrong?"

"It's all good little lupa," he called. "I'm riding him as we speak!"

"I assume you mean in his Dragon form?" I teased and Leon howled a laugh.

"You never know. Maybe I finally tamed the beast and have him writhing beneath me in ecstasy while he fists the bedsheets and begs for more."

A Dragon roared in the background and I laughed as a crash of thunder followed his protest.

"Alright, alright, we are currently flying through the clouds, working up a storm for you and Roary so that we can smash that fence with the lightning bolt of dreams."

"Perfetto," I said with a grin. "I've just gotta neutralise the Order Suppressant and the riot will take off in full force. Half the guards are locked in their quarters and we'll be climbing on up out of here in no time."

"See you soon then, little Wolf!" Leon whooped with laughter and Dante roared again, making my heart thunder in anticipation as the call disconnected and I turned to grin at Roary.

"My brother is up there too?" he asked, his golden eyes lighting and I nodded.

"This is really happening, Roar. Just a little bit longer and you and me will be laying on the beach sunning ourselves while the world tries to hunt us down."

"Let's get moving then," he said, the excitement in him clear and making me want to jump up and down and squeal like a kid at Christmas. "I'll come with you down to maintenance."

"You can't," I disagreed. "Plunger is going to start digging just as soon as he gets to the other end of that tunnel. He can't breach the surface until we're all with him and I don't trust Gustard to wait for us. But if they all end up above ground before Dante is ready to take out the fence when we're all there then the guards in the watch towers might spot them. I need someone I can trust to take charge of them and make sure they wait for me, Sin and Ethan to catch up."

"Pudding and Sonny can-"

"No, Roar," I demanded, grabbing his hand and tugging him around to face me. "I don't trust them. I don't trust anyone in here. No one but you."

His lips parted as he looked down at me and my pulse raced at the way his golden gaze seemed to be drinking me in. For a moment, my own gaze fell to his mouth and the aching, yearning, pining need that I felt for this man surged up in me so much that I was certain I would drown in it.

"Take this," I breathed, pulling a shank from my pocket which I'd made using a broken wall bracket from one of the bookshelves last week. "Gustard is dangerous and unpredictable. If anything happened to you, Roar, it would kill me. I can't-"

Roary caught the front of my jumpsuit and yanked me towards him, his mouth meeting mine in a blaze of fire that was powerful enough to consume me.

I gasped as the shank fell from my fingers and for a moment I didn't even kiss him back, I just fell apart in his arms, every wall and barrier I'd tried to construct around my shattered heart to keep him out falling down like it was made of nothing but sand.

And then my lips parted for his tongue and a moan of purest need and longing escaped me as I was destroyed for him in the best possible way, winding my arms around his neck and pushing my hands into his hair as he held my face between his big hands.

A deep and endless ache rose up inside me, only to be filled by him and everything I'd always wished and dreamed he'd be to me.

There were so many words passing between us in that kiss, so many moments that we should have shared and were promising to share now. All the things we were always meant to be to one another.

Roary pulled back, tilting my chin up so that I was looking

at him and I almost flinched, expecting him to tell me not to read into that, that it didn't mean anything and I was still just a dumb kid, or-

"I love you, Rosa. I love you in all the ways I thought I shouldn't and I'm sick of being afraid of that. I'm sick of wanting you and not having you. Of needing you and not owning you. I meant it when I said I wanted to run away to a desert island with you. But I'd stay in Darkmore for the rest of my life if this was the only place where you were too."

"Roary," I breathed, my heart pounding so fast that it deafened me as energy skipped and thrummed through my limbs and I tried to figure out what the hell I was supposed to say to that.

"It's okay," he growled. "I'm not asking you to say it. I just had to stop lying to myself, to you. I needed to tell you in case-"

"I've been in love with you since I was fourteen years old, Roar," I said, laughing at how fucking stupid that made me sound. "When I was just a dumb kid who annoyed you and you were this irresistible life-force that drew me in with every single thing you did. I used to look at you and tell myself you'd see me one day, that I'd stop being some silly little girl and maybe you'd look my way and see..."

"Everything," he finished for me, leaning in and kissing me again. "I see everything, Rosa. I'm just not sure I deserve that much."

The others had already headed off into the tunnels and time was ticking by and no matter how much I may have wanted to stay there in that moment forever and drink in the way he was looking at me and really seeing me, I knew we had to move.

"You need to go, Roar," I breathed, sliding my hands back down his chest as I tried to find the strength to move out of his arms. But I'd waited to be in them for so damn long that I didn't even know if I could leave now.

"Run fast, Rosa," he growled. "I won't let any of those assholes do a thing until you get there."

I grinned at him and he kissed me one last, punishing,

breath-stealing, earth-shattering time before releasing me and picking up the shank.

I was smirking like a stronzo when I turned and crawled into the tunnel, but I didn't even care. Roary motherfucking Night just told me he loved me. There wasn't a thing in this world that could sour my mood right now.

I crawled into the dark and took the righthand fork which curved down towards the maintenance level, getting to my feet as the tunnel widened out and glancing back at Roary as he turned to follow the others into the tunnel that led to the surface.

"Look after yourself, Rosa," he commanded in a low growl that made my toes curl and I laughed as I turned and jogged away into the dark.

It was cold in the tunnels and I tried not to shiver as I moved faster. This was it. I just needed to dose the ipump 500 with the ingredients Sin and Ethan had managed to get for me and instead of pumping suppressant up into the prison, the tank would start pumping antidote. Then every mean mother-fucker in this place would be able to shift and cause as much havoc as they liked while the guards scrambled to do a damn thing about it.

I kept going down floor after floor until I reached the wall that led into the maintenance level where I fell still, holding my breath as I listened to make sure there wasn't any sound coming from the other side of it.

A soft thump caught my ear followed by what sounded like retreating footsteps and I froze, heart in my throat as I waited to see if there was someone close by or not. We might be on the home stretch, but if I was caught now, the whole plan would fall to shit in a matter of moments.

I counted to thirty, but there was no more sound from beyond the wall and we didn't have any time to spare.

I bit down on my tongue, closed my eyes and carefully felt for the gaps in the edge of the mortar surrounding the brick in front of me.

I eased it back towards me, cringing at the sound of the bricks grinding together despite how slowly I was moving.

When it finally came free, I lowered it to the ground by my feet and moved to peer out through the hole with my pulse racing.

The maintenance room was dimly lit in red as usual and seemed completely empty. I couldn't hear anything beyond the constant whirring of the machinery either.

I blew out a long breath and started pulling more bricks from the wall, moving faster and faster as I worked to make a hole big enough for me to fit through.

A dull thump sounded in the distance like a door closing and I froze for a moment before hurrying on again when no more noise came.

I hopped out of the opening the moment it was big enough, landing softly on the stone floor within the maintenance chamber and glancing around. I had no way of knowing what time it was, but I needed to get my ass moving if I wanted to make the most use of Jerome's interference with the FIB. The moment the Fae Investigation Bureau were on our asses, we needed to be fleeing via stardust or we'd never get away. And as the protocol for escapees from Darkmore was shoot first ask questions later, I had no intention of letting them catch up to us.

I skirted the dark room and quickly made my way to the ipump 500. The bastardo who had tried to ruin everything. *We meet again my old friend.*

I forced myself to concentrate as I flipped open the control panel and started keying in the commands I needed to bypass the security system on it and unlock the intake chute. I'd been studying the information Dante had sent me on the back of his letters day and night until I was dreaming about it. I was a damn ipump expert.

A deep *bing-bong* sounded from the machine in confirmation of my command and I leapt out of my fucking skin as I spun around to check for any sign of anyone who might have heard that noise.

The chute slowly opened as I stood there fearing for my life and I pulled the ingredients from my pocket with shaking fingers before feeding them into the machine one by one as fast as I could.

The ipump powered up as the chute closed again, the sound of the engine churning and mixing everything together growing louder and making my mouth dry out as I began to back away from it.

The moment it started pumping again I had to fight the urge to whoop with excitement and satisfied the urge by jumping up and down and silently thanking the stars instead.

The sound of footsteps approaching cut my celebration short and I gasped as I darted away from the ipump and ran into the shadows beyond it with my heart thrashing against my ribs.

The distinctive buzz of static from a guards' radio came next and I pressed my back to the side of another machine and held my breath as the footsteps drew closer.

"Inmates causing unrest in the Mess Hall. All units stand by to respond if the situation worsens," Lyle's voice came over the speaker.

But the guard just snorted dismissively and kept walking, their footsteps drawing closer and closer to my hiding place as I was forced to hold my breath and pray to everything I'd ever believed in for help. Because if they found me here now, none of us were getting out of Darkmore Penitentiary.

I was down on level three by the Magic Compound, hiding in the shadows as I held a bunch of lemons in my arms. I'd planned on giving some to Rosalie and the rest of The Daring Anacondas, but I hadn't spotted them once the fight had broken out and I knew I needed to act fast. They'd be down in the library by now. I tossed most of them on the floor and pocketed two while I waited for footsteps to head this way, the quiet pressing in on my ears.

Come on, kitty kitty. Where are you my pretty?

A radio crackled and a male voice carried from it, but I wasn't paying attention to what they said. A guard answered the call and I lowered down to the vent behind me, breathing in deep, sucking in that gas and hoping my wild girl had gotten to the Order Suppressant tank already. As the guard drew closer, I sucked in air through puckered lips, hurriedly trying to awaken the Incubus in me and regain my power.

I could feel it giving me what I needed and I swallowed a manic laugh as my beautiful, sexy ass Order was returned to me. *Welcome back, honeypie.*

Officer Rind stepped past me and I leapt out behind him like a ghost in the night, snatching his shock baton from his hip and whacking it over his head so hard that he crumpled at my feet. I grinned darkly as he groaned, whacking him again to make sure his lights were firmly out before lifting him by the arms and hurrying to drag him down the corridor, humming The Daring Anacondas theme tune I'd been working on as I went. The sound of more footfalls headed this way and I fell quiet, my humming dying mid-tune.

I was on a serious time limit now and for more reasons than one. So I had to get a move on if I was going to pull this off. My wild girl was relying on me and there was no way I'd let her down.

I continued the theme tune in my head to help me focus. *Flash bang! It's an anaconda in your face. Flash bang! They're gonna break out from this place. Flash bang! There's a snake up in the grass. Flash bang! It's gonna bite ya in the ass.*

I dragged Rind around the corner as more footsteps approached and orders were barked between them. I reached the guard's elevator, lifting up Rind's hand and slamming it against the scanner, pinching him in the crook of his elbow and making him set off a few flickers of magic in his palm. It beeped as it opened and I hauled him inside, stripping off my jumpsuit as the doors closed and swapping my clothes for his.

When he lay at my feet with my jumpsuit scrunched up on his chest and a cock drawn on his face from the pen I'd found in his pocket, I shifted into Officer Cain and grinned darkly. I cupped my ass in my palms, squeezing his muscular buttocks like I'd thought about every time he walked past me with one of his serious scowls. *Mmm yeah, Cain worked out and I was here for it.*

I pushed one lemon into my pocket and lengthened my lil Vampy fangs before taking a bite out of the other one, the juices dribbling down my chin. Rosalie wasn't the only one who lusted after Cain in this place. And I'd had a dirty dream or two about him myself, so taking his form was as easy as taking nuts from a Squirrel Shifter – you just had to slap 'em a few times and they gave them up.

I punched in the number for level seven and started descending through the prison, rubbing the lemon juice on any exposed skin I had before leaning down and shoving the half eaten lemon into Rind's mouth.

"Delicious, thank you Officer Cain," I imitated his voice with a smirk then stood upright and clasped my hands behind my back all formal like.

When the doors opened, I pressed the button for the guards' quarters to send Rindipoos up to his friends then strolled on out into the corridor, gazing at the beautiful sight before me. The door to the Belorian's cage.

I smiled widely, striding toward it like a cocky asshole, revelling in the sensation of being a big man in this prison. It felt good. I wasn't surprised the guards walked around this place like their balls were made of solid gold if they felt this powerful all the time.

"Hello beasty," I purred at the door, excitement trickling through me as I prepared to put my Vampy strength to fun use and rip that collar from its neck.

Rosalie and I had our own secret language. And she'd clearly wanted more chaos tonight to keep the guards busy. I was more than happy to supply that, especially when she'd asked me to do it so plainly. A no from her was a secret yes to me. And she'd really impressed how much she needed me to do this. Yup, we wouldn't get out of Darkmore without my help. No siree.

I took Rind's radio from my hip, twirling it between my fingers before bringing it my mouth, clearing my throat then pressing the call button. "Code brown! Release the Belorian! Release it now!"

ARIES. VAMPIRE. FIRE.
COMMANDING OFFICER
CAIN
DARKMORE
PENITENTIARY

I headed out of my room in sweatpants and a t-shirt, figuring I'd grab something to eat and get an early night. I'd taken two shifts in a row and though it helped to keep me distracted from the curse, I was only Fae and I needed to sleep eventually. I headed down to the rec area and frowned as I found that some fucking lazy asshole had left their baton and radio on the coffee table. Was it really that hard to put them back in their fucking locker?

"Repeat the order, Cain, static on the line," Lyle's voice came across the radio, sounding frantic.

What the fuck?

"I said code brown! Release the Belorian, release it fucking now!" My own voice sounded in reply and I turned to stone, trying to work out how that was possible. And what the fuck was going on. *Code brown? There was no code brown.*

I snatched the radio from the table as my heart thundered and I pressed the button. "Hold that order," I barked at Lyle.

"Sir?" his voice came down the line. "You want me to hold it?"

"Yes," I snapped, but my voice didn't make it through as the other fucker impersonating me held their call button down and kept the line open on their end, shutting me out.

"Yes, release it, release it!" he demanded sounding far too peppy to actually be me, but he was either doing one hell of an impersonation or – or-

"Release it!" he begged again.

"*Fuck*," I snapped, holding my own call button down as I

tried to stop Lyle before it was too late. "Don't release it!" But I wasn't getting through, the fucker was still blocking the line.

Fear pumped through me, spreading into every bone in my body.

I cursed and shot down the hallways to the security office, shoving it open and finding Lyle sitting in front of the CCTV screens across the wall.

"Lyle!" I barked. "That wasn't me on the radio."

"It wasn't?" he gasped.

"No, please tell me you didn't release the Belorian," I growled, but the paleness of his face gave me his answer even before he said it.

"I'm sorry, I-I let it out," he stammered, sweat beading on his brow.

"Then use the collar to send it back!" I demanded.

Lyle hastily started typing commands into the console before him but as he hit the execute button, a message flashed up on the screen.

Signal lost. Unable to complete command.

"By the stars, what the fuck is going on?" I took in the riot spilling through half the prison on the cameras, my breaths coming heavily as I absorbed the chaos taking place downstairs. *Holy fucking shit.*

My heart sank like a fifty ton rock as Fae all across the cameras started shifting, their Orders spilling from their flesh, their jumpsuits torn to ribbons at their feet. My worst nightmare was materialising right before my eyes and I was frozen by the monumental problem staring me in the face.

"No," I gasped, my mind struggling to catch up and figure out a solution to the absolute mayhem unfolding before me.

My eyes hooked on a guard hurrying up the stairs away from the Belorian's cage, a wide grin pulling at his face. *My* face. What? How? Who?

Realisation struck me like a punch to the gut.

That piece of shit!

"Sin Wilder," I hissed, pointing him out. "His Order's free and he's impersonating me."

"Oh my stars," Lyle breathed as he gazed at the carnage, the guards using magical force to try and wrangle the masses, but with all their Orders loose, we were totally fucking outnumbered. They'd overrun Darkmore in less than an hour if we didn't act fast.

"Something's happened to the Order Suppressant," I growled, finding myself hunting for Rosalie in the crowds, but there were blind spots all over this prison. She could be anywhere. And why did my gut tell me she was somehow at the heart of all this?

The curse mark throbbed on my arm as anger at her twisted through me. I didn't know how, but I was sure she was to blame for some of this. Where there was trouble, that girl seemed to reside. And as my mind hooked on that thought, the curse punished me for it and I could feel the vines growing across my chest, laying claim to more of my body. Pain splintered through me and I blinked hard, trying to force it back, needing to fight it off now more than ever.

I managed to keep it at bay as I took a steadying breath and backed up towards the exit while Lyle continued to gape at the cameras, apparently too shellshocked to do anything but stare on at the madness.

"I have to get down to the Order Suppressant tank. Keep trying to send the Belorian back to its cage." I shot back into the hall, tearing towards the open elevator at the other end.

My heart lurched as I spotted Rind's body on the floor of it with a dick drawn on his unconscious face and a lemon stuffed in his mouth. I knew without a doubt who'd put him there; the same guy walking around in a guards' uniform wearing my star-damned skin.

Before I made it into the elevator, a metal shutter slammed down over it right in my fucking face. I collided with it, unable to slow in time and I stumbled back with a curse. It was the only fucking way out of here, and this shutter was only supposed to come down if an override code was entered in an emergency.

Fuck!

My head spun as the curse rose up again and nightmares flickered through my head, pain bursting through my skull.

I was half aware of my knees hitting the floor as darkness descended on me and I fought to stay awake, desperate not to succumb to its power at this most crucial moment. The warden wasn't here tonight. Which meant I was in charge.

So I had to get up.

Restore order.

Find Rosalie...

But the curse overwhelmed me and I fell into a sea of pain as I was punished for the girl I'd hurt at the worst moment possible. Darkness washed through me as I passed out and I was forced to let go of the world around me.

I'd headed back upstairs, searching every level, cursing as our time ticked down. But Rosalie couldn't leave without Sin and I sure as shit couldn't leave without Rosalie. So where had that fucking Incubus gotten to?

I made it up to level three where the Magic Compound was, shoving through a bunch of inmates and hurrying toward a huge Bear who was fighting ferociously with a Centaur. I was almost trampled by the Centaur's hooves as he charged down the Bear and I fought the urge to shift too as I felt my Wolf living freely in my chest now. Rosalie had pulled it off, the Order Suppressant was no longer pumping into the prison. My beautiful, clever mate was going to be fucking famous for this.

I was not going to let her down on the promise I'd made. She'd poured blood, sweat and tears into this plan and fucking Sin was not going to ruin it.

The Bear's huge, clawed paw swiped backwards, nearly catching me by accident and I growled angrily.

I swear to the stars, Wilder, if I die up here in this riot while I'm looking for you, I'll haunt your ass forevermore.

I had to duck into an alcove as the Centaur was thrown into a herd of Griffins who flapped their wings indignantly. My heart hammered as time ticked by and I wasn't any closer to finding that asshole. I went to move again and my foot slipped on something round. I looked down at the pile of lemons sitting there with a frown pinching my brow.

"What the...oh fuck no," I came to a realisation with my heart thundering in my chest. I'd seen Sin running out of the

Mess Hall with something in his arms. He'd done this before. And I knew for a fact that the Belorian hated lemons, so I snatched one up and shoved it in my pocket.

I shook my head, cursing through my teeth as I raced down the corridor back the way I'd come and into the stairwell. I sprinted past a pride of Lions and through the chaos which was fast spreading onto every level of the prison.

"Halt!" a guard shouted from behind me and a vine snared my arm, yanking me to a stop.

I turned, spotting Officer Kato there, raising another hand to cast magic. I clawed at the vine around my arm, trying to tug it free, refusing to be caught. I had to return to Rosalie. I had to get out of here. I wasn't going to forfeit my fucking freedom for anything.

Another vine came at me, then another and another, throwing me against the wall as Kato worked to incapacitate me. I bit through one of the vines with my teeth while tearing another from my body as more and more were sent my way. I growled in fury, preparing to shift, but before I had to, a rogue Minotaur charged up the stairs, his horned head bowed and he head butted Kato out of his way, sending him crashing onto his back. I ripped the remaining vines off of me, thanking my lucky stars before running down the stairs full pelt while Kato called for help.

"Sin!" I bellowed as I made it to level six. I was closing in on the Belorian's cage, hoping upon hope that I was going to get there before that monster was let loose.

A shredded guard's uniform and a lemon sat together on the steps that led down to the dreaded level where the monster lived. I slowed my pace, moving silently over the steps with my heart thrashing in my chest.

A guttural growl made my skin prickle and I pressed my back to the wall as I made it to the edge of the stairwell. I threw a glance around the wall and saw a terrifying sight. Not one, but *two* Belorians stood there, seeming to be communicating with clicks of their teeth. Their bodies were grey and smooth and their six legs tapered to razor sharp talons which could cut a man in half. A large collar lay broken on the ground between them and my heart stuttered at the sight of the only thing that could return those creatures to the cage.

There was no sign of Sin so I turned, trying to slip quietly away, not daring to breathe. But as I took two steps away from them, a whoop of laughter rang somewhere ahead of me and my heart lurched in my chest.

A couple of guys came into view, their skin shimmering with scales revealing their Siren Orders.

"They'll never find us down here, Colin!" one of them cried and a roar sounded behind me that made my heart bunch up into my throat.

I started running, the sound of those creatures approaching making fear tumble through my flesh.

I shoved past Colin and his friend, needing to get the fuck away as fast possible.

"Woah, what's the hurry bro?" one of them called after me, but their following screams told me they'd seen exactly what the hurry was.

I knew how quickly those things moved and fuck, I was not going to waste a single second in getting away. I leapt up step after step, the sound of the Sirens running after me followed by another roar.

Fuck this. I needed to get back to the library. Maybe Sin was there by now. Maybe I was chasing him in circles and risking my own neck for fucking nothing. But I couldn't lead this monster there so I passed by level six with a curse, planning to hide on level five in the gym until the Belorian moved on before returning to the library.

Someone collided with me and I was shoved off of the stairs onto level five and I growled as the Siren surged ahead of me and my knees hit the floor. I got to my feet as the other Siren flew past me and I glanced back, coming face to face with two Belorians, their jaws wet with venom and their eyeless faces trained on me.

The one on the left released a high pitched shriek, racing forwards and I turned tail and fled, adrenaline crashing through me as I ran for my fucking life towards the gym doors. The other Belorian charged past me, leaving me to the mercy of its friend as it hunted the two Sirens.

"Come on Colin!" one of the guys roared, but Colin was knocked to the ground by a vicious swipe of the Belorian's front legs. His terrified screams were cut off as a mouth of serrated teeth clamped down over his head and sickness churned my gut.

I don't die like this. Not like this!

The Belorian chasing me swiped at my head the same way its companion had just done to Colin and I ducked, skidding across the floor to get away. Sharp talons slammed into the ground by my leg, slicing through my jumpsuit and pinning me in place. I twisted away, trying to rip the leg of my suit as another clawed foot slammed down in front of me, caging me between its legs. I took the lemon from my pocket, but the Belorian knocked it from my hand before I could manage to slice it open.

A deep growl left its body and suddenly the beast swiped me up between its front legs, crushing me against its icily cold body. I punched and kicked and thrashed, expecting teeth to find my flesh at any moment and end me. But the beast turned and started running for the stairs instead, releasing low grunts as it moved. I kept fighting for my life, my fear making every punch powerful, but not enough to dent this vile creature's impenetrable flesh. I wouldn't give up though. I was *not* going to be dinner for this disgusting monster when my mate was waiting for me. And a whole life was waiting for *us*.

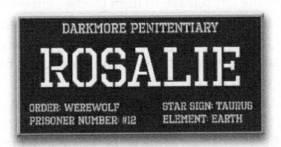

I held my breath as the guards' footsteps stalked away, both thanking and cursing Sin for the chaos he was causing upstairs by setting the fucking Belorian free again. Because I knew that had been him. From the moment I'd heard Cain sounding peppy over the guard's radio, I'd known exactly who was up there setting the Belorian loose. Mason Cain had never been and never would be peppy a day in his fucking life. I was going to beat the shit out of that motherfucker when I saw him and then kiss the fuck out of him for happening to distract the guard who had almost found me while I hid in the shadows for so freaking long I'd lost count of the time. And that was time we didn't have to spare.

I gave it to the count of thirty then slipped out of my hiding place, hugging the shadows at the side of the room as I ducked beneath a thick pipe which protruded from the side of the ipump 500 and sent the Order Suppressant - or antidote as the case now was - up into the main prison. Unfortunately for me, there weren't vents down here on the maintenance level because prisoners weren't supposed to be down here, so I was stuck in Fae form until I could get back up to the library and reclaim my inner Wolf.

I skirted the huge machine, hopped over a crate of cleaning supplies and dropped down on the other side, but as I landed, my boot connected with a metal bucket and the damn thing fell to the ground with a loud crash.

My heart leapt up into my throat and I froze half a second before the guard's voice rang out, filling the huge chamber.

"Who's there?" he demanded and my pulse pounded even harder as I recognised that old pervertito, Nixon.

I didn't wait around to let him find me, turning away and racing across the room as fast as I could run, my mind fixed on the tunnel. If I could just get inside maybe I could get the bricks back into place before he found me. Or I could just fucking run and hope for the best. Either way, I couldn't fight against a guard with his magic thrumming through his veins while mine was locked down deep inside me.

I leapt around a corner, spotting the tunnel on the far side of another machine and started running for it, but before I could reach it, Nixon lunged into my path with his shock baton raised.

"You!" he growled, thrusting the weapon at me and pressing his thumb on the button so that a thousand volts of electricity slammed into my body and I was thrown clean off of my feet, crashing to the ground in a heap.

I gasped as pain ricocheted through my body and Nixon stalked towards me with a deep and throaty chuckle. A hit from that thing should have been enough to paralyse me for several minutes, but I was Rosalie Oscura; I'd been raised in pain and had trained with a Storm Dragon for this exact scenario and nothing was going to keep me down at this asshole's mercy.

"Well look what I found down here where she shouldn't be. A bitch who overstepped the line. If you'd just told me you were already sucking Cain's cock for protection then I could have come up with an-"

I swung my leg around the second he got close enough to me, a cry of rage leaving my lips as I took out the backs of his knees and he crashed down onto his back with a curse of fury.

I leapt up instantly, pressing my advantage as I pounced on him, throwing my fists into his face with a furious snarl as I pinned him beneath me and he fought to buck me off.

The shock baton struck me again, the electricity tearing into my body and knocking me off of the stronzo so that my head cracked against the machine beside us.

Nixon cursed as the electricity shocked him too, but he hadn't taken a powerful enough hit to incapacitate him via me.

I gritted my teeth and pushed myself to my hands and knees a moment before his boot collided with my gut and the air was forced from my lungs as pain spiralled through my side.

Nixon drove the shock baton at me again and I lunged at it with a howl of fury, my hands locking around it just as he deployed the lightning strike and it slammed into my body again.

I held on with a snarl of pure and raw determination and Nixon's eyes widened in disbelief as the power of the strike faded and I managed to rip the baton out of his hands.

I swung it at the side of his knee with all of my strength and Nixon screamed in pain as something cracked and he stumbled backwards.

I was back on my feet within moments, raising the baton and aiming for his head, but before I could land the blow, he threw a hand out at me and I was struck with the power of a tornado as he hit me with a blast of air magic that lifted me clean off of my feet.

I was thrown right across the room, the lightning baton ripped from my grasp and hurtling away a moment before my back hit the wall and pain splintered up my spine.

I crumpled to the floor, a whimper of pain escaping me before I could bite it back and I forced myself upright again with a curse.

I couldn't see Nixon beyond the machines in the middle of the huge space, so I turned to my left and took off as fast as I could.

My footsteps pounded across the stone floor and I growled in frustration beneath my breath as I realised I couldn't hear him at all anymore. He must have been using a silencing bubble to hide his own movements and I got the sinking feeling that I was being hunted down here in the dark.

I ducked left and right, skirting whatever machines I could manage while trying to make my way back around to the tunnel entrance. It was my only hope. I had to get away from here, from him, back into the tunnels and up, up, up all the way to freedom.

"Where are you running to, poppet?" Nixon's voice came from somewhere to my right and I gasped as I turned, finding him hovering near the ceiling as he used his air magic to lift himself up above everything to find me.

His lips curved up into a cruel and predatory smile and I didn't even have the chance to yell out before another blast of wind slammed into me and threw me against a water tank in the corner of the room.

The pressure of the magic increased as it drove me up against the tank and no matter how much I writhed and fought against it, I couldn't break free of the hold it had on me.

Nixon used his air magic to lower himself down to the ground in front of me, smirking at me with his eyes hooded as his gaze trailed down my body.

"I think we should pick up where we left off the last time I had you in a position like this," he purred.

"Fuck you," I snarled.

"You're supposed to say 'yes, Nixy'," he said with a chuckle.

"I'm going to kill you," I swore. "I'm going to rip your face off with my bare hands and then tear into your chest and claw your beating heart from your body and stuff it into your mouth for you to choke on."

"The words you're looking for are 'yes Nixy'," he repeated, ignoring my threat like I hadn't even made it. "How about we play a little game? You're going to apologise for how rude you were for attacking me. And you're going to show me just how sorry you are by pleasing me the way I like." He rubbed a hand over his crotch and licked his lips in that toad-like way which gave away his Order as he surveyed me.

"Fuck you," I hissed. "I wouldn't touch your rancid dick if it was the key to my freedom from this place."

"You'll learn to love my dick," Nixon replied with a shake of his head. "You'll learn to love it and beg for it and purr 'yes,

Nixy'," for me on command. You'll do it or I'll be telling the warden that I found you down here messing with the Order Suppressant tank right when the rest of the prison suddenly gained access to their inner animal. How many years do you think she will slap onto your sentence for that?"

A sick feeling rose in my mouth as he moved closer and my upper lip peeled back in disgust.

"I'd take ten lifetimes in this hell before I ever let you touch me," I hissed.

"In my experience, the feisty ones usually lose all of that bravado once I'm inside them," he said, increasing the pressure of his air magic as it pinned me back against the tank. "Shall we find out if you will too?"

Nixon moved forward to grab me and I did the only thing I had left within my power as I started screaming and screaming. I'd never in my life needed help the way I did right then, but I would do whatever the hell it took to make sure this motherfucker never got to lay a hand on me.

Nixon's fist collided with my face and his air magic released me so that I could fall to the floor with the taste of blood coating my tongue.

"You're going to beg for it," he said in a low, dangerous tone. "You're going to say 'please, Nixy' before I give it to you." His booted foot swung into my gut and I cried out at the pain as I rolled away from him again.

"Fuck you." I leapt up and tried to run, but I collided with a solid air shield before I could get more than a few paces and Nixon's fist connected with my jaw as I whirled back around to face him.

That motherfucker had trapped me here with him and as I recovered from his strike to my face, I knew that I was going to have to fight him if I wanted to escape here at all.

I leapt at him with a murderous howl and he grinned as my fist collided with another air shield which he'd placed around himself, sending pain splintering through my hand which made me almost certain I'd broken something.

Nixon punched me again as I tried to recover and then flung me away with the force of his air magic before I collided with the shield trapping me once more and fell to the ground with a gasp of pain.

I couldn't fight him without magic. I was as useless as a fly beating its wings against a glass jar. But I wouldn't give up. I wouldn't give in. I was Rosalie Oscura and I hadn't begged for death at my father's hands so I certainly wouldn't do it for this scumbag.

"A morte e ritorno," I growled, a promise in my words even more forceful than I'd ever spoken them before.

"Just say it," he urged, the look in his eyes saying he was sure I would in the end. "*Please*, Nixy.'"

I spat blood from my mouth, my chest heaving as I panted and I parted my lips on another scream as I refused to give in to him. I'd die first. But I was starting to think that he was okay with that option too.

DARKMORE PENITENTIARY

ETHAN

ORDER· WEREWOLF
PRISONER NUMBER· #1

STAR SIGN· CANCER
ELEMENT· WATER

Pain seared through my flesh and I wondered what fresh hell I was being subjected to now as the Belorian ran with me in its arms. Maybe its body was designed to inflict pain, channelling it into me. Maybe I was dying. Because my head was spinning and I felt like I was being punched and kicked and-

"It's me," the Belorian grunted and I screamed, thrashing harder, sure I'd lost my mind. One of its poisonous spines must have cut me and now I was in the grip of death, never to see my beautiful mate again. It was going to carry me off to some dark corner of the prison and suck me dry like a fly in the clasp of a spider.

The beast rounded into a corridor and dropped me on my back, leaning down in my face with a hundred sharp teeth glinting at me.

"Argh!" I roared, throwing a furious punch at the fleshy place above its open jaws and I swear it made a noise like *ow*.

The monster shifted above me and I was suddenly lying beneath the widened legs of a very naked, very smug looking Sin.

"Hey buddy!" he cried happily and I winced as he reached down and pulled me to my feet, my mind taking a moment to catch up with the fact I was no longer about to be eaten, though the agony in my limbs lingered on.

"Sin?" I breathed unsteadily, unsure what the fuck I'd just witnessed.

"I shifted into the Belorian's sexy fantasy so he didn't eat me." He beamed. "Time to go." He caught my arm, dragging me through two frosted glass doors and I realised we were back at the library. "Come on, we can't be late."

"Why the fuck did you let that thing out?" I snarled furiously as he half dragged me down the aisle between the shelves which led towards the tunnel.

"Me and Rosalie had a secret plan," he said with a smirk.

"No," I snapped. "There was no plan. She told you not to release it."

He just laughed like I was the crazy one and I tried to focus on the positives as we made it to the tunnel. I had Sin. He was fine. Fucking nutty as a pecan, but still fine. And I could beat him up for this bullshit later. For now, we had to run for our lives.

We crawled into the tunnel side by side, standing up as it opened out and the passage forked before us. One way led up to the surface and the other down to the maintenance level. Despite all the adrenaline still washing through my veins for nearly thinking I was a dead man, a smile pulled at my mouth. This was it. We were getting out.

But as I took one step into the tunnel that led toward our freedom, a blood-curdling scream rang out from the passage that ran down to maintenance. Pain flared through my body again and I crumpled forward with a sickening realisation. Sin hadn't hurt me in his Belorian form, I'd been feeling her pain all along. How could I have been so fucking stupid?

"Rosalie needs us," I gasped through the pain.

Before I could think, I was stripping out of my clothes and running in her direction with Sin Wilder beside me and a common cause uniting us. *I'm coming Rosalie!*

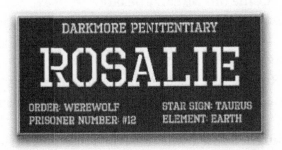

I wheezed through the pain of what I was certain were broken ribs on my right side as I crawled away from Nixon and his mocking gaze and my mind whirled with the desperate need for some kind of plan, but I was fresh out of ideas and starting to think I really might die here at the hands of this fucking cowardly piece of shit.

If I'd had my magic at my fingertips he would have been bleeding out at my feet the moment this had begun. But as it was, I felt like a mortal playing war against a god.

"If you had to face me Fae on Fae you'd be choking on your own intestines right now you pezzo di merda," I snarled as I crawled away from him and managed to get to my feet again.

I was bloody and bruised but never broken. There was no chance of that. I needed to get away from him, I needed to escape this place and never look back.

Nixon pouted sadly as he stalked after me. "Just think how sweet it will feel when I'm tender with you," he purred. "Think of how I can heal you once you've made Nixy happy."

I backed up again, but he used his air magic to stop me, licking his lips as he looked me over with a thoughtful expression.

"Maybe once we get started you'll realise how nice it can be to be my friend?" he suggested and vomit honest to the stars rose up in my throat.

My skin began to glow with the pale light of the moon as my Moon Wolf gifts rose up in my body at the desperate need in me to escape and the moment Nixon's hand tried to close on my arm, his fingers just passed right through me as if I wasn't there at all.

His lips parted in shock and confusion and I smirked triumphantly half a second before I caught sight of an enormous grey monster behind him with six legs and a gaping jaw full of razor sharp teeth and a scream of utter terror escaped my lips.

Nixon whirled around as the Belorian slammed its claws down against the top of his air shield with a murderous shriek and I leapt away from it even as the magic managed to hold.

Nixon cursed, throwing all of his power into trying to keep the monster back as he turned away from me and I froze as I stared up at it, fear paralysing me for a moment.

A deep, low howl snapped me out of my momentary panic as the Belorian continued to slam its claws against the top of the air shield and I grabbed the back of Nixon's hair before slamming his head against the water tank beside us with all of my strength.

Nixon cried out and his air shield shattered, letting the Belorian lunge at us with a shriek of hunger.

I leapt away, running with the hopes that it would go for Nixon first and suddenly coming face to face with an enormous black Wolf.

Ethan barked a greeting before leaping over me and I turned to look back at Nixon and the Belorian. Except it wasn't a Belorian anymore. It was a butt naked Sin Wilder who had the guard held by the throat as he tried to squeeze the life out of him.

Nixon twisted around and threw his hands into Sin's chest so the Incubus was thrown off of him by his magic, sailing through the air overhead where he shifted right above me into a purple Pegasus with an enormous dick dangling down between his legs.

Relief spilled through me at finding the two of them here and I was so glad to see them that I didn't even mind the huge horse dick almost hitting me in the back of the head as Sin dove towards the ground again and charged at Nixon with his head lowered, a glittering silver horn aimed right at the guard's ass.

Ethan pounced at Nixon with his teeth bared but another

blast of air magic threw the two of them back again before they could get to him.

Nixon ripped the radio from his belt and lifted it to his mouth. "I need help!" he barked. "I'm down on-"

Sin shifted into a man with ice white hair and two dicks, flinging his hand towards Nixon and shooting a bolt of electricity from his fingertips which punctured the air shield before slamming into the radio and destroying it.

I raced forward with a yell as I spotted my opportunity to take him out and I could feel Ethan running behind me too. Fuck fighting Fae on Fae. This stronzo was too much of a coward to come at me with my magic intact so I'd come at him with my men at my back and show him exactly who he was fucking with.

Nixon threw a hand out and I managed to dive aside before the blast of wind shot over my shoulder, but Ethan's howl of fury said he'd been knocked back once more.

Sin shifted again, turning into something so small that I couldn't even see him anymore and Nixon's attention moved to me.

I punched him in the face before he grabbed my hair and threw me up against the water tank. I slammed my foot down on his instep and he cursed loudly before throwing me away with another blast of wind.

I fell down heavily, crashing into a box of tools that spilled everywhere around me and my gaze locked on a screwdriver as it rolled across the floor in front of me.

Ethan thundered towards Nixon on furious paws and I snatched the screwdriver up as I got to my feet and tore after him too.

Nixon cast air at us again, but it was little more than a strong breeze and his eyes bugged out of his face as he realised he was tapped out.

I howled in victory as Ethan pounced and Nixon screamed, throwing his hands up and expelling one final blast of air which managed to knock Ethan away again.

Sin suddenly materialised behind him, locking a thick arm around Nixon's neck and immobilising him a moment before I drove the screwdriver into his chest.

I screamed as I stabbed him over and over, blood flying and my complete fury at this monster filling me for a few moments of utter bloodlust which seemed to consume me entirely.

I released the screwdriver while it was still lodged in his chest, stumbling back with a howl just as Ethan reappeared at my side and shifted back into Fae form.

Nixon was still thrashing in Sin's grip, his eyes wild as he saw his death coming on swift wings and Ethan yanked the cuff remote from the chain around his neck. I watched as he quickly tapped a few buttons on it then grabbed Nixon's hand, forcing him to press down on the device to release his magical signature.

The light of my cuffs died out a second before they fell from my wrists altogether and I groaned in pleasure as my connection to my magic returned to me like a flood of the most wondrous ecstasy.

Sin laughed loudly, shifting his grip on Nixon and ripping the screwdriver from his chest before using his fire magic to melt the metal and reform it into a blade. Nixon screamed a moment before Sin swiped the blade across his throat and blood sprayed everywhere as Sin dropped him to the ground between us.

I gasped as I stared at the two naked, bloodstained men before me and realised I owed them my life. But I wanted to give them that and so much more. I wanted to make them both mine in whatever ways I could. And I was pretty sure that this had been the first step into sealing that fate for us.

"Any chance there's time for a victory fuck?" Sin suggested with a hopeful glint in his eye that said it wasn't a complete joke.

"I think it might be better if we just get the hell out of here and save that for later, yeah?" I suggested with a shaky laugh and Ethan smirked at me as he stepped forward and pulled me into his arms.

"You gave me a real scare there, love," he murmured as he nuzzled against me and the Wolf in me wagged her tail like a contented pup at the feeling of his flesh against mine.

"I knew you'd come save me," I replied softly, realising that there was truth in those words. Ethan would always come when I needed him, just as I would for him. The stars had given us that gift.

Healing magic swept from him into me and I groaned as all of the injuries I'd gained were healed away while I stole a moment in my mate's arms.

Sin wound his arms around us too and nuzzled against my hair the same way Ethan was and somehow that made this moment feel even sweeter.

"Just a quick hand job then?" Sin whispered and I laughed, slapping his chest to tell him off.

"I think this is the part where we run," I reminded him and he groaned like a kid who had just been told he couldn't have candy for breakfast.

"Alright then. Let's get the fuck out of here."

We hurried along the tunnel, climbing higher and higher toward the surface, but it narrowed again at this end until we were forced to crawl. Plunger hadn't had time to make this part of the passage tall enough for anything else, but Claud managed to move along at my side as we followed right behind Plunger, trying to avoid looking directly at his naked ass in our faces. It was pitch black in here, but Plunger's weird mole nose glowed red like fucking Rudolph's so I could see enough.

"This way, follow my hiney," Plunger called. "Almost there."

I turned, looking back at Gustard who was hot on my heels, his eyes glittering with excitement as we drew closer to freedom. Brett, Sonny and Esme were following his crew with Pudding bringing up the rear. There was no sign of Rosalie yet and my gut clenched tighter the further we got. She should have caught up to us by now with Sin and Ethan. Where the fuck were they?

I feared what would happen if we got to the surface before they reached us. I wasn't going anywhere without Rosalie and neither was anyone else.

"She'd better hurry," Gustard said under his breath.

"We'll have to wait before we go up top," I growled for the hundredth time and Gustard answered me with silence as usual.

But Dante wasn't going to fry the fence until he had eyes on his cousin, and I wasn't going to let Gustard make any stupid decisions and ruin this entire operation. If it came to it, I'd be making sure he and his psycho friends never saw the moonlight waiting for us above ground. We had no intention of letting them actually escape anyway. The shank Rosalie had given me felt heavy in my pocket and the weight of it made me feel a whole lot better about having that piece of shit at my back.

"Ah here we are," Plunger announced, but I didn't stop in time and my cheek collided with the sagging skin of his ass as he stopped moving.

"For fuck's sake," I growled, backing up a bit, but Gustard was so close behind me that there was nowhere to go.

"She'll catch up," Claud murmured, clearly reading my mood and I nodded to him.

He smiled warmly, but there was a flicker of concern in his eyes. I didn't think any of us would be able to relax until we were far beyond the fences and stardusting to another part of Solaria. I sure as shit wouldn't anyway. I wanted Rosalie in my arms and I intended on never leaving her side again. Being parted from her now at this most crucial moment was agony.

"What's the hold up?" Gustard snapped.

"We've reached the end of my tunnel, pet," Plunger answered. "Gotta get digging into the moist dirt again." His ass wiggled back and forth in front of me and I recoiled in disgust.

Plunger started digging with his curved claws, swallowing the dirt as he went and the tunnel opened up surprisingly quickly in front of us. We moved along at a steady pace, climbing higher as Plunger used his whole body to pat down the walls, the thick skin on his shifted form perfect for slapping against the mud to keep it in place. Totally fucking gross, but seriously effective.

"Mmm I can taste the surface soil," Plunger announced. "We're almost there."

I crept after him, continually looking back over my shoulder or straining my ears for the sound of Rosalie's voice, but it never came. *Where are you, baby? Hurry up.*

"Oh my, there's a bit of a tingle in the rock up here," Plunger called.

"What do you mean?" I asked, but I felt it too as I passed

through a ring of dark rock and a tingle trickled through my skin. "What is that?"

"We might be close to an electrical source," Plunger said, but he didn't sound convinced.

I frowned as we continued on, deeper and deeper into the dark. I didn't like the feeling of being so confined down here, especially as the tunnel was narrowing and my shoulders were getting almost too wide for the space. Claud had to fall back behind me and I growled at Plunger irritably.

"Make it wider," I demanded.

"Some of us are much bigger than a little Mole Rat," Pudding's voice called from the back of the group.

"Yeah, yeah," Plunger muttered. "It takes longer if I make it wider."

"Well we have time, we're still waiting for Rosa," I said firmly and Plunger waved his ass in answer to that but started widening the tunnel again as we moved.

A faint tremor sounded somewhere off in the ground and I frowned up at the ceiling of mud above me, praying it wasn't going to cave in on our heads.

The tremor grew louder and I swallowed the ball rising in my throat.

"You sure this tunnel's safe?" I hissed at Plunger.

"Safe?" he tsked. "Of course it's safe."

"Then what's that noise?" I growled as another tremor ran through the earth beneath me.

Plunger stopped moving, turning his head left and right, up and down, his mole nose twitching as he tried to locate the source of the noise.

Another tremor ran through the wall on my left and I swear there was something moving through the ground. But that couldn't be right.

"Oh bless my balls," Plunger breathed, sounding fearful and my pulse quickened.

"What is it?" I demanded.

A noise like an explosion ripped through the tunnel behind

me and I swung my head around as dirt was thrown over me. Beyond Gustard, a huge, slithering, snake-like body was slicing through our tunnel, tearing its own path through the middle of us with its gaping, toothy mouth wide. A shout of fear got lodged in my throat as I took in the monstrous creature and suddenly realised the wetness coating my skin wasn't dirt. It was blood.

"Move!" Gustard roared and the worm creature disappeared back into the ground, its tail flicking out behind it so that I could see the other members of our team again through a fog of debris. One of Gustard's men was missing and the other two were screaming, trying to turn back as panic lit their eyes. My breaths came heavily as I tried to figure out what to do. The only thing we *could* do.

"Plunger! Go!" I bellowed and the Mole Shifter dove forward, starting to dig faster than he ever had in his life.

I crawled along behind him at a quick pace and someone managed to get Gustard's men moving after us too. There was nowhere else to go but forward. We had to get out of here.

Another tremor made my heart judder and Plunger suddenly leapt backwards just before a huge worm sliced across the path in front of him, tearing a huge tunnel into the ground.

Plunger scrambled out into the large space it had left behind, able to get to his feet, then he ran off in the direction it had come from with a wail of fright, leaving us all in the total, impenetrable dark.

ARIES. VAMPIRE. FIRE.

COMMANDING OFFICER

CAIN

DARKMORE
PENITENTIARY

I woke on the floor, groaning as I came to, released from a nightmare of my past as everything slowly drew back together in my mind. There was a more important nightmare I needed to return to, one where I was a man and not a boy with bloody hands and an aching heart. I pushed myself up to my knees with a grunt, the pain in my arm from the curse mark ebbing away, but still needling at me. It felt different this time though, like it was urging me to move.

I got to my feet, growling at the sight of the barrier still barring my way to the elevator and my ears rang with the far-away sound of a whirring alarm. Everything swept back to me at once.

The Incubus.

The riot.

The fucking Order Suppressant.

I twisted around, tearing down the corridor toward the warden's office and throwing my shoulder against it, breaking the lock as I forced my way inside. She wasn't working tonight, which meant I was officially in charge and I wasn't going to remain stuck up here unable to help. I needed to get down to the maintenance level to find out what had happened to the Order Suppressing gas and there was only one way to do that now.

I hurried over to the warden's perfectly organised desk and tapped the panel on one side of it, bringing up the emergency code entry. I clicked on the button for the escape tunnel. It was a well kept secret by the guards and a failsafe in case of this exact sort of situation.

I typed in the code and a clunk sounded behind me somewhere in the wall, but before I turned to face the open hatch, my eyes snagged on a handwritten note on the desk.

Subject for Project OTIF
12: Rosalie Oscura

I frowned, knowing I had no time to dwell on this, but I didn't like seeing Rosalie's name on that note. At the bottom were scribbled words that made my gut clench.

Transference is in the final stage of testing. Strong host needed.

I clenched my jaw, forcing myself to turn away from that note and head to the hatch which had opened in the wall. I climbed into the small space and took a metal ladder down to the tunnel, dropping onto the floor with a metallic dong. The long tunnel was lit with low blue lighting, guiding the way forward and I didn't waste any more time. I shot along it with my Vampire speed, using the passage to cross the entire length of the prison.

I met another hatch in the wall on the other side of Darkmore and twisted the metal wheel on its surface to open it. I pushed it wide and poked my head out into the elevator shaft that gave access into the prison. No one would be using the elevator tonight, so I swung my leg out onto the ladder beside the hatch, throwing a look down into the endless darkness below before I started climbing down.

I used my speed to descend quickly, heading into the depths of the prison, keeping an eye on the numbers on the wall which marked each floor. When I was down to level eight, I reached over to the hatch, twisting the wheel to open it and pushing it wide. I moved into a crawl space that led to another ladder and took that down the final two levels to maintenance. I opened the hatch beneath my feet and lowered the extendable ladder down from the ceiling to the floor below, hurrying into the maintenance room.

All was quiet, the familiar sound of humming pipes and whirring machinery filling my ears.

I shot through the maze of equipment and slowed in front of the Order Suppressant tank, gazing at the panel on the front of it. The word *warning* flashed in bright red letters on the screen and I frowned, tapping in a code to gain access to the manual override. It was going to need to be flushed but that process could take hours. And we didn't have hours. There were inmates running all over this prison and it wouldn't be long before they overwhelmed the guards. I cursed, having no choice but to press the buttons to start the reboot process. We still had our magic and they didn't. If I could get a plan in place and get the guards working together, maybe we could herd them into the Order Yard.

A puddle of something dark and red seeped out of an aisle to my left. I sucked in a breath at the sight of blood, shooting around the corner and my eyes fell on a mutilated guard on the floor.

"Fuck," I cursed, hurrying forward and turning him over onto his back. Nixon's lifeless eyes looked up at me, his features still twisted with pain in death.

I grimaced, releasing him and standing up, not giving a shit about that asshole leaving this world. Good riddance to bad rubbish. But my heart was still thumping wildly, because someone had done this. Someone had been down here, killed a guard and fucked with the tank. A distant scream called to me and I frowned in confusion, shooting across the room in the direction it was coming from, finding myself standing in front of a wall, with one of the bricks sticking out of it at an awkward angle. I reached up, tugging on it and a bunch of bricks fell from it at my feet.

My lips parted in shock and I leaned inside the hole that was revealed, gazing up at a tunnel that disappeared into the dark.

"Holy shit!" I cursed then shoved more of the bricks aside and climbed into the passage, using my Vampire speed to chase after the culprit.

Whoever the fuck had done this, clearly had a plan. They'd managed to build this tunnel, so what if they'd gotten further than that? What if someone was trying to do the impossible and escape from Darkmore?

My fangs grew sharp and I snarled as I hunted them down.

Nixon's blood had still been warm. So they couldn't be far. And I swore on the stars, I was going to catch the asshole who thought they could get away with this and teach them a lesson they wouldn't forget.

"Is it weird that I'm naked and underground?" Sin asked, his voice echoing as we scrambled up through the tunnel from the maintenance level and tried to move as fast as we could up the steep incline in the dark. "I've been naked in pretty much every place that you can think of, but never underground like this. It feels naughty, like I'm a grave robber and you're a pair of dirty zombies come to gobble me up."

"Well I'm not naked," I reminded him. "So Ethan will have to do the gobbling."

"I'm good with that so long as you're watching, wild girl," Sin purred and I bit my lip on a laugh, not minding that idea one bit.

"Keep dreaming," Ethan growled. "You'll be the one sucking my cock in that situation. I'm top dog in this little three way we have going."

"Oh, I like the sound of that," Sin said. "I can suck your dick while you eat our girl's pussy and she sucks my dick. It'll be some kind of circle situation...or a triangle I guess...maybe if she's sitting on your face and I'm-"

"What was that?" I hissed, interrupting him as a tremor ran through the tunnel surrounding us and the three of us fell still.

"I didn't hear anything aside from this asshole prattling on, love," Ethan said after a moment, taking my hand in the dark. "What do you think you heard?"

"It was more like I felt it," I whispered, straining my ears as I laid my free hand on the tunnel wall and tried to see if I could feel it again.

I reached into the wall with my earth magic, seeking out any signs that the tunnel might be collapsing or anything like that, but the structure seemed sound.

A distant scream caught my ear as the three of us stood there listening and I sucked in a sharp breath.

"Who was that?" I hissed.

"Probably just someone in the riots," Ethan muttered. "Don't forget this idiot set the Belorian free."

"On that note, I'm gonna kick your ass when we get out of here, Sin," I growled and we started moving again.

We had to be close to the library and once we reached it, we just needed to hurry on up the other tunnel to meet the others, dig our way out of here, avoid the guards on patrol in the watch towers, hope that Dante really could take out a fence designed to be indestructible, run across a field which was likely filled with even more traps and pitfalls and meet up with my cousin to stardust the fuck out of here. Easy.

"I'm gonna hold you to that, wild girl," Sin said excitedly and I cursed him beneath my breath.

"Maybe I won't be sucking your dick in that triangle situation you're dreaming up either," I added as he clearly wasn't concerned about the ass kicking.

"Shit, anyone would think you didn't want the Belorian set loose!" he growled like I was the one being unreasonable here and a snarl of frustration left my lips.

"I didn't. I told you that clear as fucking day," I insisted. As we rounded a corner and the light from the library lit the tunnel ahead at last.

"Yeah, but you gave me the secret look again," he protested.

"There is no secret look, Sin," I hissed but we all fell silent as a deep and guttural roar sounded from somewhere up ahead.

I threw a silencing bubble around us as my heart lurched with fear and Ethan shifted past me, casting ice from his fingertips until he'd hung a wall of it before us, thin enough to see through. He filled the air around us with crystals of ice so that the temperature plummeted and a shiver chased along my skin.

We crept forward with Ethan moving the barrier of ice ahead of us and chills which had nothing to do with the temperature raced down my spine.

As we reached the hole in the wall where the entrance to the library opened up before us, Ethan bent down and grabbed his jumpsuit from the floor, tossing his boxers to Sin as he pulled it on. The Incubus rolled his eyes, clearly not caring about putting his dick away, but the thing was damn distracting, so I was in agreement with Ethan on that choice.

While they were putting their clothes on, I squatted down and crawled towards the opening where Ethan had placed the ice barrier and peered out into the brightly lit room.

I sucked in a sharp breath as the Belorian scuttled by right outside and I backed up suddenly, crashing into Ethan's legs with a curse.

"Don't worry about the poor beastie," Sin said as he bent down to get a look too. "He's just hungry and horny and lonely. I was actually thinking we could bring him with us, but the tunnels might be a bit tight..."

"There is something seriously wrong with you," Ethan growled and I bit my lip as the creature scuttled into sight again, slowly turning its head like it was searching for something. Searching for *us*.

"It can't see our body heat through that ice, right?" I whispered even though the silencing bubble was still hiding any sounds we made, but something about speaking at full volume in front of that creature seemed like a terrible fucking idea to me.

"I got you, love. That thing can't see us," Ethan swore and I nodded as I stayed where I was, wondering if I should just cave in this part of the tunnel to make sure it couldn't follow us as I glanced towards the passage that led to the surface.

Just as I looked that way, a blood curdling scream echoed down to me and my eyes widened in fright as more screams followed it.

"What the-" I began, but before I could complete that thought, a hard body crashed into me and I was the one screaming as I was lifted clean off of my feet and carried straight towards the hole which led back to the library.

Cain's familiar scent wrapped around me half a second before we crashed through the wall of ice Ethan had constructed and fell sprawling to the ground between the bookshelves on the other side of it.

"Mason!" I yelled, fighting to break free of him as he wrestled me down and pinned me beneath him.

"I should have known it would be you!" he snarled in my face, his eyes wild with fury as Ethan and Sin started yelling from behind us.

"You have to get off of me," I growled. "The Belori-"

"Don't you tell me what I should or shouldn't do!" Cain bellowed. "To think I actually believed that you-"

A huge clawed foot slammed into him, launching him off of me and I shrieked in terror as the Belorian hurled him away across the room before its eyeless face turned my way.

I threw my hands up, a cage of thorns growing up to surround me just seconds before the Belorian lunged at me and a scream ripped from my lips again as its teeth sank into the thorny branches and started ripping them aside in its desperation to get to me.

"Hey, big boy, remember me?" Sin yelled from somewhere behind me and the Belorian's attack stalled as it whirled its head around and I caught sight of Sin shifting into the monster's version of a wet dream just before the thing lurched away from me and Sin took off with what I swear was a monster's version of a flirtatious giggle as he made it chase him.

Ethan appeared above me a moment later, a layer of ice falling over the two of us as he used his magic to chill our flesh and I quickly disbanded the thorny cage surrounding me and let him pull me to my feet.

"We need to go, love," he growled, tugging me towards the tunnel as I looked back over my shoulder to see where Sin had ended up.

I let Ethan pull me towards the hole in the wall again, but before we made it more than a few steps, Cain shot in front of us and planted himself in our way, flames coiling around his arms.

"Don't you dare take another step," he snarled, the fury in his eyes a wild and fearsome thing.

"Mason," I breathed, pushing my way between him and Ethan as my mate formed twin daggers of ice in his hands and bared his teeth in a threatening way.

"Don't be an idiot, Cain," Ethan snarled. "You can't possibly expect to win against the three of us with our magic and Orders intact. Move aside unless you want to die in a futile attempt to achieve the impossible."

Cain bristled at the suggestion that he couldn't win against us and my heart thrashed as I saw that demon in his eyes which he'd unleashed against Christopher and the others to protect me.

"Just let us go," I begged. "We don't want to hurt you."

The fire flared brighter and a roar of fury echoed through the room from the Belorian while Sin started cursing somewhere behind us, clearly back in his Fae form.

"You were always planning this, weren't you?" Cain demanded, his gaze fixed on me and filled with betrayal. "Every time we were down on the maintenance level. Every time you were whispering things in my ear and trying to get me to tell you about the way this place was run-"

"Of course she was playing you, you fucking idiot," Ethan growled. "What else did you think it was? You can't have seriously thought she *liked* you?"

I opened my mouth to protest, but before I could, the Belorian shrieked behind us and launched itself straight for Cain who threw a massive fireball out and away from himself in retaliation.

Ethan roared a challenge as he threw one of his daggers at the beast, followed by a flood of water.

Sin hollered like a madman and a tornado tore through the library at his command, sending shelves tumbling as all of the combined magic collided with the force of a tsunami and knocked me off of my feet.

I was swept away on a sea of wind and water and I cried out in fright as I lost sight of everyone in the carnage.

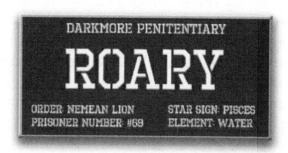

I ran along one of the tunnels created by the bloodthirsty worms with Claud at my side and screams ringing through my skull. These tunnels were unstable and the whole ground seemed to shake as earth tumbled from the ceiling and cascaded over me. I couldn't see shit and was running with one hand against the wall as I tried to find a way out. But the only way we were getting out of here was if we found our way back to the tunnel we'd originally come from. I just didn't know how we were going to manage that when we were as blind as bats without Plunger's light to guide us.

"Keep going, Roary," Claud breathed in encouragement, his voice shaking a little. "We'll make it out. We just have to keep going."

"We will. We've gotta fucking live," I said in agreement.

My heart jerked almost painfully in my chest as more screams called from behind us, but I didn't slow, following the tunnel we were in as it curved sharply to the right. I was fairly sure it was heading in the right direction so I quickened my pace, pulling Claud along with me as fear licked along my spine. We were trying to be as quiet as possible, unsure how those things hunted, but every step we took sounded as loud as gunfire in my ears.

A dim red light appeared up ahead and I raced towards it with hope in my heart, sure it must be Plunger.

"*Hey,*" I hissed to try and grab his attention, but he didn't slow, carving a tunnel into the wall ahead of us to try and get away.

Gustard suddenly spilled out of a passage to my right made by the worms, his perfectly ironed jumpsuit now splattered with blood and his hair a mess which fell forward into his eyes. One of his men was hot on his heels, but there was no sign of the other one.

"Those things ate Ronaldo," Gustard cursed. "You and your mutt whore have led me to my death." He lunged at me, throwing a punch into my gut and I growled, shoving him back a step just as a loud tremor sounded close by.

I lurched away from Gustard, dragging Claud to the opposite side of the tunnel as the rumblings grew louder. My heart leapt as one of those vile worms burst through the wall opposite me. It paused, its face nothing but two tiny white eyes with a flat nose that sucked in air above its wide mouth and I got the feeling it knew we were all here. It smelled like rotten eggs and I fought down the bile rising in my throat as its breath washed over us.

I carefully pulled the shank from my pocket, ready to defend myself with everything I had if it came to it.

It turned its face towards Gustard and I prayed it would get busy eating him so we could make a run for it. Plunger was still burrowing into his own tunnel, the light from his nose slowly fading with him as he made a break for it.

The worm suddenly released a grumbling noise and lunged for Gustard. The bastard grabbed his own man, swinging him around in front of him and the worm devoured him with a sucking, slurping sound, the guy still screaming from inside it as I fled with Claud on my heels.

I reached the tunnel Plunger had made, shoving Claud ahead of me and following him as we had to crawl into it. The sound of someone chasing behind me told me Gustard had avoided death and was right on my heels. I clenched my teeth in irritation over that fact, moving faster and faster as the tunnel started sloping down beneath us.

The red light ahead of us suddenly lit up a wider space and Claud scrambled to his feet before grabbing my arm and pulling me up after him. If I wasn't mistaken, we were in our tunnel from earlier but much further down it. There was no way of getting to the surface now. I knew that in my heart and my gut sank like a stone as we all started running down the passage as fast as we could. The sound of footfalls up ahead filled me with relief and I looked over Plunger's head, spotting Esme, Brett and Sonny racing along together. The tunnel was too small for any of us to shift, our Order forms far bigger than our Fae forms, and I feared we might bring the whole roof down on our heads if we attempted it.

Tremors shook the walls all around us as we sprinted along, moving as fast as fucking possible to try and get back to the prison.

I wasn't going to die here in some hole in the ground. I had to return to Rosa. I'd bared my heart to her. And I would not leave this world until I'd claimed her as mine.

The tunnel curved sharply to the left and Claud suddenly turned around and pushed me back, making me slip on the damp mud beneath my feet, my ass hitting the ground. A worm lunged at him from behind, its monstrous mouth closing around his legs. He screamed wildly and I shouted out in horror, diving forward and catching hold of his hand, dropping the shank in my desperation to save him.

"Don't let go!" I commanded him and another strangled scream escaped him as the worm slurped and sucked him deeper into the depths of its horrible mouth.

I kicked at the beast, refusing to let go of my friend, but with every inch I gained, the worm took more and more of him from me. I was losing him and I cursed and fought to try and hold on as he continued to scream in agony.

A heavy body slammed into me and Pudding's hands closed over mine, trying to cling to Claud, lending me his strength as we heaved him backwards together. The worm whipped its huge ugly head sideways, ripping Claud's hands from our grip and with a horrible gurgling sound, it swallowed my friend and his screams were silenced forever.

"No!" I roared.

He'd been the only person I truly trusted in this place since I'd arrived. He had a family waiting for him beyond Darkmore, a life. Fuck. No no *no*.

The creature came at us next and I felt around for my weapon in a panic, barely able to see anything as the red light beyond the worm grew fainter and fainter while Plunger left us to die.

A rock grazed my palm instead of the shank and I snatched it up, throwing it hard at the worm's ugly fucking face, making it shriek in pain. Pudding caught on, picking up rocks of his own and managed to throw one right into its eye.

The worm turned away, lurching towards the opposite wall and cutting a hole into it, making the entire tunnel shudder as it slithered away into the mud. I got up with a shaky breath and Pudding started forward at a slow pace, gazing warily down the tunnel it had disappeared into. The roof above us rumbled and dirt started falling heavily over us, making dread wash through me.

"Run!" I shouted at Pudding, shoving him forward and he moved faster than I'd ever seen him move as the tunnel started collapsing behind us.

We sprinted down, down, down, chasing after the low glimmer of Plunger's nose in the dark, having no idea where the others had all gone or if they'd been eaten too as death chased us, the heavy crash of rock and mud following us a hair's breadth behind my back.

I thought of Rosa and ran with determined strides. I would make it back to her. I had to. Because she owned my heart and soul and I'd barely had time to earn the love she'd offered me. We had so much lost time to make up for. Fate surely wouldn't take me from her now.

Someone was yelling my name but my head was ringing from the impact it had just made with a wall and it took me a few moments to recognise who it was.

"Let's just go," Ethan demanded as he grabbed my hand and hauled me to my feet. "Once we're in the tunnel just use your earth magic to cave in the entrance and he won't be able to follow us anyway."

I nodded, pressing a hand to my temple for a moment as I healed away the damage of the wound which was making me dizzy and my thoughts quickly sharpened.

We were standing in a dome of ice that Ethan had cast to hide us from the Belorian and I whipped around as I looked through the glassy structure, hunting for Sin.

"We need Sin," I said firmly. "Jerome will kill us and everyone we love if we leave here without him."

Not that that was the only reason I was determined to get the Incubus out of here with us anymore, but it was the simplest way to make it clear to Ethan that this wasn't up for any kind of discussion.

"Let's find him then," Ethan agreed, waving a hand to dispel the ice surrounding us and then taking my hand so that he could use his magic to lower our body temperatures.

The Belorian roared somewhere beyond the stacks of books to our right and I yanked on Ethan's hand as I threw my free hand out before us and cast a wooden stairway to grow up out of the carpet for us to climb. We raced up it until we were on a level with the tops of the bookshelves and I made a bridge for us to cross over between them.

I fell still as I spotted the Belorian by the door with Sin racing away from it, casting a halo of fire in place above his head to lure it his way.

"What the hell is he doing?" I demanded.

"I'd guess he's drawing it away from you, love. You have a way of making crazy motherfuckers like you."

I sucked in a breath as the monster leapt at him and Sin shifted, suddenly becoming the female version of the creature in the blink of an eye and shaking his ass about before racing out of the library doors with the Belorian hot on his heels.

"Sin!" I yelled, but before I could chase after him, a blur of motion whipped towards me and Cain ripped me out of Ethan's arms, knocking me clean off of the bridge I'd created and crashing down towards the floor.

I threw a hand out and made a bed of leaves to catch us as we fell, struggling wildly beneath Cain as he fought to pin me down in them.

"Just let us go," I begged, not because I thought he could stop me but because I really didn't want to have to hurt him.

"Why the fuck would I do that? You played me, used me, fucked me like a whore and were going to run off into the night without ever even thinking of me again," he snarled furiously.

"That's not true," I growled. "I told you where you could find me. I wanted you to come to Mount Lupa."

Cain's brow furrowed in confusion for the briefest moment and his grip on me slackened a little just before Ethan blasted him with a surge of water magic that had him tumbling off of me.

I gasped as I scrambled back up to my feet, leaping in front of Ethan as he forged a spear out of ice and raised it in his hand ready to throw.

"Leave him," I commanded, the bark of an Alpha in my tone enough to make my mate pause.

"He won't stop coming after us, love," he protested, his arm tensing for the blow and Cain took his chance to shoot away.

"Get Sin," I commanded. "I can deal with Cain."

Ethan hesitated for half a second, his gaze locking with mine for a heartbeat before he nodded once and raced away towards the doors.

Cain tore around the room and I cursed as I summoned whips into my hands forged from vines.

He shot at me, throwing a handful of flames my way and I ducked beneath them before whipping my arm at him and shooting a vine after him.

He dodged to the left then shot more fire my way as he leapt over the vine, this time making the fireball so big that it blocked my view of him. But I knew this beast well enough to know his moves now and as he chased the fireball directly towards me, I gritted my teeth and stood my ground, throwing a shield of dirt up between us to absorb the blow and letting my vines fall to the floor forgotten.

The fire exploded over the top of my head and Cain smashed straight through my shield, dirt scattering over me a moment before he collided with me and he drove me against the wall at my back.

He snarled at me, fangs bared, fury and betrayal glistening in his eyes as I made no move to fight him off, my arms hanging loose at my sides and his fingers biting into my waist.

"It wasn't a lie," I said in rough voice, making him pause just long enough for me to lean forward and press my lips to his, letting him taste the truth of those words and all of the confusing, fucked up things I shouldn't have been feeling for him in the movement of my mouth against his.

His hands tightened around my waist as he pushed me back into the wall, growling as he kissed me and a single tear spilled from my eye, racing down my cheek and falling against his jaw.

Cain pulled back as he felt it, frowning at me in confusion before he tried to lift his hand to touch me and realised he couldn't.

The vines I'd coiled around his hands were tight and impenetrable. They immobilised each of his fingers and locked his magic down, rendering it useless.

Cain snarled in fury as he tried to break the vines with brute force, throwing his Vampire strength into ripping them from the floor where I'd grown the roots deep and strong. It was no use. I'd been taught how to immobilise an enemy by the King of the Oscura Clan. No one could break those bonds unless I let them free.

"Bitch!" Cain roared in my face, his features written in heart-break and betrayal.

"I just want to be free," I replied, another tear slipping down my cheek. "I didn't mean for us to happen. But I'm not sad that it did."

Cain opened his mouth to reply just as the door banged open and Sin whooped with excitement as he raced back towards us with Ethan at his side.

"Beastie is having a feast of the Watchers," Sin called. "He's as happy as a bioweapon at a barbecue!"

I slipped away from Cain as he looked at me like I was a stranger. A stranger he hated with more fury than I'd ever known even in him.

"I have to go," I breathed as he glared at me.

Ethan and Sin appeared between the shelves and Sin laughed with a dark and terrifying excitement as he spotted Cain rooted in place, helpless and at our mercy. He ignited twin flames in his hands and his eyes danced with shadows as he stalked towards the guard with murder written all over his face.

"No," I commanded, stepping into his path. "If you hurt him, Sin Wilder, I'll kill you."

Sin's lips parted in shock then turned into a pout just as fast. "I know you wanna bang him, wild girl, but that bastard will hunt us to the ends of the earth if we leave him alive."

I raised my chin, glaring at him as I warned him to back down. "Maybe I like the hunt."

Ethan shook his head like he didn't know what to make of me then grabbed my hand and yanked me towards the tunnel at the back of the room.

"We need to hurry, love," he urged and I nodded, shooting one final look back at Cain as I ran along at his side.

Cain's jaw was working furiously and it seemed like he had something to say, but we didn't have the time to find out what it was.

"You'll never get out of here!" he shouted just as I dropped down to crawl into the hole behind the bookshelf.

"Just watch us, asshole," Ethan called back dismissively.

"I mean it," Cain snarled. "We switched on the new bioweapon today. There's a magical forcefield beneath the ground surrounding the entire prison. If you pass through it, you're dead."

"What?" I gasped, whipping back around with my heart in my throat and I stared at him. "What kind of bioweapon?"

Cain just glared at me, but fuck that.

I stormed back towards him and punched him as hard as I could, making his head wheel sideways and his lip split open.

"The man I love is in that tunnel," I snarled with a fear coursing through me unlike anything I'd ever known before. "So you're going to tell me what the fuck you're talking about or I'll tear the truth right out of you with my bare hands."

Cain glared at me with his lip pulling back, looking like that declaration had hurt him more than my punch had. "Love? Aren't there enough men here between the three of us for you? What other poor fucker have you tricked into falling for your lies? If this is what it feels like to be loved by you then I feel sorry for him, because you're nothing but a selfish, manipulative liar. I don't believe you're even capable of feeling anything close to love for anyone other than yourself."

The Wolf in me reared her head and bared her teeth as I prepared to go all in on this stronzo just as a scream echoed through the tunnels and I whirled back around towards it.

Ethan backed away from the hole in the wall just as Esme fell through it and started sobbing as she scrambled away.

"What is it?" I gasped as I raced towards her and Sonny and

Brett launched themselves through right on her ass.

"Giant fucking teeth worm things," Sonny choked out, his eyes wild as he grabbed Brett's arm and hauled him away from the hole. I'd never seen him run from a single thing in all the time I'd known him and that horror in his eyes had every instinct in my body bursting to attention.

"Where's Roary?" I demanded, fear unlike anything I'd ever felt before taking me captive as I advanced on them and the three of them shook their heads hopelessly.

"Everyone's dead," Sonny choked out. "Those things ate them."

"They *ate* them!" Esme shrieked again, clutching her tits as she backed up further like she was afraid for their safety.

"*No*," I hissed, because it wasn't true. It wasn't. Roary wasn't dead. There wasn't any way that fate would be that fucking cruel as to steal him from me after everything I'd already suffered through in my life. After everything *he'd* suffered through. I wouldn't believe it. I couldn't. If I even entertained the idea, I was going to fracture into a thousand pieces and wither away into nothing at all.

My heart leapt and pounded to a murderous rhythm as I shook my head in denial, trying to figure out how the fuck this had happened, what the fuck had happened.

"You told me they weren't switching the new system on until Sunday," I snarled, twisting around and pointing at Cain as I tried to get my head around what the fuck was happening and how we were going to fix it. Because it had to be fixable. No way was I considering any alternative. Roary was okay and we were getting out of here tonight to start our lives again. It wasn't over. I couldn't accept that this was how tonight ended. After all the promises I'd made to him. This was not how this went down. I'd rearrange the stars myself to save him if I had to.

"*By* Sunday. And it's not like I had any reason to keep you updated," Cain spat back bitterly. "Maybe you should have let me in on this little plan of yours if you were going to rely on my help so heavily."

"Fuck you," Sin snarled, stalking towards him, but I shot him a warning glare as I took off towards the tunnel.

"I'm getting Roary out of there," I said defiantly as I headed forward, my earth magic rippling beneath my flesh. I'd be able to find him using it, track his location using the vibrations of his footsteps and-

A figure appeared in the tunnel before I could climb into it and my heart lifted with hope before dashing to pieces again as fucking Gustard threw himself out of the hole, swiftly followed by Pudding. Of course the cockroach had survived, though he looked thoroughly shaken and was covered in blood which didn't seem to be his.

"Where's Roary?" I demanded and Gustard laughed bitterly.

"Dead. Along with everyone else. Thanks to you and your bullshit plan." He lunged at me in fury, but Ethan swung at him before he even got close, his fist colliding with Gustard's cheek and knocking him back on his ass.

"No," I refused again in a furious growl because it wasn't true. I wouldn't let it be true. If Roary was dead then I would be as well. My heart had belonged to him for so long that there was simply no chance that it could still be beating if it wasn't doing so for him.

A deep rumble came from the tunnel and I gasped hopefully as I looked back to it for a sign of the man who made my heart race with nothing more than a thought. But instead of seeing him racing down the tunnel back to me, an enormous worm burst from the darkness, a gaping mouth full of sharp teeth lunging straight at me as I threw my hands out and directed my magic at it with a cry of fear.

The tunnel trembled around the creature, the sides of it caving in as I reduced the whole structure to nothing, tightening my fists with a scream as the tunnel collapsed and I sealed it up with a layer of the thickest, sharpest stone I could create, carving the monster in two before burying it.

"No," I gasped, lunging to my feet as Ethan grabbed my arm

and pulled me back with a hard jerk. Tears streamed down my cheeks as the reality of what I'd just done crashed into me and I realised that Roary was gone.

"It's too late, love," Ethan growled as I fought against him, kicking and screaming as I refused to accept that my Lion wasn't coming back to me.

I was screaming so loud that it was ripping my throat raw. I couldn't accept it. How could that be the truth? I'd come all this way to save him. I'd only taken this job because of him. The Lion who had stolen my heart before he even knew I existed and had become so much more than a perfect fantasy to me. He was the person in this place who I'd been able to rely on from day one, my rock, my heart, my fucking soul. If he was dead, then I was too. The grief of it was too much to bear. It was too fucking much-

A deafening boom sounded behind us and the force of it almost knocked me from my feet as a chunk of the wall was blasted apart and a very naked, very disgusting Plunger fell into the room with Roary tumbling in right behind him.

Ethan released me as he sucked in a surprised gasp and I launched myself at Roary with a howl of relief as I leapt on him, wrapping my arms and legs around him and squeezing him so tight that I was in danger of breaking bones.

"I thought I lost you," I gasped, gripping his face between my hands and kissing him hard and demandingly as he tugged me close. My entire body was trembling with grief and relief and fear, but he held me tight enough that it couldn't consume me.

"It's a lot harder than that to kill me, little pup," he teased as he knocked his forehead against mine and I couldn't even find it in me to chew him out for calling me a pup because he was right here where he belonged and my heart was pounding in relief at having him close again and I was painting the lines of his face with my fingers as I made certain that he was okay.

"So what now, wild girl?" Sin asked casually like this was any normal day and our entire escape plan hadn't just gone to shit.

Roary placed me down and I tried to make my brain work,

to figure out something, anything that we could do to salvage this utter fucking carnage that had been the perfect plan.

I swiped a hand over my face as I looked around at the devastation we'd caused in here, thought about Nixon's body down in maintenance, not to mention my CO who was still rooted to the floor watching everything we were doing. We were fucked. No two ways about it.

Cain glared at me with this bitter, hateful look that had ice bleeding through my veins. "So this is it? The great Rosalie Oscura's amazing master plan? Looks to me like all you've done here is make a fucking mess and earned all of you a life sentence in this hell. Not to mention several months in the hole," he scoffed and I got to my feet, pulling Roary up beside me as I looked between the Fae I'd promised freedom to and read the disappointment in their eyes. The acceptance. But fuck that.

"How long do we have before the FIB bust in here to take the prison back by force?" I demanded, striding up to Cain with my jaw set.

"Just give up now. We'll go easier on you. Though not by much," he snarled back.

"Answer me, boss man. And don't forget I'm the only thing standing between you and death right now, so you might want to be polite about it."

Cain bared his fangs at me and I bared my teeth right back in a smug as fuck grin that I knew would only piss him off more. But I wasn't smug. I was drowning. Everything I'd done, all of my best laid plans, it had all gone to shit. And if I couldn't come up with some miraculous way to fix this then I really was going to end up stuck in this hell for years and years while my life passed me by.

Cain's gaze roamed over my face and the hatred eased from his eyes, giving me a glimpse of the hurt living in him. I'd ripped his heart out and there was a time I wouldn't have cared about that. But now it hurt as fiercely as if I'd ripped my own heart out too.

"How long?" I whispered again just for him and his jaw

pulsed like he was considering answering me or not.

"Three days," he finally replied in a deadened tone. "From the moment the FIB are informed about the uprising, they will give the guards three days to fix the situation ourselves so long as we're giving them regular updates. After that, they'll fill the place with so many FIB agents that you won't be able to move for them. And believe me, if you think the guards are bad, you really haven't seen anything in comparison to what those fuckers will do."

I smiled and turned away from him to address the rest of the room. "You hear that guys? Sounds to me like we've got three days with no guards and the full run of the prison to execute plan B and get our asses topside. Anyone else think that sounds too easy?"

Ethan folded his arms. "The prison is on lockdown, the Belorian is loose, every psychopath in here has access to their Order form, there are still at least a hundred guards hanging around the place looking to lock us all back up, not to mention *this* motherfucker who literally knows what we're planning to do and we are going to have to somehow keep him captive - assuming you aren't changing your mind about killing him. And the world's most ruthless federal organisation are on their way here to round us up and throw us in the hole in three days' time," he pointed out with a frown. "And you somehow think that getting out of here is going to be easy, love?"

"You're fucking delusional, Twelve." Cain growled as he looked between us. "How the fuck do you expect to get out of here? This place was built to keep monsters like all of you locked up for life."

"Simple, stronzo," I purred, turning around to look at him and smiling widely at the pure fucking rage in his eyes as Sin chuckled in that deliciously dark way of his. "You just became our ticket out of here."

__Author Note__

Heeeeey guys, how was that? You okay? The end got a bit intense there didn't it? Don't worry though, we would never kill Roary...in book 2. That's more of an end of series death, don't you think? Not that we are saying we would do that of course, but never say never, am I right? Are you crying over Claud? Maybe wondering if you remember him from book 1 or not? It did kinda suck for him though, gotta be a pretty awful death to be gobbled up by tooth worms I reckon.

Can we get a round of applause for the fact that we didn't ruin cakes for anyone in this one? In fact, I do believe that no food was harmed in the making of this book! (woohoo!!) oh...there was that Plunger putting pubes in the oatmeal bit though now I come to think of it, oh and his past experience where he dunked his dipper in chocolate ice cream. But that's okay because I'm sure none of you eat either of those things regularly or anything, so you definitely won't be wondering if you have a curly grey hair swimming in it or not the next time you're chowing down on your breakfast or dessert. On that note, who made a wish on the pubes? If you did, was the wish that we wouldn't crush your soul with this one? Did it come true? I think this one was pretty low on the soul crushing for the most part. At least we left you with hope. I mean, it's not a whole lot of hope but there's a sliver there for sure.

Side note, do we have any bunnies here who were looking out for all of those tasty easter eggs? Did you pick up a hint or two for the other books in the Solaria world? I hope you enjoyed them if you did! And if you haven't read the other books in this series yet then come on over and get reading Dark Fae and Zodiac Academy. I promise that even if the stories may make your heart hurt from time to time, they'll make you smile too. And then come shout at us in the discussion groups and share your theories with us because we loooooove seeing what you're all guessing and giggling over your right and wrong answers.

On a serious note, we would really like to take this opportunity to thank each and every one of you for sticking with us throughout this crazy journey to co-authored madness that we've been on over the last year and a half. Caroline and I have been dreaming about being authors since we were little kids (we're sisters if you didn't already know that) and you are responsible for making those dreams become reality with your love and support for our books and characters and we love and appreciate each and every one of you so, so much. This year has been kicking us all in the lady balls as hard as it can in as many ways as it can and we have taken so much pleasure in bringing smiles to all of you via the written word and drawing you into the crazy worlds that exist inside our minds. The places we create may be a little dark and depraved at times, but they're fun and free and full of possibilities too. So welcome to the madness of our internal monologues and we really hope you'll stay with us for many more books to come!

Lots of love,
Susanne & Caroline xxx